'Love, family, war and struggle power this touching story' *Woman & Home*

'A rich, sweeping epic which tells the story of the women and men who built America dream by dream. I don't know how Adriana goes into her family's attic and emerges with these amazing stories, I'm just happy she does. If you're meeting her work for the first time, get ready for a lifelong love affair. *The Shoemaker's Wife* is utterly splendid' Kathryn Stockett, bestselling author of *The Help*

'This hymn to Italian New York is a treat' *Elle*

'A real page turner' Sarah Jessica Parker

'Delightfully charismatic . . . exuberant and stylish' *Independent on Sunday*

'Yum yum – if novels were food, this one would be fudge. A joyous blend of Italian-American warmth and whiplash New York wit. The perfect read' *The Times*

'Utterly addictive' *Glamour*

'Quirky and charming . . . If you are not a fan already, you will be after this' *Company*

'An old-fashioned, romantic tale of two star-tangled lovers . . . but also a paean to artisanal work, food, friendship and family . . . Trigiani is a master of palpable and visual detail' *Washington Post*

'Breathtaking . . . sparkles in exquisite details and vivid descriptions' *Huffington Post*

'Within the pages of this novel is a gloriously romantic yet sensible world that seamlessly blends practicality and beauty . . . exquisite writing and a story enriched by the power of abiding love . . . Trigiani's very best' *USA Today*

fiction

Encore, Valentine

Very Valentine

Home to Big Stone Gap

Rococo

The Queen of the Big Time

Lucia, Lucia

Milk Glass Moon

Big Cherry Holler

Big Stone Gap

young adult fiction

Viola in Reel Life

Viola in the Spotlight

nonfiction

The Wisdom of my Grandmothers

Cooking with My Sisters (coauthor)

The Shoemaker's Wife

ADRIANA TRIGIANI

**SIMON &
SCHUSTER**

London · New York · Sydney · Toronto · New Delhi

A CBS COMPANY

First published in Great Britain by Simon & Schuster UK Ltd, 2012
This paperback edition first published by Simon & Schuster UK Ltd, 2012
A CBS Company

1 3 5 7 9 10 8 6 4 2

Simon & Schuster UK Ltd
1st Floor
222 Gray's Inn Road
London WC1X 8HB

Simon & Schuster Australia
Sydney

A CIP catalogue record for this book is available from the British Library

ISBN: 978-1-84983-077-5
eBook ISBN: 978-1-84983-424-7

Typeset by Hewer Text UK Ltd, Edinburgh
Printed and bound in Great Britain by CPI Group (UK) Ltd, Croydon, CR0 4YY

IN MEMORY OF MONSIGNOR DON ANDREA SPADA
WHO LOVED THE MOUNTAIN

PART ONE

the italian alps

A GOLD RING
Un Anello d'oro

The scalloped hem of Caterina Lazzari's blue velvet coat grazed the fresh-fallen snow, leaving a pale pink path on the bricks as she walked across the empty piazza. The only sound was the soft, rhythmic sweep of her footsteps, like hands dusting flour across an old wooden cutting board.

All around her, the Italian Alps loomed like silver daggers against a pewter sky. The rising winter sun, a pinprick of gold buried in the expanse of gray, barely flickered. In the first light of morning, dressed in blue, Caterina looked like a bird.

She turned, exhaling a long breath into the cold winter air.

"Ciro?" she called out. "Eduardo!"

She heard her sons' laughter echo across the empty colonnade, but couldn't place them. She surveyed the columns of the open portico. This wasn't a morning for hide-and-seek, or for playing games. She called to them again. Her mind swam with all she had accomplished, big chores and small errands, attending to a slew of overwhelming details, documents filed and keys returned, all the while stretching the few lire she had left to meet her obligations.

The first stage of widowhood is paperwork.

Caterina had never imagined she would be standing here alone, on the first day of 1905, with nothing before her but the small hope of eventual reinvention. Every single promise made to her had been broken.

Caterina looked up as a window on the second floor of the shoe shop opened and an old woman shook a rag rug out into the cold air. Caterina caught her eye. The woman looked away, pulled the rug back inside, and slammed the window shut.

Her younger son, Ciro, peered around one of the columns. His blue-green eyes were the exact color of his father's, as deep and clear as the water of Sestri Levante. At ten years old, he was a replica of Carlo Lazzari, with big hands and feet and thick sandy brown hair. He was the strongest boy in Vilminore. When the village children went down into the valley to collect sticks bundled to sell for kindling, Ciro always had the heaviest haul strapped to his back because he could carry it.

Caterina felt a pang whenever she looked at him; in Ciro's face was all she had lost and would never recover. "Here." She pointed to the ground beside her black leather boot. "Now."

Ciro picked up his father's leather duffel and, running to his mother, called to his brother, who hid behind the statuary.

Eduardo, at eleven, resembled his mother's people, the Montini family, dark-eyed, tall, and willowy. He too picked up his satchel and ran to join them.

At the foot of the mountain, in the city of Bergamo, where Caterina had been born thirty-two years ago, the Montini family had set up a printing press that churned out linen writing paper, engraved calling cards, and small books in a shop on Via Borgo Palazzo. They had a house and a garden. As she closed her eyes, she saw her parents sitting at an alfresco table under their grape arbor, eating ricotta and honey sandwiches on thick, fresh bread. Caterina remembered all they were and all they had.

The boys dropped their suitcases in the snow.

"Sorry, Mama," Ciro said. He looked up at his mother and knew for certain that she was the most beautiful woman in the world. Her skin had the scent of peaches and felt like satin. His mother's long hair fell into soft, romantic waves, and ever since he could remember, as he lay in her arms, he had twisted a lock until it became a single shiny black rope.

"You look pretty," Ciro said earnestly. Whenever Caterina was sad, he tried to cheer her up with compliments.

Caterina smiled. "Every son thinks his mother is beautiful." Her cheeks turned pink in the cold as the tip of her aquiline nose turned bright red. "Even when she isn't."

Caterina fished in her purse for a small mirror and a chamois puff. The tip of red disappeared as she powdered it. She pursed her lips and looked down at her boys with a critical eye. She straightened Eduardo's collar, and pulled Ciro's coat sleeve over his wrist. The coat was too small for him, and no amount of pulling would add the two inches at the cuff to make it fit properly. "You just keep growing, Ciro."

"I'm sorry, Mama."

She remembered when she had their coats made for them, along with pin-cord trousers and white cotton shirts. There had been tufted blankets in their cribs when they were born, a layette of soft cotton gowns with pearl buttons. Wooden toys. Picture books. Her sons had long outgrown the clothes, and there was no replacing them.

Eduardo had one pair of wool pants and a coat given to him by a neighbor. Ciro wore the clean but ill-fitting clothes of his father, the hems on the work pants three inches deep, tacked with ragged stitches because sewing was not one of Caterina's talents. Ciro's belt was tightened on the last grommet, but still too loose to function properly.

"Where are we going, Mama?" Ciro asked as he followed his mother.

"She told you a hundred times. You don't listen." Eduardo lifted his brother's duffel and carried it.

"You must listen *for* him," Caterina reminded Eduardo.

"We're going to stay at the convent of San Nicola."

"Why do we have to live with nuns?" Ciro complained.

Caterina turned and faced her sons. They looked up at her, hoping for an explanation that would make sense of all the mysterious goings-on of the past few days. They weren't even sure what questions to ask, or what information they needed to know, but they were certain there must have been some reason behind Mama's strange behavior. She had been anxious. She wept through the night when she thought her sons were asleep. She had written lots of letters, more in the last week than they could ever remember her writing.

Caterina knew that if she shared the truth, she would have failed them. A good mother should never knowingly fail her children, not when she is all they have left in the world. Besides, in the years to come, Ciro would remember only the facts, while Eduardo would paint them with a soft brush. Neither version would be true, so what did it matter?

Caterina could not bear the responsibility of making every decision alone. In the fog of grief, she had to be sensible, and think of every possible alternative for her boys. In her mental state, she could not take care of her sons, and she knew it. She made lists of names, recalling every contact in her family's past and her husband's, any name that might be helpful. She scanned the list, knowing many of them probably needed as much help as she did. Years of poverty had depleted the region, and forced many to move down to Bergamo and Milan in search of work.

After much thought, she remembered that her father had printed missals for every parish in the Lombardy region, and as far south as Milan. He had donated his services as an indulgence to the Holy Roman Church, expecting no payment in return. Caterina used the old favor to secure a place for her sons with the sisters of San Nicola.

Caterina placed a hand on each of their shoulders.

"Listen to me. This is the most important thing I will ever tell you. Do as you're told. Do whatever the nuns ask you to do. Do it well. You must also do more than they ask of you. Anticipate. Look around. Do chores *before* the sisters ask.

"When Sister asks you to gather wood, do it immediately. No complaining! Help one another—make yourselves indispensable.

"Chop the wood, carry it inside, and build the fire without asking. Check the damper before lighting the kindling. And when the fire is out, clean the ash pit and close the flue. Sweep up so it looks like a picture. Prepare the hearth for the next fire with dry logs and kindling. Put the broom and the dustpan and the poker away. Don't wait for Sister to remind you.

"Make yourselves useful and stay out of trouble. Be pious and pray. Sit in the front pew during mass and sit at the farthest end of the bench during dinner. Take your portions last, and never seconds. You are there because of their kindness, not because I could pay them to keep you. Do you understand?"

"Yes, Mama," Eduardo said.

Caterina placed her hand on Eduardo's face and smiled. He put his arm around his mother's waist and held on tight. Then she pulled Ciro close. Her soft coat felt good against his face. "I know you can be good."

"I can't," Ciro sputtered, as he pulled away from his mother's embrace, "and I won't."

"Ciro."

"This is a bad idea, Mama. We don't belong there," Ciro pleaded.

"We have no place to stay," Eduardo said practically. "We belong wherever Mama puts us."

"Listen to your brother. This is the best I can do right now. When summer comes, I will come up the mountain and take you home."

"Back to our house?" Ciro asked.

"No. Somewhere new. Maybe we'll move up the mountain to Endine."

"Papa took us to the lake there."

"Yes, the town with the lake. Remember?"

The boys nodded that they did. Eduardo rubbed his hands together to warm them. They were rough and pink from the cold.

"Here. Take my gloves." Caterina removed her elbow-length black gloves. She helped Eduardo's hands into them, pulling them up and under his short sleeves. "Better?"

Eduardo closed his eyes; the heat from his mother's gloves traveled up his arms and through his entire body until he was enveloped in her warmth. He pushed his hair back with his hand, the scent of the brushed cotton, clean lemon and freesia, reassuring him.

"What do you have for me, Mama?" Ciro asked.

"You have Papa's gloves to keep you warm." She smiled. "But you want something of Mama's too?"

"Please."

"Give me your hand."

Ciro pulled his father's leather glove off with his teeth.

Caterina slid a gold signet ring off her smallest finger and placed it on Ciro's ring finger. "This was given to me by my papa."

Ciro looked down at the ring. A swirling, artful *C* in an oval of heavy yellow gold gleamed in the early morning light. He closed his fist, the gold band still warm from his mother's hand.

The stone facade of the convent of San Nicola was forbidding. Grand pilasters topped with statues of saints wearing expressions of hollow grief towered over the walkway. The thick walnut door had a sharp peak like a bishop's hat, Eduardo observed as he pushed the door open. Caterina and Ciro followed him inside into a small vestibule. They stomped the snow off their shoes on a mat made of woven driftwood branches. Caterina reached up and rang a small brass bell on a chain.

"They're probably praying. That's all they do in here. Pray all day," Ciro said as he peered through a crack in the door.

"How do you know what they do?" Eduardo asked.

The door opened. Sister Domenica looked down at the boys, sizing them up.

She was short and shaped like a dinner bell. Her black-and-white habit with a full skirt made her seem wider still. She placed her hands on her hips.

"I'm Signora Lazzari," Caterina said. "These are my sons. Eduardo and Ciro." Eduardo bowed to the nun. Ciro ducked his head quickly as if saying a fast prayer. Really, it was the mole on Sister's chin he wished to pray away.

"Follow me," the nun said.

Sister Domenica pointed to a bench, indicating where the boys should sit and wait. Caterina followed Sister into another room behind a thick wooden door, closing it behind her. Eduardo stared straight ahead while Ciro craned his neck, looking around.

"She's signing us away," Ciro whispered. "Just like Papa's saddle."

"That's not true," his brother whispered back.

Ciro inspected the foyer, a round room with two deep alcoves, one holding a shrine to Mary, the Blessed Mother, and the other, to Saint Francis of Assisi. Mary definitely had more votive candles lit at her feet. Ciro figured it meant you could always count on a woman. He took a deep breath. "I'm hungry."

"You're always hungry."

"I can't help it."

"Don't think about it."

"It's *all* I think about."

"You have a simple mind."

"No, I don't. Just because I'm strong, doesn't mean I'm stupid."

"I didn't say you were stupid. You're *simple*."

The scent of fresh vanilla and sweet butter filled the convent. Ciro closed his eyes and inhaled. He really *was* hungry. "Is this like the story Mama told us about the soldiers who got lost in the desert and saw a waterfall where there was none?" Ciro stood to follow the scent. He peered around the wall. "Or is there a cake baking somewhere?"

"Sit down," Eduardo ordered.

Ciro ignored him and walked down the long corridor.

"Get back here!" Eduardo whispered.

The walnut doors along the arcade were closed, and streams of faint light came through the overhead transoms. At the far end of the hallway, through a glass door, Ciro saw a cloister connecting the main convent to the workhouses. He ran down the arcade toward the light. When he made it to the door, he looked through the glass and saw a barren patch of earth, probably a garden, hemmed by a dense gnarl of gray fig trees dusted with snow.

Ciro turned toward the delicious scent and found the convent kitchen, tucked in the corner off the main hallway. The door to the kitchen was propped open with a brick. A shimmering collection of pots hung over a long wooden farm table. Ciro looked back to see if Eduardo had followed him. Alone and free, Ciro took a chance and ran to the kitchen doorway and peered inside. The kitchen was as warm as the hottest summer day. Ciro let the waves of heat roll over him.

A beautiful woman, much younger than his mother, was working at the table. She wore a long jumper of gray-striped wool with a white cotton apron tied over it. Her black hair was wrapped tightly into a chignon and tucked under a black kerchief. Her dark brown eyes squinted as she rolled a long skein of pasta on a smooth marble work slab. She hummed a tune as she took a small knife and whittled away tiny stars of dough, unaware that Ciro was watching her. Her long fingers moved surely and deftly with the knife. Soon, a batch of tiny pasta beads began to pile up on the board. Ciro decided that all women are beautiful, except maybe the old ones like Sister Domenica. "*Corallini*?" Ciro asked.

The young woman looked up and smiled at the little boy in the big clothes. "*Stelline*," she corrected him, holding up a small piece of dough carved into the shape of a star. She scooped up a pile of the little stars and threw them into a big bowl.

"What are you making?"

"Baked custard."

"It smells like cake in the hallway."

"That's the butter and the nutmeg. The custard is better than cake. It's so delicious it pulls angels off their perches. At least that's what I tell the other sisters. Did it make you hungry?"

"I was already hungry."

The woman laughed. "Who are you?"

"Who are *you*?" He narrowed his eyes.

"I'm Sister Teresa."

"I'm sorry, Sister. But, you . . . you look like a girl. You don't look like a nun."

"I don't wear a nice habit when I'm cooking. What's your name?"

Ciro sat on a stool across from the nun. "Ciro Augustus Lazzari," he said proudly.

"That's a big name. Are you a Roman emperor?"

"Nope." Ciro remembered he was speaking with a nun. "Sister."

"How old are you?"

"Ten. I'm big for my age. I pull the rope at the water wheel in town."

"That's impressive."

"I'm the only boy my age who can. They call me an ox."

Sister Teresa reached behind the table and pulled a heel of bread from a bin. She slathered it with soft butter and handed it to the boy. As Ciro ate, she swiftly carved more stars from the dough and added them to the large bowl filled with a batter of milk, eggs, sugar, vanilla, and nutmeg. She stirred the ingredients evenly with a large enamel spoon. Ciro watched the creamy folds of custard, now speckled with stars, lap over one another as the mixture thickened. Sister poured the custard into ceramic cups on a metal tray without spilling a drop. "Are you visiting?"

"We've been sent here to work because we're poor."

"Everyone in Vilminore di Scalve is poor. Even the nuns."

"We're *really* poor. We don't have a house anymore. We ate all the chickens, and Mama sold the cow. She sold a painting and all the books. Didn't get much. And that money has almost run out."

"It's the same story in every village in the Alps."

"We won't stay long. My mother is going to the city, and she'll come and get us this summer." Ciro looked over at the deep wood-burning oven and figured that he would have to stoke and clean it until his mother returned. He wondered how many fireplaces there were in the convent. He imagined there were lots of them. He'd probably spend every hour of daylight chopping wood and building fires.

"What brought you to the convent?"

"Mama can't stop crying."

"Why?"

"She misses Papa."

Sister lifted the tray of custard cups and placed them in the oven. She checked the surface of several other baked custard cups on a cooling rack. What a lovely thing, to work in a warm kitchen in the cold winter and make food. Ciro imagined that people who work in kitchens are never hungry.

"Where did your father go?"

"They say he died, but I don't think so," Ciro said.

"Why don't you believe them?" Sister wiped her hands on a moppeen and leaned on the table so she might be eye to eye with the boy.

"Eduardo read the letter that was sent to Mama from America. They say Papa died in a mine, but they never found his body. That's why I don't think Papa is dead."

"Sometimes—," she began.

Ciro interrupted her. "I know all about it—sometimes a man dies, and there's no body. Dynamite can go off in a mine and people inside blow up, or a body can burn in a fire or disappear down a hole, or drown in a slag river inside the mountain. Or you get hurt and you can't walk and you get stuck underground and you die of starvation because nobody came to find you and animals eat you and nothing is left but bones. I know every which way there is to die—but my papa would not die like that. He was strong. He could beat up anyone, and he could lift more than any man in Vilminore di Scalve. He's not dead."

"Well, I'd like to meet him someday."

"You will. He'll come back. You'll see." Ciro hoped his father was alive, and his heart ached at the possibility that he might never see him again. He remembered how he could always find his father easily in a crowd because he was so tall, he towered over everyone in the village.

Carlo Lazzari was so strong he was able to carry both sons simultane-ously, one on each hip, like sacks of flour up and down the steep moun-tain trails. He felled trees with an ax, and cut lumber as easily as Sister cut the dough. He built a dam at the base of the Vertova waterfall. Other men helped, but Carlo Lazzari was the leader.

Sister Teresa broke a fresh egg into a cup and added a teaspoon of sugar. She poured fresh cream into the cup and whisked it until there was a creamy foam on the surface. "Here." She gave it to Ciro. He sipped it, then drank it down until the cup was empty.

"How's that stomach now?"

"Full." Ciro smiled.

"Would you like to help me cook sometime?"

"Boys don't cook."

"That's not true. All the great chefs in Paris are men. Women are not allowed in the Cordon Bleu. That's a famous cooking school in France," Sister Teresa told him.

Eduardo burst into the kitchen. "Come on, Ciro. We have to go!"

Sister Teresa smiled at him. "You must be Eduardo."

"Yes, I am."

"She's a nun," Ciro told his brother.

Eduardo bowed his head. "I'm sorry, Sister."

"Are you hungry too?"

Eduardo shook his head that he wasn't.

"Did your mother tell you that you shouldn't be any trouble?" Sister asked.

He nodded that she had.

Sister Teresa reached back into the metal bin and took a wedge of bread and buttered it. She gave it to Eduardo, who ate it hungrily.

"My brother won't ask for *anything*," Ciro explained. "Can he have an egg and cream with sugar too?" He turned to his brother. "You'll like it."

Sister smiled and took a fresh egg, sugar, and some more cream and whipped it with a whisk. She gave it to Eduardo, who slowly sipped the egg cream, savoring every drop until the cup was empty.

"Thank you, Sister," Eduardo said.

"We thought the convent would be horrible." Ciro placed his own and Eduardo's cup in the sink.

"If you behave and say your prayers, I don't think you'll have any trouble."

Sister Domenica stood in the doorway of the kitchen with Caterina. Eduardo gasped when he saw them and quickly bowed to the old nun. Ciro couldn't understand why his brother was afraid of everyone and everything. Couldn't he see that Sister Domenica was harmless? With her starched coutil bib and black skirts, she resembled the black-and-white-checked globe made from Carrara marble that Mama used as a paperweight. Ciro wasn't afraid of any nun, and besides this one was just an old lady with a wooden cross hanging from her waist like a giant key.

"I have found two capable young men to help me in the kitchen," Sister Teresa said.

"Eduardo is going to help me in the office," Sister Domenica said to Sister Teresa. "And Ciro will work in the chapel. I need a strong boy who can do heavy lifting."

"I need a strong boy who can make cheese." Sister Teresa winked at Sister Domenica.

"I can do both," Ciro said proudly.

Caterina put her hands on Ciro's shoulders. "My boys will do whatever you need, Sister."

*   *   *

Just a few miles up the mountain, above Vilminore di Scalve, the village of Schilpario clung to the mountainside like a gray icicle. Even the dead were buried on a slope, in sepulchers protected by a high granite retaining wall covered in vines.

There was no formal piazza or grand colonnade in Schilpario, no fountains or statuaries as in Vilminore di Scalve, just sturdy, plain alpine structures of wood and stucco that could endure the harsh winters. The stucco was painted in candy colors of lemon yellow, cherry red, and plum. The bright colors were set into the gray mountain like whimsical tiles.

Schilpario was a mining town where rich veins of iron ore and barite were carved out of the earth and carted down to Milan for sale. Every job in the village was in service to the towns below, including the building and maintenance of the chutes that harnessed the rushing water of Stream Vò that was piped down the cliffs.

The farms provided fresh meat for the butchers in the city. Every family had a smokehouse where sausage, salami, prosciutto, and sleeves of ham were cured. The mountain people were sustained through the long winters by the contents of their root cellars filled with bins of plentiful chestnuts, which carpeted the mountain paths like glassy brown stones. They also survived on eggs from their chicken coops, and milk and cream from their cows. They churned their own butter and made their own cheese, and what they could not sell, they ate.

The mountain forests high above the village were loaded with porcini and other mushrooms of all kinds, as well as coveted truffles, gathered in late summer and sold at a premium to middlemen from France, who in turn sold them to the great chefs in the elegant cities of Europe. The family pig was used to locate the truffles growing in the ground. Even the smallest children were taught how to hunt for truffles from a very early age, combing the woods on their hands and knees, a linen sack tied loosely around their waists, searching for the fragrant bulbs nestled deep in the earth around the roots of old trees.

Schilpario was one of the last villages to the north, which lay in the shadow of the Pizzo Camino, the highest peak in the Alps, where the snow did not melt, even in summer. So high in the cliffs, the people looked down on the clouds, which moved through the valley below like rosettes of meringue.

When spring came, the ice-covered cliffs below the peak thawed, turning bright green as mugo pine and juniper trees sprouted new branches. The deep gorge of the valley filled with fields of yellow buttercups. The village women gathered herbs to make medicine: chamomile for tea to soothe nerves, wild dandelion for blood curing, fragrant peppermint for stomach ills, and golden nettle to bring down fevers.

The Passo Presolana was the lone ribbon of road connecting Schilpario to Vilminore di Scalve and down the mountain to the city of Bergamo. It had been built in the eleventh century, a rustic one-way path to be traveled on foot. Eventually the road was widened to accommodate a horse and carriage, but only in warm weather, as it was treacherous in winter.

Marco Ravanelli knew every cleft and curve of the pass, every natural stone overpass that provided shelter, each small village along the way, every farm, river, and lake, as he had accompanied his father, who ran a horse and carriage service, up and down the mountain since he was a boy.

Marco, the coachman of Schilpario, was slim and of medium height, with a thick black mustache that offset his handsome features. As he plunged two long sticks into the ice, he steadied himself on the path between the stone house he rented and the barn that he owned. He was careful not to fall, as he couldn't afford a broken leg or any sort of injury. He was thirty-three years old and responsible for a wife and six children, the youngest, Stella, just born.

Enza, his eldest, followed behind him, plunging her own set of sticks into the ice to steady herself. Enza had just turned ten, but she could do anything a woman twice her age could do and perhaps better, especially sewing. Her small fingers moved deftly and with precision, creating small, nearly invisible stitches on straight seams. Her natural talent was a marvel to her mother, who couldn't sew nearly as fast.

Enza's chestnut brown hair had not been cut, and it grazed her waist in two shiny braids that lay flat and neat like reins. Her heart-shaped face resembled her mother's, full cheeks, skin the color of fresh cream, and perfectly shaped lips with a defined Cupid's bow. Enza's light brown eyes sparkled like amber buttons.

The eldest daughter in a family with many children never has a real childhood.

Enza had learned how to hitch a horse as soon as she grew tall enough to reach the carriage. She knew how to make a paste from chestnuts for pies, pasta dough from potatoes for gnocchi, how to churn butter, wring a chicken's neck, wash clothes and mend them. Whenever Enza found time to play, she used it to sew. Fabric was expensive, so she taught herself to dye cotton muslin to create colorful designs that she would then sew into garments for the family.

When summer came, she picked blackberries and raspberries and made dyes from their inky pulp. She pleated and pinched the coarse cotton, painting the dyes onto the fabric, and then let them dry in the sun, setting the colors. Plain cotton muslin became beautiful as Enza dyed it into shades of lavender, delicate pink, and slate blue. She decorated the colorful fabric with embellishments and embroidery.

There were no dolls to play with, but who needed one when there were two babies in cribs to care for, plus three more children in the middle, one crawling and two more walking, as well as plenty of tasks to occupy the dark winter days?

The stable was cold, so Marco and Enza threw themselves into their chores. As Papa brushed Cipi, their beloved horse, Enza polished the bench on the governess cart. The cart was smaller than a regular carriage, seated only two, and was painted a sophisticated black, to emphasize the graceful curves of its design. Enza dusted the seat with a clean moppeen, careful to polish the trim.

Working people in service to the wealthy must pay particular attention to details. Paint must be lacquered, gold trim must dazzle, every notch, joint, and button of brass must shine. The stature and social position of the customer is reflected in the gloss that results from the servant's elbow grease. It's what the wealthy pay for; it's what they require. Marco taught Enza that everything must gleam, including the horse.

Enza placed the lap robe she had made of sturdy gold cotton on one side and brown suede on the other, on the passenger side of the cart. It would keep the paying customer warm.

"I don't think you should go, Papa."

"It's the only job I've been offered all winter."

"What if the hitch snaps?"

"It won't."

"What if Cipi falls down?"

"He'll get back up."

Marco checked the suspension on the cart. He took an oilcan and greased the springs.

"Here. Let me." Enza took the oilcan from her father and slipped under the cart to oil the gears. She was careful to give a few extra squirts, so the cart could take sudden turns and jolts on the icy mountain road without toppling.

Marco helped her out from under the cart. "The snow is always the worst on the mountain. By the time I get to Vilminore di Scalve, it will be a dusting. There's probably no snow at all down in Bergamo."

"What about the rain?"

Marco smiled. "You worry enough for your mother and me."

"Somebody has to."

"Enza."

"Sorry, Papa. We have enough flour until spring. A little sugar. Lots of chestnuts. You don't have to take this job."

"What about the rent?"

"Signor Arduini can wait. All he'll do with the money is buy more dresses for his daughter. Maria has enough."

"Now you're going to tell the richest man in town how to spend his money?"

"I wish he'd ask me. I'd tell him plenty."

Marco tried not to laugh. "I'm getting three lire to take the passenger down the mountain."

"Three lire!"

"I know. Only a fool would turn down three lire."

"Let me go with you. If you have any problems, I'll be there to help you."

"Who will help your mother with the children?"

"Battista."

"He's nine years old, and a bigger baby than Stella."

"He just likes to have fun, Papa."

"That's not a quality that gets you far in life."

"Eliana is helpful."

"She's not strong," Marco reminded her.

"But she's smart; that should account for something."

"It does, but that doesn't help your mother with the chores. Vittorio and Alma are small, and Stella is nursing. Your mama needs you here."

"All right. I'll stay. How long do you think you'll be gone?"

"One day down the mountain. I'll stay the night, and one day up the mountain."

"Two whole days—"

"For *three* lire," Marco reminded her.

Marco was ambitious. He had drawn up plans to build a deluxe carriage with three benches to transport the summer tourists who craved the quiet of the mountain summers, with their cool nights and sunny days. The pristine alpine lakes were popular for swimming. Tourists could take the healing waters in Boario if they wished, sun on the beach of the Brembo River or take the mud baths of Trescore. The new carriage would take the tourists anywhere they wanted to go! Marco pictured a modern carriage with a canopy of bold black-and-white stripes with brass bindings, while silk-ball fringe along the edge would provide a touch of glamour. Giacomina and Enza would make corduroy cushions for the benches, turquoise blue.

Marco hoped to earn enough money to finally make the Arduinis an offer on the old stone house. The rent was high, but it was close to Cipi's barn, where the carriage and equipment were stored. The Ravanellis couldn't live in the barn. They needed the house.

Signor Arduini was getting older; soon his son would take over as padrone. The wooden box filled with folded parchments of surveyed land lots in Schilpario would be handed down and managed by the next generation of Arduinis. There had been signs that Marco should seriously consider buying the house. Sometimes after Marco delivered the rent, Signor Arduini would implore him to buy their house before his death, before his son took over and a potential sale might be off the table for good. It was Signore's desire to sell that had motivated Marco to expand his business; the present carriage would not provide the profit needed to buy the house.

Buying the house on Via Scalina was Marco's dream for his family.

        .   .   .

Marco arrived in Vilminore on time. Across the piazza, he saw his customer waiting for him, a nun by her side. Resting on the ground next to her was a small brown duffel. Caterina's blue coat stood out against the pink and gray of winter. Marco was relieved that his customer had been waiting for him, as arranged. Lately, most of his fares had not honored their appointments, a sign of how dire the poverty in these mountains had become, as travelers attempted to pass on foot.

Marco guided Cipi across the piazza to the entrance of San Nicola, then jumped off his perch, greeted the nun, and helped Caterina Lazzari into the governess cart. He placed her suitcases inside the drop box by her feet and flipped the cover shut, draped the lap robe over her blue coat, and secured the canopy.

Sister Domenica handed him an envelope, which he tucked into his pocket. He thanked her before climbing into the cart on the driver's side. The nun went back inside the convent.

As Marco guided the horse across the piazza, he heard a boy calling out for his mother. Caterina Lazzari asked Marco to stop as Ciro, out of breath, ran up to the side of the carriage. She looked down at her son. "Go back inside, Ciro. It's cold."

"Mama, don't forget to write to me."

"Every week. I promise. And you must write to me."

"I will, Mama."

"Be a good boy and listen to the sisters. It won't be long until summer."

Marco snapped the reins and guided Cipi down the main street to the mountain road. Ciro watched his mother go. He wanted to run after the cart, grab the handle, and hoist himself up on to the seat, but his mother did not look back at him, nor did she lean over the side, holding out her hand, beckoning him to join her, as she had done on every carriage ride, train trip, or swing as long as he could remember.

All Ciro could see was his mother's choice to ride away from him, to leave him there like a broken chair on the side of the road waiting for the junkman. As she rode off, he saw the frame of her collar and the back of her neck, straight as the stem of a rose. Soon she became a blue blur in the distance as the cart turned toward the entrance road to the Passo Presolana.

Ciro's chest heaved when she disappeared from view. He longed to open his mouth and cry out for his mother, but what good would that do? Ciro hadn't learned the difference between sadness and anger. He just knew that he would have liked to smash everything in sight—the statuary, the vendor's bin, and the windows in every shop on the colonnade.

Ciro was angry about every bad decision his mother had made since his father left, including selling everything Papa owned, including his gun and his belt buckle. He was angry that Eduardo was tolerant in the face of every setback and went along with everything their mother said. And now Ciro was furious that he had to live in a *convent*, which for him, was like asking *un pesce di abitare in un albero* (a fish to live in a tree). Nothing his mother had done made sense. Her explanations were not satisfactory. All he knew and had heard was that he must be good, and who decides what is good?

"Come inside, Ciro." Eduardo held the door open.

"Leave me alone."

"*Now*, Ciro." Eduardo stepped outside, closing the door behind him. "I mean it."

Eduardo's tone ignited Ciro's temper like a match to dry kindling. He was not Ciro's mother or father. Ciro turned to his brother and tackled him. Eduardo's head cracked against the bricks as Ciro pummeled him with his fists. Ciro heard the solid landing of the blows, but didn't hold back, only hit his brother harder in his rage. Eduardo curled up into a ball to protect his face and rolled from his back onto his knees, crying out, "It won't make her come back."

Ciro's strength gave out, and he fell onto the ground next to his brother. Eduardo held his knees tight as Ciro knelt and placed his face in his hands. He didn't want Eduardo to see him cry. Ciro also knew if he began to weep, he wouldn't stop.

Eduardo stood and pulled down the short cuffs on his shirt. He smoothed his pants and lifted them up by the waist. He patted his hair back into place. "They'll throw us out if we fight."

"Let them! I'm going to run away. I'm not going to stay here." Ciro's eyes darted around as he planned his escape. There were at least six ways out of the piazza. Once he was free of this town, he could go way up the mountain to Monte Isola, or a few miles down the road to Lovere. Someone might take him in.

Eduardo hung his head and began to cry. "Don't leave me here alone."

Ciro looked at his brother, the only family he had, and felt worse for him than he did for himself. "Stop crying," he said.

The full morning sun was up, the shopkeepers were opening their doors, lifting their shades, and rolling their carts on to the colonnade. Vendors dressed in shades of flat gray, the color of the low stone wall that encased the village, pushed hand carts painted bright red, yellow, and white filled with bins of polished walnuts, silver pails filled with braids of fresh white cheese in clean, icy water, spools of colorful silk thread on wooden dowels, fresh loaves of bread in baskets, packets of herbs in linen sacks for poultice—all manner of needs for sale.

The presence of the others helped Eduardo gain control of his emotions. He dried his tears with his sleeve. He looked out to where the main road curved to connect to the pass, but it held no meaning for him; it wouldn't lead him or his brother out of their situation. The morning mist had lifted, and the air was so cold that Eduardo could barely breathe. "Where would we go?"

"We could follow Mama. We could change her mind."

"Mama can't take care of us right now."

"But she's our *mother*," Ciro argued.

"A mother who can't take care of her children is useless." Eduardo held the door open for Ciro. "Come on."

Ciro entered the convent with his heart heavy with need for his mother's embrace and a deep shame for having hit his brother. After all, their tenure at San Nicola wasn't Eduardo's choice, and the events that had led them there were not his fault either.

Maybe these nuns could be of some use, Ciro thought. Maybe they could pray their mother back *before* the summer—Ciro would ask them to offer up their rosaries for her. But something told him that all the glass beads on the mountain wouldn't bring Caterina home. No matter how Eduardo might reassure him, Ciro was certain he would never see his mother again.

Ciro cried himself to sleep that night, and in the morning found Eduardo sleeping on the floor next to him, as the cots provided by the nuns were too small to hold both of them. Even when he grew to be a young man, Ciro would never forget this small act of kindness, which Eduardo would repeat night after night for months. Eduardo's love was the only security Ciro would ever know. Sister Teresa would feed them, Sister Domenica would assign them chores, and Sister Ercolina would teach them Latin, but it was Eduardo who would look out for Ciro's heart and try to make up for the loss of their mother.

2

A RED BOOK
Un Libro Rosso

Halfway down the mountain, in the early afternoon, Marco stopped to rest Cipi on the outskirts of Clusone. He helped Caterina down from the cart. She thanked him—the first time she had spoken directly to him since the trip began that morning.

Marco opened a tin and offered her a fresh, crusty roll, thin slivers of salami, and a bottle of sweet soda. Caterina took a handkerchief tucked inside her sleeve and placed the bread and salami on it while Marco opened the bottle of soda. She took a small bite of the biscuit and chewed slowly.

Marco had been a coachman since he was a boy. His father had taught him how to take care of horses, shoe and feed them, build and maintain equipment, and serve customers, and he still followed his father's advice: *The coachman must know his place and speak only when spoken to. Half the negotiated fare is collected at the beginning of the trip, the balance at the end. A coachman should engage a strong horse and provide a clean carriage with the feed stored out of sight. There should be several rest points on a long journey, announced to the customer beforehand. Food and drink should be provided, as well as pipe tobacco, snuff, cigarettes, and matches. The coachman should be familiar with the route, and know the location of way stations in case of illness or accident. Once the destination is reached, the coachman is responsible for the secure delivery of the customer's belongings.*

This particular afternoon, Marco forgot the rule about conversing with passengers. He was thinking of his children, and knowing that Signora Lazzari was also a mother, he sensed that she might be simpatico. The little boy she'd left behind tore at Marco's heart. Caterina was stoic until the carriage reached the cleft of the pass. It was only then that she wept.

"I told my daughter that it wouldn't snow beyond Valle di Scalve." Marco looked out over the expanse of the valley, frozen over in white ice, the hills curved like sculpted marble. The road ahead seemed clear; the only danger Marco foresaw was the occasional patch of black ice.

"You were right." Caterina took the biscuit and broke it in half, giving the other half to Marco.

"Thank you," he said.

She took a bite.

"Do you have a daughter?" Marco asked.

"No. Two boys. You saw Ciro, and there's Eduardo. He's a year older."

"Was he at the convent too?"

She nodded that he was. Marco looked at Caterina, roughly his own age, and decided that she was taking the years better than he. The early mornings tending the animals, the long days working in the iron ore mine for little return, and the constant anxiety about how to provide for his family had made Marco feel and look older than his age. There had been a time when a beautiful woman like Caterina could turn his head. In the right circumstances, she still could.

"I always wanted a daughter," she admitted.

"My eldest is a good girl. She helps her mother and me, and she doesn't complain. Enza is ten years old, and already so wise. I have two sons and three more girls."

"You must have a farm."

"No, no, just the cart and the horse."

Caterina couldn't imagine why Marco would have six children unless he needed to put them to work on a farm. A couple of strong boys was all he would need to keep a carting business with a livery stable going. "You must have a good wife."

"A very good wife. And your husband?" Marco realized that he was asking very personal questions, inappropriate for a lady like Caterina. "I only ask because you left your boys at the convent," he explained.

"I am a widow," Caterina offered, but she did not elaborate.

Caterina's station in life—once as the daughter of a prominent family, then as a young wife and mother, and now as a widow—required her to hold herself to standards of decorum. A lady didn't confide in a coachman, even when she may very well have been even poorer than he.

"The sisters of San Nicola are very kind," Marco said.

"Yes, they are." Caterina was sure he was referring to the envelope that Sister Domenica had given to him, which paid for this trip. For Caterina, the nuns had been more than generous. They had taken the boys on short notice and made her arrangements as well.

"Your boys should do very well there."

"I hope they will."

"Many years ago, when I was a boy, the nuns of San Nicola gave me a remembrance card. I still carry it with me." Marco reached into his pocket and handed her a small illustrated card trimmed in gold.

"A talisman." Caterina's father used to print cards like this one, depicting the Holy Family protected by angels. They were distributed on feast days or at funerals, often with the name of the dead embossed upon the back. Her eyes filled with tears at the memory of the boxes of them in her father's print shop. "I understand why this gives you comfort. Are you a believer?"

"Yes, I am," Marco said.

"Not me. Not anymore." Caterina handed the card back to Marco. If only the image on the card were true. She had long given up on the angels and saints. Their power to soothe her had died with her husband. She climbed back up into the carriage without Marco's help, suddenly impatient with the length of the journey. "How much longer is the trip?"

"We'll be in Bergamo by nightfall."

They continued down the Passo Presolana, over Pointe Nossa, through Colzate, past Vertova, for a final rest stop in Nembro, where Signora Lazzari changed out of her traveling clothes and into a proper dress before arriving in Bergamo. Marco surmised the appointment Signora was to keep must be important. She fixed her hair, her hat, and her gown, which once had been stylish but now was worn along the hem and cuffs. The coachman and his customer did not exchange another word.

.   .   .

Enza closed the wooden shutters on the window at the front of the house. As she threw the latch, cold wind whistled through the slats. With the hearth crackling behind her, stoked with wood and a few pieces of coal, and the laundry kettle about to boil, the kitchen was filled with a warm and welcome mist.

This was Enza's favorite time of day, when night had fallen in Schilpario and the children were in bed. Baby Stella slept in a woven basket draped with a soft white blanket. Her face looked like a pink peach by the firelight.

Giacomina, Enza's mother, a capable woman with a sweet face and soft hands, stirred a pot of milk on the fire. She wore her long brown hair with a center part and two braids, wrapped neatly in a bun at the base of her neck.

Giacomina stooped over the flame until the milk foamed and placed the pan on a stone trivet. She lifted two ceramic cups from the shelf, placing them on the table, dropped a pat of butter in each cup, and poured the milk on top. Reaching up to pull a small bottle of homemade brandy from the shelf, she put a teaspoon in her cup, a couple of drops in Enza's. She stirred the mixture and ladled the foam left in the pan on top.

"This will warm you up." Giacomina gave Enza her cup. They sat down at the end of their dining table, made from wide planks of alder, with matching benches on either side. How Enza wished she could buy her mother a dining room suite made from polished mahogany with fabric seats, and a new set of china to dress the table, just like Signora Arduini had at her house.

"Papa should be back by now."

"You know the trip back up the mountain is always longer." Mama sipped her milk. "I'll wait up for him. You can go to bed."

"I have wash to do." Enza shrugged.

Giacomina smiled. The laundry could wait, but Enza wanted an excuse to be awake when her father returned. It was always the same.

Enza couldn't sleep until all the members of the family were safe inside, asleep in their beds.

"Mama, tell me a story." Enza reached across the table and took Giacomina's hand. She spun her mother's gold wedding band around her finger, feeling the grooves of the tiny carved rosebuds etched into the gold. Enza believed it was the most beautiful piece of jewelry in the world.

"I'm tired, Enza."

"Please. The story of your wedding day."

Enza had heard the love story so many times that her own mother and father had become as magical to her as figures in her favorite book, drawn in exquisite detail and eternally young in the telling. Enza studied the photograph of her parents on their wedding day as if it were a map. In a sense it was, as they were creating a destination, a life together. The bride and groom sat stiffly in two chairs. Mama held a bouquet of mountain asters tightly as Papa rested his hand on her shoulder.

"Your papa came to see me one Sunday when I was sixteen and he was seventeen," Giacomina began the familiar story. "He drove the governess cart—at that time, it belonged to his father. It was painted white in those days, and that morning, he had filled it with fresh flowers. There was barely room for your papa on the bench.

"Cipi, just three years old, had pink ribbons braided through his mane. Papa arrived at our house, threw off the reins, leaped off the bench, came into the house, and asked my papa if he could marry me. I was the last daughter in my family to marry. My papa had married off five daughters, and by the time it was my turn, he barely looked up from his pipe. He just said yes, and we went to the priest, that was that."

"And Papa said—"

"Your father told me that he wanted seven sons and seven daughters."

"And you said—"

"Seven children will be enough."

"And now we have six."

"God owes us one more," Giacomina teased.

"I think we have enough children around here, Mama. We barely have enough food as it is, and I don't see God showing up at the door with a sack of flour. "

Mama smiled. She had grown to appreciate Enza's wry sense of humor. Her eldest daughter had a mature view of the world, and she was worried that Enza was overly concerned with adult problems.

Enza went to the fire to check the iron kettle suspended on the spit and filled with bubbling hot water, melted down from snow. A second pot, resting on the hearth, filled with clean hot water, was used to rinse the clothes. Enza lifted the pot off the fire and placed it on the floor. She picked up a wooden basket full of nightshirts and placed them into the kettle to soak, added lye, and stirred the laundry with a metal rod, careful not to splash the lye onto her skin. As she stirred, the nightshirts turned bright white.

Enza poured off the excess water into an empty pot and hauled it to the far end of the kitchen, where her father had made a chute in the floor, feeding into a pipe that released water down the mountainside. She wrung the nightshirts by hand and gave them to her mother, who hung them on a rope by the fire, mother and daughter making quick work of a big chore. The lye, sweetened with a few drops of lavender oil, filled the room with the fresh scent of summer.

Giacomina and Enza heard footsteps on the landing. They ran to the door, opening it wide. Marco was on the porch, brushing the snow off his boots.

"Papa! You made it!"

Marco came into the house and embraced Giacomina. "Signor Arduini came for the rent this morning," she whispered.

"What did you tell him?" Papa lifted Enza off the ground and kissed her.

"I told him to wait and speak to my husband."

"Did he smile?" Marco asked his wife.

"No."

"Well, he just did. I stopped at his house and paid him the rent. On time, with thirty-five minutes to spare."

Enza and Giacomina embraced Marco. "Did you girls think that I would let you down?"

"I wasn't sure," Enza said truthfully. "That's a big mountain and there's a lot of snow, and we have an old horse. And sometimes, even when you do a good job, passengers only pay the first half of the fare, and you get stuck for the rest."

Marco laughed. "Not this time." Papa placed two crisp lire and a small gold coin on the dining table. Enza touched each bill and spun the gold coin, thrilled at the treasure.

Giacomina lifted a warming pan from the hearth filled with her husband's dinner. She served her husband a casserole of buttery polenta and sweet sausage, and poured him a glass of brandy.

"Where did you take the passenger, Papa?"

"To Domenico Picarazzi, the doctor."

"I wonder why she needs a doctor." Giacomina placed a heel of bread next to his plate. "Did she seem ill?"

"No." Marco sipped his brandy. "But she's suffering. I think she must have just become a widow. She had just placed her sons in the convent in Vilminore."

"Poor things," Giacomina said.

"Don't think about taking them in, Mina."

Enza noticed that her father used her mother's nickname whenever he didn't want to do something.

"Two boys. Around Enza's age: ten and eleven."

Giacomina's heart broke at the thought of the lonely boys.

"Mama, we can't take them," Enza said.

"Why not?"

"Because it's two more children, and God only plans to send you one more."

Marco laughed as Enza stacked the laundry pots and kettles next to the hearth. She kissed her mother and father goodnight and climbed the ladder up to the loft to sleep.

Enza tiptoed in the dark past the crib where Stella slept and over to her brothers and other sister, who slept on one large straw mattress, their bodies crisscrossed like a basket weave. She found her place on the far side of the bed and lay down to sleep. The sound of the gentle breathing of her brothers and sisters soothed her.

Enza prayed without making the sign of the cross, saying her rosary, or reciting the familiar litanies from vespers in Latin. Instead she called on the angels, thanking them for bringing her father home safely. She imagined her angels looked a lot like the gold-leafed putti holding sheaves of wheat over the tabernacle at the church of Barzesto, with faces that resembled that of her baby sister Stella.

Enza prayed to stay near her mother and father. She wanted to live with them always, and never marry or become a mother herself. She couldn't imagine ever being that brave, courageous enough to stand away from all she knew to choose something different. She wanted to live in the same village she had been born in, just like her mother. She wanted to hold every baby on the day he was born and bury every old person on the day he died. She wanted to wake up every day to live and work in the shadows of il Pizzo Camino, Corno Stella, and Pizzo dei Tre Signorei, the holy trinity of mountain peaks that she had been in awe of her whole life.

Enza prayed that she could help her mother take care of the children, and maybe one more when God sent him. She hoped the new baby would be a boy, so Battista and Vittorio would feel less outnumbered. She prayed for patience, because babies are a lot of work.

Enza prayed for her father to make enough lire to buy the house, so they wouldn't have to live in fear of the padrone any longer. When the first of the month arrived, so would Signor Arduini. Enza dreaded it, as there were times when Marco could not pay the rent. So Enza used to imagine her father's empty pockets filled with gold coins. Her imagination helped her avoid despair; the things that frightened her could be willed away. Enza imagined a satisfactory outcome to every problem, and thus far, the world had obeyed her will. Her family was warm, safe, and fed tonight, the rent was paid, and there was money in the tin box that had been empty for too long.

Throughout the day, she pictured her father as he came up the mountain, imagining each curve of the road, the rest stops where Cipi ate oats and Papa enjoyed a smoke. She imagined each clop of the hooves that led her father safely back up the pass, one after the other, like the consistent ticking of a clock. In her mind's eye, she willed Marco home to Schilpario, safely, surely, and without incident, and with the promised three lire in his pocket that would get his family through the long winter.

Enza knew how lucky she was, and how sad it was that everyone on the mountain did not share that luck. Her papa had done a good job, and he had been paid. For now, all was well. When she dreamed that night, she would imagine the young widow who suffered the loss of her husband and now her sons. *Poverella*, she thought.

3

A SILVER MIRROR
Uno Specchio d'Argento

Six winters had passed since Caterina Lazzari left her sons at the convent.

The terrible winter of 1909–10 finally came to an end, like a penance fulfilled. Spring arrived, bringing a daisy sun and warm breezes, thawing every cliff, trail, and ridge, releasing rushing streams of clear, cold water down the mountainside like flowing blue hair ribbons on a girl.

It seemed that all the residents of Vilminore had come outside and taken a moment to lift their faces to the apricot sky, absorb the warmth of it. There was much to do, now that spring had arrived. It was time to open the windows, roll up the rugs, wash the linens, and prepare the gardens.

The nuns of San Nicola never rested.

When Caterina did not return for them the summer after she left them at San Nicola, her sons had learned not to count on her promises. They let the disappointment wash over them like the waterfall showers they took in the lake above Vilminore. When they finally received a letter from their mother, cloistered in a convent without a return address, they stopped begging Sister Ercolina to let them go to her, since that was clearly impossible. Instead, they vowed to find her as soon as their time at San Nicola was done. No matter how long it might take, Eduardo was determined to bring his mother back to Vilminore. When the sisters told them Caterina was "getting better," they believed she would. They imagined their mother in the care of the nuns in some far-away place, because Sister Ercolina assured them this was true.

Besides the upkeep and care of the convent and church of San Nicola, the sisters ran the local school, Parrocchia di Santa Maria Assunta e di San Pietro Apostolo. They were responsible for the housekeeping of the rectory and providing meals for the new village priest, Don Raphael Gregorio. They also did his laundry, maintained his vestments, and took care of the altar linens. The nuns were no different from any of the working people on the mountain, except that their padrone wore a Roman collar.

The Lazzari brothers, now teenagers, were as much a part of convent life as the nuns themselves. They were aware of all they missed, but instead of grieving for their father and pining for their mother, they learned to use their emotions to fuel their ambition. They learned how to fend off sadness and quell despair by staying busy like the sisters of San Nicola. This life lesson, learned by the sisters' example, would carry them through.

The Lazzari brothers made themselves indispensable to the nuns, just as Caterina had hoped. Ciro had taken over most of the chores assigned to Ignazio Farino, the old convent handyman, who, at nearly sixty, was looking for a pipe, a shade tree, and an endless summer. Ciro rose early and worked until night, tending the fireplaces, milking the cow, churning the butter, twisting fresh braids of *scamorza* cheese, chopping wood, shoveling coal, washing windows, scrubbing floors, while Eduardo, the scholar with a gentle nature, was chosen to work as a secretary in the convent office. His artful penmanship was put to use answering correspondence and placing marks on report cards. Eduardo also hand-printed the programs for holiday masses and high holy days in elegant calligraphy. Eduardo, certainly the more devout of the two brothers, also rose at dawn to serve the daily mass in the chapel and ring the chimes in early evening to summon the sisters to vespers.

Ciro was a strapping fifteen-year-old, having grown to nearly six feet tall. The convent diet of eggs, pasta, and wild game had made him robust and healthy. With his sandy brown hair and blue-green eyes, he made a vivid contrast to the dark, regal Italian natives of these mountains. His thick eyebrows, straight nose, and full lips were characteristic of the

Swiss, who resided just over the border to the north. Ciro's tempera-ment, however, remained pure Latin. The sisters had tamed his quick temper by forcing him to sit quietly and say the rosary. He learned per-sistence and discipline by their example, and humility from his desire to please the women that took him in. There wasn't anything Ciro wouldn't do for the sisters of San Nicola.

Without social connections, opportunities, or a family business to inherit, Ciro and Eduardo had to create their own luck. Eduardo studied Latin, Greek, and the classics with Sister Ercolina as Ciro maintained the buildings and gardens. The Lazzari boys were convent-trained in every respect, their excellent manners learned at the table with the nuns. They had grown up without the benefit of close family, which had robbed them of much but also bestowed a certain self-sufficiency and maturity.

Ciro balanced a long wooden dowel draped with freshly pressed altar linens on his shoulder as he crossed the busy piazza. Children played close by as their mothers swept the stoops, hung out the wash, beat the rugs, and prepared the urns and flower boxes for spring plantings. The scent of fresh earth troweled into window boxes filled the air. The release after months of isolation was palpable; it was as if the mountain villages exhaled an enormous breath, finally free of the bitter cold and the layers of wool clothing that came with it.

A group of boys whistled as Ciro passed.

"Careful with Sister Domenica's pantaloons," a boy teased.

Ciro turned to them and made as if to butt them with the linens. "Nuns don't wear pantaloons, but your sister does."

The boys laughed. Ciro kept moving, and hollered back, "Say hello to Magdalena for me."

Ciro carried himself like a general in full regalia, when in fact he wore secondhand clothes from the donation bin. He found a pair of melton pants and a chambray work shirt that fit, but shoes were always a prob-lem. Ciro Lazzari had huge feet, so he was always searching the donation bin for bigger sizes. A brass ring on his belt loop was festooned with keys to every door in the convent and church, which jingled as he walked.

Don Gregorio insisted that altar linens be delivered through the side entrance so as not to interfere with worshippers who came in and out of the church during the day and might be compelled to put an extra coin into the poor box.

Ciro entered the sacristy, a small room off the altar. The scent of incense and beeswax filled the space like sachet in a drawer. A beam of pink light from a small rose window cut across a plain oak table in the center of the room. Along the wall, there was a standing closet for vestments.

A full-length mirror in a silver frame was hung behind the door. Ciro remembered the day the mirror showed up. He thought it odd that the priest needed a mirror; after all, there had been none in this sacristy since the fourteenth century. Don Gregorio had installed the mirror himself, Ciro found out; his vanity did not extend to asking Ciro to hang it.

A man who needs a mirror is looking for something.

Ciro placed the linens on the table, then went to the door and looked out into the church. The pews were empty except for Signora Patricia D'Andrea, the oldest and most devout parishioner in Vilminore. Her white lace mantilla was draped over her head, bowed in prayer, which gave her the look of a sad lily.

Ciro walked out into the church to replace the used altar linens. Signora D'Andrea caught his eye and glared at him. He sighed and went to the front of the altar, bowed his head, paused, genuflected, and made an obligatory sign of the cross. He looked out at Signora, who nodded her approval, and bowed his head reverently to her.

A smile curved across her lips.

Ciro carefully folded the used linens into a tight bundle and took them into the sacristy. He untied the satin ribbons, lifted the fresh linens off the dowel, and went back into the church, carrying the embroidered white altar cloth like a bridesmaid in charge of lifting the bride's train on her wedding day.

Ciro centered the freshly starched linens on the altar. He placed the gold candlesticks on opposite corners of the altar, anchoring the linens. He reached into his pocket for a small knife, with which he trimmed the wax drippings from the candle until the taper was smooth. This gesture was in honor of his mother, who reminded him to do whatever needed to be done without anyone having to ask.

Before he went, he looked out at Signora and winked at her. She blushed. Ciro, the convent orphan, had grown up to be an effective flirt. For his part, it was simply instinct. Ciro greeted every woman he passed, tipped his secondhand hat, eagerly assisted them with their parcels, and inquired about their families. He talked to girls his own age with a natural ease that other boys admired.

Ciro charmed the women of the village, from the schoolgirls with their waxy curls to the widowed grandmothers clutching their prayer missals. He was comfortable in the company of women. Sometimes he thought he understood women better than he did his own sex. Surely he knew more about girls than Eduardo, who was so innocent. Ciro wondered what would become of his brother if he ever had to leave his convent home. Ciro imagined that he was strong enough to face the worst, but Eduardo was not. An intellectual like Eduardo needed the convent library, desk, and lamp and the connections that came through church correspondence. Ciro, on the other hand, would be able to survive in the outside world; Iggy and the sisters had taught him a trade. He could farm, make repairs, and build anything from wood with his hands. Life beyond the convent would be difficult, but Ciro had the skills to build a life.

Don Raphael Gregorio pushed the sacristy door open. He placed the tins from the poor box on the table. Don Gregorio was thirty years old, a newly minted priest. He wore a long black cassock, affixed with a hundred small ebony buttons from collar to hem. Ciro wondered if the priest appreciated how many times Sister Ercolina went over the button loops with the pressing iron to have them lie flat.

"Do you have the plantings ready for the garden?" Don Gregorio wanted to know. The priest's bright white Roman collar offset his thick black hair. His aristocratic face, strong chin, small, straight nose, and heavy-lidded brown eyes gave him the sleepy look of a Romeo instead of the earnest gaze of a wise man of God.

"Yes, Father." Ciro bowed his head in deference to the priest, as the nuns had taught him.

"I want the walkway planted with daffodils."

"I got your note, Padre." Ciro smiled. "I will take care of everything." Ciro lifted the dowel off the table. "May I go, Don Gregorio?"

"You may," the priest answered.

Ciro pushed the door open.

"I'd like to see you at mass sometime," Don Gregorio said.

"Padre, you know how it is. If I don't milk the cow, there's no cream. And if I don't gather the eggs, the sisters can't make the bread. And if they can't make the bread, we don't eat."

Don Gregorio smiled. "You could do your chores and still find time to attend mass."

"I guess that's true, Father."

"So I'll see you at mass?"

"I spend a lot of time in church sweeping up, washing windows. I figure if God is looking for me, He knows where to find me."

"My job is to teach you to seek Him, not the other way around."

"I understand. You have your job, and I have mine."

Ciro bowed his head respectfully. He hoisted the empty wooden dowel to his shoulder like a rifle, took the bundle of linens to be washed and pressed, and went. Don Gregorio heard Ciro whistle as he went down the path that would soon be planted with yellow flowers, just as he had ordered.

·   ·   ·

Ciro pushed open the door to the room he and Eduardo shared in the garden workhouse. At first the boys had lived in the main convent, in a cell on the main floor. The room was small and noisy; the constant shuffle of the nuns in transit from the convent to the chapel kept the boys awake, while the gusts of winter from the entrance door opening and closing made the room drafty. They were happy when the nuns decided to give them a permanent space away from the main convent.

The sisters had moved the boys out to the garden workhouse in a large room with good light, knowing that growing boys needed privacy and a quiet place to study. Sister Teresa and Sister Anna Isabelle had done their best to make the room cozy. They cleared the cluttered storage room of flowerpots, cutting bins, and old-fashioned garden tools that hung on the walls like sculptures. The nuns installed two neat cots with a wool blanket for each boy and pillows as flat as the communion wafers. There was a desk and an oil lamp, a ceramic pitcher and bowl on a stand near the desk. As it goes with the ranks of the working religious, their basic needs were met, and nothing more.

Eduardo was studying when Ciro came in and fell onto his cot.

"I prepped every fireplace."

"Thanks." Eduardo didn't look up from his book.

"I caught a glimpse of Sister Anna Isabelle in her robe." Ciro rolled over on his back and unsnapped the key ring from his belt loop.

"I hope you looked away."

"Had to. I can't be unfaithful."

"To God?"

"Hell, no. I'm in love with Sister Teresa," Ciro teased.

"You're in love with her chestnut ravioli."

"That too. Any woman who can make eating chestnuts bearable through a long winter is the woman for me."

"It's the herbs. A lot of sage and cinnamon."

"How do you know?"

"I watch when she cooks."

"If you'd ever get your head out a book, you might be able to get a girl."

"Only two things interest you. Girls and your next meal." Eduardo smiled.

"What's wrong with that?"

"You have a good mind, Ciro."

"I use it!"

"You could use it more."

"I'd rather get by on my looks, like Don Gregorio."

"He's more than his appearance. He's an educated man. A consecrated man. You need to respect him."

"And you shouldn't be afraid of him."

"I'm not afraid of him. I honor him."

"Ugh. The Holy Roman Church is of no interest to me." Ciro kicked off his shoes. "Bells, candles, men in dresses. Did you see Concetta Martocci on the colonnade?"

"Yes."

"What a beauty. That blond hair. That face." Ciro looked off, remembering her. "And that figure." Ciro whistled.

"She's been in the same class at Santa Maria Assunta for three years. She's not very bright."

"Maybe she doesn't want to sit around and read all the time. Maybe she wants to see the world. Maybe she wants me to take her for a ride."

"Take her on your bicycle."

"You really don't know anything about girls. You have to offer them the best and nothing less."

"Who's teaching you the ways of women? Iggy?"

"Sister Teresa. She told me that women deserve respect."

"She's correct."

"I don't know about all of that." It seemed to Ciro that respect wasn't something to spread around like hay on the icy walkways in winter. Maybe it should be earned.

"If you showed a little spiritual initiative, if you bothered to go to mass once in a while, maybe Don Gregorio would loan you the cart," Eduardo said.

"You're on good terms with him. Ask him if I can borrow it."

"You'll have to walk, then. I'm not asking him."

"Saving your favors for something more important?"

"What could be more important than Concetta Martocci?" Eduardo said drily. "Let's think. The priest's cart delivers medicine to the sick. Takes old people to see the doctor. Takes food to the poor—"

"All right, all right. I understand. My heart's desire is not an act of mercy."

"Not even close."

"I'll just have to think of other ways to impress her."

"You work on that, and I'll study Pliny," Eduardo said, pulling the lamp close to his book.

.   .   .

Every Friday morning, Don Gregorio said mass for the children of the school. They walked into church silently and reverently, in two lines, the youngest students first, led by Sister Domenica and Sister Ercolina.

The girls wore gray wool jumpers, white blouses, and blue muslin aprons, while the boys wore dark blue slacks and white shirts. On weekends their mothers washed the navy-and-white uniforms and hung them on clotheslines throughout the village. From a distance, drying in the sun, they resembled maritime flags.

Ciro stood behind a pillar in the overhead gallery of San Nicola, above the pews and out of the sight line of Don Gregorio. Only two boys Ciro's age remained in school; most had quit by the age of eleven to work in the mines. Roberto LaPenna and Antonio Baratta were the exception, and at fifteen, they planned to become doctors. Roberto and Antonio processed to the front of the church, genuflected, and went into the sacristy to put on their red robes to serve the mass for Don Gregorio.

Ciro watched the teenage girls file into a pew. Anna Calabrese, studious and plain, had lovely legs, slender ankles, and small feet; Maria DeCaro, lanky and nervous, had a long waist and slim hips; chubby Liliana Gandolfo had full breasts, nice hands, and a perpetual look of indifference in her brown eyes.

Finally, Concetta Martocci, the most beautiful girl in Vilminore, slipped into the pew on the end. The sight of her filled Ciro with longing. Concetta was usually late to mass, so Ciro figured she was about as devout as he was. Her nonchalance extended to every aspect of her unstudied beauty.

Concetta's blond hair, the exact color of the gold embroidery on Don Gregorio's vestments, hung loosely over her shoulders, pulled off her face with two slim braids wrapped around her head like a laurel wreath. She was delicate and pale, her coloring like vanilla cake with a dusting of powdered sugar. Her deep blue eyes were the shade of the ripples on Lake Endine, her inky eyelashes like the black sand that colored the shoreline. She was curvy but small-boned. Ciro imagined he could carry her easily.

Ciro slid down the pillar to the floor, leaned back against the column, and peered through the railing as he reveled in the unobstructed view of his object of desire for a full, uninterrupted hour.

As Concetta followed the mass, she would glance up and look at the rose window over the altar, then down to the words in the open missal in her hands.

O salutaris Hostia,
Quae caeli pandas ostium,
Bella premut hostilia,
Da robur, fer auxilium.

Ciro imagined kissing Concetta's dewy pink lips as they pronounced the rote Latin. Who invented women? Ciro wondered as he observed her. Ciro may not have believed in the promises of the Holy Roman Church, but he had to admit that God was on to something if He invented beauty.

God made girls, and that made Him a genius, Ciro thought as the girls rose from the kneeler and filed into the main aisle.

Ciro peered around the column to watch Concetta kneel at the communion rail. Don Gregorio slipped the small communion wafer onto Concetta's tongue, and she bowed her head and made the sign of the cross before rising. Her smallest movements had an anticipatory quality. Ciro didn't take his eyes off her as she followed the other girls back to the pew.

Sensing his stare, Concetta looked up into the gallery. Ciro caught her eye and smiled at her. Concetta pursed her lips, then bowed her head in prayer.

Don Gregorio intoned, *"Per omnia saecula saeculorum."*

The students responded, "Amen." They rose from the kneelers and sat back in the pews.

Liliana leaned over and whispered something to Concetta, who smiled. Ciro took in the smile, a bonus on this spring morning—usually there were no smiles during mass. One brief glimpse of her white teeth and perfect dimple made getting up at dawn to open the church worth the effort.

Ciro planned his day around the hope of running into Concetta. He might change course on a morning errand for a glimpse of her walking from the school to the church. He'd go hungry and miss supper for a quick "Ciao, Concetta" as she strolled by with her family during *la passeggiata*. One smile from her was enough to keep him going; she inspired him to do better, to *be* better. He hoped to impress Concetta with aspects of his character she might not have seen, like the fine manners drilled into him by the nuns. Good manners in young men seemed to matter to young ladies. If Ciro got the chance, he knew he could make Concetta happy. He remembered, in the deepest shadows of his memory, his father doing the same for his mother.

The students knelt for the final blessing.

"*Dominus vobiscum.*" Don Gregorio extended his arms heavenward.

The students responded, "*Et cum spiritu tuo.*"

"*Vade in pace.*" Don Gregorio made the sign of the cross in the air.

Ciro watched as Concetta slipped the missal into the holder in the back of the pew. Mass had ended. Ciro was to go in peace. But he wouldn't, not anytime soon, not as long as Concetta Martocci was in the world.

.   .   .

There was a field of orange lilies near the waterfall above Schilpario where the Ravanelli children played. When the spring came, the sun burned hot, but the mountain breezes were cool and invigorating. Those days *di caldo e freddo* only lasted until Easter, and Enza took full advantage of them. She gathered up her brothers and sisters every afternoon and took them up the mountain.

The aftereffects of the harsh winter were apparent in the landscape, mottled from the assault of heavy rain, snow, and ice. Pale green shoots pushed through the brown branches as tangled mounds of low brush in the ravines thawed out in the sun. The depressions in the earth along the trail where water had pooled and frozen were now pits of black mud. The rushing waters had left thick striae of silt as the snow melted too fast and overflowed down the cliffs. But it didn't matter; after months of gray, everywhere she looked, Enza saw green.

Enza was relieved every year when spring arrived at last. These majestic mountains were terrifying in the winter; the glittering snow could turn dangerous as wily avalanches buried houses and rendered roads impassable. There was the constant fear of sudden and prolonged isolation, food shortages, and sickness gripping families who might need medicine and had no access to a doctor.

It was as if the sun set the village free.

In spring, the children scattered through the Alps like dandelion puffs. The mornings were filled with chores—fetching water, gathering sticks, scrubbing clothes, hanging the wash, and prepping the garden. The afternoons were spent at play, as the children flew kites made of strips of old muslin, floated in the shallow pool under the waterfall, or read in the shade of the pine trees.

Primavera in the Italian Alps was like a jewelry box opened in sunlight. Clusters of red peonies like ruffles of taffeta framed pale green fields, while wild white orchids climbed up the glittering graphite mountain walls. The first buds of white allium lined the trail as clusters of pink rhododendron blossoms burst through the dark green foliage.

There was no hunger in the spring and summer; the mountain provided food and drink, as the children plucked sweet blackberries from the thickets and cupped their hands and drank the clean, cold water of the streams.

The girls collected baskets of wild pink asters to place in the outdoor shrine at the feet of the statue of Mary while the boys found smooth lavender fieldstones to haul down the mountain to enclose their families' garden. The children took all their meals alfresco, and their naps in the mountain grass.

Spring was the gift after the deprivation of the long winter, and summer was the highest dream of all, with its hot sun, sapphire sky and blue lakes, and tourists with their pockets full of silver to spend on holiday. The children welcomed the visitors, who generously tipped them for carrying their bags or running errands. In return, the children offered them small baskets of raspberries and fresh lemonade.

Enza hauled the food hamper up the mountain, following the path to the lake. She inhaled the crisp mountain air tinged with sweet pine and felt the hot sun on her neck. She smiled because the chores of the morning were behind her, and she had a new book to read. *The Scarlet Pimpernel* was nestled in the basket next to the fresh cakes her mother baked. Her teacher, Professore Mauricio Trabuco, had given it to her as a prize for having the best marks in her class.

"Come on, Stella." Enza turned to look for her baby sister, who lagged behind. Stella was five years old, with long, wavy hair that Enza braided every morning. She had stopped on the path and picked a yellow buttercup. "There are lots of flowers in the field."

"But I like this one," Stella said.

"So pick it," Enza said impatiently. "*Andiamo*."

Stella yanked the yellow buttercup, held it tightly, and ran ahead of her sister on the path, scrambling up a steep knob on all fours and disappearing through the brush to follow her brothers and sisters.

"Be careful!" Enza called to her as she took the hike up the path herself. When Enza reached the top, she saw her brothers and sisters running across the green field to the waterfall. Battista rolled the cuffs of his pants. Vittorio did the same, then followed Battista into the shallow wading pool, which came up past his ankles. They began to splash, then wrestle in the water, laughing as they went.

Eliana climbed a tree in the distance, looping her long arms around the branches and hoisting herself higher and higher. Alma and Stella, on the ground, clapped for their sister to reach the top.

Enza put the basket down beside a wild thatch of orange blossoms. She flipped the lid, pulled out a muslin tablecloth, unfolded it, and laid it out on the ground, smoothing the edges. She dug in the basket for her book while keeping her eyes on her brothers and sisters, and pulled it out to read. When she saw that the children were safe at play, she lay down on her back on the edge of the cloth.

Enza held the book over her face as she read, blocking the bright sun. Soon she was in France, in the times of guillotines, palace intrigue, and a mysterious man who signs his name with a quick sketch of a red flower.

Enza read the first chapter, and then the second. She rested the book on her chest, closed her eyes. She saw herself in the book wearing a red silk shantung gown, with hair that twirled up like smooth meringue, her cheeks powdered with hot pink rouge. Enza wondered what it would be like if she lived in another place at another time, with another family, fulfilling a destiny different from her own. Who would she be? What might she become?

"We're hungry," Alma said.

"Is it time to eat?" Enza asked.

Alma looked up at the sun. "It's one o'clock."

"That looks like a pretty good guess. You're right. It's lunchtime. Go and get your brothers and sisters."

Alma ran off to do as she was told while Enza unloaded the hamper. Mama had made sandwiches of mozzarella, tomato, and fresh dandelion drizzled in honey and wrapped them in fresh linen napkins. There were two sandwiches for each child, and an extra for each of the boys. There was a jug with fresh lemonade, and slices of golden pound cake.

Enza set out the feast as her brothers and sisters gathered around. The boys, wet from wading in the pool, were careful to kneel on the outer edge of the cloth. Enza pulled Stella onto her lap.

"She's not a baby anymore," Alma said to Enza.

"I'm going to keep her a baby forever," Enza said. "Every family needs a baby."

"I'm five." Stella held up five fingers.

"This is going to be a bad year for porcini," Battista said as he ate his sandwich. "This ground is too wet."

"It's too soon," Enza told him. "Don't worry about the porcini. You have to help Papa this summer."

"I'd rather hunt truffles."

"You can do both."

"I want to make lots and lots of money. I'm gonna sell truffles to the Frenchmen. They're suckers," Battista said.

"You have such big plans. I'm impressed," Eliana said, though clearly she was not.

"I'll help Papa," Vittorio said.

"We'll *all* help Papa. He's going to get a lot of fares this summer," Enza said.

"Good luck. Cipi won't last the summer," Battista said.

"Don't say that." Alma's eyes filled with tears.

"Don't upset your sister," Enza said. "Nobody knows how long Cipi will be around. You have to leave that up to God and Saint Francis."

"Will Cipi go to heaven?" Stella asked.

"Someday he will," Enza answered quietly.

"I want to go wading." Alma stood.

The sun, high on the ridge, burned hot on the children. Even Enza felt the heat as she followed the children to the wading pool, where she took off her shoes and long woolen knee socks. She hiked up her skirt, tied it under her shirtwaist, and waded into the pool. The cold water grazed her ankles. Enza jumped as the frigid water tickled her feet.

"Let's dance!" Stella said. Soon all the children were splashing in the cold, shallow water. Stella fell into the pool and laughed. Enza scooped her up, holding her close as Alma, Eliana, Battista, and Vittorio waded over to the waterfall to let the cold water rush over them.

Through the clear water of the pool, Enza saw something odd. As Enza leaned over to set Stella down, the child's thin legs were magnified in the sunlight. Enza saw blue veins and splotchy maroon pools underneath Stella's skin, darker in places, a network of them from ankle to thigh.

"Stand up, Stella."

Stella stood in the water, the ends of her pigtails dripping like wet paintbrushes. Enza checked the back of her legs in the unforgiving light, where she saw more bruises that extended up to the top of Stella's thighs. In a panic, Enza checked her sister's back, and upper arms. There, too, were the bruises, like blue stones visible on the lake bottom in shallow waters.

"Eli, come here!" Enza shouted to her sister. Eliana, reedy, tall, and athletic at thirteen, trudged over in the shallow water.

"What?" She looked at Enza, pushing her hair off her face.

"Do you see these bruises?"

Eliana looked at them.

"Who hit her?" Enza insisted.

"Nobody hits Stella."

"Did she fall?"

"I don't know."

"Battista!" Enza shouted. Battista and Vittorio were at the far end of the falls, peeling lichen off the stones. Enza waved them over. She gathered up Stella, took her to the cloth spread on the ground, and dried her off with her apron. Stella's teeth chattered, and, frightened by Enza's quick movements, she began to cry.

"What did I do?" Stella wailed.

Enza pulled her close. "Nothing, *bella*, nothing." She looked up at Eliana. "We have to go home." Her tone changed. "Now."

A feeling of dread came over Enza as she watched her sister gather the children.

Enza counted the heads of her brothers and sisters just as her mother did when they went to neighboring villages for feast days, careful to keep track of every child, careful not to lose one to the gypsies, or in a large crowd.

Stella nestled into the warmth of her older sister, holding her tight.

Mama always said a good family has one heartbeat. No one knows you like the people you live with, and no one will take up your cause to the outside world quite like your blood relatives. Enza knew Battista's moods, Eliana's courage, Vittorio's ego, Alma's restlessness, and Stella's peaceful nature. When one laughed, eventually they all did. When one was afraid, they did whatever they could do to shore up the other's courage. When one was sick, soon they all felt the pain.

There was an especially deep bond between the eldest and the youngest. Enza and Stella were the beginning and end, the alpha and omega, the bookends that held all the family stories from start to finish as well as the various shades and hues of personality and temperament. As Enza held Stella closely and rocked her, the children silently gathered the lunch, cleaned up the napkins, and repacked the basket. Enza could feel Stella's warm breath in the crook of her neck.

The boys hoisted the food hamper, while the girls helped Stella onto Enza's back, to carry her back down the mountain. Eliana followed, keeping her hand on the small of Stella's back, while Alma led them, kicking away any rocks or sticks on the path that could trip Enza as she carried Stella. A small tear trickled down Enza's face. She had prayed for spring to come, but now she was afraid it had brought with it the worst of luck.

4

A POT DE CRÈME
Vasotto di Budino

There was a strange moon the night after Stella got the bruises. Filmy and mustard colored, it flickered in and out of the clouds like a warning light, reminding Enza of the oil lamp Marco used when he traveled by cart in bad weather.

Enza hoped the moon was a sign that the angels were present, hovering over Stella, ambivalent about whether to take her sister's soul or leave her behind on earth. Enza knelt at the head of the bed, wove her fingers together, closed her eyes, and prayed. Certainly the angels would hear her and let her sister stay on the mountain. She wished she could shoo the angel of death away like a fat winter fly.

Marco and Giacomina sat on either side of Stella's makeshift bed in the main room, never taking their eyes from their daughter. The boys, unable to sit still, stayed busy doing chores. Battista, tall and lean, stooped over and stoked the fire, while Vittorio hauled the wood. Eliana and Alma sat in the corner, knees to their chests, watching, hoping.

The local priest, Don Federico Martinelli, was an old man. He had no hair and a long face whose expression did little to comfort them. He knelt at the foot of Stella's bed through the night, praying the rosary. The soft drone of his voice did not waver as he pinched his shiny green beads one after the other, kissing the soft silver cross, and beginning the Hail Marys anew as the hours passed.

Marco had gone to Signor Arduini as Stella grew weaker, begging for any help he might provide. Signor Arduini sent for the doctor in Lizzola, who came quickly by horse. The doctor examined Stella, gave her medicine for fever, spoke with Marco and Giacomina, and promised to return in the morning.

Enza tried to read the doctor's face as he whispered with her parents, but he gave no indication what the outcome would be. There appeared to be no urgency, but Enza knew that didn't mean anything. Doctors are like priests, she knew. Whether it's an affliction of the body or the soul, there is little that surprises them, and they rarely, if ever, show what they are thinking.

Enza grabbed the doctor's arm as he went through the door. He turned to look at her, but she could not speak. He nodded kindly and went outside.

Enza peered out into the night through the window slats, certain that if Stella made it until sunrise, she would live; the doctor would return as promised, declare a miracle, and life would be as it always had been. Hadn't this been true for the Maj boy, who was lost on the road to Trescore for three days, then found? Hadn't the Ferrante baby, sick with jaundice for sixteen days, eventually recovered? Hadn't the Capovilla family survived after four children had the whooping cough in the winter of 1903? There were so many stories of miracles on the mountain. Surely Stella Ravanelli would become one of those stories told over and over again in the villages, assuring everyone who lived so high and close to the sky that God would not abandon them. Years from now, when Stella was grown and had her own family, wouldn't she tell the story of the night she survived the terrible bruises and the fever?

Enza couldn't imagine their home without Stella, who had always been special. Stella wasn't named for a saint or a relative like the rest of the children, but for the stars that had shimmered overhead on the summer night she was born.

Enza pictured Stella healthy, but she could not maintain the image, her mind filling with doubt. She battled helpless feelings of injustice through the night. In her mind, Stella's dilemma was unfair. After all, her family had paid their marker in this life. They were poor, humble hard workers who helped others and lived the gospel. They had done everything right. Now it was God's turn to reward them for their piety. Enza closed her eyes and imagined the angels and saints surrounding her sister, making her well.

Enza even pictured her family in the future. She imagined her mother and father as grandparents and her brothers and sisters with families of their own. Battista would teach the children the trails, Eliana would show them how to balance on the stone fence on one foot, Alma would instruct the girls in sewing, Vittorio would teach the boys how to shoe the horse, Stella would show them how to paint, Mama would keep the garden, and Papa would hitch the cart and take the children for rides. Their lives on the mountain would go forward as they always had; they would grow old together and happily in greater numbers, with a homestead that they owned free and clear.

La famiglia èterna.

Enza was mystified as she watched Stella's labored breathing. She had taken the medicine from the doctor. Why was her sister getting worse?

Stella's color was all but gone, the pink of her cheeks now an odd gray and her lips turned chalky white. When she opened her eyes, they were unfocused, the pupils like two black rosary beads.

Giacomina dabbed her daughter's lips with a damp cloth and stroked her hair. Occasionally the soft din of Hail Marys said in unison was cut by a moan from Stella that sent a knife through Enza's heart. Finally, unable to take another moment of watching her sister wither away, Enza stood and ran outside.

Enza ran to the end of Via Scalina. She buried her face in her hands and wept for Stella. There is no worse feeling than being unable to assuage the suffering of the innocent. Enza could not erase Stella's expression of fear as she grew weaker, and the helpless look on her mother's face. Giacomina had been through many fevers and long nights of worry for her children, but this time was altogether different; it had a velocity of its own.

Enza soon felt her father's hands on her shoulders. As she turned, Marco took her into his arms and wept with her.

God had abandoned them, the angels had taken their leave, and the saints had turned away. Now Enza understood the truth of those terrible hours. They had not been waiting for Stella to get well; they were watching her die. For the first time in her life, in almost sixteen years of surviving blizzards, spring floods, and want, Enza was unlucky. The strong arms of her father could no longer protect her, and her mother's touch had lost its power to heal.

*   *   *

Enza and Marco returned to the house. The fire had all but died out, and the morning sun was pulling itself up over Pizzo Camino, flooding the room with light. Eliana and Alma stood at the head of the bed, Vittorio and Battista on either side. After hours on his knees, the old priest stood up and kissed the silver cross on his rosary for the last time.

Giacomina draped herself over Stella's body as she wept into her daughter's hair. The mother then lifted her child into her arms, pulling her close and rocking her as she had done every night before the child went to sleep. Stella's lifeless arms dangled outstretched from her mother's body, palms up as if to be received by the angels who were nowhere to be found in the hours before her death. Stella's brown eyes were open, her thick eyelashes framing her vacant stare. Her lips had turned pale blue like the underside of a shell.

Marco leaned over his wife and put his arms around her, unable to comfort her. He felt the strong hand of miserable failure upon him. Not only had the doctor in Lizzola, the priest, and the church failed him; he had not been pious enough in the eyes of God to spare his own daughter.

There was a sacrament happening in their midst, the uninvited moment of complete surrender to the spirit world, as life passes and death takes its hold. It was a sacred pause, a swinging bridge over the most perilous chasm, a moment that lasted only a second or two, where Stella was still theirs before she was gone to God. It was in this moment that Enza screamed, loud enough for God to hear, "No!" But it was too late; the little girl was gone, her soul returned to the stars she had been named for just five years ago.

Was all of this somehow her fault? Enza had planned the picnic that day. As the eldest, she had packed the hamper and led them up the mountain. *She* had wanted to read a book in the bright sun. *She* had allowed the children to play in the pond under the rush of the spring waterfalls. *She* had failed Stella, and now she had failed the whole family. Now Enza looked around for someone to absolve her of her irresponsibility, to forgive her for the mistakes she had made, but no one stepped forward to break the bondage of her massive guilt. She needed the arms of her mother and father around her, but they were filled with Stella.

Giacomina's pain was so deep that her back began to heave, her entire body to rise and fall, just as it had when she birthed this child. She cradled her daughter's lifeless body, feeling the last warmth of her. A father mourns, but a mother, whose child is born of her body, remembers the soft kisses that become the act of two loving bodies joined together in sweet privacy, which begets the first flutter of joyous pregnancy, to the soft, slippery kicks as the baby grows in her belly, to the moment when her body opens up to bring a new life to the world, and yields to a despair that will never leave her.

Stella was Giacomina's winged angel child, quick to laugh, impertinent with facts she learned from her less wise older siblings, and in total tune with the magic of the world, a curly-haired fairy who danced on the surface of life, soaking up the details of the world around her with a sense of wonder, identifying the possibilities in everything she touched, as she examined glittery mountain grass, hummed along with musical night winds, or embraced the miracle of water at every opportunity, to splash, bathe, and revel in it. And, as fleeting as a sun shower that moves through quickly on the sweet breath of a summer breeze, she was gone.

· · ·

The hand-painted statues of Saint Michael the warrior, Saint Francis of Assisi with the lamb, Mary the Mother of Jesus crushing the green snake, Saint Anthony holding lilies in one hand and the baby Jesus in the other, Saint Joseph in a carpenter's apron, and the Pietà, a grieving mother holding her dying son in shades of gray, were lined up in the bright sun in the garden at the church of San Nicola for their annual bath.

Ciro imagined that this was what the devout think heaven will be. Upon their deaths, they will proceed to a garden, filled with a seraphim of perfect saints, with unlined faces and thick hair, waiting to greet them in white light, wearing robes of purple, blue, and green, their smooth, long-fingered plaster hands indicating where to go.

Don Gregorio may have found Ciro's lack of devotion odd, but Ciro thought the believers were the strange ones, with their relics, incense, and holy oils whose mystical powers did more to raise questions in his mind than provide answers.

Ciro mixed the special cleaning paste he had invented in an old tin drum. Through trial and error, Ciro had created this paste to clean and polish the statues and delicate ornamentation of the church. For this special chore, Ciro mixed a cup of fresh, wet clay from the riverbed of Stream Vò, a few drops of olive oil, and a handful of crushed lavender buds in a drum. He put his hands in the mixture and squeezed it through his fingers until it became a soft putty. After rinsing his hands in a bucket of cold water, he picked up a moppeen, twisted the end around three fingers, and dipped the cloth into the paste.

"*Va bene*, Saint Michael, you're first." Ciro made small circular motions, gently rubbing the paste onto the base of the statue. The gold lettering, "San Michele," gleamed as Ciro polished the surface.

Of all the statues in San Nicola, Ciro felt the closest kinship with Saint Michael. His strong legs, broad shoulders, and silver sword raised high to battle evil appealed to Ciro's sense of adventure and aspirations for courage. Plus, Saint Michael's sandy hair and blue-green eyes reminded Ciro of his own. As he buffed the golden jaw of the saint, he decided that of all of God's army, this was the man who could win Concetta Martocci. The rest of the male saints, holding doves or walking with lambs or balancing a baby on one arm, would not be as effective. Saint Anthony was too gentle, Saint Joseph was too old, and Saint John, too angry. No, Michael was the only warrior who could have wooed a beautiful girl and won her heart.

Ignazio Farino rounded the corner, pushing a small handcart loaded with small blue river stones. Slight of build, with a long nose and thin lips, Iggy wore lederhosen with thick wool knee socks and an alpine hat with a *merlo* feather stuck in the faded band. He looked more like an old boy than an old man.

"*Che bella*." He looked up at the statue of Mary perched upon the globe and gave a whistle.

"Is she your favorite, Iggy?" Ciro asked.

"She's the Queen of Heaven, isn't she?" Ignazio sat down on the garden wall and looked up at the statue. "I used to gaze—I mean, *gaze*—at her face when I was a boy. And I used to pray to God to send me a beautiful wife that looked like the Virgin Mary in the church of San Nicola. The prettiest girl in Vilminore was taken, so I took a hike up the mountain and married the prettiest girl in Azzone. She had the golden hair. Pretty on the outside, but"—he pulled a hand-rolled cigarette from his pocket—"so complicated within. Don't marry a beautiful woman, Ciro. It's too much work."

"I know how to take care of a woman," Ciro said confidently.

"You think you do. Then you get the ring on her hand, and the story changes. Women change. Men stay as they are, and women change."

"How so?"

"In every way. In manner." Iggy bowed from the waist. "In personality. In their desire for you." He thrust his body forward as if to stop a runaway wheelbarrow. "At first, oh, *si, si, si*, they want you. Then they want the garden, the home, the children. And then they weary of their own dreams and look to you to make them happy." He threw up his hands. "It's never enough, Ciro. Never enough. Believe me, eventually, you run out of ways to make a woman happy."

"I don't care. It would be my honor to try."

"You say that now," Ignazio said. "Don't do as I did. Do *better*. Fall in love with a plain girl. Plain girls never turn bitter. They appreciate their portion, no matter how meager. A small pearl is enough. They never long for the diamond. Beautiful girls have high expectations. You bring them daisies, and they want roses. You buy them a hat, and they want the matching coat. It's a well so deep you cannot fill it. I know. I've tried."

"Plain or pretty, I don't care. I just want a girl to love. And I want her to love me." Ciro rinsed Saint Michael's cape with clean water.

"You want. You want. You just wait." Iggy puffed.

Ciro buffed the plaster with a dry towel. "I'm finding it very difficult to wait."

"Because you're young. The young have everything but wisdom."

"What does wisdom get you?" Ciro asked.

"Patience."

"I don't want wisdom. I don't want to grow old to get it. I just want to be happy."

"I wish I could give you my experience, so you might not have to endure what I have known in my life. I was like you. I didn't believe the old men. I should have listened to them."

"Tell me what I don't know, Iggy."

"Love is like *pot de crème*." Iggy stirred an imaginary pot with a spoon. "You see Signora Maria Nilo make it in the window of her *pasticceria*." Iggy wiggled his hips like Signora. "You see her stir the chocolate. You see the caramel cascade from the spoon into the baking dish. It looks *delicioso*. You want it, you can taste it. You pass by the shop every day and think, I want that *pot de crème* more than anything. I would fight for it. I would kill for it. I would die for one taste. One day, you get paid, you go for your *pot de crème*. You eat it fast, you go for another, and another. You eat every spoonful in the bowl. And soon the thing you wanted most in the world has made you sick. Love and *pot de crème*—the same."

Ciro laughed. "You'd have a hard time convincing a starving man when he hasn't had his fill. Love is the only dream worth pursuing. I'd work so hard for love. I'd make a future! I'd build her a house with seven fireplaces. We would have a big family—five sons and one daughter. You need at least one daughter to tend to the mother in old age."

"You've got it all figured out, Ciro," Ignazio said. "I've taken what life has given me"—Ignazio put his hands in the air as if to measure the scope of his world—"and I did not ask for more. It's *more* that will get you in trouble."

"That's a shame," Ciro said. "All I want is more. I earn my room and board, but I want to earn money."

"How much do you need?"

"If I had a lira for starters, that would be good."

"Really? One lira?" Ignazio smiled. "I've got a job for you."

Ciro washed down the Pietà with a damp cloth. "I'm listening."

"Father Martinelli needs a grave dug up in Schilpario." Iggy lit his cigarette.

"How much?"

"He'll give you two lire, and you kick back one. The church always has to get their cut."

"Of course they do." Ciro nodded. "But only one lira to dig a grave?" Ciro couldn't help but wonder why Ignazio couldn't cut a better deal. Now he understood why Ignazio hadn't graduated beyond his job as convent handyman.

Ignazio took a smooth drag off of his cigarette. "Hey, better than nothing." He offered Ciro a puff of his cigarette. Ciro took it, inhaling the smooth tobacco. "Don Gregorio has you dig for nothing. What are you going to do with your lira? You need shoes." Ignazio looked down at Ciro's shoes.

"I'm going to buy Concetta Martocci a cameo brooch."

"Don't waste your money. You need new shoes!"

"I can go barefoot, but I can't live without love." Ciro laughs. "How will I get to Schilpario?"

"Don Gregorio says you can take the cart."

Ciro's eyes lit up. If he could take the cart, maybe he could work in a ride with Concetta. "I'll do it. But I want the cart for the whole day."

"*Va bene.*"

"You'll fix it with Don Gregorio?" Ciro asked.

"I'll take care of it." Ignazio threw the butt of his cigarette onto the path. He stamped it and kicked it into the shrubs, where one small orange ember released its last spark and went out.

.   .   .

Ciro propped open the front doors of San Nicola to let the crisp spring air play through the church like the chords of the Lenten kyries. Every surface gleamed. The nuns would like to believe their ward scrubbed the church and everything in it for the honor and glory of God, but the truth was, Ciro was hoping to impress Don Gregorio so he'd give him use of the rectory cart and horse whenever he asked.

The young handyman rubbed the mahogany pews with lemon wax, washed the stained glass windows with hot water and white vinegar, scoured the marble floors and buffed the brass tabernacle. He wire-whisked the candle drippings off the wrought-iron votive holders and refilled the pockets with fresh candles. The scent of beeswax filled the alcove of saints like the rosewater Concetta Martocci sprinkled on the laundry before she did the ironing. He knew this for sure because when she passed, the air filled with her perfume.

The saint statues looked brand new. Ciro had returned the gloss to the creamy faces, and the colors to their robes and sandals. He hoisted Saint Joseph into place upon his perch in the alcove, then rolled the votive candle cart in front of him and stood back, pleased with the results of his hard work. He turned when he heard footsteps on the marble floor. Peering out from the alcove, he saw Concetta Martocci genuflect in the aisle and move into a pew about halfway between the altar and the entrance. Ciro's heart began to race. A white lace mantilla was draped over her hair. She wore a long gray serge skirt and a white blouse, the palette of an innocent dove.

Ciro looked down at his work clothes, taking in the wet hems of his pants, the shadows of soot along the seams, his ill-fitting boots and filthy work shirt, which looked like a handyman's paint palette—smears of clay putty, brass polish, and black streaks of smudges from charred candlewicks. A white polishing rag was stuck in the shirt pocket where a starched handkerchief should go.

He ran his hands through his thick hair, then looked at his fingernails, black half moons under every nail. Concetta turned and looked at him, then turned back to face the altar. This type of meeting, just the two of them alone in the church, was rare. A conversation with Concetta was nearly impossible to engineer. She had a stern father, a devout uncle, a few brothers, and a gaggle of girlfriends that surrounded her, as tight as the knot on the ties of a pinafore.

Ciro pulled the rag from his pocket and tucked it behind Saint Michael. He unsnapped the brass key ring from his belt loop and placed it on the rag. He walked up the center aisle of the church, genuflected, joined her in the pew, knelt beside her, and folded his hands in prayer.

"*Ciao*," he whispered.

"*Ciao*," she whispered back. A smile crossed her perfect pink lips. The lace of the mantilla made a soft frame around her face, as though she were a painting. He looked down at his dirty hands and folded his fingers into fists to hide the nails. "I just cleaned the church," he said, explaining his appearance.

"I can tell. The tabernacle is like a mirror," she said appreciatively.

"That's on purpose. Don Gregorio likes to look at his own reflection."

Concetta frowned.

"I'm just joking. Don Gregorio is a holy man." Sometimes Ciro was happy that he actually paid attention to things his brother Eduardo said, so he added, "A *consecrated* man."

She nodded in agreement and pulled a string of white opal rosary beads from her skirt pocket and held them. "I'm here for the novena," she said, looking up at the rose window behind the altar.

"Novena is on Thursdays," Ciro said.

"Oh," she said. "I'll just say my rosary alone, then."

"Would you like to see the garden?" Ciro asked. "We could go for a walk. You can pray in the garden."

"I'd rather pray in church."

"But God is everywhere. Don't you listen in mass?"

"Of course." She smiled.

"No, you don't. You whisper with Liliana."

"You shouldn't watch us."

"I'm not watching Don Gregorio."

"Maybe you should." She slipped back off the kneeler and sat on the pew. Ciro did the same. He looked down at Concetta's lovely hands. A slim, plain gold bracelet dangled from her wrist.

"I didn't invite you to sit with me," she whispered.

"You're right. How ill-mannered of me. May I sit with you, Concetta Martocci?"

"You may," she said.

They sat in silence. Ciro realized that he hadn't drawn a deep breath since Concetta entered the church. He exhaled slowly, then took in the wondrous scent of Concetta's skin, sweet vanilla and white roses. He was finally, at last, grateful to God for something, the nearness of Concetta.

"Do you like living in the convent?" she asked shyly.

Ciro's chest tightened. The last thing he wanted from this girl was pity.

"It's a good life. We work hard. We have a nice room. Don Gregorio loans me the cart whenever I want it."

"He does?"

"Of course." Ciro puffed up with pride.

"You're very lucky."

"I'd like to take a ride to Clusone sometime."

"I have an aunt there," she said.

"You do? I could take you to see her."

"Maybe." She smiled.

A *maybe* from Concetta was better than a *yes* from any of the hundreds of other girls who lived on this mountain. Ciro was elated, but tried not to show it. Ignazio had taught him to hold back, to refrain from showing a girl how much you care. Girls, according to Iggy, prefer boys who *don't* like them. This made no sense to Ciro, but he decided to follow Iggy's advice, if at the end of the game he might win Concetta's heart. Ciro turned to her. "I wish I could stay, but I promised Sister Domenica I would make a delivery for her before dinner."

"*Va bene.*" Concetta smiled again.

"You're very beautiful," Ciro whispered.

Concetta grinned. "You're very dirty."

"I won't be the next time I see you," he said. "And I *will* see you again."

Ciro stood and exited the pew, remembering to genuflect as he left. He looked at Concetta a final time, bowing his head to her, remembering the manners the nuns taught him to use in the presence of a lady. Concetta nodded her head before she turned to the gold tabernacle, which Ciro had spent the greater part of the afternoon buffing to a high polish. Ciro practically skipped out of the church into the piazza.

The afternoon sun burned low, a purple peony in the powder blue sky. Ciro ran across the piazza from the church to the convent, noting that the colors of his world had changed for the better. He threw open the front door, grabbed Sister Domenica's parcel for Signor Longaretti, and made his way up the hill to deliver it.

Ciro passed folks who greeted him, but he did not hear them. All he could think about was Concetta and the possibility of a long ride to Clusone alone with her. He imagined the lunch he would pack, the way he would take her hand, and how he would tell her all the things he had stored in his heart. His nails would be smooth and round and pink, the nail bed as white as snow, because he would soak them with a little bleach. Concetta Martocci would only see Ciro at his best going forward.

He would kiss her.

Ciro dropped the package at Signor Longaretti's door. When he returned to the convent, Eduardo was busy in their room, studying.

Eduardo looked at Ciro. "You run around the village looking like that?"

"Leave me alone. I cleaned San Nicola today." Ciro flopped onto the bed.

"You must have done a good job. Every bit of dirt is on your clothes."

"All right, all right, I'll take a good soak."

"Use lye," Eduardo said.

"What's for dinner?"

"Roast chicken," Eduardo replied. "I'll tell Sister Teresa how hard you worked, and she'll make sure you get extra. I need the keys to the chapel. I finished the mass cards for Sister."

Ciro reached down to hand his brother the ring of keys. "Agh," he said, "I left them at church."

"Well, go get them. Sister wants these in the pews before dinner."

Ciro ran back to the church across the piazza. The evening had a chill to it, and Ciro shivered, thinking he should have grabbed his coat. When he got to the church, he found the front entrance door locked, so he went around to the side entrance to the sacristy. He pushed the door open.

He could not believe what he saw.

Concetta Martocci was in the arms of Don Gregorio. The priest kissed her ravenously. Her gray skirt was lifted, exposing the smooth calf of her tawny leg. Her delicate foot was extended as she stood on her toes. In his arms, Concetta looked like a dove caught in the black branches of winter. Ciro stopped breathing; he swallowed air and choked.

"Ciro!" Don Gregorio looked up and let go of Concetta, who glided away from him as if she was on ice.

"I . . . I left my keys in the vestibule. The entrance door was locked." Ciro felt his face flush.

"Go and get your keys then," Don Gregorio said calmly as he smoothed the placket of buttons on his cassock. Ciro pushed past them and into the church. Embarrassment quickly gave way to anger and then fury.

Ciro ran down the center aisle, not bothering to bow or genuflect.

When he reached the vestibule, he grabbed his key ring and the rag from behind the statue, stuffing both in his pockets, wanting to break free of this place as quickly as he could. The church's grand beauty and the attention Ciro had lavished on every detail that afternoon meant nothing to him now. It was plaster, paint, brass, and wood.

Ciro had unbolted the main door to go when he felt Don Gregorio behind him.

"You are never to speak of what you saw," the priest whispered with contempt.

Ciro turned to face him. "Really, Father? You're going to issue an order? With what authority?" Ciro took a deep breath. "You disgust me. If it weren't for the sisters, I'd take an ax to your church."

"Don't threaten me. And don't ever come back to San Nicola. You are discharged of your duties here."

Ciro stepped forward, within inches of Don Gregorio's face. "We'll see about that."

Don Gregorio grabbed Ciro by the collar. In turn, Ciro grabbed the soft black linen of Don Gregorio's cassock with his dirty hands. "You call yourself a priest."

Don Gregorio loosened his grip on Ciro's shirt, and dropped his hands. Ciro looked him in the eye and then spit on the floor at Don Gregorio's feet. To think that all of Ciro's hard work had been for the honor and glory of this undeserving shepherd of a most ignorant flock! Ciro unlocked the entrance door and walked out into the dark. He heard Don Gregorio bolt the church door behind him.

Don Gregorio looked down at his cassock, the chest placket rumpled and smeared with dirt where Ciro had grabbed it. He dipped his fingers in the holy water font, brushed the clay-colored smudges away, and smoothed his hair before turning back up the aisle to the sacristy, to his Concetta.

Concetta leaned against the table, her arms folded across her chest. She had twisted her golden hair into a knot on the back of her head, and buttoned her sweater over her blouse.

"You see why you cannot speak with boys?" the priest said sternly. He paced back and forth across the floor.

"Yes, Don Gregorio."

"He took your conversation as interest in him," Don Gregorio said angrily. "You encouraged him, and now he feels betrayed."

Concetta Martocci placed her hands in her pockets and looked down at the floor. "How is that my fault?" She took a deep breath.

"You led him on."

"I did no such thing."

"He sat with you."

"He works in the church!" she said defensively.

"The nuns have coddled him. He's arrogant. He doesn't take the sacraments or attend mass regularly. He's too familiar with the congregation."

She smiled. "You're jealous of Ciro Lazzari? I don't believe it."

Don Gregorio put his arms around her and pulled her close. He kissed her neck and then her cheek, but as he grazed her lips, she pulled away.

"He saw you kiss me." Concetta patted her skirt. "What if he tells?"

"I'll take care of it." Don Gregorio reached out to stroke Concetta's arm.

"I'd better go," she said, her voice making it clear she'd rather not. "My mother is expecting me."

"Will I see you tomorrow?"

Concetta looked at Don Gregorio. He was handsome and polished in ways the boys from the mountain would never be. His kiss was not clumsy like Flavio Tironi's, behind the fourth pillar of the colonnade at the feast last summer, nor were his hands sweaty or his conversation banal. Don Gregorio was well traveled, full of observations and political opinions, and told fascinating stories about places she had never seen, but intended to. He was an educated man, a graduate of the seminary. He was as familiar with the streets of Rome as she was with the roads of Vilminore.

Don Gregorio saw something in her that no teacher or tutor had bothered to find. He did not press her to study mathematics or bore her with science. Instead, he had made her hungry to see the world beyond the mountains, places he knew would delight her like the pink beaches of Rimini, the shops on the Ponte Vecchio in Firenze, and the purple cliffs of Capri. He loaned her books of stories, not ones filled with dull academics but red-leather-bound novels with plots of sweeping romance and adventure.

Don Gregorio had dinner every Sunday afternoon with the Martocci family. The perfect guest, he arrived after mass and stayed until dusk. He paid special attention to Concetta's grandmother, listening patiently to her complaints about her health and every detail of her aches and pains. He blessed their fields and their house, administered sacraments, encouraged the family to be devout, to perform acts of mercy in the village, and to support the church.

Concetta had loved Don Gregorio from afar, instantly, from the first day he arrived in Vilminore. Over the course of the next several months, she had found moments alone with Don Gregorio exhilarating. She spent her school hours conniving ways to go to the church, in the hopes of seeing him.

The boys of San Nicola were generally dull and unkempt; they worked in the mines or in the fields, and had simple ideas about how to live. They were boys like Ciro Lazzari, the church handyman who wore rags and casually joined her in the church pew as though he'd bought a ticket next to her on a carnival bench and therefore earned the right to talk to her.

All her life, Concetta had been taught to choose the best in all things, whether it was a yard of linen to make an apron or the finest distilled lemon water to wash her hair. She knew Don Gregorio was a holy man who took vows, but he was also the most powerful and sophisticated man on the mountain. She wanted him. At fifteen she would give up the notion of a life with a husband and children of her own to stay home with her mother and see Don Gregorio whenever she could. She was besotted with the priest, thrilled to share stolen moments with him, and encouraged by his attention. To spend the occasional long afternoon and the weekly meal in his company would bring her happiness, she believed with all her heart.

"Make sure Ciro doesn't tell anyone about us," Concetta implored. "If my father were to find out . . . if anyone . . ."

Don Gregorio took Concetta in his arms and kissed her to reassure her. Once she was in his arms, risk was meaningless. Her proper upbringing, strict morals, and common sense held no power against his kiss. The rules she had promised her mother to respect until marriage dissipated in the air like smoke from an urn of incense. She told herself she had nothing to fear. No one would believe a servant over the word of a consecrated man.

Don Gregorio kissed her neck. Concetta let him; then, slowly, she pulled away. She did not linger, but pulled the lace mantilla over her head and slipped out of the sacristy into the night.

5

A STRAY DOG
Un Cane Randagio

Three small roast chickens surrounded by strips of potatoes and cubes of carrots rested in the center of a platter. Several large ceramic bowls were filled with a puree of chestnuts, made with butter, cream, and salt. Sister Teresa had learned to stretch meals with chestnuts, which were roasted to make crust in place of flour, pureed to fill tortellini, or boiled, mashed, and served as a hearty side dish. By spring, the nuns and Lazzari boys had had their fill of them.

Ciro burst into the kitchen. "Sister?" he cried out.

Sister Teresa emerged from the pantry. "What's the matter?"

"We must go to Sister Ercolina," he said, out of breath. "*Now.*"

"What happened?" Sister Teresa handed Ciro a hot towel.

"I saw something at San Nicola." Ciro mopped his face, and then cleaned his hands. "Don Gregorio. He was with Concetta Martocci." Ciro felt his face flush with embarrassment. "In the sacristy. I just caught them."

"I see." Sister Teresa took the towel from Ciro and threw it back into the pot of hot water on the fire. She poured Ciro a glass of water and motioned for him to sit. "You don't have to explain."

"You *know*?"

"I'm not surprised," she said, evenly.

Frustrated, Ciro raised his voice. "Are you telling me that vows have no meaning?"

"Some of us struggle with vows; for others, it's easier," she said carefully. "Humans are capable of divine acts. But sometimes they sin."

"There's no excuse for him. Do something!"

"I have no sway over the priest."

"Then go to Sister Ercolina and tell her what I saw. Bring me in. I'll give her the details. She can go to the Mother Abbess. She'll punish him but good!"

"Oh, I see. You want him punished." Sister Teresa sat. "Is it your love for Concetta Martocci that drives you, or your dislike of Don Gregorio?"

"I am done with Concetta, after what I saw—how could I . . ." Ciro held his head in his hands. The pangs of unrequited love stung his heart for the first time. There was nothing worse than never having the opportunity to express true romantic feelings to the person who inspired them. Today, he had been as close as he had ever been! For months, he had imagined Concetta getting to know him, returning his feelings, eventually falling in love with him. How many kisses he had planned, in as many places as he could imagine. To know that she had chosen another was almost too much for his young heart to bear. And the village priest, no less!

"Poor girl. She believes whatever he's telling her."

"I knew he was a fake. There is nothing mystical happening in San Nicola. It's all a show. A pageant of perfection. He cares too much about his vestments and the linens and what flowers will grow along the path in the garden. He's particular about the wrong things. He runs San Nicola like a storefront! That priest is like one of those oily peddlers from the south who come north to the lakes to sell cheap jewelry during the summer. They sweet-talk the ladies and take their good money for glass beads. The way the schoolgirls gather around Don Gregorio, fawning over him, is no different."

"Yes, it's true, he's handsome and he uses it," Sister said. "Concetta is being duped. But you should never look down on someone for trusting the wrong person. It could happen to any of us."

"I thought she was intelligent."

"And why did you think that?" Sister Teresa had tutored Concetta since she was six years old. She knew exactly how little interest Concetta had taken in her studies and how much energy she had expended in the quest for physical beauty and sartorial elegance. Far more effort went into her pursuit of glamour than into developing her intellect, character, or common sense.

"I thought she was . . . everything."

"I'm sorry. Even those we love can disappoint us."

"I know that now," Ciro said.

"Priests aren't perfect . . . ," Sister Teresa began. "Ciro, Don Gregorio already knows his shortcomings, far better than you ever will."

"He doesn't think he has any! He runs the church like he's king."

Sister Teresa took a deep breath. "Don Raphael Gregorio was neither distinguished academically nor admired for his spiritual acumen in the seminary. From all reports, he glided through on his good manners and pleasant personality. After he took his final vows, he wasn't assigned to the cathedral in Milan. He was not chosen to write for the Vatican newspaper. He was not selected to be the bishop's envoy or the cardinal's secretary. He was sent to the poorest village on the highest peak in the most northern Alps of Italy. He's a good-looking sap, and he knows it. He's just exactly smart enough to know that he can only be important in a place where he has no competition. He says mass like I read a recipe aloud as I'm cooking."

"He's a consecrated man! He's supposed to be better!"

"Ciro, you can't go by the costume."

"Then why does Sister take pains ironing his vestments? Why do I have to carry the altar linens on a dowel? We make the man look good."

"A cassock does not make a man a priest, any more than a fine dress makes a woman truly beautiful—or good or generous or intelligent. Don't confuse the way someone looks with the way they *are*. Grace is a rare thing. I wear the habit not because I *am* pious but because I'm *trying* to be. I left my mother and father when I was twelve years old to become a nun. I had a great desire to see the world, and now, I am doing penance for my selfishness. Who knew I'd see the world through the drain of an old sink and across the surface of a wooden chopping board? But here it is, and here I am. In my zeal to be a part of a grand adventure, I traded my mother's kitchen for this one."

Sister Teresa cooked three meals a day for the nuns, and also prepared the meals for Don Gregorio. She was up at 3:00 a.m. baking bread, which Ciro knew because he was up milking the cows. It seemed that Sister Teresa had the workload of a wife and mother, without the love and respect that went with it.

"Why do you stay?" Ciro asked.

Sister Teresa smiled. She really was beautiful when she smiled; her pink cheeks glowed, and her brown eyes twinkled. She placed her hands on Ciro's. "I'm hoping that God will find me."

Sister Teresa stood and threw a moppeen over her shoulder. She handed Ciro the platter to carry to the dining room and loaded the bowls of chestnut puree onto a large tray.

"It's not so bad. We eat, don't we?"

"Yes, Sister."

"There's never enough chicken, but we manage. God's love fills us up, that's what Sister Ercolina says. You have to find the thing that fills you up, Ciro. What fills you up? Do you know?"

Ciro Lazzari thought he knew what filled him up, but the last person he would tell was a nun. If Ciro understood anything about himself, it was his desire to woo and win a girl's heart. "I thought it was Concetta," he said.

"I'm sorry. Sometimes we get our hearts broken, only to have the right person come along to mend them," Sister said.

Ciro wasn't ready to let go of Concetta Martocci. He couldn't say why he loved her, he only knew that he did. The goal of winning her heart inspired him to work harder, longer, and more diligently so he might make enough money to take her places and buy her pretty things. Now what would he work for?

Ciro imagined Concetta in full, filling in the details of her life outside of what he observed in fleeting glimpses of her on the piazza, in school, or in church. He wondered how she spent her time away from San Nicola. He imagined her bedroom, with a round window, a white rocking chair, and a soft feather bed surrounded by a wallpaper of tiny pink roses. He wondered what she wished for—an elegant gold chain, a small emerald ring, or a fur capelet to wear over her winter coat? What would she become? Did she see herself working in a shop on the colonnade? Would she want a house on Via Donzetti or a farm above the village in Alta Vilminore?

Ciro pleaded, "Let's get rid of Don Gregorio. Help me do it. He's an infidel. You know how the church works. Help me get the job done. I would do it for you."

"Let me think about it," Sister Teresa said.

Seeing Concetta in the arms of another did not make Ciro jealous, it made him sad. He had hoped for a kiss for so long, and now he would never know one from the girl he had longed for from the first moment he saw her. The village priest had stolen any chance for his happiness outright, and Ciro wanted Don Gregorio to pay.

.   .   .

Ciro set off on foot for Schilpario to the north. The five-mile hike over the pass would take him about an hour, so he gave himself plenty of time to make it to the church to speak with Don Martinelli after the funeral and receive instructions for the grave-digging.

Sister Teresa packed a few fresh rolls, sliced salami, a hunk of Parmesan cheese, and a canteen of water. Ciro was frustrated that he was forced to walk to Schilpario, but after his run-in with Don Gregorio, he knew he would never ride in the church carriage again. He wondered who would take care of the rectory stable now that he had been fired. He felt for Iggy, who was getting older and counted on his young companion to do the heavy lifting. The word had spread quickly that Ciro was no longer working at the church, a bit of news in a village longing for it.

The Passo Presolana curved like a copper coil up the perimeter of the mountain, snaking under stone overpasses and widening where the lip of the gorge extended over the rocks. Ciro walked through a long tunnel carved into the mountain, its stone walls once jagged from dynamite blasts but now covered in green moss. Ciro kept his eyes on the far entrance, an oval of bright light capping the darkness.

Suddenly he heard the pounding of hooves. Ciro could make out the silhouettes of a team of horses pulling a covered carriage as it entered the tunnel. The horses plowed on at full gallop. Ciro heard the driver shout, "*Sbrigati!*" to him as he froze in their sightline. Ciro threw himself against the wet wall of the tunnel, clinging to it, arms outstretched.

The galloping horses raced past, the wheels of the carriage inches from Ciro's feet as it barely negotiated the hairpin turn.

The deafening sound of the hooves diminished in the distance, and Ciro leaned over, placed his hands on his knees, and attempted to regain his breath, his heart pounding. The idea of certain death skirted only seconds ago sent a chill through him.

As soon as he had regained his composure, he made his way out of the tunnel and continued his climb up the mountain. The Alps blossomed with the fresh buds of spring; on one side the cliffs were draped in white button daisies, while on the other, the rocky sides of the perilous gorge were blanketed in a mesh of vines. Ciro wished he had taken Eduardo up on his offer of company, as the journey was turning out to be longer and more treacherous than he imagined, but his brother was busy preparing the liturgy for Easter week.

Ciro whistled, climbing a steep crook in the road. As he passed a deep gulley where the road dropped off, he heard something rustle in the brush. He looked down into the pit, a crevice filled with thick foliage, and stepped back. There were wolves in these mountains, and he imagined that if they were half as hungry as the poor people who lived in these villages, he might not make it to Schilpario after all. He sprinted up the road when he heard another rustling, this time closer, as if he were being followed. Ciro broke into a run and was soon followed by a small barking dog, a wiry black-and-white mutt with a long face and alert brown eyes.

Ciro stopped. Catching his breath, he asked, "Who are you?"

The dog barked.

"Go home, boy." Ciro surveyed the stretch of road. He was too far outside Vilminore for the dog to belong to anyone there, and besides, the dog was thin, so it was doubtful he'd been in the care of an owner for a while.

Ciro knelt. "I have to dig a grave, boy."

The dog looked up at him.

"Where do you live?"

The dog stuck out his pink tongue and panted.

"Oh, I get it. You're an orphan boy like me." Ciro scratched the dog behind the ears. His fur was clean, but matted tightly, like thick wool.

Ciro opened his canteen of water and poured some into his hand for the dog to drink. The dog lapped up the water and then shook his head, splashing the remains all over Ciro.

"Hey!" Ciro stood, wiping his face with his sleeve. "*Non spruzzarmi!*"

He turned to walk up the road. The dog followed him.

"Go home, boy."

The dog ignored the command and followed Ciro up the mountain. The rest of the climb went by quickly as Ciro tossed sticks for his new friend to fetch. Back and forth, back and forth, the dog made a game of Ciro's climb higher and higher into the Alps. Ciro had begun to appreciate the dog's company just as the journey ended. The entrance to the village of Schilpario was in sight.

Ciro's destination, the church of Sant'Antonio da Padova, built with large blocks of sandstone from the mountain, anchored the entrance to the village. From the church courtyard Ciro saw an enormous waterwheel below, spinning furiously as rushing torrents from the mountain streams spilled over the slats and into a clear pool. The deep field behind the waterwheel gave a sense of length and breadth to this village, nestled at the foot of Pizzo Camino.

Ciro peered down the empty street. The town was eerily quiet. He looked up at the windows and saw no faces in them. The shop doors were locked, and the shades were down. It was as though the village had been abandoned. Ciro began to doubt Iggy's instructions.

The stray dog followed Ciro to the entrance of the church. Ciro looked down at him. "Look, I have a job here. Go find a family to take you in."

The dog looked up at Ciro as if to say, What family?

Ciro opened the door to the church. He looked back at the dog, who sat back on his hind legs to wait. Ciro shook his head and smiled.

Ciro entered the church, removing his cap. The vestibule was full, ten people deep. Ciro worked his way through the crowd to the back of the church. Every pew was filled. Rows of mourners stood in the aisles. The alcoves overflowed with people, and the stairs up to the choir loft were full. Ciro soon realized that the entire population of the village was standing in the church. Ciro had been hired to bury someone very important, a padrone, a *sindaco*, or perhaps a bishop.

Ciro was tall enough to see over the heads of the mourners. He looked down the long center aisle to the foot of the altar, where a small open casket rested. To his horror, Ciro realized that he had come to bury not an old man, but a child. Kneeling before the casket was the family, a mother and father and their children. They were dressed in clean, neatly pressed work clothes, but in no way would their humble appearance justify this elaborate funeral or the standing-room-only attendance. Ciro was surprised to see such a poor family, one of his own station, so exalted in church.

.   .   .

Giacomina knelt before the casket, placing her hands upon it as if to comfort a sleeping child in a cradle. Giacomina had never had the seventh baby she had promised her husband. How strange that she was thinking about the baby that had never been born as her own lay in her casket. The scent and sounds of a new baby in the house always sweetened the surroundings. The older children had their enchantments, and it was a pleasure to tend to them, but a baby brings a focus to the home. A new baby binds a family together anew.

Giacomina had believed that the absence of a seventh baby shielded the other six from harm. She had made a deal with God Almighty. In exchange for that seventh joy she had prayed for but not received, He would hold the six she had close and safe. But God had broken His promise. As she took in the faces of her children, she realized that she could not comfort them. Their loss was as catastrophic as her own.

.   .   .

Enza gripped her mother's hand tightly as she knelt before the casket, taking in for the last time Stella's sweet face and unruly curls. How many times Enza had stood at the foot of the crib when Stella was a baby, peering up at her as she slept! She did not look that different to Enza now.

Enza would hold the image of her baby sister in her heart like the curl of Stella's hair that she had clipped and placed in a locket before the priest allowed the mourners into the church. Enza began to list all the things Stella had accomplished during her short life. Stella was learning to read.

She knew the alphabet. She could recite her prayers, the Hail Mary, the Glory Be, and the Our Father. She knew the song "Ninna Nanna" and could dance the bergamasca. She was learning about nature; she could identify the poisonous red berries of the sagrada plant as well as the edible plumberries that grew wild on the cliffs. She knew the difference between alpine deer and wild elk from drawings in Papa's book.

Stella knew about heaven, but it had been presented like a land of make-believe, a castle in the clouds where angels lived. Enza wondered if Stella understood what was happening as she lay dying. It was too cruel to imagine Stella's last thoughts.

Life, Enza decided, is not about what you get, but what is taken from you. It's in the things we lose that we discover what we most treasure. Enza's most profound wish was that she might have kept Stella safe, that she had not failed her baby sister, that they would not have to face the years ahead without her.

Enza vowed never to forget Stella, not for a day.

The priest struck a long match and ignited the incense in the gold urn until streams of gray smoke curled from the open squares of the brass cup. He gently lowered the cap and lifted the urn on its rope chain, swinging it gently as he walked around the casket, anointing it, until puffs of smoke obscured the tiny casket, which now resembled a small golden ship sailing through clouds. The family encircled the casket as they had Stella's bed.

The priest looked all around the church, unable to figure out a way to move the vast crowd through the cathedral so each mourner might pass the casket and pay their final respects. Ciro quickly grasped the problem. He nudged two young men and motioned for them to join him.

Ciro walked up the aisle with the boys, and, slipping behind the altar to the far side of the church, he motioned for the two young men to do the same on the other side of the church. They unbolted the side doors, top and bottom, letting in the fresh mountain air and beams of sunlight that immediately dispelled the gloom. The mourners formed a line and began to process past the casket and out from either side. The priest nodded his approval to Ciro.

Ciro observed the eldest daughter rise from her kneeling position to stand behind her grieving mother, placing her hands on her shoulders to comfort her. He looked away; to see such deep connection between mother and child awoke a particular grief of his own. He slipped out the side door through the crowd. Once outdoors, he took in the cool, fresh air. He figured it would take most of the afternoon to move the mourners through the cemetery after the final benediction. It would be hours before he could begin to dig the grave, and nightfall before he would return to Vilminore.

Hearing a dog whimper, Ciro looked up and saw his stray running around the side of the church toward him. He leaned down, and the dog nuzzled his hand.

"Hey, Spruzzo," he whispered, happy for the company.

Ciro reached back into his knapsack and broke off a bit of salami for the dog as the mourners filed out of the church and into the streets of Schilpario in waves of black and gray, like low storm clouds off the cliffs.

A group of children left the church together. Ciro immediately recognized them as orphans. They were led by a nun whose hands were folded into her billowing black sleeves, her head bowed as she went. The sight of the children, moving quickly as if to ward off attention as they followed the nun, tore at his heart. He missed his own mother. Ciro had learned that the pain of her abandonment was only lying dormant; suddenly, when he was most unaware, the sight of a child around the age he was when Caterina left him at the convent would open the old wound again, piercing his fragile soul.

Ciro imagined his mother in a gold carriage, led by a team of black horses, stopping in front of the convent on a winter morning. Caterina would be wearing her best coat, of the deepest midnight blue velvet. She would reach down and extend her hands to her sons, beckoning them to join her. In this dream, Ciro and Eduardo were young boys again. This time, she wouldn't leave them behind; instead, she would scoop them up and place them on the seat of the carriage. The driver would turn to them: their father, Carlo, smiling with the contentment of a happy man with a clear conscience, who needs nothing in this world but a woman who loves him and the family they have made together.

6

A BLUE ANGEL
Un Angelo Azzurro

A silver mist settled over the cemetery of Sant'Antonio da Padova as the sun sank behind the mountain. The wrought-iron gates of the cemetery were propped open, revealing a flat field cluttered with headstones and surrounded along the periphery by a series of crypts.

Prominent families had built ornate marble and granite mausoleums that featured outdoor altars, open porticoes, and hand-painted frescoes. There were also simple, spare structures in the Roman style, with columns offsetting crypts inlaid with gold lettering.

Ciro knew that grave-digging in Schilpario would be difficult. Barite and iron mines lay beneath the village, which meant that the ground was loaded with shale. Even as his shovel struck rock again and again, he persisted, excavating white limestone hunks that looked like oversize pearls and stacked them by the grave.

Stella's casket rested nearby on the marble floor of a mausoleum entrance. It was covered in a blessed cloth, ready to be placed in the grave when Ciro's work was done.

Spruzzo sat on the edge of the open grave and watched his new master make steady progress, the mound of dirt next to the headstone growing higher and higher. Earlier, after final rites were performed at the graveside, the casket had been lowered into the shallow grave and covered with greenery. As soon as the last mourners left, Ciro removed the spray, lifted the casket out of the grave, and commenced digging seven feet into the earth. After two hours of digging, the shale gave way to dry earth, and Ciro dug the last two feet into the pit in no time at all.

Ciro climbed out of the grave to retrieve the casket.

Years ago, the Ravanelli family had purchased a small plot and marked it with a delicate sculpted angel of blue marble. Ciro preferred the Ravanellis' plot, elegant in its simplicity, to the fancy mausoleums.

Ciro lifted the small casket and set it down beside the pit. He placed it gently on the ground and jumped into the grave.

"Here. Let me help," a girl said.

Ciro peeked up from the ragged hem of the grave to see the eldest Ravanelli daughter standing over him. In this light, she seemed ethereal, like an angel herself. Her long black hair was loose, and her eyes pierced through the mist, black as jet beads. She wore a starched white apron over her paisley dress. Wiping her tears away with her handkerchief, she stuffed it into her sleeve before kneeling.

Ciro could see that the girl needed to help, that the finality of burying the casket would give her some peace. "Okay," he said. "You lift one end, and I'll take the other."

Carefully, they lifted Stella's casket together. Ciro placed it gently in the grave and positioned it in the earth firmly before climbing out. Enza knelt on the ground and bowed her head. Ciro waited for her to finish her prayer.

"You might want to go now," Ciro said softly.

"I want to be here."

Ciro looked around. "But I have to cover the casket now," he said gently, as he leaned against the shovel.

"I know."

"Are you sure?"

Enza nodded that she was sure. "I don't want to leave my sister."

Spruzzo whined. Enza extended her hand, and the dog trotted over to her.

"There's some food in my knapsack," Ciro told her.

Enza opened the burlap sack and found the end of the sausage Sister Teresa had packed for him.

"If you're hungry, help yourself," he offered.

"*Grazie.*" She smiled at him.

Enza's smile filled Ciro with a feeling of warmth as he stood next to the mound of cold earth. He smiled back at her.

Enza fed Spruzzo bits of sausage as Ciro shoveled. He layered the ground evenly, until the surface on top was smooth and level with the other graves. When he was done, Enza helped him move the limestone rocks off to the side.

When they were done, Enza replaced the spray over the fresh grave until barely any earth showed through the quilt of green juniper and pine that the ladies of the church had gathered. Enza lifted long, fresh green branches of myrtle from a stack she had gathered that morning and made an edge around the grave, framing the grave in deepest green. She stood back; it looked lovely, she thought.

Ciro gathered the shovel and pick as Enza folded the holy cloth carefully.

"I have to return that to the priest," Ciro said.

"I know." Enza tucked it under her arm. "They use it at every funeral."

"Do you press the linens?" Ciro asked.

"Sometimes. The ladies of the village alternate between the linens and tending to meals for the priest."

"No nuns in Schilpario?"

"Just the one who runs the orphanage. And she's too busy to do extra chores."

Enza led Ciro out of the cemetery. Spruzzo followed behind, wagging his tail as he went.

"I can take it from here," Ciro said to her. "Unless . . . you want to show me the way." He smiled to invite her along.

"The rectory is behind the church," Enza said. "Like it is in every village in every province in Italy."

"You don't have to tell me about churches."

"Are you studying to be a priest?" Enza assumed he might be because he wore the clothes of the poor, and many entered the religious life because it was a good alternative to a life in the mines, or other hard-labor jobs on the mountain like stonecutting.

"Do I look like a priest?" Ciro asked her.

"I don't know. Priests look like everyone else."

"Well, let's just say I will never be a priest."

"So you're a grave digger?"

"This is my first, and hopefully my last, time." He realized how that sounded, so he said, "I'm sorry."

"I understand. It's not a pleasant job." Enza smiled. "I'm Enza."

"I'm Ciro."

"Where are you from?"

"Vilminore."

"We go there during the feast. Do you live in the village or on a farm?"

"I live in the convent." It surprised him that he so readily admitted where he lived. Usually, when talking to girls, he was reluctant to tell them about San Nicola and how he had grown up.

"Are you an orphan?" Enza asked.

"My mother left us there."

"Us? You have brothers and sisters?"

"One brother, Eduardo," he said. "Not like you. What's that like, to be from a big family?" he asked.

"Noisy." She smiled.

"Like the convent."

"I thought the nuns were quiet."

"Me too. Until I lived with them."

"So none of the piety rubbed off on you?"

"Not much." Ciro smiled. "But that's not their fault. It's just that I don't think prayers are answered very often, if at all."

"But that's why you need faith."

"The nuns keep telling me I need it, but where am I supposed to find it?"

"In your heart, I guess."

"There are other things in my heart."

"Like what?" Enza asked.

"Maybe you'll find out someday," Ciro said shyly. Enza picked up a stick and tossed it up the road, and Spruzzo ran to fetch it.

They walked up the road and into town. Enza noticed that their strides were similar as they walked together. She didn't find herself skipping to keep up with him, even though he was bigger and taller than she.

"Was your mother ill?" Enza asked.

"No. My father died, and she couldn't take care of us anymore."

"How sad for her," Enza said.

In all these years, Ciro had never thought about his mother's feelings. Enza's observation opened up his heart to think about what his mother had gone through. Maybe she missed her sons as much as they longed for her.

"How did you come to dig my sister's grave?" Enza asked.

"Iggy Farino sent me. He's the caretaker at San Nicola. I work for him." Throughout the long day, Ciro had wondered what had caused Stella's death. Even though he overheard conversations, little was said when it came to the death of children. "I don't mean to cause you any further sadness. But I'd like to know what happened to your sister."

"A fever. And she had terrible bruises. It happened so fast. By the time I carried her from the waterfall back to our house, the fever had consumed her. I kept hoping the doctor could help," Enza said. "But he couldn't. We'll never know."

"Maybe that's for the best," Ciro said gently.

"There are two kinds of people in this world. Those who want to know the facts, and those who want to make up a nice story to feel better. I wish I was the kind who made up stories," Enza admitted. "I was taking care of Stella the day before she died."

"You shouldn't blame yourself," Ciro said. "Maybe you shouldn't blame anyone, but accept that this is your sister's story, and the ending belongs to her."

"I wish I believed that."

"If you look around to find meaning in everything that happens, you will end up disappointed. Sometimes there aren't reasons behind the terrible things that go on. I ask myself, If I knew all the answers, would it help? I lie awake and wonder why I don't have parents and wonder what will become of my brother and me. But when the morning comes, I realize that there's nothing to be done about what has already happened. I can only get up and do my chores and push through the day and find the good in it."

"Stella was a big part of our happiness." Enza's voice broke. "I never want to forget her." Enza stifled her tears.

"You won't. I know a little about that. When you lose someone, they take a bigger place in your heart, not a smaller one. Every day it grows, because you don't stop loving them. You wish you could talk to them. You need their advice. But life doesn't always give us what we need, and it's difficult. It is for me, anyway."

"Me too," Enza said.

As they walked in the twilight, Ciro decided that Enza was more beautiful than Concetta Martocci. Enza was dark, like an inky lake in the moonlight, whereas Concetta was lacy and airy, like columbine in the spring. Ciro decided he preferred the mystery.

Enza had slender limbs and lovely hands. She moved gracefully and was well-spoken. Her cheekbones, straight nose, and strong chin were typically northern Italian. But she had something that Ciro had not seen in any girl before—she was *curious*. Enza was alert; she drank in the details of the world around her, sensitive to the feelings of others and quick to respond to them. He saw this in church that morning, and now, in conversation. In contrast, Concetta Martocci poured her energy into the cultivation of her beauty and the power it brought her.

Ciro had met Enza at her most vulnerable, and he wanted to help her. He felt compelled to do whatever he could for her. He had used his physical power when he worked, but now he wanted to share his emotional strength. There were no awkward moments with Enza; they seemed to have an immediate and comfortable connection. He hoped the walk back to the rectory took longer than he remembered; he wanted more time with this beautiful girl.

"Are you in school?" he asked.

"I'm fifteen. I finished school last year."

He noted happily that they were the same age. "You help your mother with the house?"

"I help my father in the stable."

"But you're a girl."

Enza shrugged. "I've always helped my father."

"Is your father a blacksmith?"

"He drives a carriage to and from Bergamo. We have an old horse and a pretty nice carriage."

"You're lucky to have a carriage." Ciro smiled. "If I had a carriage and horse, I would go to every village in the Alps. I'd take trips to Bergamo and Milan every chance I got."

"How about over the border to Switzerland? You look like the Swiss. The light hair."

"No, I'm Italian. Lazzari is my name."

"The Swiss have Italian surnames sometimes."

"You like the Swiss? Then I'll be Swiss," Ciro teased.

Enza walked ahead of Ciro, then turned on her heel to him. "Do you flirt with all the girls you meet?"

"Some." He laughed. "You just ask a question like that?"

"Only when I'm interested in the answer."

"There's a girl I know," Ciro admitted. He thought of Concetta, and he was disappointed all over again. The kiss between Don Gregorio and the girl he was enamored of burned in his memory like the image of hell in the fresco over the altar.

"Just one?"

"Concetta Martocci," Ciro said softly.

"Concetta. What a beautiful name."

"*Si,*" he said. "It suits her. She's small and blond." He glanced at Enza, who was almost as tall as he was. Ciro continued, "And I used to watch her in church. The truth is, I looked for her everywhere. I'd wait on the colonnade for her to go by. Sometimes for hours."

"Did she return your feelings?"

"Almost."

It was Enza's turn to laugh. "I'm sorry, I just never heard anyone describe love in terms of *almost.*"

"Well, I loved her from afar, let's say. But it turns out that she loves someone else."

"So your love story has a sad ending."

Ciro shrugged. "She's not the only girl in Vilminore."

"You keep telling yourself that," Enza said. "You can be the Prince of the Alps, wooing girls with your charm and your shovel."

"Now you're making fun of me!" Ciro cried.

"Not at all. I don't think you have anything to worry about. There are lots of girls in the Alps. Pretty ones in Azzone, and more up the mountain. Or go to Lucerne. The girls are blond there, and petite and pretty. Just like you like them."

"Are you trying to get rid of me?" Ciro stopped and put his hands in his pockets.

Enza faced Ciro. She reached behind her apron and tightened the bow. Then she smoothed the front placket with her hands. "You should have what you want. Everyone should."

"And what do you want?" Ciro asked her.

"I want to stay on this mountain. And I want to be with my parents until they're old." Enza took a breath. "Before I go to sleep, I picture my family. Everyone is safe and healthy. There's enough flour in the bin and sugar in the jar. Our chickens decide it's a good day, and they lay enough eggs to make a cake. That's all I want."

"You don't wish for a gold chain or a new hat?"

"Sometimes. I like pretty things. But if I had to choose, I'd rather have my family." Enza put her hands in her apron pockets.

"Have your parents made a match for you?"

"If they have, they haven't told me who he is." Enza smiled. How odd that Ciro asked her this question on this day, of all days. Stella's death had forced her to grow up, or at least ponder the choices that lay ahead in adulthood. But now she realized that to have a full life, you must commit to building one.

"Maybe they haven't chosen him yet." Ciro leaned against the shovel.

"I wouldn't want my parents to make a match for me. I want to choose who I will love. And I want—more than anything—to see my sister again." Enza began to cry but stopped herself. "So I'm going to do my best in this life so that I'm sure to see her in the next one. I'm going to work hard, tell the truth, and be of some use to the people who care about me. I'm going to try, anyway." Enza took the handkerchief out of her sleeve, turned away from Ciro, and wiped her tears away.

Ciro instinctively moved toward her and put his arms around her. Even though he had been thinking for the past several minutes how to get his arms around her, he was surprised to realize that the urge to comfort her came from a place of authentic compassion, not simply desire.

The scent of the earth and his skin enfolded her as he pulled her close.

Enza felt a sense of relief in his arms. This kindness from Ciro felt good after a day of comforting others. She leaned into him and released her burdens, crying until the tears stopped. She closed her eyes and let him hold her tight.

A feeling of contentment washed over Ciro as he held her. Enza seemed to fit naturally in his arms. There was a familiarity between them that made him feel useful. He discovered a purpose in her arms that he had never known before.

Ciro's worth had always been measured by how hard he worked, how many chores he could complete from the time the sun came up until it went down. His diligence was his calling card and the foundation of his fine reputation; he had built his sense of self-worth one task at a time.

Ciro hadn't had any idea how capable he would feel, caring for a person rather than completing a chore. He felt a deep well open in his heart. He believed that a girl could be a thrilling mystery, but he couldn't have guessed she could also be a true companion, that conversation with her would fulfill him, or that he might even learn something from her.

Enza pulled away from his embrace. "You came to dig a grave, not to talk to me."

"But I found you," he said, took her into his arms, and kissed her. As his lips caressed hers, his mind rushed over the events of the day. He tried to remember when he had first seen her. Had he seen other girls in the crowd first and then found her, or was she the only girl he noticed? How did he get this far, how was she allowing him to kiss her when his hands were dirty and he was hardly at his best? Would there ever come a time when he would woo a girl pressed, polished, and as shiny as a glass button?

Enza felt her heart race as their lips touched, the sadness of the day quelled by the unexpected meeting with this boy from Vilminore. Maybe their kisses, breath exchanged for breath, could show her a way to live in the shadow of the sorrow of this day. Maybe her darkest moments had found some light; perhaps he could redeem her grief and replace it with connection. Maybe this boy was some kind of peculiar angel, tall and strong, with freckles from working in the sun and calluses on his hands, so unlike the soft hands of the wealthy and learned. After all, he had made Stella secure in the earth. Maybe he had been sent to place her sister in the mountain she knew and loved, making her an eternal part of it.

But it didn't matter what he was, or where he came from. Enza was sure he had a good heart, raised as he had been by the sisters in the convent, and he filled a yearning within her. There would be time later to wonder why she had let a boy she hardly knew kiss her on Via Scalina. For her, there was no hesitancy, because there was no mystery. She understood him, though she wasn't sure why.

In this small village, though, there were rules about courting. The thought of a neighbor seeing her, here in the open, kissing a boy quickly brought her to her senses. As usual, her practical nature won over her romantic heart.

"But you love someone else," she said, making an excuse to step away from him, even though she didn't want to.

"Sister Teresa says that when one girl breaks your heart, another comes along to mend it."

Enza smiled. "I'm the best seamstress in Schilpario. Everyone says so. But I don't know how to help you mend your broken heart. I have one of my own, you know." Enza ran up the stairs of the rectory and rang the bell. Ciro bounded up after her.

Father Martinelli came to the door. He seemed so much smaller in the doorway than he had at the altar. His white vestment robes and gold sash had made him seem like a giant, but in his black cassock, he had shrunk to the size of an ink blotter.

"Your cloth, Don Martinelli."

"*Va bene. Buona sera.*" Don Martinelli began to close the door. Ciro put his foot in the door frame to prevent the priest from closing it.

"Ignazio Farino says you're to pay me two lire."

"You're an expensive grave digger."

Father dug in his pocket and handed Ciro two lire. Ciro handed one lira back to Don Martinelli. "For the church." Ciro said. Don Martinelli took the money, grunted, and closed the door.

"That was kind of you," Enza said.

"Don't think highly of me. That was the deal," Ciro said.

Enza looked up at the night sky, an expanse of lavender with streaks of gold that looked like embroidered threads. A beautiful heaven had welcomed her sister's soul tonight.

"Where did you stable your horse?" she asked.

"I walked."

"From Vilminore? You can't possibly walk over the pass when it's dark. You could get trampled, or worse."

Spruzzo wheezed.

"And what about your dog?"

"He's not my dog."

"But he follows you everywhere."

"Because I couldn't get rid of him. He followed me up here over the pass. I made the mistake of feeding him."

"He chose you." Enza knelt down to pet Spruzzo.

Ciro knelt down next to her. "I'd rather *you* chose me."

Enza looked into Ciro's eyes, and couldn't decide if this young man was the type who said pretty things to all the girls, or if he really liked *her*. He wouldn't be the first boy to take advantage of a sad girl, but Enza decided that she had to trust what she saw in him instead of thinking the worst.

"You know this church is named for Sant'Antonio di Padova, the saint of lost things. That's a sign. Spruzzo was lost, he found you, and he meant to. You have to keep him."

"Or what?"

"Or Sant'Antonio will forget you. And when you need him most, when you're lost, he won't help you find your way."

When Enza spoke of the saints, Ciro almost wanted to believe in them. He couldn't imagine such a personal faith, where saints were at the ready to do the bidding of those on earth. Ciro had buffed every statue at San Nicola, and never once felt the power behind the plaster images. How did this mountain girl know with certainty that the heavenly hosts were watching over her?

"Come with me," she said. "I'll take you home."

"You can drive a carriage?"

"Since I was eleven," Enza said proudly.

"This I have to see."

Enza and Ciro walked up Via Scalina together, following Spruzzo, who trotted ahead as though he'd been officially adopted. Oil lamps lit the path to the entrance of the Ravanellis' old stone house. The yard was filled with small groups of visitors who had come to be with the family. Inside, the house overflowed with more neighbors and friends, who had brought food and comfort to the family.

"Let me talk to my father," she said. "I need his permission."

Ciro followed Enza into the Ravanelli home while Spruzzo waited outside on the grass.

Ciro's mouth watered as he looked at the table, filled with an array of homemade breads and rolls, fresh cheese, prosciutto, cold polenta, and platters of tortellini, small purses of pasta filled with sausage. On the mantel over the hearth, he saw several cakes in tin pans, reminding him of the holiday baking at the convent. Ciro delivered Sister Teresa's rum cakes throughout Vilminore every December. An enamel pot of coffee rested on a trivet, and a pitcher of cream was set nearby. Every bench and chair was filled with company from the village.

There were children everywhere, climbing the ladder to the loft, running under the table, playing tag as they ran through the house to the outdoors. It occurred to him that a terrible day had been made whole by the laughter of children after the loss of one of their own.

Ciro felt the sudden sting of regret for all that he had missed in his own home, with family and friends filling rooms and making a life. The simply furnished house was clean and welcoming, and the friends seemed devoted. What more does a man need to be happy? Ciro wondered.

A woman around the same age as Giacomina poured her coffee, while Marco stood in a circle with several men who tried to keep his mind off his grief with stories from the mines. Ciro remembered them at the foot of the altar that morning , a lump forming in his throat.

Enza made her way to her father. She whispered in Marco's ear, and he nodded and looked over at Ciro, sizing him up, as Enza went to her mother and knelt before her. She patted her mother's hand and kissed her on the cheek.

Enza collected two pears, several small sandwiches, and a *cavazune* pie filled with ricotta and honey, placing them in a starched moppeen. She joined Ciro at the door. "Papa said we can take the carriage."

"Before we go, may I pay my respects to your parents?" Ciro asked.

Every feeling Enza had in her heart had been expanded that day. She was surprised by Ciro's grace and also moved by it. "Of course," she said quietly.

Enza tied a knot in the moppeen and placed the food on the table. She took Ciro to meet her father. Ciro shook his hand and offered his condolences. Then Enza took Ciro to meet her mother. Ciro repeated his kind sympathies and remembered to bow his head to the lady of the house.

Ciro followed Enza down a stone path to the stable as Spruzzo barked outside the stable door. Enza grabbed a small oil lamp and went into the barn, where the light turned everything inside a milky gold— the hay, the walls, the trough, the horse. Cipi stood in his stall, covered by a blanket.

"You can pull the muslin cover off the carriage," Enza said, lifting the blanket off Cipi. The horse nuzzled her neck.

"You want me to hitch the carriage?" Ciro asked.

"I can do it." Enza led Cipi out of his stall to the carriage hitch. "You can feed him."

Ciro lifted a bucket of oats from the feeder trough and positioned it where Cipi could gobble it down.

Enza opened the stable doors and attached the oil lamp to the hook on the carriage. She went to the water pump outside the doors and pumped fresh water for Spruzzo, who lapped it up hungrily. Then she washed her hands and face, wiping her face on her apron. Ciro did the same, wiping his own face on his bandana.

She climbed up onto the carriage bench. "Don't forget supper." Ciro picked up the food and climbed next to Enza, who picked up the reins as Spruzzo jumped up on to the seat and sat between them.

Enza snapped the reins; Cipi trotted out of the barn and onto the main road that weaved through Schilpario. The heart of the village, a corridor of buildings that lined either side of the road, was drenched in pale blue moonlight. The carriage passed through the narrow stone street until the walls of the town gave way to the entrance of the Passo Presolana.

The road unspooled down the mountain before them like a black velvet ribbon, the carriage lamp throwing a strong beam of white light into the darkness to guide them. Ciro watched as Enza deftly controlled the reins. She sat up high, with perfect posture, guiding Cipi through the night.

"Tell me about your ring," Enza said.

Ciro twisted the gold signet ring on his smallest finger. "I'm afraid I'm going to outgrow it altogether."

"Have you had it very long?"

"Since my mother left. It belonged to her."

"It suits you."

"It's all I have from my family."

"That's not true," Enza said. "I'll bet you have her eyes, or her smile, or her coloring."

"No, I look like my father." Whenever anyone else asked about his mother, Ciro changed the subject, but Enza asked about Caterina in a manner that didn't feel like prying. "My brother looks like our mother." He added, "I'm not at all like her, really."

"You should eat," Enza said. "You must be starving."

Ciro took a bite of the bread and cheese. "I'm always hungry."

"What's it like, living in the convent? When I was a little girl, I thought about becoming a nun."

Ciro draped his arm over the back of the carriage seat around Enza. "You shouldn't kiss boys, then."

"Don't look so smug."

"How can you tell how I look? It's dark out here."

"I can see just fine. The lamp is loaded with oil." Enza loosened the reins on Cipi, who slowed to a more leisurely jog.

"You don't even have to direct him. He knows the way," Ciro observed.

"Papa takes this route when business is good."

"And how is business?"

"Terrible. But the summer is coming, and it's always better then."

"Will I see you this summer?" Ciro asked.

"We go up to Lake Endine."

Ciro sat up. "You do?"

"We stay with our cousins. You could come with us," Enza offered.

"I would never impose," Ciro said.

"My brothers would love the company. They go fishing. They hike and go in caves. Battista says that there are caves with blue sand up on the mountain."

"I've heard of those caves! Do you go fishing?" Ciro asked.

"No, I cook and clean and help my aunt with her babies. Just like your nuns. A lot of work, and I'm paid in fresh figs," Enza joked.

Enza took the turn onto the piazza in Vilminore. A few of the townspeople were out after *la passeggiata*. Old men played cards on small tables on the colonnade as a mother pushed a pram, soothing her baby. Cipi's hooves clicked across the piazza as Ciro took the reins and guided the carriage to the entrance of the convent.

"Thank you for the ride," Ciro said. "I wish you didn't have to go back alone."

"Don't worry about me. Cipi knows the road. Remember?"

"I'd better go," Ciro said, yet he didn't move. He wasn't ready to get out of the carriage, or for this night to end.

"I'm not going to kiss you again," Enza said gently.

"But . . . ," Ciro said.

Enza gave him the moppeen with the food.

"Good night, Ciro. Remember, Sant'Antonio will take good care of you if you take care of Spruzzo."

"When will I see you again?"

"Whenever you want. You know where I live."

"The yellow house on Via Scalina," Ciro said.

He climbed down from the carriage, his arms full of Spruzzo and the remnants of supper. He turned to say something more to Enza, but Cipi had trotted out into the piazza and was heading for the road.

Enza's dark hair flew behind her like a veil. How small she looked, high on the driver's bench! As the carriage turned off onto the pass, the lamplight threw a sheen on the wooden side of the carriage. "Wait!" Ciro called out, but she was gone.

I know that carriage, he thought.

It looked like the carriage that had taken his mother away. Could it be the same one? Ciro had felt there was something fated about meeting

Enza, and now he knew. He couldn't wait to tell Eduardo, who might remember the carriage in more detail than he. Or maybe he was just imagining things on this day of grave-digging and tears.

The smattering of clouds over the moon floated away, leaving a gold coin in the sky. Lucky moon. Tonight, Ciro thought, life was pretty good. If he were the praying kind, he might even thank God for his good fortune. He had a lira in his pocket. He had met a pretty girl, and he'd kissed her. It wasn't like any of the other kisses he'd ever had, nor was she like any of the other girls who had come before her. Enza *listened* to him, and this was a gift sweeter than any kiss. But it would take Ciro many years to realize it.

. . .

Ciro pushed the convent door open and entered the vestibule. Eduardo jumped up from the bench. "You're back. *Grazie Dio.*"

"What's the matter?"

"What is that?" Eduardo looked down at the dog.

"This is Spruzzo."

"You can't have a dog in the convent."

"He's for Sister Teresa. She says there's a rat in the kitchen."

Ciro turned to head out to the workhouse. Eduardo stopped him. "They're waiting for us in the kitchen."

"*They?*"

"The nuns."

Ciro followed Eduardo. "What's going on?" he asked. A sense of unease displaced the contentment he had felt moments before.

The kitchen door was closed, but light spilled through the cracks in the doorjamb. Ciro told Spruzzo to stay outside as Eduardo pushed it open.

The nuns had gathered around Sister Teresa's worktable. Some sat on stools, while others stood. Sister Teresa stood off to the side, a look of worry on her face.

"Are we taking a vote?" Ciro asked. "Because if we are, I vote to plant more olives next year than grapes."

The nuns, who usually appreciated Ciro's jokes, were in no mood for them tonight.

"Okay, before you punish me, for *whatever* I've done—" Ciro took the lira from his pocket. "For you." He handed it to Sister Domenica, whose white hair stuck out of her wimple, a sure sign she'd been in a rush to get to this meeting.

"Thank you," she said. The sisters murmured their gratitude.

"We have a very serious problem," Sister Ercolina said as she adjusted her wire-rimmed glasses and stood tall and reedy, like a palm frond on Easter Sunday. She crossed her arms across her chest inside her sleeves. "We have loved having you boys here. Eduardo, you have been a wonderful student, and Ciro, we don't know how we would have handled the garden and the chickens and the maintenance of the convent and the church without you—"

"This is about Don Gregorio, isn't it?" Ciro interrupted her, but his mouth was so dry, he could barely swallow. He picked up the pitcher and poured himself a glass of water.

"He has asked to have you removed from the convent immediately," Sister said.

Ciro looked at Eduardo, whose face had turned as white as the flour in the enamel bin. Ciro placed his hands on the table and nodded his head in disbelief. The Lazzari boys had lived in two homes in their young lives. The first had been taken from them because their father had died, and their mother could not build a life for them alone. Now, it was Ciro's own actions against the village priest that had caused them to lose their home. The boys had grown accustomed to their role in service to these good and poor nuns. They felt long work hours in exchange for their room and board was a fair trade. They had became part of this community, and grown to feel affection for it. The nuns were purposeful in their motherly care of the boys, making certain they celebrated holidays and feast days as they might have with their parents. Now, the security that had given them confidence and a place in the world had been taken away.

"I hope you told Don Gregorio to drop dead," Ciro said.

The novitiates gasped.

"He's a *priest*," Sister Ercolina said.

"He's also a fraud who takes advantage of young girls. You press his vestments, but he is not worthy of them. You—" Ciro turned and searched the eyes of his family of nuns. "You are worthy. Every single one of you. You *serve*. Don Gregorio *takes*."

Eduardo gripped Ciro's arm.

"My brother and I"—Ciro's voice broke—"thank you for taking us in. We'll never forget you. You should not suffer because I was honest with Don Gregorio. My brother and I will pack up and find another place to stay."

Sister Ercolina's eyes filled with tears. "You won't be together, Ciro."

"Don Gregorio has seen to it that you will be separated," Sister Teresa cried.

"Ciro, he has arranged to send you to the boys' workhouse in Parma," Sister Domenica began. "I argued that you had done nothing wrong, and that you don't belong there with boys who steal and do worse, but he was vehement."

"So the infidel punishes us instead of doing penance for his own sin. And this, dear sisters, is the man who represents God on earth? I have no words."

"He deserves our respect," Sister Domenica said, but the steady look in her eyes told Ciro the words were bitter in her mouth.

"Sister, you can give him yours, but he will never have mine."

Sister Ercolina looked around, then fixed her gaze on Ciro. "I am not here to debate the power of the village priest, I am here to help you. We have all gathered to help you."

"That's why we meet in secret in the kitchen." Ciro looked around at their faces, the same sweet faces with whom he and Eduardo had shared dinner since the first night they came to the convent. He could not imagine his life without them, nor could he accept the loss of his brother. Fury rose within him. "He would never think to look for us here. The saint of pots and pans is not one he calls upon. No, the saints of gold, frankincense, and *lire* are more his style."

"Stop it," Eduardo said sadly. "Listen to Sister."

Sister Teresa stepped forward. "Ciro, we have a plan to help you."

"What about Eduardo?"

"Eduardo is reporting to the seminary of Sant'Agostino in Rome."

Ciro turned to his brother in disbelief. "You're going into the seminary?"

Eduardo nodded. "I am."

"When were you going to tell me?"

Eduardo's eyes filled with tears. "I've been thinking about it. And now I will leave the convent when you do."

"So you've been sacrificed on the altar of the priesthood in exchange for me?"

Sister Teresa stepped in. "Don Gregorio insists you both leave the mountain."

"Of course—I saw too much."

"But we have a plan of our own. Sister Anna Isabelle has an uncle who is a very good shoemaker."

"Oh, come on," Ciro blurted.

"Ciro—," Eduardo warned.

"It was either apprentice with him or go to the workhouse in Parma. That's not a place for a fine young man with a good mind and a good heart." Sister Teresa began to cry.

"We have to protect you," Sister Ercolina said. "We promised your mother."

The weight of what had transpired on this day finally settled on Ciro. This wasn't really their home, and the nuns weren't truly family. The security they had provided was only on loan.

"Is this shoemaker in Rome, so I can be near Eduardo?" Ciro asked, accepting his fate. Ciro would work anywhere, for anyone, as long as he could be close to Eduardo.

"No, Ciro," Sister Teresa said.

"Milan, then?"

"America," Sister Teresa said, as her voice broke.

. . .

The cot creaked as Ciro rolled over in the dark. "You awake?"

"I can't sleep," Eduardo said.

"Probably a good idea. Keep your eyes open. Don Gregorio will come in here and stab us in our cots," Ciro said. "No, he wouldn't. He's too much of a coward."

Eduardo laughed. "Do you take nothing seriously?"

"It hurts too much."

"I know," Eduardo said.

"Do you really want to be a priest?"

"Yes, Ciro, I do. Though I'm not worthy of it."

"*They* are not worthy of *you*."

"Well, either way, they're about to find out." Eduardo's wry tone made Ciro laugh.

"I suppose there were signs. You served every morning mass, and you never missed vespers. And I saw you read your missal every night."

"I'll do my best to be one of them. I'll become a priest, and then I'll be able to help you should you ever need me. It doesn't hurt to have a brother with an education and a good position in the church."

"I would have been proud of you no matter what you became."

"You are pure of spirit, Ciro. You always have been."

"Right," Ciro joked. "And what does it say in the Beatitudes? The pure of spirit inherit what? The shoes?"

"I didn't think you knew what the Beatitudes were."

"I guess some of your dogma soaked in after all."

"There's another reason for me to become a priest. I can find Mama and take care of her. The church provides for the families of the clergy."

"You're going to give up everything for the chance it might help Mama?" Ciro asked.

"Yes, Ciro. It's the first vow I ever took."

"If I could, I would help. That was always our plan. But now the Holy Roman Church has ruined that, too," Ciro said. "I miss her."

Eduardo got up, went to Ciro's cot, and lay down on the floor next to him, as he had every night when they first arrived at the convent. The nearness of Eduardo was all it took to soothe Ciro. And tonight, it still did.

"When you find her, no matter where I am, I will come home to you," Ciro said.

Spruzzo jumped up on Ciro's cot and nestled at his feet. Ciro lay back and crossed his arms behind his head, staring at the wooden beams on the ceiling, with their spikes and hooks sticking out where pots and tools and loops of rope once hung. He wondered how soon the nuns would put all the equipment back into this room after they had left. The sisters reconfigured the space inside the convent like wealthy women in the city changed their hats.

This old room wouldn't be empty for long.

The winter bulbs asleep in pots, the urns, the buckets, the wreaths of wire, the spirals of rope, and the bowed wooden frames of the grape arbors would find their way back onto the shelves, as the trowels, rakes, and shovels would dangle from the hooks once more. It would be as though the Lazzari brothers had never lived at San Nicola.

.   .   .

One day, when Ciro took a walk up the hill to Via Bonicelli, he had seen that a new family had moved into the house where he and Eduardo were born. Sometimes Ciro would climb the hill just to look at the house, so as not to forget the details of the only place his family had ever lived. Eventually, he stopped going, and now he knew why.

Memories take the place of rooms. The sisters would fold up the cots, roll the rug, and put the lamp back into the office. The ceramic wash-basin and pitcher would be returned to the sisters' quarters in the guest room. Will the nuns even think of us when we are gone? Ciro wondered as he lay in the dark.

Ciro knew every street in Vilminore, every house and every garden. He would study their architectural details, creating his own perfect home in his mind's eye. He'd imagine a staircase here, a veranda there, windows with small panes that swung out, a garden with an arbor for grapes, and a patch of sod to grow a fig tree. He preferred a house built of stone to one of stucco and pine. He'd live at the end of the street, high on the mountain, with a good view of the valley below. He'd open his windows in the morning and let the fresh breeze through, as the sunlight filled every room, as bright as the petal of a daffodil. Light would fill every corner, and happiness would fill every room. The love of a good wife and children would fill his heart.

All Ciro knew of America was what he had heard in the village. There was a lot of boasting about the potential there, the money to be made, the fortunes to be built. But for all its promise, America had not returned their father home to the mountain. America had become, in Ciro's mind, almost like heaven, a place he could only see in his dreams. He had longed for his father and pictured him alive still, imagined their reunion. Maybe his father was filling his purse to return to the mountain to buy them a fine house. Maybe his father had had a plan, and something had prevented him from seeing it through. Anything but death in the mine, anything but that. Ciro still believed his father was alive. He vowed to find his father and bring him home. Maybe his father had grown to love America and didn't want to return to the mountain. *That* particular thought always brought Ciro pain. Ciro imagined America loud and crowded, and wondered if there were gardens and sun.

Southern Italians had flocked there to America to find work; fewer had emigrated from the Alps. Maybe that trip down the mountain was long and treacherous because it should be made rarely, if at all. It seemed to Ciro that a man had all he needed in the shadow of Pizzo Camino, so long as he was lucky enough to find love and a job to sustain his family.

Ciro was sure of one thing; he would only stay in America until the scandal blew over, not one day more. He vowed that he and Eduardo would return to Vilminore together, someday, to live on the mountain where they were born. Nothing would separate them, not even the Holy Roman Church. The Lazzari boys were blood brothers, and as their mother left them on that winter day, together, so they would remain, even when an ocean separated them.

7

A STRAW HAT

Un Capello di Paglia

The nuns kept Ciro out of sight for two days as they plotted to save him from the work camp in Parma. As the sun set behind the mountain, Sister Domenica, Sister Ercolina, and Sister Teresa carried trays across the piazza from the convent to the rectory.

Sister Ercolina shivered as they approached the rectory. "What did you make?" Sister Ercolina asked Sister Teresa.

"Veal," said Sister Teresa.

"It's his favorite meal," Sister Domenica said softly.

"Of course it is. It's the most expensive meat." Sister Ercolina sighed.

"I know. I bribed the butcher," Sister Teresa said.

Sister Domenica unlocked the door to the rectory kitchen. Sister Teresa lit the oil lamps, while Sister Ercolina placed a tray on a butcher-block worktable in the center of the room. The marble floor was pristine, the walls painted bright white. Fine copper pots, a deep stove, and a double enamel sink filled the wall under the windows. The rectory kitchen had the scent of fresh paint. Only rarely was food cooked here; the nuns bussed every meal over from the convent.

Sister Teresa placed Don Gregorio's dinner on the counter. She gathered the china, silver, and cloth napkins from the open shelves and pushed through the swinging doors into the dining room. Sister Domenica followed her, lighting candles in silver holders. The formal dining room was splendid, its walls adorned with a wallpaper of pale green stripes, staggered with oil paintings in gold-leaf frames.

The mahogany dining room table, which seated twenty, was polished to a mirror shine. The nuns had embroidered the seats of the chairs by hand in a pattern of lilies of the valley, surrounded by ivy vines, on a field of navy blue.

The nuns worked silently and swiftly, setting a place for Don Gregorio.

Sister Ercolina entered the dining room, checking her watch. "May I call Don Gregorio to supper?"

"Yes, Sister." Sister Domenica folded her arms into her habit sleeves, took her place by the sideboard, and looked straight ahead.

Sister Teresa entered the dining room with Don Gregorio's meal, warm under its silver dome. She positioned it on the starched linen place mat and took her place next to Sister Domenica.

Sister Ercolina entered the dining room and stood on the opposite wall, facing Teresa and Domenica.

Don Gregorio entered. "Let us pray," he said without looking at the nuns. He made a sweeping sign of the cross, his hands cutting a swath through the air as he said,

> *Benedice, Domine,*
> *nos et haec tua dona*
> *quae de tua largitate sumus sumpturi*
> *per Christum Dominum nostrum. Amen.*

The nuns made the sign of the cross with him, and Don Gregorio took his seat as Sister Teresa moved forward to serve him. She lifted the silver dome off the plate, and Sister Domenica took it from her. They returned to their stations by the server.

"What a beautiful cut of veal," Don Gregorio said.

"Thank you, Don Gregorio," Sister Teresa said.

"Why am I deserving of such an opulent meal in the midst of Lent?"

"Don Gregorio, you must keep your strength up during Easter week."

"Have you set the schedule for the house blessings, Sister Ercolina?"

"Yes, Father. We have the LaPenna and Baratta boys accompanying you. We thought you should begin in Vilminore Alta this year and work your way down the mountain. Ignazio will drive you in the carriage. We have the silver polished, and the urns ready for your blessing of the holy water."

"Have the palms arrived?"

"They were shipped from Greece, and we expect them any day now," Sister assured him.

"And the linens for Good Friday?"

"They are pressed and stored in the sacristy."

"And my vestments?"

"Hanging in the chifforobe in the sacristy." Sister Ercolina cleared her throat. "Are you expecting any visitors during Holy Week, Father?"

"I've sent a letter to the priest in Azzone to concelebrate Easter mass with me. I understand the choir has been practicing."

"Yes, they sound wonderful." Sister Ercolina motioned to Sister Teresa to refill Don Gregorio's wineglass.

"Sisters, I'd like to speak to Sister Ercolina alone, please."

Sister Domenica and Sister Teresa nodded and left quietly through the door to the kitchen, closing the door behind them.

"You may sit, Sister Ercolina."

Sister Ercolina pulled a chair out from the table and sat on the edge of it.

"Have you taken care of the Lazzari boy?" he asked.

"Which one?" Sister Ercolina said innocently.

"Eduardo." The priest was impatient.

"I sent the letter to the seminary weeks ago. They are willing to take him now. Eduardo is a very pious young man," Sister Ercolina said.

"I can see that. I believe he'll do very well there."

"He has been a great help to us at the convent." She added, "And I know you will miss his expert planning of the liturgy and music for Sunday mass. He really is quite talented."

"I agree with you. That's why I recommended him," Don Gregorio said.

On the other side of the door, Sister Teresa and Sister Domenica listened to the conversation.

"What are they saying?" Domenica asked.

"They're talking about Eduardo. Don Gregorio is taking full credit for Eduardo's admission into the seminary."

"Really? He applied months ago with Sister Ercolina's recommendation."

Sister Ercolina folded her hands on her lap. Don Gregorio tore a bit of bread from the loaf and sopped up gravy, made with butter, red wine, and mushrooms.

"And the other one?" He bit the bread and chewed.

"They are willing to take Ciro at the workhouse in Parma."

"Good."

"But we need a little help from you."

"What do you need?" he asked grudgingly. He picked up his glass of wine and sipped it.

"We need one hundred lire."

"What!" Don Gregorio placed his wineglass on the table.

"There is usually a waiting period at the workhouse, and they are willing to waive it, but we have to pay them for the privilege. I told them the matter was urgent, and that you want Ciro off the mountain as soon as possible—"

"I do," Don Gregorio said defiantly.

"They won't take him without it. I need the money tonight."

Don Gregorio eyed her suspiciously.

"Father, you asked me to make the arrangements quickly, and I was not to question you," Sister Ercolina pressed. "I have done as you have asked."

"Yes, of course, we must do what's right for San Nicola."

Sister Teresa and Sister Domenica entered to clear the plates. Sister Domenica carried a silver tray with a dish of baked custard for dessert.

"If you don't mind, I am going to skip dessert tonight," he said. "Sister Teresa, I need to speak to you alone."

Sister Teresa looked at Sister Ercolina nervously.

The older nuns nodded and retreated into the kitchen, closing the door behind them.

"Did you get the money?" Sister Domenica whispered frantically.

Sister Ercolina nodded. "He said he would give it to me. I hope that Sister Teresa corroborates what I've told him."

"Don't worry about her. She's as smooth as custard." Sister Domenica lifted a spoon and ate Don Gregorio's dessert.

In the dining room, Sister Teresa stood in front of Don Gregorio. She folded her hands and stared straight ahead.

"Sister Teresa, I would like to know why you went to Signora Martocci about their daughter."

"I was concerned, Father."

"You believed the little story that the Lazzari boy was spreading about me?"

"He has been at the convent since he was a boy, Father, and I've never known him to be dishonest."

"He's a liar," Don Gregorio said.

"Father, if you're trying to upset me, or cause me to doubt my own instincts, you won't succeed."

"You upset the Martocci family and caused them great distress. The sin of envy has swept through this village. Or perhaps it is you who has embarked upon an inappropriate relationship?"

"I assure you that is not the case. He's like a son to me." Sister Teresa raised her voice defensively.

"I would call that an inappropriate relationship. You're a nun, not his mother. Had I been the priest here when their mother dropped them off, I wouldn't have allowed them to stay. You're not running an orphanage over there."

"We minister to the poor in whatever capacity they need us."

"You're here to service the church, Sister Teresa. Now go and send in Sister Ercolina."

Trembling with rage, Sister Teresa bowed and exited to the kitchen. In a moment, Sister Ercolina stood at the table, facing Don Gregorio.

"I want you to transfer Sister Teresa from our parish."

"I'm sorry, Father." Sister Ercolina was firm and clear—she had done enough horse trading for one night. "Sister Teresa is a good nun, and an excellent cook. I think you might remember when Sister Beatrice was the cook. We practically starved."

"Have someone else deliver my meals, then." Don Gregorio checked his watch.

"Of course, Father." Sister Ercolina was relieved to have saved Teresa. "But first, I need the one hundred lire," she said placidly.

"Oh, yes." Don Gregorio didn't make a move.

"I'll wait."

Don Gregorio got up and went out the door to the living room. Sister Ercolina reached down into her habit pocket and gripped her rosary. She bowed her head and prayed. After a few minutes, Don Gregorio returned.

"Here." He handed Sister Ercolina the money. "But it's an enormous amount. You've been taken advantage of."

"You gave me an urgent command, Don Gregorio. Perhaps you would prefer that Ciro—"

"No," he snapped. "It's a small price to pay to clean up this village."

Sister Ercolina put the money in her pocket. "Good night, Don Gregorio," she said, and went.

As Sister Ercolina joined her friends in the kitchen, she placed her fingers over her lips, smiling. The nuns lifted the trays and extinguished the oil lamp. Sister Ercolina opened the door and showed the sisters out.

That night, the sisters of San Nicola filed into their pews in the convent chapel. Ciro and Eduardo joined them, taking seats behind them. Sister Ercolina entered from the sacristy. She closed the door and faced them.

Sister Ercolina began with a heavy heart. "The arrangements have been made. This Saturday, Ignazio is going to take you both down to Bergamo, in the church cart."

"I'm allowed in Don Gregorio's cart? I thought he'd make me walk barefoot down the mountain, hauling a giant cross like Jesus on Golgotha."

"Ciro, I'm going to ask you to hold your tongue until I finish talking."

"I'm sorry, Sister." Ciro smiled.

"Eduardo, your train ticket will be waiting for you at the station. You will join four other seminarians. When you reach Rome, you will proceed with them to your new home in the seminary at Sant'Agostino. Ciro, the ticket waiting for you at the train station will take you to Venice. From there, you will sail to Le Havre, France, where you will purchase a one-way ticket to New York on the SS *Chicago*."

"Have you secured me a spot as an indentured servant? I only had one lira, and I gave it to Sister Domenica, who may have already squandered it on a bottle of Cuban rum."

"Ciro!" Sister Domenica laughed. The nuns giggled.

"No, your passage will cost one hundred lire." The sisters gasped at Sister Ercolina's defiance.

"Sister Anna Isabelle's family wired us to let us know that they will meet you in Manhattan at South Port 64 after you have been processed through Ellis Island. Take this letter." She gave it to Ciro. "And this money." She gave Ciro the lire. "There are two extra lire for you."

"Thank you," Ciro said. He held the envelope and the money and looked at his brother. "You've all sacrificed for me, and I'm not worthy."

"You are worthy, Ciro. But, I must ask you something in return. And I must ask you, Eduardo, and all the sisters, to hold a confidence for me. I told Don Gregorio that you were being sent to the work camp in Parma."

The sisters gasped; they had never known Ercolina to lie.

"I prayed about it, and I must follow my conscience in this matter. I believe you to be an honorable young man, Ciro. It's ironic that in order to take care of you, I had to lie. But the priest's power is absolute, and a thousand years of begging him to change his mind would not have turned the result in your favor. You should never have been punished for telling the truth."

"Thank you, Sister." Sister Teresa was full of emotion.

"I'm asking you to forgive me, and to pray for Eduardo and Ciro as they leave us to start their new lives. And also, please pray for Don Gregorio, who needs your intercessions on his behalf."

"You had me until you asked us to pray for the padre," Ciro muttered.

Sister Ercolina snapped, "Ciro, you realize, had you ever met me halfway, I'd be sending you to the seminary with Eduardo."

"Better to ship me off on a boat to America. I don't think the Holy Roman Church and I are a match."

"That would be my conclusion also, Ciro." Sister Ercolina smiled.

*   *   *

The rectory carriage was parked outside the entrance of the convent. The sun was not yet up over Vilminore; only the farmers and the town baker were up this early. Sunrise was an hour away.

Ignazio Farino drank a cup of strong coffee and hot milk and dipped a heel of day-old bread into it in the convent kitchen while Sister Teresa prepared eggs on the stove. Ciro and Eduardo joined them in the kitchen.

"It's the last supper, Sister," Ciro joked.

"I didn't know a sense of humor was awake this early." Eduardo pulled out a work stool and sat. Ciro poured his brother a cup of coffee, and then one for himself.

"Thank you for getting up early to milk the cows," Sister Teresa said to Ciro.

"I'm going to New York City. I don't know when I'll see another cow."

"That's a talent that you can use anywhere in the world," Ignazio assured Ciro. "They drink a lot of milk in America, I hear."

"I'm going to be a shoemaker, Iggy."

"I've always wanted a pair of black leather boots with blue spats and gray pearl buttons. I'll tell you what, I'll have my wife take a pencil and draw my feet on butcher paper. I'll send you the patterns and you can make the shoes. And you"—Ignazio turned to Eduardo—"You can pray for me and arrange some indulgences, if and when I need them."

"You'll always be in my prayers, Iggy," Eduardo said.

Ignazio finished his coffee and headed outside to prepare the cart for the trip down the mountain. He had agreed to transport several boxes for the Longarettis and deliver a collection of missals to the church in Clusone.

"I'm going to go and pack up my books. Thank you, Sister." Eduardo took his plate to the sink.

"I'll be right there," Ciro said to Eduardo.

Sister Teresa turned away from Ciro and cleaned the frying pan on the griddle.

"The pan is clean, Sister."

"I can't look at you, Ciro."

Ciro looked away, trying not to cry. The only sound was the soft sizzle of the pot of boiling water in the fireplace. Finally, Ciro said, "You knew this day would come. I just hoped to live up the road and visit a lot. Bring my wife over and my children. Maybe stop in and be of some use to you."

"You're going so far away."

"If only Don Gregorio knew how far."

Sister Teresa smiled, knowing this was the last bit of humor from Ciro that would brighten her mornings. "He'll never find out, but even if he does, you'll be safe."

"Do you know what happened to Concetta?" Ciro asked quietly.

"Her mother didn't believe me until Concetta admitted the whole thing. The relationship between the Martoccis and the priest has ended. Concetta won't see the priest any longer. That's why Don Gregorio is so angry at us. We ruined his happy arrangement."

"I loved Concetta, you know."

"I know."

Ciro tried to lighten the mood, for Sister Teresa's sake and his own. "I can't believe Sister Ercolina shook Don Gregorio down for one hundred lire. He didn't even know what hit him. I wish she would've asked for two hundred, and then you could've gotten some cows and pigs for the convent."

"Sister only takes what she needs. It's the secret to happiness, you know. Only take what you need."

"I'll remember that," Ciro smiled. "I guess I should say good-bye. I will write to you. One day, I promise, I will return to Vilminore. This is my home, and I plan to grow old here."

"I'll be so happy to see you when you come back."

"Thank you for all you've done for me." Ciro embraced Sister Teresa. Her eyes filled with tears.

Ciro wiped his own tears on his sleeve. "You have been my mother and my friend. You have been on my side from the day I arrived here. Eduardo will always do well because he knows how to follow rules. I never could, but you protected me and made it seem as though I was. I'll never forget you. It's only fitting that I leave you with a special gift so you'll always remember me."

"Absolutely not, Ciro."

"Oh, yes, Sister."

Ciro whistled. "Come on, boy."

Spruzzo bounded into the kitchen.

"Spruzzo will keep you company. You can feed him bits of salami, just like you fed me. He won't talk back, and he won't hound you for seconds. He will be happy with whatever you give him. Promise me you'll be as good to him as you were to me."

Sister Teresa's tears gave way to a hearty laugh. "All right, all right. But when you come back, he's all yours."

"Absolutely." Ciro hugged Sister Teresa one last time, then slowly walked out the door. Ciro did not look back. He wanted to, but he knew that the greatest gift he could give Sister Teresa was to forge ahead and take a bold step into his new life. He knew that she hoped above all he would be brave; courage would keep him from harm.

Spruzzo looked up at Sister Teresa. She sat down on the work stool, lifted her apron to her face, and cried into it. She had vowed to be true only to God, and then to her community, but she hadn't counted on raising a hungry little boy who had walked into the convent kitchen and won her heart. No mother had ever loved a son more.

. . .

The bells in the tower above the convent chapel rang out over the valley as the rectory carriage made the turn on the ridge above Valle di Scalve. Iggy pulled the reins tightly as Eduardo and Ciro looked up the mountain at Vilminore for the last time.

Ciro's eyes did not linger on the landscape, as he vowed to return quickly. Eduardo knew differently, taking a few moments to commit the green cliffs to memory. He was certain the antiquities of Rome could never be this beautiful.

"Those bells are for you boys," Ignazio said. "If I didn't have to drive you down the mountain, it would have been me working the ropes in the tower to say good-bye to you. I'm deaf in one ear from ringing those chimes."

"I'm sorry you have to scrub the church from now on," Ciro said.

"You left it so clean, I think I can get to next Easter without a major scouring," Iggy said. "Now, Ciro, when you get to America, remember that every other person you meet is trying to trick you out of what's in your pocket. Only drink wine with your spaghetti and never alone at a bar. When a woman seems interested in you quickly, she is looking to take advantage of you. Ask for your wages in cash, and if they pay by paper, don't let them take a cut for cashing your check. Open a bank account as soon as you get there, with ten lire. Leave it there, but never add to the sum. Every man needs a bank, but the bank doesn't need your money."

"I'll only have two lire after I pay my passage," Ciro reminded him.

Ignazio reached into his pocket and gave Ciro eight lire. "Now you have ten."

"I can't take this."

"Trust me, Mother Church will never miss it." Iggy winked as Eduardo rolled his eyes and made the sign of the cross.

"Thanks, Iggy." Ciro put the money in his pocket.

"I always felt for you boys. I remember your father, and I know he would be very proud of you."

Eduardo and Ciro looked at one another. Whenever they asked Iggy about their father, he made a joke or told a funny story.

"What do you remember about him?" Eduardo asked.

Iggy took his eyes off the road and looked at the boys. He believed dwelling on the past and revisiting the pain would make their loss worse, so he had kept quiet all these years. Today, though, Iggy wanted to share all he knew. "He never set foot in church. You must get your devotion from the Montini side. Anyway, his people were from Sestri Levante originally, down in the Gulf of Genoa. He came up to Bergamo to find work. At that time, they were building the train station, and there were many jobs. Your mother's people had a printing shop, and he would walk by on his way to work and see your mother in the window. He fell in love with her and that was that."

"Why did they come to Vilminore?"

"Your father got a job in the mines. But then he was told he could get twice the wages for the same job in America. And your mother came from some means, and he felt that he had to provide her with a life like the one she knew as a girl. So he set off to make his fortune."

"Do you know where he went?"

"He went to a place in America called the Iron Range, in Minnesota."

"Do you know how he died?"

"I know only what you boys have been told, that he died in a mining accident."

"But they never found his body," Ciro said, a phrase repeated whenever he spoke of his father.

"Ciro," Iggy said solemnly, "you're a man now. It's not good for you to believe that he'll return. Put your hopes in something real, something that will bring you happiness."

Ciro stared ahead, wondering what, if anything, would ever bring him happiness. Eduardo nudged Ciro to say something.

"*Va bene*, Iggy," Ciro said.

"You just do your best, and life will follow. That's what my papa used to tell me."

*   *   *

They stopped in Clusone to deliver a package to the local stonemason. Iggy tied the horse to the railing outside the post office. Eduardo and Ciro sat on the bench and ate their lunch. Ciro squinted and looked across the street, taking in the homes staggered on the hillside like dollhouses, painted yellow and white, pale blue with eggshell trim, moss green with black shutters. Ciro never tired of looking at houses. He was fascinated by their design and longed for the permanence they represented.

Across the street, a girl closed the door of a white house with dark blue trim. She pulled on a straw hat with a long red ribbon and tied it under her chin. Ciro saw the ruffles of her white skirt as they grazed the top of her brown leather ankle boots. She turned and walked out onto the street. It was Concetta Martocci.

"Where are you going?" Eduardo called out as Ciro leaped from the bench. "We'll be late for the train!"

"I'll be right back."

Ciro ran across the road and followed her. Concetta turned and saw him, then quickened her pace.

"No, please . . . stop, Concetta!" Ciro called after her.

"I don't want to talk to you," she said as Ciro raced alongside her, until he overtook her. She stopped.

"I never meant to hurt you," Ciro said.

"Too late for that." Concetta moved around him and kept walking.

"Why are you in Clusone? Did Don Gregorio send you away?"

"No, my mother decided it was best. I'm staying with my aunt."

"He should have been the one to leave, not you and not me."

Concetta stopped and faced Ciro. "Why did you have to ruin everything?"

"He was taking advantage of you!"

"No, he wasn't. I didn't want to end up a miner's wife, I wanted something more for myself." Concetta's eyes burned with tears.

"You couldn't make a life with him," Ciro said, frustrated by her ignorance. "He's a priest."

"Just so you understand," Concetta said, "I never would have fallen in love with you. I don't like the way you would strut on the piazza, lifting stones and hauling wood, talking loudly and making jokes. Your clothes were always dirty, and when you'd eat, you ate with both hands and hungrily, as though you would never eat another meal again. I watched you too, Ciro, just like you watched me, and I was not impressed. You deserve the work camp. Maybe they can straighten you out."

"Maybe they can." Instead of defending himself, instead of trying to convince her to see what he believed to be true, he surrendered. What had always been impossible would remain so forever.

Eduardo waved to Ciro from across the road.

"Good-bye, Concetta," Ciro said as he turned to the carriage. He didn't look back, but this time it was because he didn't want to.

. . .

In the days that followed Stella's death, Giacomina hardly spoke. She took care of the house, washed the clothes, and cooked the meals as she had always done, but joy was lost along with her baby girl. She knew that she should be grateful that she had five other healthy children, but the comfort of many could never make up for the loss of one.

Slowly, Enza was beginning to feel the suffocating bonds of her grief break loose. She picked up after the children and took care of chores her mother usually attended to. Marco kept busy running the carriage from Schilpario to Bergamo.

"I have a package to deliver to Vilminore," Marco said as he came into the house before supper.

"I'll take it for you, Papa," Enza volunteered. She had waited a week to hear from Ciro Lazzari. He had promised to come to see her, and she believed he meant it.

A practical girl never pines; she takes action, Enza told herself. She knew Ciro lived at the convent in Vilminore.

As she hitched up the carriage and the horse, she remembered the camaraderie she had felt with Ciro the night they drove down to Vilminore. He was easy to be with, and she loved the way he looked, that offbeat thick sandy hair, the funny ring of keys on his pants loop, and the red bandana tied around his neck, just like the miners wear after they've cleaned up after a long shift. He was original, on a mountain where that was rare.

Ciro had taken Enza's mind off her despair the day of Stella's funeral. He had given her something to look forward to, something beyond that terrible day. In his kiss there was hope.

As she took Cipi out of the stable, he found the road and instinctively headed south in the direction of Vilminore. The wind cooled her face as Cipi settled into a trot on the pass. The night she took the ride with Ciro, it had been pitch-black, but the lamp threw plenty of light to see. She savored their conversation, and often, when doing her chores, she remembered the words he said to her, and how hopeful he was that she might kiss him again.

Now, she wished she had. Because one kiss is not enough. Neither is one conversation. Enza had so much more to say to Ciro Lazzari.

As she entered the village of Vilminore, she guided the carriage to the entrance of the convent, where she had left Ciro the week before. She felt confident, but more importantly, she felt the excitement of the possibility of their reunion. Surely he would be happy to see her. Hadn't he said he wanted to see her again? Even if he didn't, even if he was cold and abrupt, at least she would know his feelings. She would happily stop imagining his kisses every time she put down her book, or remembering his arms around her when she hung up the wash.

Enza jumped off the carriage bench and onto the ground. She rang the bell at the convent entrance and waited. Soon, Sister Domenica answered the door.

"Sister, my name is Enza Ravanelli. I'm from Schilpario."

"Is there something I can do for you?"

"I'm looking for Ciro Lazzari."

"Ciro?" Sister's eyes darted around suspiciously. "What do you want with Ciro?"

"I met him the day my sister was buried. He dug the grave."

"I remember."

"And I wanted to thank him."

"He doesn't live here anymore," Sister Domenica said softly.

"Where did he go?"

"I'd rather not say," Sister said.

"I see." Enza looked down at her hands. Ciro had probably gone off on a great adventure. Maybe he'd gone south to the port cities to work on the fishing boats, or west to work in the marble mines. All Enza knew was that he'd left without saying good-bye, which told her that he didn't feel the same about her as she did him.

"Maybe I can get a message to him," Sister said softly, looking around the piazza.

"There's no message, Sister. I'm sorry to have bothered you."

Enza climbed back on the bench, checked the address of the package, and guided Cipi across the piazza and up the street to deliver it. She began to cry, and wasn't sure why. Really, what had she thought would happen? What had she hoped he would say?

As she reached the road on the outskirts of Vilminore, Cipi stopped and waited. He didn't know which way to turn, and Enza had given him little direction with the reins. She sat high on the bench and looked out over the valley and wondered what she could have done differently when it came to Ciro Lazzari.

8

A FRIAR'S ROBE
Una Tonaca del Frate

It was a Tiepolo blue sky with smatters of creamy clouds the morning Ignazio Farino bid farewell to the Lazzari brothers at the train station in Bergamo before turning the horse and cart back up the mountain to return to Vilminore di Scalve.

Iggy looked back at the boys several times from his perch on the carriage bench, until the road took a turn and he could no longer see them. The boys watched Iggy go, bowed like the crook of a cane, until he had disappeared.

Orphans have many parents.

Eduardo and Ciro made their way through the station to the platforms. Eduardo's black wool pants and white shirt were pressed. His boiled wool jacket in forest green with gold epaulets on the shoulders looked a bit like a castoff from a defunct alpine regiment, but it was clean and without moth holes, so it would do, until he made it to the seminary and was assigned vestments.

Ciro wore navy blue corduroy work pants and a mended and starched chambray shirt under a gray wool topcoat with black piping. Sister Ercolina had retrieved the coat from a donation bag left on the convent steps, and Sister Anna Isabelle had lined it in a few yards of silk paisley left over from a sewing project to make bedding for a wedding gift to the town's mayor.

That morning, in the first light of dawn, Sister Domenica had given each boy a haircut, after which she vigorously rubbed their scalps with the juice of a fresh lemon mixed with a bit of clear alcohol. Ciro commented that when Sister Domenica was in charge, beauty hurt.

The nuns had laundered, pressed, and mended the boys' clothes before packing them. The clean underclothes in their duffel bags, along with handkerchiefs embroidered with their initials by Sister Teresa and socks knitted by Sister Domenica, would provide them with the basics until they arrived at their destinations. The sisters did their best to prepare the boys for the outside world, at least on the surface of things.

Eduardo checked the large station clock, its black Roman numerals set on a mother-of-pearl face. Everything seemed more important in Bergamo than it did on the mountain; even the telling of time had a certain elegance.

They had already begun to miss their village. As the boys surveyed the station, they were aware of all they were leaving behind. A long black train parked on the tracks had a series of wooden step stools placed outside the open doors reminded Eduardo of the nuns' shoes left outside their doors to be collected for polishing.

Passengers rushing to make their train gently jostled the boys. Eduardo and Ciro did their best to step out of the way, but their apologies went unheeded.

The people were so different here. The parade of well-dressed men that milled around the platform bore no resemblance to the journeymen and laborers on the mountain. The nobility of Bergamo wore custom-made three-piece suits topped with dress coats of silk wool and dapper felt fedoras wrapped with broad bands of dark grosgrain ribbon, accented with small feathers or a tucked knot. The men in Vilminore also wore hats, but they were strictly utilitarian, straw in the summer to ward off the sun and wool in the winter to keep them warm.

The elite wore shoes of dyed calfskin with insets of pebbled leather, some with laces, others with buttoned spats. They carried satchels made of the finest embossed suede. The women were also dressed stylishly, in long skirts and fitted waistcoats. They wore dramatic hats with extravagant plumes, clouds of net dolloped over the wide brims and tied under the chin with satin bows. They seemed to move slowly, as if underwater, the only sound they made the rustle of their skirts and the click of their high-buttoned shoes, which grazed the pavement in muted taps as they passed.

Eduardo looked around for the four young men who would accompany him to the seminary in Rome, checking a slip of paper to remind himself of their names.

"Here," Ciro said, handing his brother the three lire Iggy had given him.

"No, no, put it away, Ciro."

"Take it," Ciro insisted.

"I don't need money where I'm going," Eduardo assured him.

Distraught at the thought of leaving his brother, Eduardo stared at the great clock, willing time to stand still. He wanted to give his brother something to remember him by, to bind the two together when they were apart.

Ciro looked down at his mother's signet ring with its swirling engraved *C*.

"And don't offer me your ring, either," Eduardo said.

Ciro laughed. "How did you guess?"

"You're the most generous person I know. You would give me your shoes if you could. And you wouldn't complain if you had to walk to Venice barefoot."

"Yeah, except my feet are twice the size of yours," Ciro said.

"Lucky for me, because those are ugly shoes."

"That's all Sister Domenica could find in the bin." Ciro shrugged. "Besides, when you become a priest, they'll give you the cassock, the collar, and the black slippers. You'll never want for clothes, that's for sure."

"No cassocks for the Franciscans. Just brown robes of burlap tied with an old rope. And sandals."

"If you're going to go to all this trouble to become a priest, I wish you'd join a fancy order. You deserve the fine linens of the Vincennes like Don Gregorio. You're a poor orphan becoming a poor priest. You're like a crab going sideways."

"That's the idea, Ciro." Eduardo smiled. "Jesus wasn't known for his embroidered vestments."

"And what will become of me?" Ciro asked quietly.

"Sister Anna Isabelle's family will take good care of you." Eduardo's voice broke, hoping what he said would prove true. It had always been his job to take care of Ciro. How could he trust anyone else to do it? "It goes that way, you know. There isn't anything they can do for her as a nun who has taken a vow of poverty, so instead they will do for you, because she asked. We're very lucky, Ciro."

"Really? You would call us lucky?" Ciro believed fate had been against them at every turn. Had he remembered his keys that night, he would not have discovered Concetta and the priest, which had set all these horrible events in motion.

"Yes, brother. We've made it this far." Eduardo looked up and down the tracks, trying not to cry.

The Lazzari boys stood on the platform, having never been apart, not for a day or night of their lives. Little had gone unsaid between them. They had been one other's counselors and confidants. In many ways, Eduardo had been Ciro's parent, setting his moral compass, helping him navigate convent life, prompting him to study, all the while encouraging him to see the good in people and the possibilities of the world beyond the piazza in Vilminore.

Eduardo was now seventeen, and he possessed a contemplative air and a humble attitude. For a young man, he was unusually solemn, as well as empathetic.

Ciro would turn sixteen on the ship to America. He was over six feet tall, the pugilistic stance and comedic expressions of his youth replaced with a grown-up masculine prowess that made him appear much older. Eduardo sized up Ciro and was reassured that his younger brother could take care of himself physically. But he worried that Ciro was too trusting and could be taken advantage of by people less honorable than he. It was always the young men of gentle natures who acknowledged the worst in the world; strong boys like Ciro never did.

"You know, Ciro," Eduardo began slowly, "I never felt I really lost Papa, because you look so much like him. Sometimes when I was studying late at night and I would look over at you sleeping, I would remember him lying on the grass, taking siesta. And I would swear Papa had never really left us because he was alive in you. But you are like him in more ways than your appearance. You have a mind like him too."

"I do?" Ciro wished he could remember more details about his father. He remembered his laugh, and the way he held a cigarette, but beyond that, very little.

"You always tell the truth. You stand up for the weak. And you're not afraid of taking chances. When the sisters told us that we had to leave, and they told you that you had to go to America, you didn't flinch. You didn't cry. You didn't try to make a better deal for yourself, you just accepted their offer."

"Maybe that makes me a pushover," Ciro said.

"No, it makes you wise. Like Papa, you aren't afraid of trying something new. I don't have that kind of daring in my nature, but you do. I'm not going to worry about you in America."

"Liar."

"Let's put it this way, I'm going to *try* not to worry about you."

"Well, I wish I could say the same." Ciro said. "Keep your eyes open, Eduardo. Holy men sometimes aren't. Don't let them push you around or make you feel like you're not one of them. You're smarter than the keenest of their lot. Take charge. Show them what you can do."

"I'll do my best."

"I'll work hard because it's all I know," Ciro said. "But, everything we do, everything we make, is done so we might to return to the mountain. *Together.*"

Eduardo nodded in agreement. "Pray for me."

"Papa said something to me the night before he left, and I wrote it in my missal, so I would never forget it." Eduardo's eyes glinted with tears as he opened his leather-bound black missal to the first page. He handed it to Ciro. In a young boy's measured script, Eduardo had written:

> *Beware the things of this world that*
> *can mean everything or nothing.*

Ciro closed the book and handed it back to Eduardo. "You've never been without this missal. It belongs to you. Keep it."

Eduardo placed it in Ciro's hands firmly. "No, it's your turn now. When you read it, you will think of me. Besides, I know you aren't one for daily mass—"

"Or Sunday mass."

"Or any mass!" Eduardo grinned. "But if you'll read the missal, I think you'll find some comfort."

Ciro closed the missal. "The sisters of San Nicola, my brother, and the world conspire to turn me into a good Catholic. To all of you, I say, good luck."

The whistles of an incoming train pierced the air. An attendant climbed a ladder and wrote the new arrival on the station's giant blackboard:

ROMA

"I have to go," Eduardo said, his voice breaking. "That's my train."

The brothers embraced. They held one another a long time, until Eduardo straightened his back and gently released his brother.

"You go to track two for the train to Venice—"

"I know, I know, then the ferry to Le Havre. Eduardo?"

Eduardo picked up his satchel. "Yes?"

"I've never been to France."

"Ciro?"

"Yeah?"

"You've never been to Venice, either."

Ciro put his hands on his hips. "Do you think anyone can tell? Do I look like a goat herder from the Alps?"

"Only when you wear lederhosen." Eduardo slung his satchel over his shoulder. "Be careful in America, Ciro. Don't let anyone take advantage of you. Watch your money. Ask questions."

"I will," Ciro assured him.

"And write to me."

"I promise."

Four young men, similar in countenance and age to Eduardo, each carrying a single satchel, boarded the train for Rome. Eduardo turned to follow them. "Your new brothers are waiting for you," Ciro said.

"They will never be my brothers," Eduardo said. "I only have one."

Ciro watched as Eduardo slowly disappeared into the crowd.

"And don't you forget it!" Ciro shouted, waving the missal, before he, too, crossed the platform and boarded a train to take him to his new life.

PART TWO

manhattan

9

A LINEN HANDKERCHIEF
Un Fazzolletto di Lino

Two days after he left Eduardo at the train station in Bergamo, Ciro made his way up the plank of the SS *Chicago* in Le Havre, hauling his duffel over his back. His impression of the French port city was limited to the view of the canal, with its bobbing dinghies nipping at the hulls of ocean liners lashed to the docks. The pier was cluttered with passengers filing up the planks of the ships with their luggage. Behind a wall of fishing net, swarms of loved ones waved their handkerchiefs and tipped their hats as they bid their final good-byes.

There was no one to see Ciro off on his journey. For an ebullient young man who had never known a stranger, he was subdued and sober as he made his connections. Ciro bought a meal of cold polenta and hot milk before boarding. He skipped the sausage, so the hearty meal only cost him a few *centesimi*. He hoped to arrive in America with his small purse intact.

The attendant took Ciro's ticket and directed him belowdecks to the men's third-class compartment. Ciro was relieved the sexes were segregated on this ship, as Sister Ercolina had told him about grim steerage accommodations where men, women, and children stayed in one large room, separated only by squares drawn on the ship's floor with paint.

Ciro pushed the metal door to his cell open, dropped his head, and stooped to enter. The room was five by five feet, with a small cot jammed against the wall. Ciro could not stand up in it, and there was no window. But it was clean enough, with a scent of saltwater.

Ciro sat down on the cot and opened his duffel. The fragrance of the convent laundry—lavender and starch—enveloped him, fresh as the mountain air of Vilminore. He snapped the satchel shut quickly, hoping to preserve the scent; this was all he had left to remind him of his life in San Nicola.

The ship creaked in the harbor as it floated in place, rubbing against the pilings. For the first time since he'd boarded the train in Bergamo, Ciro exhaled. The anxiety of changing trains, meeting the ferry in Venice, and processing his ticket once he arrived in La Havre had kept him in a state of highest alert. During the day, he dared not nap or let his mind wander, for fear he would miss a train or ferry and bungle the trip entirely.

The first night, he'd slept in a church in Venice; on the second, he found a spot between shops on the boardwalk in Le Havre. Now only the ocean kept him from the start of his new life. He had avoided conversation with strangers, having been warned about the swindlers who preyed on unsuspecting passengers. He would like to see anyone try to get his money. He tucked it carefully in a pouch around his neck, then pinned it to the inside of his undershirt for safekeeping.

Ciro's heart ached for all he was leaving behind, especially the company and counsel of Eduardo, the person who had made him feel safe in the world. None of the events of the past week had seemed real as they were happening, but now that he was alone, Ciro felt the finality of all of it. Ciro had been punished for something he had seen, not something he had done. He was aboard this ship because he had no advocate and was an orphan. The nuns had spared him the work camp, but the priest had levied a far worse punishment when he separated one brother from the other. Ciro buried his face in his sleeve and wept.

It was in the release of his sadness that Eduardo's reassuring words flooded back to Ciro. He took stock of his situation. He knew how to work hard. Hadn't the nuns marveled at his strength and stamina? He looked down at his hands, replicas of his father's. Ciro was a common laborer, but he was intelligent; he could read and write, thanks to Eduardo. He knew how to cut a fair business deal because of Iggy. He had mastered self-denial and sacrifice through convent living. He would live frugally in America and save his money, thus speeding his return to the mountain. In this instance, his banishment was also his ticket to adventure, to his future.

Ciro would show the priest what he was made of by making something of himself. He would eat just enough to maintain his strength, pay as little as possible for his accommodations, and avoid temptation. A full purse cannot be denied; a full purse has power and a voice. Ciro learned that, watching the collection plate being passed in San Nicola.

Ciro poured water from his canteen onto his clean handkerchief and washed his face. He placed his duffel neatly under the cot. He locked the cell door before he climbed back up the steps to the deck. He was not going to isolate himself because Don Gregorio mandated it. Ciro decided to throw himself into the experience of the crossing, so he positioned himself on the promenade and watched the passengers board, dazzled by the variety of people who climbed the plank.

Whenever there was a festival in Vilminore, hundreds of visitors from nearby towns emptied into the village. The revelers were hardworking mountain people who toiled in the mines or on the farm, just like the people who lived in Vilminore. There was no discernible difference in wealth or status. Men worked to provide for the table and had to work the same amount of hours to get it. But even among the padrones of the Italian Alps, there was nothing that compared to the opulence Ciro watched sashay up the plank of the SS *Chicago*.

The wealthy Europeans were beautifully dressed in pastel linens and pale silks, followed by maids and errand boys who carried their luggage. The servants were dressed better than anyone Ciro knew in Vilminore. His eyes fell upon an older woman, dressed in a wide-brimmed straw hat. A servant followed her, balancing two leather hatboxes, one in each hand. She was followed by a second maid who pushed a canvas dress box on wheels, as tall as she, up the plank. Ciro had never seen such service. His first observation was that the rich didn't carry their own weight.

Ciro heard a variety of Italian dialects. Ciro's own, the Bergamasque of the Lombardy region, was heavily influenced by the Swiss that bordered them to the north. The Venetians, by contrast, had low, rolling vowels and enunciated clearly, something Ciro was quick to pick up as influenced by the French. He heard all manners of Italian spoken—Barese, Tuscan, Calabrese, and Sicilian. The world was noisy. As Ciro looked around, he was the only person who seemed to be listening.

Sometimes there was no need for words. Ciro watched as young women floated through the crowd. Perhaps it was their lace shift dresses, or the soft sway of the cream-colored tulle on their hats, but they appeared light and airborne, moving like a dizzy constellation of white butterflies that hovered over the fields of Alta Vilminore in the springtime.

Ciro saw people he had only read about in books. Turks wore starched tunics in shades of indigo, the color of the waves of the Adriatic, embroidered with silver thread. Portuguese laborers, squat and muscular, wore overalls, straw hats, and looks of defiance. French nuns, wearing white winged wimples, skimmed down the steps into steerage like a flock of gray pigeons.

The sisters of San Nicola had taught Ciro to seek the nuns dressed like them, *le bianconere*, the "black-and-whites" who wore a large wooden cross on rosary beads draped from the waist. He had been instructed to approach them and explain his connection. The sisters promised he would never be turned away from any convent of their order, if he ever found himself without a place to stay.

Two old British men wearing rumpled wool suits with plaid vests, the uniforms of *il professore*, climbed the steps to first class, speaking proper English. An Italian family, with grandmother in tow, headed to second class. She directed her grandsons on the proper technique for hauling the food hampers. It occurred to Ciro that men pretended to run the family, but in truth, the women were in charge. He wondered why this family was emigrating, as it appeared that they were doing well in Italy. It occurred to Ciro that most people were not on the run as he was. Perhaps they were looking for an adventure, just for its own sake. He could not imagine the luxury of that.

"*Ciao.*"

"*Ciao,*" Ciro said as he turned to face a man of thirty, with thick brown hair, who wore an immaculate white uniform with colorful bars across the pocket.

"Are you the captain?" Ciro asked.

"The bursar. I'm Massimo Zito." The man smiled. "I hire the crew here."

"You speak Italian," Ciro said, his ears ringing from the circus of sounds around him. "*My* Italian."

"And French, Spanish, Portuguese, and English. And a little Arabic."

"The only language I speak is Italian," Ciro told him. "And Latin, only because my brother insisted I learn it."

"Why are you going to America?"

"To make money," Ciro said. "Is there any other reason?"

"*Si, Si.* America has lovely women. Do you like blondes? The gold in their hair glitters like the gold in the streets. Brunettes? Like chestnuts, they're everywhere. Redheads? Like apples in trees, available by the bushel. They work in factories and crack their gum."

"They can do whatever they want, as long as they talk to me." Ciro laughed.

A lovely young woman wearing an apricot dress with periwinkle calfskin boots glided up the plank into first class. Ciro and Massimo watched her go.

"I hope this trip takes a lifetime if all the girls on board are that beautiful," Ciro said.

Massimo laughed. "It's a brief lifetime. We'll arrive in nine days. Are you alone?"

"Yes, Signore," Ciro said.

"Are you looking for a job?"

"That depends," Ciro said. "What position are you offering?"

"I need another man in the boiler room. Shoveling coal."

"What are you paying?" Ciro looked off in the bustle below and squinted nonchalantly, just as Iggy had taught him. Never show the padrone you want the job.

"I can pay you three dollars American for nine days' work."

"Three dollars?" Ciro shook his head. "I'm sorry. Can't do it."

"Why not?"

"I need ten dollars for that job," Ciro said. He gazed out over the docks absently, though his heart raced.

"That's crazy." Massimo's voice went up an octave.

Ciro had no idea how hard the job in the belly of the ship would be; he only knew that he was strong, and certainly knew his way around a shovel. If he had dug a grave in a poor village for two lire, surely one American dollar was a fair daily wage for shoveling coal aboard an ocean liner. Ciro talked himself into his firm counteroffer with logic. "Ten dollars, Signor Zito," Ciro replied evenly.

"You're out of your mind. Eight dollars," Massimo countered.

Ciro turned to face Massimo. "I suppose it would be *difficile* to find someone to shovel the coal at this point. I mean, we're about to shove off here. You don't have time to go and empty the local jail, or pick up an ambitious boy on the street who wants to take a ride to America. From the looks of the French boys, you'd be hard pressed to find one strong enough to do the work. They're as lean as the overpriced baguettes they sell on the pier. I can appreciate the bind you're in. How about this—I'll take the eight dollars, if you'll also refund the fare I paid to ride this boat."

"You expect one hundred lire plus eight dollars?"

"I'm sure the rest of the crew gets their room and board for free. Including you." Ciro leaned over the railing and studied the middle distance, awaiting Massimo's counteroffer.

Finally, Massimo sighed. "You're going to do very well in America."

Waves of blistering heat greeted Ciro as Massimo Zito unhinged the entrance door to the furnace room. When the good sisters of Vilminore had taught Ciro about hell, he imagined an open pit with flames. The belly of the SS *Chicago* came close to their description.

The massive boiler room extended the length of the ship under a low steel-beamed ceiling. It held the mechanics for the coal ovens that heated the water that fed the steam engine. The storage bins for the coal were as deep as the ship, funneled through a large chute that led to the coal pit in the boiler room. From there, the crew shoveled the coal into the furnace. It would take 570 tons of coal to produce enough steam for the SS *Chicago*'s transatlantic voyage, shoveled round the clock by thirty men in twelve-hour shifts. Ciro was the thirtieth hire.

Massimo Zito pulled the overseer off the job to meet Ciro. Christie

Benet, a Frenchman and the boss of the operation, was covered in coal dust. The deep furrows of his brow seemed engraved in black ink, making the whites of his eyes look bright and menacing in contrast.

"He'll do," Benet told Massimo. He turned to Ciro. "There's a pair of overalls in the pump room." Benet turned back to the open mouth of the pit. Ciro was in awe of the mighty furnace, but more so of his good fortune. He had secured his first job, and he hadn't yet set foot in America.

Massimo Zito took good care of the workers. Occasionally the men received the leftovers from first class, so Ciro sampled his first croissant, steamed asparagus, and boiled shrimp.

The men were allowed to bathe at the shift change before dawn. They climbed up to the second tier of the ship and, in an area cordoned off by bamboo screens, used one of the fire hoses as a showerhead and lye soap to scour off the coal dust. By the end of the week, Ciro noticed that the lye soap could not strip all of the coal-dust residue off his skin. His hands, face, and ears had a gray pallor where the dust had embedded itself in his pores. He understood why his fellow workers looked far older than he, when they were actually close in age. This was brutal work that took a toll on the body immediately.

Ciro pulled on a clean jumpsuit in the deck changing area before returning down to the pit. He took a moment to look out over the water. As the sun rose over the Atlantic, the sea took on a glistening coral patina. The distant horizon appeared fringed in gold. Ciro lit a cigarette and took a long, slow drag off it. It was his sixteenth birthday that morning, and he took a quiet moment to celebrate it.

"Two more days," said Luigi Latini, who had worked beside Ciro in the pit from the first day. Luigi was from the south, the province of Foggia on the Adriatic. He was of medium height, and built like a sturdy square box. At twenty, he looked out for Ciro like a reliable older brother. Luigi had a small nose and large brown eyes, which gave him the appearance of a thoughtful rabbit.

"It's almost over, Luigi." Ciro handed him the cigarette.

"Where are you going?"

"I'm meeting a family who has sponsored me. They live in Manhattan. How about you?"

"I'm going to Mingo Junction, Ohio. My parents made a match. I'm going to marry Alberta Patenza," Luigi said as he handed the cigarette back to Ciro.

"Have you met her?"

"Only her picture. *Che bella.*"

"Have you written to her?"

"Oh, yes, many times." Luigi said.

"You seem worried for a man who has a beautiful girl waiting for him."

"What if she's *brutta*? You know, there are stories. Parents make a match through letters, and they switch the pictures. Suddenly Philomena is replaced by Graciela. That sort of thing. You could end up with a *faccia di bow wow* when you thought you were getting a princess."

"I hope that doesn't happen to you."

Luigi shrugged. "If it does, I run."

Ciro laughed. "If you can run as fast as you shovel coal, you'll do all right."

"In photographs, Alberta's nose is small, like mine." Luigi rubbed the ridge of his nose with his fingers. "I need to keep this nose in the family. If I marry a girl with a big nose, then I have big-nosed babies, and I don't want that."

Ciro laughed. Luigi wasn't the only man with a list of what he wanted in a wife. Ciro had been amending his list since he first noticed girls. He didn't much care about her nose, but he did want a girl who was sweet, kind, and moved through the world with grace. She had to be beautiful, because like any work of art, beauty reveals new aspects over time. "You will have your small-nosed babies, Luigi," Ciro said, taking the last drag off the cigarette before flicking it into the ocean. The orange tip flashed then went out in midair. "Everyone should have what they want." Ciro leaned against the railing and remembered who had given him that bit of wisdom. Enza Ravanelli of Schilpario. The sky was cobalt blue the night he kissed her. He had been carrying a shovel exactly like the one he used to load coal into the pit of the SS *Chicago*.

Ciro had begun to notice the overlapping themes of his life. The seemingly disparate pieces of his experience weren't so separate after all. Happenstance and accidents didn't seem so random. The mystery of the connections intrigued him, but he wasn't going to agonize about them, and he had not yet reached an age where he was interested in analyzing them either. He figured that all the threads of his experience would eventually be sewn together, taking shape in harmony and form to create a glorious work of art. But who would sew those pieces together? Who would make him whole? That was something Ciro thought about a lot.

Before he went to sleep, Ciro thought about girls instead of praying. Girls were a kind of religion to him. He visualized their sweet charms and the haunting details of their beauty, black eyes obscured by a tulle veil, a graceful hand on the stem of a parasol, or Concetta Martocci's small ankles the night he caught her with the priest. These fleeting memories soothed him, but lately, as he drifted into sleep, his thoughts had gone to Enza Ravanelli, whose kiss he remembered with particular delight. When he thought of Enza, he didn't imagine her lips, her eyes, or her hands. Rather, he saw her in full, standing before him in the blue night air, every aspect of her beauty revealed in the light.

10

A GREEN TREE

Un Albero Verde

The morning the SS *Chicago* pulled into the docks of lower Manhattan, it felt to Ciro as if a champagne cork had been popped over New York City, drenching the harbor in gold confetti as sprays of sea foam showered the decks. Even the tugboats conspired to make a smooth transition as they nudged the ocean liner deftly into position without lurching or grinding against the pilings. The bellows of the horn and the cheers of the passengers lined up on deck seemed to give the ship its last shot of steam as it docked in the harbor.

Ciro and Luigi took in the splendor from the third-tier balcony. The island of Manhattan, shaped like a leaf, was staggered with stone buildings, pink in the morning light. The slate blue waves of the Hudson River rolled up to the shoreline in inky folds. The city skyline seemed to move, shifting and swaying under construction, as cranes and pulleys filled the air like marionette strings. Cables hauled slabs of granite, suspended thick steel beams, and lifted planks. Grand smokestacks chuffed billows of gray into the blue sky, where it dissolved like puffs from a gentleman's pipe. Windows, too many to count, reflected prisms of light as the tracks of elevated trains circled in and around the buildings like black zippers.

Bergamo, with its bustling train station, did not compare; nor did Venice, with its crowded harbors, or Le Havre, with its frenzied ports.

Big American noise surrounded them as crowds gathered on the docks below to cheer the arrival. A drum and bugle corps played, and girls twirled striped parasols like giant wheels. Despite the fanfare, Ciro's heart was heavy. Eduardo was not there to share any of it. The louder the noise, the more shrill the din, the more lonely Ciro felt.

The metal gangplank of the *Chicago* hit the ground with a thud. The first-class passengers processed off the ship, moving slowly, preening themselves in their fresh costumes and hats without a thought to the passengers in steerage, who longed to disembark and move out of their cramped quarters into open space. The wealthy never seem to be in a hurry. Shiny black motorcars lined up to take the first-class passengers to their destinations. As the ladies climbed into the open cars in their spring hats decorated with white feathers and crystal sparkles, they resembled a box of French pastries dusted in powdered sugar.

Massimo Zito stood at the bottom of the plank with three attendants. Each émigré was instructed to pin a copy of the ship's manifest to his chest, standard procedure for all who entered from a foreign country. They were directed to a line for the ferry that would take them to Ellis Island. After a handshake of gratitude for the bursar who had given him his first job, Ciro's feet touched the ground of New York City at last.

Ciro and Luigi leaned against the railing on the ferry to Ellis Island and took in the fresh breeze as it skimmed across the Hudson, leaving a streamer of white foam on the gray river. Ciro was grateful for the company, as the ferry plowed closer to the shore of Ellis Island. On land, in the middle distance, a long gray line of immigrants filed into an enormous building, which seemed to occupy the entirety of the small island. The Statue of Liberty loomed over them like a schoolmarm herding children at her feet.

Suddenly the ferry lurched into place against the pilings of the docks, throwing the people onboard off their feet. Ciro grabbed the railing, steadied himself, and looped his duffel through his arms. Ciro and Luigi followed signs with red arrows into the reception hall of the main building, weaving in and out of the crowd with nothing to slow them down, as they were not tending to children, or herding grandparents, or keeping a family together.

The guard at the door, a brusque, heavyset woman in a gray uniform with a long plait of white hair down her back, glanced down at their papers. Ciro reached into his duffel and handed her a sealed envelope from Sister Ercolina. She ripped open the envelope, scanned the letter, and snapped it on to her clipboard.

"You"—the guard pointed to Luigi—"go there." Luigi followed her finger and joined a line. "And you"—she pointed to Ciro—"there." Ciro got in line next to Luigi. The lines were long and didn't move.

"Welcome to America," Luigi said as he surveyed the hundreds on line. "At this rate, I won't see Mingo Junction till next week."

A deafening chatter reverberated throughout the massive hall. Ciro was in awe of the building, an architectural wonder. No cathedral ever stood so tall, with vaulted ceilings so high. The arched windows were so close to the sun, they filled the atrium with bright natural light. Ciro looked up at the windows and wondered how they were washed. Under his feet, a polished terra-cotta brick floor glistened, the golden hue of the bricks reminding him of the convent floor he'd polished as a boy.

Ciro observed hundreds of people standing in twelve long single-file lines, separated by waist-high iron bars, their duffels stacked around them like sandbags in a gulley. There were Hungarians, Russians, the French, and many Greeks, all waiting patiently on their best behavior. Mostly he saw Italians, perhaps because he was looking for them.

Ciro couldn't imagine that there was a single person left in southern Italy. Surely they were all here under this massive roof—Calabrese, Sicilian, Barese, and Neopolitan, old, young, newborn. Beyond the lines, he saw doctors examining one immigrant after another, tapping their backs, checking their tonsils, grazing their fingertips across their necks. A peasant mother cried out when a nurse took her baby, swaddled in flannel. An officer who spoke Italian quickly came to her aid, and allowed the woman off the line to accompany her child.

"There's a nursery in the back," Ciro heard a woman explain as she mopped her face with a bandana. "All the babies go there. They have milk."

Ciro took off his coat and undid his scarf to prepare for his examination. His line had begun to move. He looked back at Luigi, who had barely budged. A nurse motioned Ciro forward.

"Height?" the nurse asked in Italian.

"Six foot two," Ciro answered.

"Weight?"

"One hundred and ninety pounds," he said.

"Markings?"

"None."

"Whooping cough?"

"No."

"Dysentery?"

"No."

As the nurse rattled off every illness on her list, Ciro realized he'd never been sick as a child. Sister Teresa had shored him up with egg creams and chestnut paste.

The nurse flipped the page on her clipboard. "Teeth?"

"My own."

The nurse smiled. Ciro grinned back at her.

"And fine teeth they are," she said.

The doctor listened to Ciro's heart with a stethoscope, asking Ciro to move his money pouch to the side to give him access. He asked Ciro to take a deep breath and listened from the back. He checked Ciro's eyes with a small light, and his neck with his fingers. "Move him through," the doctor said in English.

Ciro moved through the metal gates to the next line. He heard attending officers asking the immigrants simple questions: Where are you from? How much is six plus six? Where does the sun rise? Where does it set? Some of the immigrants became rattled, afraid to answer incorrectly. Ciro saw that remaining calm was half the battle to earn your papers. He took a deep breath.

The attending officer looked over his paperwork, then up at Ciro. He walked Ciro to a holding pen. Ciro began to sweat, knowing that this was a bad sign. He waved at Luigi, who had progressed only a few feet from where he started. There were at least twenty people in front of Luigi who still needed their medical exam. Luigi waved back, helpless to assist.

What if Don Gregorio had figured out the nuns' plan and contacted U.S. immigration? Suddenly Ciro felt like the young orphan he was. There was no one to help, nowhere he could turn. If he were banished again, rejected from American soil, there was no telling where he would be sent, and he was certain Eduardo would never find him.

They were advised aboard ship to never leave the line at Ellis Island, and to try to draw as little attention to themselves as possible. Never get in an argument. Never push or shove. Keep your head down and your voice low. Agree to all conditions, and accommodate all requests. The goal at Ellis Island was to process through without incident and make it back into Manhattan as quickly as possible. Immigration had a thousand reasons to turn you away, from the rasp of a dry cough to a suspicious answer about your ultimate destination. You didn't want to make it easy for a coldhearted processing agent in a gray coat to send you right back to Italy.

Ciro's heart raced as the immigration officer returned with another officer to speak with him.

"Signor Lazzari?" the second officer said, in perfect Italian.

"Yes, sir."

"*Andiamo*," he said sternly.

The officer led Ciro into a small room with a table and two chairs. A poster of the United States flag hung on the windowless wall. The officer indicated that Ciro should take a seat. The officer spoke perfect Italian, though Ciro saw that the name on his jacket was American.

"Signor Lazzari," he said.

"Signor Anderson." Ciro nodded. "What have I done?" he said, looking down at his hands.

"I don't know. What have you done?"

"Nothing, sir," Ciro replied. Then, noticing the officer's gaze on his coal-gray hands, he quickly added, "I worked in the pit on the SS *Chicago* on my way over."

Signor Anderson pulled Sister Ercolina's letter from a file folder. As he read over it, Ciro panicked. "So you know the sisters of San Nicola," the officer said.

The poor sisters had tried to do right by Ciro, but instead, it seemed, they had attracted the attention of this wolf in the gray uniform. "I grew up in their orphanage," Ciro admitted.

"The diocese here in New York received a telegram. You're on our list."

Ciro swallowed, certain the telegram was from Don Gregorio. After this long trip working in the furnace in hellish heat, all was for naught. Ciro would be plucked from the group and deported. He would end up in the work camp after all. "Where am I to be sent?" he asked quietly.

"Sent? You just got here, didn't you? Those nuns wired the archbishop some kind of character reference. You're to be processed as quickly as possible." Signor Anderson made notes inside the file.

In one miraculous moment, Ciro realized that Signor Anderson wasn't the enemy; he wasn't going to send him back to Italy to the work camp. "Thank you, Signore," Ciro said.

"You have to change your name." He gave Ciro a list and said, "Choose."

> *Brown*
> *Miller*
> *Jones*
> *Smith*
> *Collins*
> *Blake*
> *Lewis*

"Take Lewis. It's an *L* name like yours."

Ciro glanced over the names and handed the list back to Mr. Anderson. "Will you send me back if I don't change my name?"

"They won't be able to pronounce your name here, kid."

"Sir, if they can say spaghetti, they can pronounce Lazzari."

Signor Anderson tried not to laugh. "Scoliaferrantella was my name," he said. "I had no choice."

"What province are you from, Signore?" Ciro asked.

"Roma."

"My brother Eduardo just entered the Sant'Agostino Seminary there. He's going to become a priest. So you see," Ciro continued, "if I give up my name, it will die. It's only my brother and me in the world. I don't want to lose Lazzari."

Signor Anderson leaned back in his chair. He fixed his eyeglasses on his prominent nose. His thick eyebrows arched as he asked, "Who is your sponsor?"

"Remo Zanetti of Thirty-six Mulberry Street."

"And your trade?"

"I'm a shoemaker's apprentice."

"How old are you?"

"Sixteen."

The officer stamped Ciro's documents for entry into the United States. The name Lazzari remained on Ciro's paperwork. "You may go. Return to the ferry line on the slip, and it will take you across to Manhattan."

Ciro held his paperwork in his hand, stamped with fresh midnight blue ink. He had everything he needed to start his new life. Part of gratitude is sharing one's good fortune, and Ciro felt compelled to do so. "Signor Anderson, I don't want to be any trouble," he began.

The officer looked up at Ciro with a look of bemused irritation. Didn't this young man understand that he was lucky? He had gotten through Ellis Island without a hitch, even his Italian surname was intact.

"Could you help my friend? His name is Luigi Latini. He worked in the furnace room with me. He's a good man. His parents made a match, and he needs to catch the train to Ohio to meet the girl. He's afraid if he doesn't get there in time, she'll marry someone else."

Anderson rolled his eyes. "Where is he?"

"Line three. In the back."

"Wait here," Anderson said. He took the file and left Ciro alone in the room.

Ciro reached into his pocket and pulled out the medal Sister Teresa had given him as a parting gift. He kissed the Sacred Heart of Jesus. Ciro hadn't found religion, but he knew to be grateful. Ciro sat back and inhaled the sweet scent of the polished oak of the walls. This room was ten times the size of his cell in steerage. Space, square footage, width and height, these were the things Ciro would remember about the passage from Italy to America.

Luigi Latini entered with Officer Anderson, his face the same pale gray hue as their immigration papers.

"Don't worry, Luigi. Officer Anderson is here to help us," Ciro said to Luigi as he took a seat next to him.

"Are you a good Catholic too, Signor Latini?" Officer Anderson smiled.

"*Si, si,*" Luigi said, looking at Ciro.

"I'm glad you didn't ask me that question, Officer Anderson." Ciro grinned.

When the officer concluded his line of questions, Ciro said, "Luigi doesn't want to be a Lewis either."

"You want to keep your name too?" Signor Anderson asked.

"May I?" Luigi looked at Ciro and then at the officer.

Officer Anderson stamped Luigi's papers. "You boys behave yourselves," he said, reaching into his pocket and handing them each a stick of gum.

"What is this, sir?" Ciro asked.

"Chewing gum."

Luigi and Ciro looked at one another, then down at the small foil-covered rectangles.

"You never had it?"

The boys shook their heads. Ciro remembered Massimo Zito said that redheads chewed gum.

"It's very American. Like hot dogs and cigarettes. Try it."

The boys unwrapped the gum, placing the pink slices in their mouths.

"Now chew."

The boys commenced chewing. Sweet bursts of clove filled their mouths. "Don't swallow the gum. You'll get worms. That's what my wife says, anyhow." He laughed.

Ciro took one last look at the registry hall as he left with Luigi. For the rest of his life, Ciro would admire the classic lines and grand scale of American architecture. Beyond the buildings, beyond this port city, he imagined there were acres to farm, plenty of coal to mine, steel to weld, tracks to lay, and roads to build. There was a job for every man who wanted to work. Luckily for Ciro, every one of those men would need a pair of shoes. Ciro was beginning to understand the concept of America, and it was changing his view of the world and of himself. A man could think clearly in a place that gave breadth to his dreams.

There were all manners of souvenirs and trinkets for sale when Ciro and Luigi disembarked from the ferry into the port of lower Manhattan. Signs advertising Sherman Turner cigars, Zilita Black tobacco, and Roisin's Doughnuts graced rolling carts selling Sally Dally Notions and Flowers by Yvonne Benne. The stands competed for the immigrant business. Ciro and Luigi came face to face with the engine of American life: *You work, and then you spend.*

Luigi purchased a small rhinestone heart brooch for his bride-to-be, while Ciro bought a bouquet of yellow roses for Mrs. Zanetti. Then they were funneled through a walkway and under an arch with a sign that read,

WELCOME TO NEW YORK

Luigi turned to Ciro. "I go to Grand Central Station to take the train to Chicago and then Ohio."

"I'm going to Mulberry Street," Ciro said.

"I'm going to learn English on the way to Chicago."

"And I'm going to learn it when I get to Little Italy. Can you believe it, Luigi? I have to go to a place called Italy to learn English," Ciro joked as they shook hands.

"You take care of yourself," Luigi said.

"Good luck with Alberta. I know she will be more beautiful than her photograph."

Luigi whistled. "*Buona fortuna,*" he said before he disappeared into the crowd headed for the el train.

Ciro stayed put and looked out over the crowd. The Zanettis were supposed to be there to greet him, holding up a sign with his name on it. He scanned the crowd but did not see his name anywhere. After a few minutes, he began to worry.

From the ship, the welcome on the ground seemed grand, but upon close inspection, the revelers greeting the immigrants were shabby. The band's red-and-blue uniforms were ill-fitting and missing buttons; their brass horns, an unpolished greenish gold, were dented and scratched. The women's dresses were dingy, the parasols they twirled, frayed. Ciro realized that the hoopla was manufactured, a theatrical show for naive eyes and nothing more.

A slim young woman in an organza dress and straw hat with silk daisies spilling from the crown approached him.

"Hello, handsome," she said in English.

"I don't understand," Ciro mumbled in Italian, keeping his eyes on the crowd for the Zanettis.

"I said, hello and welcome." She leaned in and whispered, again in English, grazing his cheek with her lips, "Do you need a place to stay?"

She wore a sweet perfume of gardenias and musk that soothed Ciro, who had been shoveling coal for days in a hot tomb. The machinations of Ellis Island had left him exhausted. She was soft and pretty and seemed taken with him. Her attention reassured him.

"Come with me," she said.

Ciro didn't need to understand her words to know he would follow her to the ends of the earth. She was around his age, her long red hair loosely braided, with red satin ribbons woven into the plaits. She had a few freckles on her creamy skin, and dark brown eyes. She wore a bright pink lip rouge, a color unlike any Ciro had ever seen.

"Do you need a job?" she said.

Ciro looked at her blankly.

"Job. Work. *Lavoro.* Job," she repeated, then took his hand and led him through the crowd. She pulled a single yellow rose from the bouquet Ciro carried, and touched the petals to her lips.

Suddenly Ciro saw his name on a sign. The man holding it was pushing anxiously through the crowd. Ciro let go of the girl's hand and waved. "Signor Zanetti!" Ciro shouted.

The girl tugged on his sleeve, motioning him toward a nearby group of men on the dock, but Ciro saw a red parasol moving through the crowd like a periscope.

"No, no, come with me," the young woman insisted, placing her calfskin-covered hand on Ciro's forearm. He remembered the soft touch of his mother's gloved hand.

"Leave him alone!" Signora Zanetti's voice cut through the din from under her parasol. "Shoo! Shoo! *Puttana!*" she said to the girl.

Carla Zanetti, stout, gray-haired, five feet tall, and sixty, burst forward from the crowd. She was followed by her husband, Remo, who was only slightly taller than she. He had a thick white mustache and a smooth bald head with a fringe of white hair above his collar.

Ciro turned to apologize to the red-haired girl, but she was gone.

"She almost got you," Remo said.

"Like a spider in a web," Carla agreed.

"Who was she?" Ciro asked, still turning his head from side to side, searching for the pretty young woman.

"It's a racket. You go with her and sign up to work in the quarries in Pennsylvania for low wages," Carla said. "She gets a cut, and you get a life of misery."

Reeling at this news, Ciro handed her the flowers. "These are for you."

Carla Zanetti smiled and took the bouquet. She cradled the flowers appreciatively.

"Well, you've won her over already, son," Remo said. "We'll take a carriage over to Mulberry Street."

Carla walked in front of the men, leading them through the crowd. Ciro looked back and caught a glimpse of the girl talking with another passenger from steerage. She leaned in and touched his arm, just as she had Ciro's. He remembered Iggy warning him about women who were too nice too soon.

The carriage careened through the streets, dodging pedestrians, carts, and motorcars. The streets of Little Italy were as narrow as shoelaces. The modest buildings, mostly three-floor structures made of wood, were potchkied together like a pair of patchwork pants. Open seams in walls were sealed with odd ends of metal, drainpipes trailed down the sides of houses in different widths, welded together with flaps of mismatched tin. Some houses were freshly whitewashed, others showed weathered layers of old paint.

The cobblestone streets were crowded with people, and when Ciro looked up, the windows were also filled with faces. Women leaned out of second-story windows to holler for their children or gossip with the neighbors. Stoops spilled over with southern Italians gathered in small groups. It was as if the belly of the ship had been sliced open and docked on the streets of Little Italy. Curls of black smoke from cheap wood puffed out of the chimneys, and the only green was the occasional tufts of treetops, scattered among the tarpaper roofs like random bouquets.

The sounds of city life were a deafening mix of whistles, horns, arguments, and music. Unaccustomed to the clatter, Ciro wondered if he could get used to it. When they arrived on Mulberry Street, he offered to pay the driver, but Remo wouldn't allow it. Ciro jumped out of the carriage and held his hand out to help Carla. Signora Zanetti nodded at her husband, impressed with Ciro's fine manners.

A barefoot boy in ragged shorts and a torn shirt approached Ciro and held out his hand. His black hair was chopped off, leaving uneven layers. His thick black eyebrows were expressive triangles, his brown eyes wide and alert.

"*Va, va!*" Carla said to the boy. But Ciro reached into his pocket and handed the boy a coin. He held the coin high and twirled down the sidewalk, joining his friends, who charged back toward Ciro. Remo pulled him into the house before Ciro had a chance to empty his pockets.

The poor of Little Italy were different from those Ciro knew. On the mountain, they wore clothes made of sturdy fabric. Boiled wool was their velvet; buttons and trim were extravagant extras added to clothing worn on feast days, at weddings, and for burial. The New York Italians used the same fabrics to make their clothing, but they accessorized with jaunty hats, gold belt buckles, and shiny buttons. The women wore lipstick and rouge, and gold rings on every finger. They spoke loudly and expressed themselves with theatrical gestures.

In the Italian Alps, this particular kind of presentation was considered ill mannered. In Ciro's village, when the vendors rolled their carts out on to the colonnade to sell their wares, there was modest stock to choose from, and little room for negotiation of the price. Here, the carts were loaded full, and customers haggled. Ciro came from a place where people were grateful to be able to purchase any small thing. Here,

everyone acted entitled to a better deal. Ciro had entered the circus; the
show was Italian, but the tent was American.

.   .   .

Back on the mountain, Enza siphoned homemade burgundy wine from
a barrel into bottles lined up on a bench in the garden. She closed her
eyes and held the bottles up to her nose, distinguishing the scent of
the woodsy barrel from the potential bitterness of the grapes. She had
begun to cork the bottles when she saw her father and Signor Arduini
entering the house.

Enza quickly untied her apron, splattered with clouds of purple, and
smoothed her hair. She slipped into the house through the back door.
As Marco took the landlord's hat and pulled out his chair, Enza removed two small glasses from the shelf, poured brandy into the glasses,
and placed them before the padrone and her father.

"I always say the Ravanelli children have the best manners on the
mountain." Signor Arduini smiled. Enza looked at him, thinking that if
she weren't so scared of him, and so anxious about the power he wielded
over her family, she might actually like him.

"Thank you," said Marco.

Enza opened a tin, placing several sweet *anginetti* cookies on a plate.
She served the men, placing two linen napkins on the table.

"I wish my daughter had Signorina's grace," Arduini said.

"Maria is a lovely young woman," Marco reassured him.

"Lovely and spoiled." Arduini sighed. "But thank you."

Enza knew all about the pampered Maria Arduini. She had made
her several gowns when she took on odd jobs in the dress shop in town.
When Maria couldn't decide upon a fabric, she would have three gowns
made instead of one.

"We're always happy to see you. What brings you here today?" Marco
asked.

"I've been meaning to come down the mountain and talk to you
about the house."

"We would like to come to terms on the sale," Marco began.

"I had hoped to sell it to you," Signor Arduini said.

Marco continued, "We hope to give you a down payment by the end of summer."

Enza placed her hand on her father's arm. "Signor Arduini, you said you *had* hoped to sell it to us. Is that still your plan?"

"I'm afraid it's no longer possible."

There was a long silence. Signor Arduini sipped the brandy.

"Signor Arduini, we had an agreement," Marco said.

"We would like to make an offer to you for the stable," Signor Arduini said, placing his glass on the table. "You know that it isn't worth much, but I'm sure we can negotiate a fair price."

"Let me understand you, Signore. You have reneged on your offer to sell us the house, but you would like to buy my stable, which has been in my family for a hundred years?" Marco asked softly.

"It's a small stable." Arduini shrugged.

Infuriated, Enza blurted, "We will never sell the stable!"

Signore Arduini looked at Marco. "Does your daughter speak for you?"

"My father has worked hard to pay a high rent to you for many years in exchange for the opportunity to buy our house outright. You promised him that you would sell as soon as we had a reasonable down payment."

"Enza." Marco put his hand on Enza's.

"My son wants the house," Arduini said.

Enza was unable to contain her anger. "Your son squanders every lira you give him. He drinks his allowance at the tavern in Azzone."

"He can raise his son as he pleases. And this is his house, Enza. He can do with it whatever he wants," Marco said.

Since Stella died, her father's ambition had all but left him. This current turn of events didn't seem to surprise him so much as reinforce his sense of helplessness in the inevitable downward spiral of bad luck.

"Signore, you are backing out of a promise. That makes you a liar." Enza seethed.

"I have been kind to this family for many years, and this is how you thank me. You allow your daughter to say whatever she likes against me. You have until the end of the month to move out."

"Just a moment ago I had the best manners on the mountain." Enza's voice broke.

Arduini stood and placed his hat on his head, a sign of disrespect while he was still inside their home. He left the house without closing the door behind him.

"We'll have to find a place to live." Marco was stunned. He'd had no idea the meeting might end this badly.

"Enough renting! Enough living in fear under the thumb of the padrone. We should buy our own house!" Enza said.

"With what?"

"Papa, I can go to America and sew. I hear the girls in the shop talking about it. They have factories and jobs for everyone. I could go and work and send the money home, and when we have enough, I'll return to take care of you and Mama."

"I'm not sending you away."

"Then come with me. You can get a job too—that's more money for our house. Battista can run the carriage service while we're gone. Everyone must work!"

Marco sat down at the table. He put his head in his hands, trying to sort through this dilemma.

"Papa, we have no choice."

Marco looked up at his daughter, too tired to argue, and too defeated to come up with an alternative.

"Papa, we deserve a home of our own. Please. Let me help you."

But Marco sipped the brandy and looked out through the open door, hoping for a miracle.

.   .   .

Ciro followed Remo and Carla Zanetti into their shop. He found a tidy operation. There was one serviceable main room, with a wide-plank wood floor and a tin ceiling overhead. The pungent scents of leather, lemon wax, and machine oil filled the room. A large worktable was positioned in the center of the room under a saw for cutting leather, surrounded by a series of bright work lights.

The far wall was lined with a sewing machine and a buffing apparatus for finishing. Floor-to-ceiling shelves were stacked with tools and supplies, and sheets of leather, bolts of fabric, and spools of thread filled the opposite wall. As workspaces went, this one was far more pleasant than the slag pit in the bottom of the SS *Chicago*. Plus, Signora Zanetti looked to be a good cook.

In the back of the shop, Remo showed Ciro a small alcove with a cot, basin, pitcher, and one straight-backed chair, all of which had been cordoned off behind a thick curtain.

"It's as nice as the convent," Ciro said as he placed his duffel on the chair. "And better than the ship."

Remo laughed. "Yes, our apartments in Little Italy are better than steerage. But just barely. It's God's way of keeping us humble." Remo opened the back door of the shop. "That's my little piece of heaven. Go ahead."

Ciro followed Remo through the open door to a small enclosed garden. Terra-cotta pots positioned along the top of the stone wall spilled over with red geraniums and orange impatiens. An elm tree with a wide trunk and deep roots filled the center of the garden. Its green leaves and thick branches reached past the roof of Remo's building, creating a canopy over the garden. There was a small white marble birdbath, gray with soot, flanked by two deep wicker armchairs.

Remo fished a cigarette out of his pocket, offering another to Ciro as both men took a seat. "This is where I come to think."

"*Va bene*," Ciro said as he looked up into the tree. He remembered the thousands of trees that blanketed the Alps; here on Mulberry Street, one tree with peeling gray bark and holes in its leaves was a cause for celebration.

"Signor Zanetti," Ciro began, "I'd like to pay you rent."

"The agreement is that you'll work for me, and I'll provide your room and board."

"I had that same agreement at the convent, and it did not end well for me. If I pay you, then I'm secure."

"I'm not looking for a boarder to pay me rent; I need an apprentice. The letter from my cousin, the nun, came at the right moment. I need help. I've tried to train a couple of boys here in the neighborhood, but they're not interested. They want the fast money. Our boys rush to line up for day work on the docks. They're assigned to crews that build bridges and lay tracks for the railroad. They work long hours and make a good wage, but they aren't learning a craft. A trade will sustain you, while a job will only feed you temporarily. I think it's important to be able to make something, whether it's shoes or sausage. Food, clothing, and shelter are the basic needs of all people. If you master a trade that serves one of those needs, you will work for a lifetime."

Ciro smiled. "I'll work hard for you, Mr. Zanetti. But to be honest with you, I have no idea if I have any talent for what you do."

"I will teach you the technique. Some of us make shoes; then there are the men who do more. They take the same skills I use in the shop to make sturdy shoes, and make art. Either way, you'll eat. The world will never run out of feet in need of a pair of shoes."

Ciro and Remo leaned back in the wicker chairs and puffed their cigarettes. The smooth tobacco calmed Ciro after his long journey. He closed his eyes and imagined he was home with Iggy, sharing a smoke in the church garden. Perhaps this little garden on Mulberry Street would be a tonic for his homesickness.

"You like girls, Ciro?" Remo cleared his throat.

"Very much," Ciro answered honestly.

"You want to be careful, Ciro," Remo said, lowering his voice.

"Oh, I understand about the red-haired girl on the dock now," Ciro said, embarrassed. "At first, I didn't. She just seemed pretty and American."

"She has a job. But I'm talking about the girls on Mulberry Street, on Hester, and on Grand. They're about your age, and sometimes there are ten children living in the same three rooms. It gets tiresome for them. The girls want to marry, as soon as possible. So they find a hardworking young man who will provide for them and take them away from the situation they come from." Remo put his cigarette out on a stone at the bottom of the tree.

"And you think the girls on Mulberry are lining up for Ciro Lazzari to take them away from their troubles?" Ciro smiled.

Remo smiled too. "There will be a few."

"Well, sir, I'm here to work," Ciro said solemnly. "I want no permanent part of this beautiful country. I want to save my money and go home to Vilminore, find a good wife there, and build a house for her with my own hands. I'd like a garden like this, and one cigarette a night in a deep, comfortable chair where I can sit and think after a hard day's work. I know it doesn't sound like much, but that would be the perfect life for me."

"So you won't be a Romeo in Little Italy?"

"I didn't say that. But I won't get serious, that I promise you."

Carla pushed through the door with a tray of popovers and three small glasses of red wine. Ciro rose and gave her his chair.

"I thought we needed to toast our new apprentice," she said.

"The Italian way," Remo said, winking at Ciro.

* * *

Every May, Our Lady of Pompeii Church on Carmine Street held the Feast of Santa Maria, in honor of the Blessed Mother. The church bells chimed the tune of "Hail Holy Queen Enthroned Above" as the vestibule doors were propped open to reveal a church overflowing with baskets of white roses. This was the most important feast day for the girls of the parish who, at sixteen, were at the peak of their adolescent beauty.

The girls wore white silk gowns and tiaras of tiny satin rosebuds woven by the women of the church sodality. Across their gowns, they wore sashes in a demure pink called ashes of roses. The street was cleared as the girls processed single file from the church on Carmine Street to Bleecker Street and back again, following the priest, the altar boys, and the men of the church carrying the statue of the Blessed Lady.

This parade was a celebration of what it meant to be both Italian and American. As Americans, they were free to march through the streets, and as Italians, they could express their devotion to Mary, the mother of all mothers. They hoped the queen of heaven would shower them with health, good fortune, and strong families in exchange for their alms. The religious aspect was only part of the celebration. It was also a chance for the young men of the village to choose the girl of their dreams from the May court.

Ciro stood on the corner in the midst of the crowd as the girls passed. The May Queen was the most beautiful girl in the parade. *Felicitá! Felicitá!* The crowd chanted her name. She wore a sheath of white silk and, upon her lustrous black curls, a long lace mantilla. Her veil fluttered on her shoulders in the breeze.

Ciro remembered a similar mantilla worn by Concetta Martocci in the church of San Nicola, the afternoon he sat with her. Ciro no longer felt the sting of regret when he thought of Concetta, just the pang of rejection. The wise man leaves the past behind like a pair of boots he has outgrown.

Ciro set his gaze upon Felicitá, as did every young man in the crowd. Ciro watched as Felicitá pulled a white rose from her bouquet and handed it to an old lady in the crowd. This simple gesture was full of grace, and Ciro took it in.

Women move through the world never knowing their power.

The next time I fall in love, Ciro thought to himself, *I will choose wisely. I will make sure that the girl loves me more than I love her.* It was in that moment, when he made that promise to himself, that he set his cap for Felicitá Cassio, the May Queen.

11

A BLESSED MEDAL

Una Medaglia Benedetta

The quarter moon peeked through the alpine trees like a snip of pink ribbon in the purple night sky. By the first day of May 1910, a few weeks after their disastrous meeting with Signor Arduini, the Ravanellis were settled into another rental two streets away from the house where their six children had been born. Enza made fast work to find another house with the help of her boss at the dress shop.

The move from Via Scalina to Via Gondolfo meant less space and a higher rent. Instead of an entire house, Marco rented the bottom floor of the Ruffino homestead, which had a small garden in the back, a patch of green grass in the front, four rooms, and a fireplace. Even though they were lucky to find a house so quickly, leaving one landlord for another was not what Marco had envisioned for his family.

Marco kept the family stable on Via Scalina, refusing to sell it to Signor Arduini. He built a low fence between the two buildings and laid a new stone path to the entrance from the street. Signor Arduini was not pleased with the situation, but Marco would not sell the barn to the man who had forced him out of his home.

When Marco passed Signor Arduini in the streets of Vilminore, he continued to show his respect and tip his hat. Signor Arduini did not return the kindness. Enza's words still burned in the padrone's gut like the perpetual flames in the coke ovens below the village. It was a fire Arduini could not put out.

The final piece of the Ravenellis' bad luck came one day while Enza was working in Signora Sabatino's dress shop. Enza remembered the day the old lady from Lake Iseo came to pick up her dress for her son's wedding. Ida Braido was small, slim and white haired, but she had the focus of a much younger woman with a project in mind.

Ida's blue eyes were clear behind her eyeglasses as she sat in the window seat, waiting for Signora Sabatino to attend to her. Enza sat behind the sewing machine, carefully feeding two sides of a cotton placket under the bobbin. Ida watched her with interest.

"Is there anything a machine can't do?" Signora Braido asked.

"Fall in love," Enza replied.

"Or die," Signora Braido mused.

"Oh, they can die all right," Signora Sabatino said as she entered from the back of the shop. "I had a buttonholer give out last week. Enza and I have the bloody thumbs to prove it."

Signora Sabatino held up the dress, a simple pale yellow sheath overlaid with organza embroidered in a pattern of small daisies around the hem.

"I did all the stitchwork by hand. No machines touched your gown," Enza assured her.

"I like it," Ida Braido said. "It's fitting for a send-off."

"I thought you were going to wear it to your son's wedding."

"I am. After the wedding he and his bride are leaving for Naples, where they are taking the SS *Imelda* to America. I am losing a son, gaining a daughter-in-law, and then losing them both."

Signora Braido opened her change purse and handed the seamstress full and final payment for the daisy dress. She went out into the street, where her son awaited with a horse cart to take her home.

"All these *pazzo* people and their dreams of America," Signora Sabatino said. "What do they think? If every Italian leaves to find a job in America, pretty soon there will be too many workers in America lining up for a few jobs. And then what? They've lost their home here, and any possibility of returning. Crazy dreams."

Signora Sabatino lifted the bin of finished mending and went to the back room.

Enza pulled her small notebook and pencil from her apron and calculated her pay against what the girls made in America. She would have to work several years for Signora Sabatino to make what she could save in one year in America. Enza tucked the notebook with the figures back into her pocket.

Enza adjusted her work lamp over the needle of her sewing machine. She flipped the bobbin switch and fed the fabric under the needle, guiding it with her hands. The silver needle pumped up and down along the chalk line of the placket. She released the bobbin switch, pulled the fabric away gently from the gears, and snipped the threads with her shears. She examined her work. She had created one flawless seam, quickly, with a sure hand, just like a master.

She had sat back in her work chair when she saw Eliana tap on the window. Enza went to the door.

"*Andiamo!*" Eliana said urgently.

"Is it Mama?" Enza's heart sank in her chest.

"No, no. The stable."

Enza called out to Signora Sabatini that she must go. She ran with Eliana from the shop to Marco's stable.

Giacomina stood by the worktable, holding Alma, who cried into her apron.

"Mama? What is it?" Enza asked, fearing that something terrible had happened to her father. She turned and saw Marco kneeling in Cipi's stall. Battista and Vittorio fought back tears as they stroked Cipi's mane.

The grand old horse lay still on the clean straw as Marco covered him with a blanket. The day they dreaded had come. Cipi was old, and finally his heart had given out.

"He's gone," Papa said, tears in his eyes.

Enza went into the stall, Vittorio and Battista moving aside as she knelt next to Cipi, whom she had known all of her life. His shiny mane was still warm, and his brown eyes, even in death, had a sweet expression, one of surrender, where there once had been one of abiding patience. Enza remembered climbing up on his back when she was a girl, grooming him as soon as her hand had grown large enough to hold the brush, and, when she grew tall enough, feeding him slices of apples from her hands. She remembered loading the carriage lamp with oil in the winter, and making bouquets of fresh flowers to attach to the carriage in summer. Cipi had pulled the carriage that carried Stella's coffin, and had taken every bride and groom from Sant'Antonio down the mountain to Bergamo after their weddings. She remembered braiding Cipi's mane with ribbons on feast days—red on Christmas, white on Easter, and pale blue for Santa Lucia. She remembered leaving the house on the night of a snowstorm and going to the barn to throw an extra blanket over him. She remembered shaking the sleigh bells on the carriage at Christmastime as Cipi pulled the children through the streets while the snow fell. She had taken excellent care of this horse, and in return, he had served her family loyally and well.

The long shadows of her brothers, sisters, mother, and father looked like tombstones against the stable wall as they stood around Cipi. Enza rested her body against the horse she had loved all of her life, taking in the clean scent of his lustrous coat.

"Thank you, Cipi," Enza whispered. "You were a good boy."

·   ·   ·

Besides having been May Queen at Our Lady of Pompeii Church, Felicitá Cassio was also the privileged daughter of a grocer in Greenwich Village who had emigrated from Sicily with his bright, sturdy wife and built a small empire that began with a fruit stand on Mott Street and eventually spread to every corner below Fourteenth Street.

As her father loved peddling fresh fruit, strawberries and cherries, Felicitá loved boys. Ciro pursued Felicitá in the weeks after the festival, but he didn't have to work too hard to win her; just as he had chosen her, Felicitá had chosen him.

She arranged to stop by and visit with her friend Elizabeth Juviler at the cheese store on Mulberry on a regular basis, with the goal of running into Ciro. When she discovered that Ciro made deliveries of boots and shoes he had repaired to the factory workers in the West Village, she made sure to take a walk across Charles Street when she knew she might run into him. Felicitá had a serious attraction to the mountain boy. She was taken with Ciro's light hair and eyes, and he was enamored of her *bella figura*, the envy of every girl in Little Italy.

Felicitá was thinking how lucky she was as she brushed Ciro's hair off his face and studied his profile as he napped. Her parents worked long hours in the business, and she had their apartment to herself during the day. An only child, she cooked and cleaned for her parents in exchange for everything a girl of sixteen desires.

Felicitá found Ciro more impressive than the compact Sicilian boys, who were attractive enough with their thick eyebrows and Roman noses, but only a couple inches taller than she. They were also too eager to please for her taste. She liked that Ciro didn't fawn over her; he was remote, yet warm, and Felicitá saw those attributes as signs of maturity. Ciro was so tall he barely fit in her small bed. Her shoes, resting nearby, could easily hide inside his.

Ciro stirred and opened his eyes. She once had a party dress the exact blue-green color of his eyes.

"You should go," she said.

"Why?" He pulled her close and rested his face in her neck.

"I don't want you to get caught." She sat up and pulled a small crystal bowl filled with her jewelry off the nightstand. She slid delicate rings—thin, embossed gold bands, others inlaid with round opals and shimmering chips of citrine—onto her fingers.

"Maybe I want to get caught," Ciro teased.

"Maybe you ought to get dressed." Felicitá fluttered her fingers, now sparkling with metal and stones. She flipped her long hair to the side and snapped on a necklace with a holy medal. "Hurry up. Papa will kill you," she said without the slightest urgency.

Ciro pulled on his pants and then his shirt.

Felicitá grabbed Ciro's hand. "I want that ring."

"You can't have it." He pulled his hand away, laughing. They'd played this game before. "Your name doesn't begin with a *C*."

"I've always wanted a signet ring. They can scrape off the *C* at the jeweler on Carmine Street. Then they can size it and carve an *F* on it. It looks like good gold. 24K?"

"I'm not giving you the ring." Ciro put his hands in his pockets.

"You don't love me." She pulled the bedsheet around her body as she knelt on the bed.

"I'll buy you a different ring."

"I want *that* one. Why won't you give it to me?"

"It belonged to my mother."

Felicitá softened. Ciro had never mentioned this detail before. "She died?"

"I don't know," Ciro answered honestly.

"You don't know where your mother is?"

"Where's yours?" Ciro shot back.

"On the corner of Sixth Avenue, selling bananas."

Ciro reached down and kissed her on the cheek. "I'll buy you something nice at Mingione's."

"I don't want another cameo."

"I thought you liked the cameo."

"It's all right. I'd rather have something with shine."

"Let your fiancé buy you a stone with shine," Ciro said.

"I'm not ready to get married."

"Your parents made a match." Ciro slipped into his shoes. "You're obligated."

"I don't always do what they say. After all, you're here—" As Felicitá stood, the sheet fell away.

Ciro took in her golden skin, soft curves, and sleek lines. She resembled the statues in the church of San Nicola. He pulled her close and buried his face in her thick hair, with its scent of sweet vanilla. "You know I'm a lost soul."

"Don't say that." Felicitá kissed his cheek. "I found you. Remember?"

Felicitá pulled on her robe and walked Ciro to the front door of the apartment. She lifted a blood orange from the bowl on the table and gave it to him, along with a good-bye kiss. Ciro slipped out of Felicitá's building and walked back to Mulberry Street.

He peeled the orange and ate it as he walked through Little Italy. The orange was sweet, the September air cool, and the sky teal blue. The seasons were changing, and so was Ciro's point of view. It was after making love, when he felt satisfied, that Ciro did his best thinking.

He thought about Felicitá. She had been good to him. Felicitá had taught him English, as she spoke both English and Italian. She mended his clothes and replaced buttons on his coat. He imagined he was in love with her, but his feelings did not consume him, and not just because she was betrothed to another. He had always believed true love would overwhelm, capture, and guide him to the safe shores of fidelity like a boat made of fine wood, varnished against the elements. But it hadn't, not yet anyway, and not with Felicitá. He was waiting to feel that deep attachment take hold within his heart. He knew for sure it existed. He remembered it on the mountain. He remembered his mother and father.

.   .   .

The wind whistled through the trees as Enza made her way up Via Scalina toward home. She heard the hinges on the gate as she passed the old house they used to rent, the light of a new family pouring out of its front windows. The Arduinis had turned around and rented it to another family as soon as the Ravanellis moved out. Next door, her father's stable was dark, the windows latched, the doors chained, and had been so since Cipi died. The night air had the scent of oncoming snow, but in October, it was early for the storms.

Enza pushed the front door of the house on Gondolfo Street open. Her mother and father sat at the farm table, which took up most of the space in the smaller kitchen of this house. Every important family document lay neatly on the table. The brown tin money box rested by Mama's accounting book, which had a series of figures recorded on a fresh page marked with the date. Papa rolled a cigarette while Mama wrote in the ledger, as Enza took off her coat and hung it on the hook.

"You're so late, Enza," Giacomina said.

"I know, Mama. It was my last day at the dress shop, and I didn't want to leave Signora with a lot of work to do." She fished in her apron pocket. "She gave me ten lire for the trip." Enza placed the money in the box on the table.

"She should've given you fifty," Giacomina said.

"Mama. It was a *gift*. You taught me to be grateful for them, no matter how small." Enza went behind her mother and wrapped her arms around her. "You're the best mother on the mountain. You taught me good manners and . . . patience. That's why I expect so little from cheap bosses like Signora Sabatino. Besides, we don't need her money. We saved all year long, and we have our passage."

"Which is the money we usually use to survive the winter."

"Mama, as soon as Papa and I get to America, we'll get jobs and start sending you money. Please don't worry," Enza said. "Your tin box will be full by Christmas."

"Maybe we should go in the spring, Enza," Marco said.

Enza was tired of arguing with her father. He agreed to the plan, and then doubted Enza's logic. Marco had had a terrible time making decisions since Stella died. Enza gradually took on more responsibility as her father grieved.

Enza spoke kindly but firmly to her father. "Papa, we've thought about this long enough. If we work hard for the rest of our lives in Schilpario, we will never save enough to buy a house. We need to make real wages. The scraps from summer tourists will never be enough. We'll go to America, make the money, and come back as soon as we can. It's the only way. Someday we'll have the life we dreamed of."

Giacomina handed an envelope to Enza. "From my cousin."

Enza read the back of the envelope: *Pietro Buffa, 318 Adams Street, Hoboken, New Jersey.* "What's he like, Mama?"

"I don't know him very well. I know that he has a wife and three sons, and the sons have wives, and some have children. There's a lot of work there for you to do."

Enza tucked the letter into her apron pocket. She would find work in a factory and, in exchange for room and board, cook and clean for the Buffa family. How hard could it be? She had been helping her mother since she could remember.

Eliana came out of the bedroom. "I wish we could all go with you."

"How long will it take you to make enough to buy a horse? Because I will keep the stable going until Papa returns," Vittorio asked from his cot.

"We'll make enough for a new horse," Enza promised. "And then enough to build our own house."

"You stay here and help Mama, and we'll be back before you know it," Marco said.

Enza smiled at her father gratefully. "As fast as we can."

"What if you like America more and forget about us?" Alma said from her loft bed above the kitchen.

"That will never happen," Papa assured her.

"I'm going to get a job sewing, and Papa will build all sorts of things: bridges, railroads."

"Whatever they need," Marco said.

"Just picture the house," Enza said. "And it will come true."

"Then we'll be like Signor Arduini," Battista said from his cot.

"Except Papa looks better in hats," Enza said.

It seemed the entire village of Schilpario came out to see Enza and Marco Ravanelli off on their journey.

Their friends showered them with gifts—small soaps scented with peppermint from the Valle di Scalve, tins of cookies, and knit gloves that Giacomina carefully wrapped in brown paper and packed into their cloth duffels.

Battista walked Marcello Casagrande's horse, a sleek black mare named Nerina, pulling the Ravanelli carriage, up to the street in front of the house. He climbed up onto the seat and took the reins.

When Enza climbed up to sit on the bench of the carriage, she looked down at the faces of neighbors and friends she had known since she was a girl, faces that expressed worry, apprehension, and support. From their smiles she drew confidence to go to America and do what she must for her family; seeing their tears, she felt regret that she could not achieve the same goal by staying at home.

Marco climbed up into the seat next to his daughter. Battista leaned forward and patted Nerina's mane.

As the carriage pulled away, Giacomina waved her handkerchief and began to cry. She had a terrible feeling about the trip, but she didn't share her worries with Enza. Enza was brave, and Giacomina would never tell her not to follow her heart's desire. But she warned Marco to take especially good care of their daughter; when she had the bad dream, it was about Enza.

The dream had recurred over several months, after Cipi's death and the decision to send Enza and Marco to America. Lately, Giacomina had dreaded falling asleep. The details were always the same, which made the dream seem true after a time. Giacomina pictured Enza aboard an ocean liner in a terrible storm, with deafening thunder and streaks of lightning illuminating sickly green waves that pummeled the ship.

Enza, in her traveling clothes, would grip the railing on the deck.

Giacomina could see every detail of her daughter's hands—the slim blue veins, the tapered fingers, the trim white nails. As the storm swirled around her, Enza cried and held on. Giacomina then appeared in her own dream, crawling across the deck to save her daughter. Just as she reached to grab Enza's cloak, a towering black wave stretching as high as a masthead bludgeoned the deck, swallowing Enza. Giacomina would call out for her lost daughter, then wake in sheer panic. Leaping out of bed, she would climb the ladder to the loft to find her daughter safely asleep. No amount of prayer would stop the nightmare, and no matter how Giacomina tried to let go of the image of her daughter aboard the ill-fated ship, she could not.

As Giacomina waved good-bye, she thought of the dream. She knew in her heart that it was the last time she would see Enza.

As Nerina clopped through the narrow streets of Schilpario, Enza turned to take one last look at Pizzo Camino, and the eternal white peaks of the Italian Alps that towered over the rolling green hills of the Orobie Prealps. She had been born and baptized on this mountain. She promised herself she would return and raise her children here; and someday, when she was old, she would be buried next to Stella under the blue angel.

It didn't occur to Enza to be sad that circumstances were so dire that she and her father had to leave their family to make enough money to buy a house. As she had always done, she would imagine the house in her dreams and build it beam by beam. The goal was to come home as quickly as possible. That dream would fuel her ambition. She would work as many hours a day as she could stand, save every penny, and return to Schilpario as soon as possible. There was no regret on this day, only hope. The Ravanellis had plenty of love, and now they wanted security. Marco and Enza would see to it that they had both.

As they passed the church of Sant'Antonio da Padova, Enza made the sign of the cross. As they approached the cemetery, she asked her brother to stop the cart.

Enza climbed down from the bench, opened the wrought-iron gate to the cemetery, and walked the gravel path to the family grave. Standing before the small angel on the marble headstone, she prayed for her sister.

Gravel crunched behind her as her father joined her by the grave.

"What it is about grief, Papa? It never leaves you."

"It's there to remind us of what we had," he answered. "It's a terrible trick played on the living."

Enza lifted a chain from around her neck and slipped a medal of the Sacred Heart off its bale. She kissed it and placed it on Stella's grave.

"We should go," Marco said. "Or we'll miss our train."

Marco put his arm around his daughter and walked her out of the cemetery.

As Nerina descended the mountain pass, the old carriage bounced over the pits and grooves in the Passo Presolana. Rainstorms had pounded the road and flooded the surface, wearing the gravel away, leaving streaks of cinnamon-colored mud. Enza would remember the exact shade of that color, and when she sewed, she would often choose a similar rich, reddish brown in wool and velvet, a hue that held meaning and memory for her.

If only Enza had known that this would be the last time she'd descend this mountain and overlook the gorge, she might have paid closer attention. If she had known that this would be the last time her mother held her in her arms, she might have clung to her more tightly. If she had known that she would not see her brothers and sisters again, she might have listened more carefully to every word said that day. In the years to come, when she yearned for the comfort of her family, she would conjure this day and try to recall omens and clues.

Enza would have done everything differently. She would have taken her time to acknowledge that one part of her life was ending and a new era had begun. She would have held Alma's hand longer, given Eliana the gold chain she had always coveted, and told one final joke to Vittorio. She would have touched her mother's face. Maybe, if she knew what lay ahead, she would never have made the decision to leave Schilpario in the first place.

Enza might also have noticed that the shadows beneath the Pizzo Camino were more menacing than they had ever been; but she didn't see them. She wasn't looking up, and she wasn't looking back; instead, she kept her eyes focused on the road ahead. She was thinking about America.

12

A FOUNTAIN PEN

Una Penna da Scrivere

The SS *Rochambeau* was twelve hours out of the port of Le Havre when Marco was summoned from steerage to the ship's hospital on the second tier.

The sleek, elegant ship was French built, with a midnight blue hull, whitewashed decks, and brass bindings. It graced the ocean like fine French couture, but below the waterline, it was no different from the worst Greek and Spanish ships. Bunk beds, three to a cell, were made of thick canvas, reeked of vomit, and were stained with the sickness of prior passengers. The accommodations in steerage were primitive, the maintenance minimal: floors swabbed with ammonia and hot water between crossings, and not much more.

There was one large dining room for third class. The rough-hewn tables and benches were nailed to the floor. It had no windows and was lit by the flames of gaslights that spit coils of black soot into the cavernous space. Meals prepared with beans, potatoes, and corn, stretched with boiled barley and served with black bread, were typical. Once, in the nine-day crossing, they were served beef stew with gristle of meat, family style.

Once a day, the passengers in the belly of the ship were encouraged to go up to the deck for fresh air and sun. Many chose to sleep on the deck through the night, to avoid the overcrowded conditions in the accommodations below. The cold night air and ocean storms, it turned out, could be as perilous to their health as the cramped conditions in the cabins below. Many contracted coughs they could not shake, influenza, and fevers, for which there was nothing but mustard plasters and weak tea.

While on the deck below, the passengers in steerage could hear the tinkling of champagne glasses, the strings of the orchestra, and the sandy shuffle of feet as the first-class passengers danced through the night above them. In the morning, they were awakened by the heady scent of fresh coffee and cinnamon rolls drenched in butter baking in the ovens in the upper-class kitchen. When the steerage passengers went below for their own breakfast, there were vats of scorched black coffee, cups of cold milk, and heels of day-old bread with butter.

The elegance and easy living of first class seemed so close. The passengers imagined what it must be like. The young girls dreamed of dancing in chiffon dresses and eating cake in the ballroom. The boys imagined vendor carts serving caramel peanuts while they played shuffleboard on the polished wood floors in the game room.

As the men below gathered on the deck to smoke, they compared plans and schemes, promising themselves that when they returned to Italy, they would return on this boat, traveling in first class as rich Americans. Their wives would have their hair done, wear peacock plumes, and douse themselves in perfume. They would stay in large suites with soft beds, a butler in attendance to steam their suits, press their shirts, and polish their shoes. French maids would turn down their beds at night.

The women, wives, mothers, and grandmothers saved their dreams for their new lives on the other side of the Atlantic. They imagined wide American streets, lush gardens, sumptuous fabrics, and large rooms in clean houses awaiting their touch. They had received the letters, they had been told the stories, and they believed domestic bliss awaited them.

The trick, it seemed, was to make it across the ocean without incident. It was simple: avoid the crooks and stay healthy. Enza Ravanelli was not so lucky.

The hospital aboard the *Rochambeau* consisted of three small rooms with bright red crosses painted on the doors. They were outfitted with clean beds on stationary lifts and well attended by a nursing staff. The porthole windows made the accommodations seem lavish compared to the dark cells in steerage.

Dr. Pierre Brissot, a lanky Frenchman with blue eyes and a permanent slope in his posture, ducked his head and left Enza in the room, to meet Marco in the hallway.

"Your daughter is very ill," Dr. Brissot said in halting Italian.

Marco could hear his heart pound in his chest.

Dr. Brissot continued, "She was brought here from her cell. Was she ill before the ship left Le Havre?"

"No, Signore."

"Has she been ill on a ship before?"

"This is the first time she has been on the sea."

"Have you traveled by motorcar?"

"Never. She drives our horse carriage. She has always been very strong." Waves of panic washed over Marco. What if he lost her, as he had lost Stella?

He barely listened to Dr. Brissot when he said, "I cannot order the ship back to Le Havre for one sick passenger in third class. I'm very sorry."

"May I see her?"

Dr. Brissot opened the door to the hospital room. Enza was curled up in the bed in a fetal position, holding her head. Marco walked over to her and placed his hand on her shoulder.

Enza tried to look up at her father, but her eyes filled with terror as she was unable to lift her head or focus her gaze.

"Oh, Enza." Marco tried to soothe her, hoping his voice didn't give away his fear.

Enza searched for the strength to tell her father she felt like a spoke in the wheel of a runaway carriage. Nausea rolled through her in waves. Sounds were deafening, each wave against the ship's hull shattering within her ear like explosions of dynamite, rock smashing against rock without reprieve.

Enza opened her mouth, but no sound came out.

"I'm here," Marco said. "Don't be afraid."

.   .   .

Night after night, Marco lay on the cold metal floor beside Enza. He slept only briefly, awakened by nurses, the clank of the engines, and Enza's agonized moans. Utter exhaustion gave way to brief nightmares as the terrible days crept by. Dr. Brissot's reports offered little encouragement. The medicines he usually prescribed for extreme motion sickness failed to have any effect on Enza. She became weaker and weaker, dangerously dehydrated. Soon her blood pressure began to plummet. Tinctures of codeine, a syrup of black cohosh, seemed to only make Enza worse.

Toward the end of the nine-day journey, Marco finally fell into a deep sleep, where he dreamed he was back in Schilpario, but instead of the green cliffs, the hillsides had been torched by fire, and the gorge was filled with black water. Marco had gathered his family to safety on a precipice, but below he saw Stella drowning in the floodwaters. Enza jumped in to save her, and she too began to flail in the black water. Marco dived into the gorge headfirst, hearing his wife and children on the cliff screaming to stop him, but it was too late.

Marco awoke in the hospital cell, feverish and disheveled. A nurse gently tapped him. "We're in the harbor, sir."

Marco could hear the muffled sounds of the cheers from the Rochambeau's passengers above, gathered on deck as the ship docked in lower Manhattan.

There was no celebration for Marco and Enza, no lingering first gaze at the soft turquoise majesty of the Statue of Liberty or awe expressed at the view of the cityscape of Manhattan. There was only the scratch of Dr. Brissot's fountain pen against the paperwork to save Enza's life once the ship was safely in the harbor.

"I've made arrangements for signorina to be taken immediately to Saint Vincent's Hospital in Greenwich Village. They may be able to stabilize her. You have to process through Ellis Island with the others."

"I must stay with my daughter."

"You'd be an illegal alien, sir. You don't want to risk that. They'll pick you up and send you right back to Italy without your daughter. Follow instructions to Ellis Island, and then join her at Saint Vincent's. They'll be doing everything they can for her. We will file her paperwork through the hospital."

Dr. Brissot bustled off to attend to his other patients, and Marco was asked to leave the room as the nurse and two of the ship staff placed Enza on a gurney to transport her off the ship.

As Enza was carried off on the stretcher through the narrow doorway, Marco reached out to touch her face. Her skin was cold to the touch, just as Stella's had been the last morning her father ever held her.

The nurse pinned the ship's manifest to Enza's sheet, per standard regulations, then handed Marco a slip of paper with the address of the hospital. In the bright sunlight, Enza looked worse, and waves of panic overtook Marco as he watched her go. He turned to the nurse in desperation.

"Is my daughter dying?"

"I don't speak Italian, sir," she replied briskly in English, but Marco understood her meaning. The nurse had avoided telling him the terrible truth.

      · · ·

As Marco stood on the interminable line at Ellis Island, he began to shake from exhaustion fueled by anxiety. He knew he must appear in control and composed to meet the immigration officer; any sign of mental illness or physical weakness would be a reason to deny him citizenship. He must act as though he was nothing but an eager laborer who had come to America to join the workforce, although at middle age, he was a less than ideal candidate in the eyes of immigration. But his heart was breaking, and his feelings of inadequacy and failure as a father were on the brink of overwhelming him.

Marco set the cap on his head at an angle, to show confidence. He placed one hand in his jacket pocket, feeling the smooth lining, a patch of rare silk sewn by Enza. His eyes filled with tears when he thought of his daughter and her efforts to improve the lot of the Ravanelli family. There was never a girl so driven to hold her family together.

Enza looked after her brothers and sisters, and she had more responsibility than most girls her age. But did his daughter have the strength to recover? What if there was an underlying cause to Enza's illness that could not be healed? What would he tell Giacomina if Enza died? The thought panicked him, as the slow pace of the line made every moment he was away from her unbearable.

Marco wished he had never agreed to come. But he knew if he had decided to stay in Schilpario, Enza would have come to America alone.

If something happened to Marco, Enza was to return home immediately, but it had never dawned on them that Enza would be the one to face catastrophe.

. . .

The Zanetti Shoe Shop had never enjoyed so much business. The small storefront on Mulberry Street stood out under a brand-new red, white, and green striped awning. The shop percolated with activity as customers stopped in for fittings, drop-offs, pickups, and repairs. Salesmen came through with sumptuous sleeves of leather, boxes of grommets, and bolts of rawhide laces. Signora Zanetti thrived on the haggling that ensued, as she bargained for supplies for the best price.

There was good reason for the boom: work had commenced on the building of the Hell's Gate Bridge in Queens. Every available man over fourteen and under sixty had signed up for round-the-clock shifts. Each new hire needed a pair of sturdy, well-made work boots that were properly soled, could withstand bad weather, and would provide safe traction on the metal parapets high over the Hudson River. Many came to Zanetti's for the best deal.

Remo taught Ciro everything he knew in the long hours they kept in the shop. Ciro learned how to sketch the patterns, cut the leather, and construct the work boots. He also became adept at finishing, polishing, and buffing the boots he had made, taking pride in the small details that would become the hallmark of his fine craftsmanship.

Carla handled the books, making sure boots bought on credit were paid off weekly. If money was due her, she made sure to collect it, even if she had to knock on apartment doors or visit a job site to do so. She reconciled the receipts and counted the money. The green cloth bank bag was soon too small for their deposits, and a second was added.

Ciro had been up since dawn, sewing vamps and hammering heels. He had spent the previous day creating small steel cups for the toes of every pair of boots.

"You need to eat," Carla said as she placed a breakfast tray on the worktable.

"I had coffee," Ciro said.

"A young man cannot grow on coffee. You need eggs. I made you a frittata. Eat."

Ciro put down the hammer and sat. Signora Zanetti was a good cook, and he appreciated her hot meals. He placed the cloth napkin on his lap.

"I'm always impressed by your manners," Carla said.

"You seem surprised I have them."

"With your background . . . ," Carla began.

Ciro smiled. He found it funny that Signora Zanetti was a snob. She tried to distance herself from other immigrants despite the fact that they shared similar histories. They had all emigrated because they were poor and had to find work. Now that the shop was successful, Signora had begun the slow, careful climb of reinvention and had even more reason to look down on her struggling fellow Italians. "My background is not so different from yours, Signora," Ciro reminded her.

Signora ignored the comment. "However you look at it, the nuns did right by you."

"I had parents too, Signora." Ciro put down the fork and napkin and placed the tray aside.

"But you were so small when they left you." Carla poured herself a cup of coffee.

Signora's comment cut through Ciro's heart. "Don't ever assume, Signora, that my brother and I were unloved. We probably got more than our portion."

"I didn't mean . . . ," Carla stammered.

"Of course you didn't." Ciro cut her off as Remo joined them in the workroom.

Ciro treated Signora with respect, but he didn't have affection for her. Her love of money offended him. In Signora's eyes, those who had money were better than those who didn't. She treated her husband, Remo, as a servant, barking orders and making decisions without consulting him. Ciro promised himself that he would never fall for a woman with a temperament like Carla Zanetti's. She was a demanding boss, but as the American saying went, she was also a tough customer.

There were nights when he thought about leaving the Zanetti Shoe

Shop and trying his luck working on the road crews in the Midwest, or going south to the coal mines. But he never seriously considered it. Something had happened over the past several months, a turn of events that Ciro had not counted on.

Ciro had fallen in love with the craft of shoemaking. Remo was a fine teacher, and a capable master craftsman. Through his instruction, Ciro discovered that he enjoyed the arithmetic of measurements, the touch of the leather and suede, the feel of the machines, and the delight of the customers when he made a boot that fit, after a lifetime of ones that didn't. Ciro began to appreciate fine workmanship as an art form unto itself. The painstaking craft of building a proper boot or shoe from simple elements gave Ciro a purpose he had never known before.

Remo saw Ciro's raw talent blossom under the techniques Remo had learned from an old master in Rome. Ciro was eager to learn everything Remo knew, and built upon that knowledge with his own insights and ideas. There were modern machines being developed, and new techniques that would take shoemaking forward in a progressive, exciting way. Ciro wanted to be a part of that.

But there were two sides to business: the creative side, handled by Remo, and the business side, closely guarded by Carla. Signora Zanetti was far less eager than her husband to share the details, or teach Ciro how to run a business. Was it her inborn sense of competition, Ciro wondered, or her secretive nature? Either way, she withheld all of her practical business knowledge. Nevertheless, Ciro picked up on Signora Zanetti's techniques of salesmanship, customer payment plans, and dealing with the bank. This Italian woman knew how to make good American money. As Ciro gained confidence in his abilities, he had begun to hunger to take his own green bag to the bank. He was thinking about money, and it was in this moment that he lost focus. The metal lathe sliced into his hand.

"Aah!" he shouted, and looked down at the bloody puncture in his palm. Carla raced for a clean rag.

"What did you do, Ciro?" Remo asked, leaping from his stool to run to Ciro's side.

Ciro wrapped a clean moppeen around his palm to staunch the bright red blood.

"Let me see the wound!" Carla insisted. She took his hand and unwound the tight cloth. A deep gash in his hand oozed fresh blood, a flap of blue skin dangling over it. "We are going to the hospital."

"Signora, I have to finish these boots," Ciro said, but his voice broke in pain.

"The boots can wait! I don't want you to lose your hand to gangrene. Hurry! Remo! Hitch the cart!"

. . .

Enza opened her eyes in a hospital room that had the scent of ammonia. For the first time since she left Le Havre, the room did not spin, and her body did not have the sensation of free-falling. She had awoken to a pounding headache, and her eyes had trouble focusing, but she was no longer in the state of agonizing constant motion. She had no memory of the transport from the ship to Saint Vincent's Hospital. She didn't remember her first ride through Greenwich Village in the back of a horse-drawn ambulance. She did not take note of the trees in bloom, or the windowboxes stuffed with yellow marigolds.

As Enza attempted to sit up, a searing pain split her head from top to bottom. "Papa?" she called out fearfully.

A slim young nun in a navy blue habit eased Enza back down onto the pillow. "Your father is not here," she said in English.

Baffled at the new language, Enza began to cry.

"Wait. Let me get Sister Josephine. She speaks Italian." The nun turned to leave. "Don't move!" The nun grabbed Enza's chart and went.

Leaning back against her pillow, Enza surveyed the room.

Her travel clothes were neatly folded on a chair. She looked down at her white hospital gown. A needle was bound with a bandage into the skin of her hand. She followed the tube to a glass jar filled with liquid. There was a small pulsing pain in her hand where the needle met the vein. She bit her dry lips. She reached for a glass of water on the small table and drank it down in a single gulp. It was not enough.

A second nun pushed the door open. "*Ciao*, Signorina," Sister Josephine said, then continued in Italian, "I'm from Avellino on the Mediterranean." Sister Josephine had a full face, tawny skin, and a straight, prominent nose. She pulled up a chair next to Enza's bed, filled the empty water glass, and gave it to Enza.

"I'm from Schilpario," Enza said in a scratchy voice, "on the mountain above Bergamo."

"I know the place. You're a long way from home. How did you get here?"

"We were on the *Rochambeau* from Le Havre, France. Can you help me find my father?"

The nun nodded, clearly relieved to find her patient so lucid. "We were informed that he had to process through Ellis Island."

"Does he know where I am?"

"Yes, he was told to meet you here at Saint Vincent's."

"How will he find me? He doesn't speak English. We were going to learn some basic phrases on the trip, but then I got sick."

"There are plenty of people in Manhattan who speak Italian."

"But what if he doesn't find someone who can?" Enza was panicked.

Sister Josephine's face showed her surprise that the daughter was in charge of the father. Yet Enza knew that Marco had not been the same man since Stella died. To be fair, no one in the family had been the same since they lost her. Enza doubted they would have made the decision to come to America if Stella had lived. She couldn't explain to Sister Josephine how loss had led to a plan, then to action, how precarious everything had seemed after Stella's sudden death, and how desperate she felt to help the Ravanellis forge a more secure life for themselves.

"Your father will find his way to you," Sister Josephine reassured her.

"Sister, what's wrong with me?" Enza asked. "Why have I been so ill?"

"Your heartbeat all but disappeared from low blood pressure in reaction to the motion. You almost died on that ship. You'll never be able to travel by boat again."

The nun's words cut worse than any pain she had endured on the crossing. The thought of never seeing her mother again was too much to bear. "I'll never be able to go home." Enza began to cry.

"You mustn't worry about that yet," Sister Josephine interjected before Enza's despair could spiral further out of control. "You just got here. First you must get well. Let me guess, you're going to Brooklyn."

"Hoboken."

"Do you have a sponsor?"

"A distant cousin on Adams Street."

"And you're going to work?"

"I sew," Enza said. "I hope I can get a job quickly."

"There are factories on every block. Hasn't anyone told you? Anything is possible in America."

"So far that hasn't been true, Sister." Enza lay back on the pillow.

"A practical girl for a change." Sister looked around and then back at Enza. "You must know that they don't give you your papers unless you're a dreamer."

"I wrote 'seamstress' as my occupation. That's what's on the ship's manifest of the *Rochambeau*," Enza said, closing her eyes. "I didn't think to write 'dreamer.' "

Marco Ravanelli stood at the railway platform in lower Manhattan with a few lire in his pocket, his duffel, Enza's suitcase, and a small slip of paper with an address upon it. The processing through Ellis Island had taken most of the day, as the Greek and Turkish onboard came with multiple family members, adding to the slow grind of the process.

For all Marco knew, Saint Vincent's Hospital might be a thousand miles away. He was exhausted from the interminable lines at Ellis Island and terrified at the uncertainty he faced. Marco wondered if the American doctors had saved Enza. His beautiful daughter, whom he had held on the day she was born in the same blanket that had held him, might already have died in the long hours he had been away from her side. He wanted to pray for his daughter's life, but he couldn't find the will or the words to do so.

Marco gave in to the emotions of the long day and cried.

The sight of this newly arrived immigrant, obviously a proud man with troubles, standing alone next to his cloth duffels in boiled wool clothing and a dingy shirt, filled a driver on the carriage line with compassion. He jumped off his perch and headed toward the man.

"Hey, Bud, you all right?"

Marco looked up at a burly American man, around his age. He wore a plaid cap, vest, and work pants. He had the flat nose of a prizefighter, and a plain gold tooth in the front of his mouth shimmered like a window. Marco was taken aback by the man's gregarious manner, but welcomed the sound of his friendly voice. "You look like you lost your best friend. You speak English?"

Marco shook his head.

"I speak a little Italian. *Spaghetti. Ravioli. Radio. Bingo.*" The stranger threw his head back and laughed. "Where are you going?"

Marco looked at him blankly.

"Do you mind?" The stranger took the piece of paper from Marco. "You have to go to the hospital?"

Marco heard the word *hospital* and nodded vigorously.

"Joe, this hospital is about two miles from here. If you didn't have the bags, you could walk. You Catholic?" The stranger made the sign of the cross.

Marco nodded, dug into his shirt, and pulled out a devotional medal on a chain he wore around his neck.

"You're Catholic, all right. You gonna work for them?" he asked. "They got a lot of jobs at the hospital. And them nuns will find you a place to stay too. They're good about that. Something about those habits makes 'em want to help people. They wear veils with wings, makes you think they're fairies, flying around doing good works. Now, just nuns I'm talking about. Not women in general, if you know what I'm saying. They don't wear the wings, and they don't fly. They got other pluses. And the first plus: they ain't nuns." The driver threw his head back again and laughed.

Marco smiled. He may not have understood the words, but the animated delivery by this stranger was entertaining.

"Tell you what I'm gonna do. I'm gonna do a good deed for the hell of it. I'm gonna give you a lift to Saint Vincent's." The stranger pointed to his horse and carriage. Marco understood the man and nodded appreciatively.

"My treat." The driver snapped his fingers. "*Regalo.*"

Marco formed his hands in the prayer position. "*Grazie, grazie.*"

"Not that I'm a good Catholic or nothin'," the man said as he picked up Marco's bags. Marco followed him to the carriage. "I'm planning on repenting at the very end of my life, when I'm takin' that last gasp. I'm the kind of guy who eats a rib eye rare on Good Friday. I know, I know, it's a mortal sin. Or maybe it's venial. See that? I don't even know the difference. The point is, I wouldn't mind seeing the face of God once I'm on the other side, but I got a hard time with rules on this one. Ya know what I mean?"

Marco shrugged.

"Hey, what am I doin', unloading on you when you got your own problems. Ya look like a sad sack, my friend, like ya just heard the most miserable opera they ever wrote."

Marco nodded.

"Ya like the opera? All them Italian guys, Puccini, Verdi . . . I know about 'em. How about the Great Caruso? He's one of youse guys too. I seen him for twenty-five cents at the Met. Standing room. Ya gotta go to the Met sometime."

As Marco climbed into the carriage, the driver hoisted the bags on to the bench next to him. The driver with the gold tooth climbed up to his perch and took the reins.

For the first time since he'd left Schilpario, Marco had caught a lucky break. He sank into the leather seat and held hope in his heart like a hundred stars.

*   *   *

Ciro practically filled up the tiny examination room on the second floor of Saint Vincent's Hospital. He was so tall, his head nearly touched the ceiling before he sat down on the table. A young nun in blue, who had introduced herself as Sister Mary Frances, wrapped a clean bandage around the stitches that sealed the wound on his hand.

Remo and Carla stood against the wall and watched her bind Ciro's hand. In the months since Ciro had arrived and breathed new life and energy into the shop, the childless couple had begun to enjoy a late-in-life experience of parenting. Even their styles in that regard were different. Remo thought of the pain Ciro was in, while Carla thought of the lost hours the accident would cost her.

"I could've used you this morning," Sister Mary Frances said as she wrapped the bright white strips of cloth around Ciro's hand. "We admitted an Italian girl, and I couldn't communicate with her."

"Is she pretty?" Ciro asked. "I'll be her translator."

"You're incorrigible," Carla said.

"How did you learn English?" Sister asked Ciro.

"The girls on Mulberry Street," Carla answered for him, and cackled.

"There you have it, Signora," Ciro said to Carla. "It pays for me to spend time with the girls. I learn English, and I learn about life."

"You know enough about life," Carla said drily.

"How bad is the wound, Sister?" Ciro asked.

"It's quite a gash. I want you to keep the wound covered, and don't think of pulling out the stitches yourself. You come back, and I'll take them out. About three weeks?"

"Three weeks in a bandage?" Ciro complained. "I have to make shoes."

"Do whatever you can one-handed," Sister told him.

. . .

Enza watched the sun as it slipped past the trees over Greenwich Village. From her hospital window on Seventh Avenue, Enza saw rows of connected houses. The colors of New York City were new to her, burnt orange and earthy browns with an apricot glaze so different from the vivid blues and soft greens of her mountain town. If light itself was different in this new country, imagine what else would be.

Sister Josephine wrote, *Enza Ravanelli*. "Is that your full name?"

"Vincenza Ravanelli." She corrected the nun without taking her eyes off the streets below. She couldn't imagine what was taking her father so long.

"Did you know this hospital is called San Vincenzo's?"

Enza turned to her and smiled.

Sister asked, "Do you believe in signs?"

"Yes, Sister."

"Me too. Well, that's a good omen."

"Where is Hoboken from here?" Enza asked.

"Not far at all. Look out the window. It's across the Hudson River, where the sun sets."

"What's it like?"

"Crowded."

"Is every place in America crowded?"

"No, there are places in America that are just wide open spaces, with nothing but rolling hills and fields. There are lots of farms in places like Indiana and Illinois."

"I'll never get that far," Enza says. "We came to make money to buy our house. As soon as we do, we'll go home."

"We all come here thinking that we'll go home. And then, this becomes home."

. . .

The driver hopped down from his perch and helped Marco with his luggage. Marco looked up at the hospital entrance; the sandstone building took up an entire block. Marco reached in his pocket for his money.

"This is on me, buddy." The driver smiled.

"Please," Marco said.

"Nope." The stranger climbed back on his perch. "*Arrivederci*, pal." He drove off into the darkness whistling, with the light heart of a man who'd just done a good deed.

Marco approached a young Irish nun who managed the arrival desk, outfitted with a telephone and a large black leather-bound book with an inkwell. A row of low benches around the outside walls of the room were filled with patients.

"*Parla Italiano*?" Marco said.

"Who are you looking for?" she replied in English.

Marco did not understand.

"Are you ill?" she asked. "You look all right. Is it a job you're after?"

Marco indicated that he didn't understand her. He grabbed a fountain pen off the desk, wrote down his daughter's name, and frantically waved it at the nun.

She read the name and checked it against her ledger. "Yes, she's here. I'll take you up to three."

Marco bowed and said, "*Mille grazie.*" He followed the nun up the stairs to the third floor, taking them two at a time. As he passed the second-floor landing, the door opened as Ciro, Remo, and Carla turned to descend the stairs.

"That guy just landed," Ciro said, watching Marco bound past them.

"Remember your first day?" Remo asked. "We almost lost you to the port hustlers wearing French perfume."

Ciro and Remo made their way down the stairs.

"Where do you think you're going?" Carla asked Remo and Ciro as she stood on the landing above them.

"Back to the shop," Remo said.

"Oh, no. We go to the chapel and give thanks for the speedy recovery of Ciro's hand."

"Carla, I have orders to fill," Remo argued.

Carla gave Remo a withering look.

"Ciro, we go to the chapel," Remo said. "Follow the padrone."

.   .   .

As Marco burst through the door to Enza's hospital room and took his daughter into his arms, his heart filled with a joy he had not known since the day she was born. For the first time since they left the mountain, he felt their luck changing. The registrar on Ellis Island had taken his information without question, the man with the gold tooth had given him a ride, and now, his daughter had recovered.

"What did the doctor say?" Marco asked.

"He wants me to stay in the hospital until my headache is gone."

"Then we'll stay."

"But I have to get to work."

"You get well, and then we'll go to Hoboken."

"The doctor wants me to walk."

Marco helped Enza into her robe. She was shaky as she stood up, but it helped to lean against her father. With his assistance she walked out into the hallway, feeling grateful to be on her feet again.

The polished aqua and white floor tiles glistened. There wasn't a corner of the hospital that was not scrubbed clean, not a handprint on the painted wall or a pile of sheets in the hallway. The nuns moved swiftly as they tended to the patients, their veils gently fluttering behind them as they went.

The doctors of Saint Vincent's were confident, not like the old man who came over the mountain on horseback from Azzone when Stella fell sick. These men were young, robust, and direct. They did their work thoroughly and quickly, weaving in and out of rooms like whip stitches. They wore crisp white lab coats and moved through the sea of nuns dressed in blue like the sails on a ship.

Against the bright walls of the hospital corridor, Marco appeared wizened. Enza felt a wave of remorse for what she had put him through. On the mountain, Marco had been like everyone else's father, a hard worker, intelligent, and devoted to his family. Here, he was just another man in need of a job. Enza felt responsible for him, and sorry that she had convinced him to come to America.

Marco and Enza reached the end of the hallway, where they found the etched glass doors of the chapel entrance. Beams of streetlight filtered through the stained glass, casting a rosy tint over the pews. A few visitors were scattered throughout the chapel; some knelt before the votive trays, while others sat in the pews and prayed. The altar was golden in the candlelight, like a lost coin on a cobblestone street.

Marco pushed the door open gently. They entered the chapel and walked up the center aisle. Enza made the sign of the cross and slid into a pew as Marco genuflected and followed her.

At last, something familiar, something that was just like home. The scent of beeswax reminded Enza of the chapel of Sant'Antonio. Over the altar, a large stained-glass mural in three parts told the story of the Annunciation in shards of midnight blue, rose red, and forest green. On the ceiling, in a china blue inset framed in gold leaf, were the words:

GOD IS CHARITY

The familiar comforted them; the altar, the pews, the kneelers, and the Latin in the missals provided them with a deserved peace at the end of their long ordeal. The Blessed Mother's outstretched arms seemed to welcome them, while Saint Vincent's black robes and wooden rosary beads gave a sense of abiding serenity to these two lost souls hungry for home.

"I was told I will never see my mountain again," Enza said quietly.

"What do they know about us?" Marco tried to bolster Enza's spirits, but when he looked at his daughter, she seemed so small to him now, so vulnerable. Marco wished Giacomina was there to counsel her. He always left the big problems to his wife; she seemed to know just what to say to the children to soothe them. He couldn't imagine how to solve this new problem. What *would* they do if Enza couldn't return home? He sighed deeply, and decided all he could do was encourage Enza to move ahead with their plan. "You have to believe," Marco said, "that we came this far for a purpose." When the words came out of his mouth, he realized he meant them as much for himself as he did for his daughter.

Enza rose from the pew and followed her father down the aisle. Marco pushed the door of the chapel open.

"Enza? Enza Ravanelli?"

Enza heard her name said aloud in a familiar accent. She looked up to see Ciro Lazzari, who she had not seen since she left him at the convent entrance months ago. Her heart began to race at the sight. For a moment, she wondered if this meeting was real, when he had only lived in her dreams.

"It *is* you!" Ciro stood back and took her in. "I don't believe it. What are you doing here? Are you here to visit? Work? Do you have people here?" As he asked her every question he could think of, Enza closed her eyes, took in the soft tones of her native language, and grew homesick on the spot.

"Who is this?" Carla Zanetti snapped.

"These are my friends from the mountain. This is Signor Ravanelli and his eldest daughter, Enza."

Carla made fast work of sizing up the Ravanellis. She could see that Enza was not another girl from Mulberry Street looking to trap a husband, have a baby, and secure an apartment. This girl was an old friend from Ciro's province; she traveled with her father, and was therefore respectable.

Ciro explained how he had met the Ravanelli family to Carla, who softened as she heard the story. Keep talking, Enza thought, drinking this conversation in like the first sips of cold water after the long journey.

"Why are you in the hospital?" Ciro asked her.

"Why are you in a chapel?" Enza countered.

Ciro threw his head back and laughed. "I was forced to give thanks that I didn't lop off my entire hand." Ciro showed her the bandage.

"My daughter fell ill on the ship," Marco explained.

"A little sea sickness," Enza said.

"She almost died," Marco corrected her. "She was in the hospital aboard ship the entire time. We were terrified. I thought I would lose her."

"I'm fine," she said to Ciro. "There's nothing to worry about now, Papa."

Carla and Remo led Marco out of the chapel, leaving Enza and Ciro alone. She took his hand in hers, tucking the loose end of the gauze under the tight bandage. "What happened to you? Are you a butcher?"

"A shoemaker's apprentice."

"That's an excellent trade. A shoemaker's children never go barefoot. Do you remember that expression from the mountain?" She smiled.

Ciro was more of everything than she remembered; taller for sure, seemingly stronger, and his eyes a more vivid color, reminding her of the cliffs above Schilpario, where the branches of the deep green juniper trees met the bright blue sky. She noticed that Ciro carried himself differently. He possessed a particular swagger, an upright posture and a deliberate carriage, which Enza eventually, when she looked back on this moment, would identify as American. He even wore the uniform of the working class—durable wool work trousers with a thin leather belt, a pressed chambray shirt worn over an undershirt, and on his feet, proper brown leather work boots with rawhide laces.

"I should have written to you," he said.

Enza took in the phrase *should have*, which she hoped meant that he *wanted* to write to her, not that he was obligated to do so. She said, "I went to the convent to see you, and the nun told me you were gone. She wouldn't say where."

"There was some trouble," he explained. "I left in a hurry. There was no time to say good-bye to anyone except the sisters."

"Well, whatever it was, I'm on your side." She smiled shyly.

"*Grazie.*" Ciro blushed. He put his hand to his face and rubbed his cheek, as if to remove the pink flush of embarrassment. Now he remembered why he liked Enza; it wasn't simply her dark beauty, it was her ability to get to the heart of things. "Are you going to Little Italy? We have a carriage. Most Italians go to Little Italy or Brooklyn."

"We're going to Hoboken."

"That's across the river," Ciro said. "It's not very far." He seemed to think the distance over. "Can you believe I found you again?"

"I don't think you were looking very hard," she teased him.

"How do you know?"

"Intuition. It must have been very hard for you to leave the mountain."

"It was." Ciro could admit this to Enza, who came from the same place. He tried not to think about the mountain very much. He threw himself into his work, and when the day was done, he carefully laid out his leather and patterns for the next day. He allowed himself little time for outside amusement. It was as if he knew that the work would sustain him more than other pursuits. "Why did you leave?" Ciro asked her.

"You remember our stone house on Via Scalina? Well, the padrone broke his promise to us. We need a new house."

Ciro nodded sympathetically.

"And how's your padrone?" She motioned down the hallways toward Carla Zanetti.

"I didn't know there were women like her in the world," Ciro admitted.

"Maybe it's good you find that out now." Enza laughed.

"There you are!" Felicitá Cassio whisked down the hallway toward them. She wore a fashionable full skirt in a dusty-purple-and-white-striped silk with a matching shirtwaist in white. The hem of the skirt was hiked an inch to reveal a small fringe of cut lace, and lavender calfskin shoes tied with matching satin bows. She wore a proper straw hat with a white grosgrain ribbon band, and kid gloves upon her hands. Enza couldn't help but admire the young woman's dress and accessories.

Felicitá took Ciro's wounded hand and kissed it. "What did you do?"

Enza's heart sank as she realized Ciro and Felicitá were sweethearts. Of course he had a girlfriend, why wouldn't he? And of course she would be beautiful. She was also stylish and bold, seemingly a perfect match for the new Ciro, the American Ciro. Enza's face burned with embarrassment. While she had been dreaming of the boy from the convent, the last thing on his mind had been the girl from Schilpario.

"I can't take my eyes off of you for a second!" Felicitá said. "Elizabetta told me you were bleeding all over Mulberry Street."

"She should sell mozzarella instead of gossiping," Ciro said, clearly embarrassed by the show of attention.

Ciro looked at Enza, who no longer met his gaze. Felicitá turned to face Enza. "I don't think we've met."

"Enza Ravanelli is a friend of mine from home," Ciro said softly. Enza glanced up at him; she'd heard something in his voice, possibly regret.

"He has such a big heart," Felicitá said, placing her gloved hand upon Ciro's chest. Enza noticed how small Felicitá's hand looked by comparison. "I'm not surprised that he makes a point to visit the sick."

Ciro was about to correct Felicitá when Marco interrupted them.

"Enza, you should rest now."

Nodding dutifully, Enza pulled the collar of her robe up around her neck. She wished her robe was made not of thick industrial cotton, but of silk charmeuse that made a soft swishing sound when a girl walked away from a handsome fellow she once had kissed.

"Enza, we'll walk you back to your room," Ciro said.

"No, no, the Zanettis are waiting for you. Besides, I know the way," Enza said as she turned to walk down the hallway. She tried to walk away quickly, but she found that the steps back to her room were painful for an altogether different reason. There was no doubt: Ciro Lazzari had fallen in love with someone else.

13

A WOODEN CLOTHESPIN
Una Molletta di Legno

The leaves of the old elm in the courtyard behind the Zanetti Shoe Shop on Mulberry Street had turned a dull gold and fallen to the ground like confetti at the end of a parade. Ciro propped the door open with a can of machine oil. The cool autumn breeze floated over the worktable, rustling the pattern paper. Ciro adjusted the overhead light to illuminate the book he was reading.

The scar on Ciro's hand from the accident with the lathe had taken almost six years to fade. By the fall of 1916, the thin red gash that crossed his lifeline on his palm had faded to pink. Ciro was concerned about the mystical implication of the placement of this wound, so he had his palm read on Bleecker Street. As Gloria Vale held his open palm, she assured him that he would have more riches in this life than his heart could hold. But, he noticed, she never told him how long this blessed life would be. When Carla heard of the palm reading, she sniffed, "Another woman charmed by Ciro Lazzari."

"I finished the order," Ciro said without looking up as Remo entered the shop.

"What are you reading?"

"A manual about how to build women's shoes. A salesman left these samples, and it got me to thinking."

In response to Remo's quizzical look, he added, "There are a lot of people in New York City, and half of them are women."

"True," Remo said. "And you'd be the first fellow to count them one by one."

Ciro laughed. "Look." He fanned a dozen small squares of leather out on the table. There was soft calfskin dyed pale green, a pebble leather the color of red licorice, and a deep brown suede the exact shade of *pot de crème*. "*Bella*, no? If we make women's shoes, we double our business on the spot. But Signora doesn't like the idea."

"Carla doesn't want women in the shop. She's afraid you'll take your mind off your work." Remo laughed. "Or that I will."

"She has it all wrong. I don't want to make ladies' shoes to meet women, I want to make them to challenge myself. And I'll take any advice you have for me. A master must be a master to the apprentice in all respects. Benvenuto Cellini said so in his autobiography."

"I haven't read a book in twenty years. Once again, the apprentice surpasses the master. I'm almost obsolete. You're not only smarter than me, you're a better shoemaker."

"Then why is your name on the door?" Ciro teased him. "You know, Cellini dictated his autobiography to his assistant."

"You should write down my wisdom before I die and it's forgotten."

"You won't be forgotten, Remo."

"You never know. That's why I want to sell everything and go home to Italy." Remo admitted, "I miss my village. I have family there. Three sisters and a brother. Lots of cousins. I have a small house. I have a crypt with my name on it."

"I thought I was the only one who dreamed of home."

"You know, Ciro, if there's a war, we don't know what side Italy will be on. It could make it very difficult for us here."

"We're Americans now," Ciro said.

"That's not what our papers say. We're welcome to stay and work; beyond that, it's up to them. Until you pass the test for citizenship, you are here at the whim and fancy of the United States government."

"If they threw me out, I would be happy to go back to Vilminore. I liked that I knew every family in my village, and that they knew me. I remember every garden and street. I knew who owned the best ground to grow sweet onions and who had the best spot to plant pear trees. I watched women hang the wash and men shoe the horses. I even watched people pray in church. I could tell who was truly penitent and who was there to show off a new hat. There's something to be said for life on the mountain."

"You dream of your mountain, and I dream of the port of Genoa. I spent every summer there with my grandmother," Remo said. "Sometimes I go through the leather and look for the exact blue of the Mediterranean."

"And I look for the green of the juniper trees. Everyone on the mountain had the same view of Pizzo Camino. We looked at the world in the same way. I can't say that about Mulberry Street."

"So many layabouts here. They don't work hard enough. They want the sparkle without doing the polish."

"Some, not all," Ciro said. Ciro heard the men leaving for construction jobs before sunrise, and watched the women tend their children. Most of the people in Little Italy worked hard to keep their families secure. "I'm lucky," Ciro admitted.

"You made your luck. Do you know how many boys I tried to train in this shop? Carla never liked anyone I tried to apprentice here. But she's never said a word against you. I think you work harder than she does."

"Don't tell her that."

"Do you think I'm crazy?" Remo looked at the doorway, hoping Carla was not coming through it.

"I am very grateful to you, Remo. You didn't have to take me in."

"Every boy deserves a second chance." Remo shrugged.

"I didn't think I needed one. I didn't do anything wrong. But I learned that it doesn't matter what I think. It's what the padrone believes—that's what counts."

"We all have a boss." Remo pointed up the stairs. "Thirty-seven years with her taught me to keep my mouth shut and follow instructions." He lowered his voice. "Don't marry a padrone, Ciro. Pick a quiet girl who likes to take care of you. An ambitious woman will kill you. There's always something that needs to be done. They keep a list. They make *you* a list. They want more, more, more, and trust me, *more, more, more* leads to an ulcer."

"Don't worry about me. I make shoes for a living, and love . . . only when it suits me."

"Smart boy," Remo said.

"What are you two talking about?" Carla asked as she entered the room with the mail. She pushed the leather samples aside. "What are these doing here?" she barked, then glanced back at Ciro.

"We're not going to make anything in this shop but work boots. Get those pipe dreams out of your head."

Ciro and Remo looked at one another and laughed.

"It's a good thing I keep the books," Carla said, undeterred. "If I left this business to you two, I might come home one day to find you making cannoli instead of boots. You're a couple of dreamers." Carla gave Ciro a letter before she climbed back up the stairs.

Ciro was thrilled when he saw that the return address was Eduardo's seminary in Rome. He excused himself and went out to the garden with the letter, put his feet up, and carefully opened the envelope. Eduardo's perfect penmanship was a work of art. Ciro handled the letter reverently.

October 13, 1916
My Dear Brother,

Thank you for the work boots you sent. I laced them up tightly and tested the steel toes you mentioned like a prima ballerina. Our old friend Iggy would not have been capable of en pointe. Of course, I examined the boots as closely as Sister Ercolina would have and was happy to see that you are every bit the craftsman you claim to be in your last letter. Bravo, Ciro, bravissimo! Though I wear the sandals of Galilee, I can still appreciate a good pair of boots!

I have some news regarding our mother.

Ciro sat forward in the old wicker chair.

This information has been relayed to me by letter from the abbess in a convent near Lake Garda where our mother has been living for the past several years. I know this will come as

a shock to you. Mama was so close to us, just a few kilome-
ters from Bergamo. But she was very sick. She went to see a
doctor in Bergamo the day she left us at the convent. He made
his diagnosis and sent her to the nuns. They have a hospi-
tal and a sanitarium there. Our mama suffered from mental
distress so severe she could not function. Papa's death had
put her in a grief state she could not overcome. Sister Ercolina
made sure that Mama got the best care, and now, I am told,
she works in the hospital there. I wrote to her and told her
about you, and about the seminary. As you know, seminar-
ians are not allowed any contact with family members except
by letter. If I could fly over these walls to see Mama in this
moment, I would, if only to write to you to tell you that I had
seen her and was assured by my own eyes that she was safe
and healthy. But, sadly, I have only the promise of the sisters
to go on. We must trust that they are taking care of her, as
they always did for us.

Ciro's heart felt heavy. He began to cry.

The news that Mama is alive is a blessing to me. I feared that
we'd never look upon her face again, not even learn what became
of her. We must be grateful for this news, and pray that we will
all be reunited someday. I keep you in my prayers, my best and
only brother, and remember how proud I am of you. Nor am I
penitent about that pride. I know what you are made of.

                                        Yours, Eduardo

Remo stood in the doorway to the garden and watched as Ciro wiped
his eyes, carefully folded the letter, and placed it back in the envelope.
He remembered the day Ciro had come off the ferry from Ellis Island.
Despite his size and abundance of energy, Ciro had been an innocent
boy. As Remo observed Ciro now, he saw a man in the wicker chair, a
man any father would be proud to call his son.

In the intervening years, Remo had grown to find as much purpose
in the exchange of knowledge from master to apprentice as Ciro. This

experience would be as close as Remo would ever come to being a father himself, and he savored the role.

"Ciro, you have a visitor," Remo said softly. "He says he's an old friend."

Ciro followed Remo back into the shop.

"You never write," Luigi Latini said to Ciro. Luigi had cropped his black hair, slicked it back with pomade, and grown a small, fashionable square mustache under his small nose.

"Luigi!" Ciro embraced his old friend. "*You* could've written to *me*! Where's your wife?" Ciro looked over Luigi to see if he had brought her.

"I don't have one."

"What happened?"

"I went to Mingo Junction as planned"—Luigi nodded sadly—"but I knew the photograph was too good to be true. I couldn't get past her nose. I tried. But I just couldn't do it. So I made up an excuse. Said I was dying and that I had weak blood. I told her father that his daughter did not deserve to be a young widow. I practically climbed into an empty casket and clutched a lily to my chest. Before they could figure out I was lying, I'd hopped a freighter and gone to Chicago. I've worked there ever since, on the roads, mixing cement. Six years I've been working on a crew. And I could work another twenty out there. They're building roads all the way to California."

"How did you find me?"

"I remembered Mulberry Street," Luigi said. "We worked so well together aboard ship, I thought maybe we could work together again."

"How touching." Carla stood in the doorway and fixed a red bandana in her white hair. "You can't stay here."

"Mama," Ciro teased, winking at Luigi. Ciro only called Signora "Mama" when he wanted something. He knew it, and so did she.

"I'm not your mother," Carla said. "There's no room here."

"Look at him. You can see the bones in his neck. Luigi barely eats. He'll have one spoon of cavatelli and no more."

"Not likely. When he tastes my cavatelli, he'll eat a pound."

"See that? Signora has invited you to dinner," Ciro said to Luigi.

"There's a boardinghouse on Grand," Carla said as she wrote

down the address. "Go get a room there and be back in an hour for dinner."

"Yes, Signora," said Luigi.

.   .   .

Enza's sixth anniversary on Adams Street in Hoboken came and went without a glass of champagne or a slice of cake, and there was surely no acknowledgment from Signora Buffa.

A few months after Enza settled in with the Buffa cousins in Hoboken, Marco Ravanelli left Hoboken for the coalfields of Pennsylvania to take a job in the mines. He was six hours away by train, and sent his pay to Enza faithfully. She, in turn, would take the money to the bank, deposit it with her own paycheck, and send a money order to her mother in Italy.

Each Christmas, Marco managed to visit his daughter. They would celebrate quietly, attend a mass, share a meal, and he would return to work, and so would she, making overtime on the holiday shifts.

A lucky break came a year into their plan. Giacomina had been willed a small parcel of land above Schilpario. The plot was just large enough to accommodate a house, but Marco seized on the opportunity. Instead of buying one of the modest storefront houses along Via Bellanca, Marco and Enza decided he would keep working in America until they had saved enough to build the kind of house Marco had dreamed of. Not a grand home, but one with a deep hearth and three windows for sunlight and five bedrooms so that Enza and her siblings could all stay and raise their families under one roof. Enza knew this change in plan would keep them in America longer than they had hoped.

Six years of combining Enza and Marco's salaries, less their expenses, was slowly beginning to fill Giacomina's money box in Schilpario. Battista and Vittorio carried on Marco's carriage route and picked up small jobs wherever they could, but without the money made in America, they would never have survived.

The letters on thin blue paper that crossed the Atlantic were filled with details of the home that was to be: a porch with a swing; two gardens, one facing east for vegetables and herbs, and the other facing west, where a patch of sunflowers would tilt their heads toward the setting sun; a common kitchen with a long farm table and many chairs; a basement to make and store wine; a deep brick oven with a hand-turned rotisserie.

Enza and Marco's venture to America would make it all possible, down to the small grace notes like handmade lace curtains. The Ravanellis were brilliant savers, used to deprivation, only spending money on their basic needs in America; everything else went to Giacomina and the house fund. The house would be the castle that would shield them from want, hurt, and further loss.

Enza longed for satin shoes and elegant hats, like all young women, but when she thought of her mother, she put her desires aside for the family's dream. She sent her father a letter each week, after she received his pay, in which she only wrote good news. She told humorous stories about the girls in the factory where she worked and the church she attended.

Enza said little about the Buffa family, because life with them was barely tolerable. She was mistreated, overworked, forced to do the cleaning, cooking, and laundry for Anna Buffa and her three daughters-in-law, who lived in the apartments above her own. While the Buffas were blood relatives of Giacomina's, they were distant third cousins, only discovered when Enza and Marco looked for connections to help them make the move to America. Anna did not consider Enza family, and she let her know it.

Enza was given a small room in the basement, a cot, and a lamp. It was indentured servitude, and the only happy moments she knew came from the friendships she made at the factory. Enza promised herself each night before sleep that once the house money had been secured, she and Marco would return to Schilpario, and life would be as it once had been. Papa would manage the carriage, and Enza would set up her own dressmaking shop. She put aside thoughts of her illness on the voyage over, vowing that she could survive a return trip. Enza's dreams of the mountain, her determination to return to the security of her mother's arms, and the memory of the laughter of her brothers and sisters got her through each day—but just barely.

Enza sealed the envelope addressed to her mother carefully, then tucked it into her apron pocket.

"Vincenza!" Signora Buffa's voice thundered from the kitchen.

"Coming!" Enza shouted back. She slipped into her shoes and climbed the basement steps.

"Where is my rent?"

Enza reached into her pocket and handed Signora one dollar in cash, for the rental of her basement room. The original agreement had been that Enza would work in exchange for her room and board, but that plan had quickly died when Pietro Buffa took a job in Illinois, taking his three sons with him, to build train tracks on a crew in the Midwest. Enza only stayed because she had heard stories of immigrant girls who left their sponsor's homes only to find themselves in the street, without a position or a place to stay.

"You're behind on the laundry. Gina needs the baby clothes." Signora Anna Buffa had thin black eyebrows, a turned-up nose, and a cruel mouth. "We're tired of waiting for you to finish your chores."

"I hang the laundry when I leave in the morning. Gina could take it down."

"She's watching the baby!" Anna shrieked.

"Maybe one of the other girls could help."

"Dora is in school! Jenny has children! It's your job!"

"Yes, Signora." Enza lifted the laundry basket and entered the kitchen.

Anna called after her, "The sun will go down and the clothes won't dry. I don't know why I took you in, you stupid girl!"

Late that evening, Anna stood by her phonograph player in the living room. She sorted through stacks of Enrico Caruso's records, shuffling through them like cards. She chose a record, placed it on the turntable, and cranked the wheel. The needle settled into the grooves as Anna poured herself a glass of whiskey. Soon the air was filled with Caruso's artistry, long, luscious notes, arias sung in Italian. The scratches on the wax records only made his voice sound sweeter, the grooves deepened from wear.

Anna played "Mattinata" over and over again at top volume, until the neighbor yelled, "*Basta!*" Then she changed the record, playing music from *Lucia di Lammermoor* until she fell asleep, the needle scouring the innermost track of the wax in an endless hiss.

Enza checked the strands of fresh pasta she had made that morning, hanging them up to dry on wooden dowels. As they dried, the powdery scent of flour wafted through the kitchen. These were the things that made Enza long for the Ravanelli kitchen in Schilpario, on days when Mama would cover the table in flour and they would knead fluffy ropes of potato pasta to make gnocchi, or roll small, delicate bundles of crepes filled with cheese and bits of sweet sausage.

Enza tried not to think about home when she did her chores. She would rather be helping her own mother than this ungrateful landlord.

Enza walked through the piles of dirty laundry on the sunporch. None of the Buffa women worked in the local factories, nor did they perform any of the usual household chores. They considered Enza their personal maid. They had adjusted quickly to having everything done for them, as if they came from homes with servants.

Enza lifted the tin washtub, filled with wet laundry she had scrubbed and rinsed by hand. She pushed the screen door open and stepped out onto the patch of grass behind the tenement, where she had strung a clothesline across the courtyard. Every bit of space behind the building had been negotiated and bartered, including the open air. Lines of rope choked the sky like strings on a harp.

Enza lifted the corners of her apron, tucking them beneath the sash. She filled the pocket with clothespins. She lifted a bleached white diaper out of the bin, snapped it, and clipped it to the clothesline. She yanked the pulley and hung the next, and the next. Enza's laundry was always the most pristine in the courtyard. She used lye soap, and finished the job with a soak in hot water and bleach.

Enza hung the underpants, pantalettes, and skirts of the Buffa women one by one. When she had first arrived, she would drop lavender oil into the rinse as she had when she washed the family's clothes in Schilpario, but after a few months, she stopped. Her extra efforts were neither appreciated nor acknowledged. She only heard complaints: there was a wrinkle in a hem, or the laundry wasn't finished fast enough. Four babies had been born in six years on Adams Street. Enza could barely keep up with the workload.

Anna Buffa played a duet from *Rigoletto* at full volume as Enza heated chicken stock on the stove. She chopped a carrot into slim discs and dropped them into the broth. Enza carefully ladled a cup of pastina into the pot, then another. The tiny dots of pasta, as small as rice, would make a hearty soup. Giacomina had taught Enza that all ingredients in soup must be chopped and diced similarly to create a smooth texture in order to feel uniform in the mouth, no one ingredient overpowering another.

Enza prepared a tray for Anna's meal. She poured a glass of wine from a homemade bottle labeled "Isabelle Bell," and set out several slices of bread, some softened butter, and the soup. She placed a cloth napkin on the tray and took it into the living room.

Anna Buffa was draped on an easy chair covered in brown chenille, one leg slung over the ottoman, the other foot on the floor. Her eyes were closed; her pale blue dress was hiked to the knees, and her lace collar was askew. Enza felt a moment of pity. Anna's once-lovely face was now etched with lines of worry, its texture slack from age, and her once-black hair was streaked with white. Anna still managed to put on lipstick each morning, but by nightfall all that was left was a pale stain of tangerine, which made her look more haggard still.

"Your dinner, Signora." Enza placed it carefully on the ottoman.

"Sit with me, Enza."

"I have so much to do." Enza forced a smile.

"I know. But sit with me."

Enza sat down on the edge of the sofa.

"How is the factory?"

"Fine."

"I should write to your mother," Anna said.

Enza wondered what had brought on this civil tone and mood. She looked over at the whiskey glass and realized that Anna had already finished it. This would explain her sudden warmth.

"You should eat your soup," Enza told her, placing a pillow behind the small of Anna's back. This was the only pampering Anna had ever received, and she relished it.

Anna placed the napkin on her lap and slowly sipped the soup. "Delicious," she said to Enza. Evidently, Anna's mood had mellowed in the glow of the amber booze.

"Thank you."

Enza looked down at Anna's swollen ankles. "You should soak your feet tonight, Signora."

"The ankles are bad again." Anna sighed.

"It's the whiskey," Enza said.

"I know. Wine is good for me, but whiskey is not."

"Hard liquor has no place to go in the body."

"How do you know this?" Anna's dark eyes narrowed suspiciously.

"My mother always said that if you drink wine made from the grapes of your own vines, it can never hurt you. But we don't have room on Adams Street for a trellis." Enza smiled.

"Evangeline Palermo grows her own grapes and makes wine in Hazelet. She'll live to be a hundred. Watch," Anna said bitterly. "Play me a record."

Enza placed Enrico Caruso singing *Tosca* on the turntable.

"Don't scratch it," Anna barked.

Enza placed the needle gently on the outer groove, then lowered the volume dial. "Signora, tell me why you like the opera."

"I had some talent myself," Anna began.

"Why don't you sing in church?" Enza asks.

"I'm better than that!" Anna hissed. "I can't waste my talent in a church choir. So I don't bother to sing at all." She was as petulant as a spoiled girl.

Enza rose from the sofa, returning to the kitchen to finish her chores. She promised herself that she would never run a household like this one. Anna's daughters-in-law took their meals upstairs at different times, and their respect for their mother-in-law was nonexistent.

Enza thought longingly of her home and how close she had been to her brothers and sisters. They had shared everything, meals, chores, and conversation. Even the mountain itself, with its majestic cliffs, rolling green fields, and well-worn trails, seemed to belong to them. The Ravanellis were truly a family; they didn't simply share an address like the Buffas.

Enza's eyes filled with tears whenever she thought of Schilpario. Her talks with her mother would go long into the night, and it surprised her to realize that Anna's family never sought her out for company or conversation. Anna Buffa doesn't know what she is missing, Enza thought. Or maybe she did. Perhaps that's why she drank whiskey and played opera music so loudly. Anna Buffa wanted to forget.

Carla cleared the dishes from the garden table. She had served a feast of rigatoni in pork sauce, hunks of fresh buttered bread, a salad of fresh greens, and glasses of Remo's homemade red wine under the old tree to Ciro and Luigi, who put in long ten-hour days without a break.

Remo roasted chestnuts on the grill. As they popped in the heat, bursting their glassy shells, he looked over at Ciro and Luigi, telling stories and making each other laugh. Ciro had seemed so much happier since Luigi arrived, as though his old friend breathed new life into him. Remo could see that Ciro hungered for the kind of friendship Luigi provided, one based upon shared memories and goals. Remo didn't want to lose Ciro in the shop, and he figured the best way to keep his apprentice was to hire his friend.

"You know, Ciro, when you were looking at the leather samples, it got me to thinking." Remo sat down. "We don't necessarily need to go into women's shoes just yet. It's a good idea, but I see it further down the line,"

"I understand," Ciro said, but there was no mistaking the quick flash of disappointment across his face.

"But we do need to expand our business, especially if I have to pay another salary." Remo looked at Luigi.

Ciro beamed. "I'm listening," he said.

"We need to take the Zanetti Shoe Shop to the job sites. Imagine if we had a cart near the Hell's Gate bridge operation. You could make repairs on-site as well as take orders for new boots. With another pair of hands, we could get a real assembly line going here, delivering shipments of new goods right back to the job site."

"We'd get the Greeks from Astoria, the Russians from Gravesend, the Irish from Brooklyn," Ciro began. "They would all wear Zanetti boots. And then we'd move the cart around the city to the construction sites for more new customers. It's a great idea."

"Luigi can be in the shop with me while he trains, and you can be out in the field expanding the business. Eventually, you two can take over," Remo continued. "The master steps aside, and the journeymen run the shop."

"This is a great opportunity," Luigi said. "What do you think, Ciro?"

"I like it," Ciro said.

"What are you boys cooking up out here?" Carla asked.

"We're about to put the Zanetti Shoe Shop on the move," Ciro explained.

"Was anyone going to check with me?"

"Say hello to the new apprentice," Ciro said. "You might want to ask the bank for an extra green bag, because this man is going to help you fill it."

Carla beamed at the thought.

.   .   .

Enza finished the last of the dinner dishes, drying them carefully and placing them on the shelf. She went from room to room, collecting the soup bowls and breadbaskets set outside their doors by Anna's daughters-in-law. When Enza returned from the night shift at dawn, the sink would be full of empty baby bottles, dirty plates, and glasses. After a long shift in the factory, Enza would have to boil the baby bottles, wash the dishes, and clean the kitchen all over again.

Enza packed a hard roll, a hunk of cheese, and an apple in her purse. She tiptoed through the house to the front door, past Signora Buffa, who snored in the bedroom, and let herself out, locking the door behind her.

She walked quickly through the dark streets of Hoboken, careful not to draw any attention to herself, not from the groups of men gathered on street corners, or from the women who sat on their stoops and fanned themselves in the night air.

Occasionally a young man would lean over a second-story balcony and whistle as she passed, and she would hear the laughter of his friends, which sent a fearful chill through her. Enza had never told her father that she worked the night shift. He would be concerned if he knew she walked the streets of Hoboken alone at night.

Enza had developed some tricks to keep safe. She would cross the street to walk near a cop on his beat, and when none could be seen, she would duck off to a side street when she sensed eyes upon her, waiting for the threat of danger to pass so she could continue the half mile undisturbed.

Meta Walker was the largest blouse factory in Hoboken. The rambling warehouse was three stories high, the first floor built of local sandstone blocks, the upper floors tacked on in shingled wood painted gray, as though a cheap paper party hat had been placed atop the stonework. Metal fire escapes snaked up the exterior, with square landings outside doors marked Exit. The runners often used the fire escapes to carry messages to the foreladies running the operators on their machines.

About three hundred girls worked in the plant, split in two shifts, keeping the factory in operation twenty-four hours a day, six days a week. The need for machine operators was constant, as was the turnover, making this plant a first stop for immigrant girls looking for a paycheck.

The factory produced various styles of ladies' cotton blouses: button-down with round-necked collars, flat-placketed with ruffles on the bodice, lace-trimmed with square collars, shirtwaist-style with half-inch stand-up collars, and the popular tuxedo style, collarless, with a flat bib and a small series of buttons.

Enza gathered a dozen white cotton blouses, tied them together with a ribbon of cotton remnant from the cutting room floor, threw them into a canvas bin filled with twenty similar bundles, and wheeled the bin to finishing. She practiced her English aloud as she pushed the bin, because no one could hear her over the roar of the machines.

"Dago girl," Joe Neal from the finishing department called out as Enza passed him. Joe Neal was the nephew of the owner. Sturdily built, around five foot ten, with pomade slicked through his thin brown hair, which was parted fashionably down the center, he grinned with the bright white teeth of the milk-fed American rich. He taunted the girls, and most were afraid of him. He strutted around the factory as if he owned it already.

"When you gonna go out with me?" Joe Neal hissed. He followed Enza as she pushed the bin.

Enza ignored him.

"Answer me, dago girl."

"Shut up," Enza said, strong and plain, as her friend Laura had taught her.

Joe Neal had worked in various departments throughout the factory, though he never lasted long. Enza was told by the other machine operators that Joe had been thrown out of military school, where he'd been sent to be straightened out. The girls warned Enza about him on the first day, and told her to avoid him. But this was impossible, since it was her job to deliver bundles to the finishing department.

Joe Neal had first attempted to flirt with Enza. When she did not respond, his taunts escalated. Now he lay in wait to bully and provoke her, choosing his moments carefully, usually when Enza was alone. He hid behind rolling racks of blouses, or stepped in front of her when she turned a corner. Night after night, Enza endured his insults. She held her head high as she passed him.

Joe Neal sat on the cutting table, legs dangling. Instead of a smile, he sneered at Enza. "Dago has airs."

"I don't speak English," Enza lied.

"I'll fix you."

Enza ignored the comment, pushing the bins filled with bundles to the end of the line. She checked the clock and headed to the lunchroom for her break.

"Over here!" Laura Heery waved to Enza from the far end of the break room, a concrete box filled with unpainted picnic tables and attached benches.

Laura was slim and reedy, a blazing candle of a girl, a redhead with vivid green eyes, a small nose covered in freckles, and perfectly shaped pink lips. Of Irish descent, Laura accentuated her height by wearing long, straight skirts and matching vests over starched blouses. Like Enza, she made all of her own clothes herself.

The girls in the factory were usually cordial during work hours, yet rarely did the friendships continue outside the cutting-room doors. Laura and Enza were the exception, having recognized their simpatico natures over an argument about fabric.

Every few months, the mill owners cleared the fabric inventory and put out ends, yardage of fabric that hadn't been used on an order, or samples dropped off by eager-to-please salesmen. These fabric pieces of various sizes and lengths, rolled on bolts, were useless to the owners but could be salvaged by an expert seamstress to create or adorn clothing.

On Enza's first day of work, she was invited to peruse the ends with the other operators. A piece of pale yellow cotton printed with small yellow rosebuds with green leaves caught Enza and Laura's eye at the same time. Laura grabbed the fabric as Enza reached for it, held it up to her face, and yelled, "Yellow and green are my colors!"

Enza was about to yell back, and instead said, "You're right. It's perfect with your skin. Take it."

Enza's act of generosity moved Laura, and from that day forward, they shared break time. Within a few months, Laura began to teach Enza to read and write English.

Enza's letters to her mother were filled with stories about Laura Heery, like the time they went to the Steel Pier in Atlantic City one Saturday afternoon. Enza had her first hot dog that day, dressed with yellow mustard and sauerkraut. Enza took pains to describe the pink sand on the beach, the one-man band on the Steel Pier, and the bicycle built for two on the boardwalk. She wrote about the wide-brimmed sun hats decorated with giant bows, whimsical felt bumblebees, and enormous silk flowers, about the bathing costumes, sleek, scoop-necked tanks with belts. Everything was new to her, and so American.

Enza had found a best friend in Laura, but so much more. They both loved well-made, fashionable clothes. They both aspired to elegance. They both took time with whatever they made, whether it was a hat or a simple skirt. They groaned when the Walkers bought cheap cotton from a middleman, and the lot of blouses made from it had to be scrapped. They were hard workers, conscientious and fair. The stories in Enza's letters proved that the values instilled in her by her mother had remained intact.

"You look awful," Laura said as she handed Enza a paper cup filled with hot coffee, light with cream, just like Enza liked it.

"I'm tired," Enza admitted as she sat.

"Signora Buffa soused again?"

"Yes." Enza sighed. "Whiskey is her only friend."

"We have to get you out of there," Laura said.

"You don't have to solve my problems."

"I want to help." Laura Heery was twenty-six, had attended classes in secretarial school, and worked as the night manager in the office. It was Laura who had shown Enza how to fill out the forms for employment, where to be sized for her work apron, where to pick up her tools, and how to earn the promotions that took her from operating the machines to becoming the lead girl in finishing. She taught Enza how to add money to her paycheck by doing additional piecework on the blouses during deadline crunches.

Laura broke a fresh, plain buttermilk doughnut in two, giving the bigger portion to Enza.

Enza said, in perfect English, "Thank you for the doughnut, Miss Heery."

"Nice." Laura laughed. "You sound like the queen."

"Thank you kindly," Enza said with a perfect inflection.

"You keep that up, and pretty soon you'll be treated like one."

Enza laughed.

"Get ready. The next thing I'm going to teach you is how to answer questions on a job interview."

"But I have a job."

Laura lowered her voice. "We can do better than this dump. And we will. But keep that under your hat."

"I will."

"And Signora Buffa still doesn't suspect anything, right? That's how they keep you on a cot in a cold basement, you know. If you don't learn English, you're dependent on them. We're about to spring you from that awful trap."

Enza confided, "I hear her say terrible things about me to her daughter-in-law. She thinks I don't understand."

"See those girls? Millie Chiarello? Great on the buttonholer. Mary Ann Johnson? Best steam presser on the floor. Lorraine DiCamillo? Nobody like her in finishing. They're competent, hard workers, but you have real talent. You have ideas. You thought of piping a white blouse in baker's twine, and the stores reordered twice, they were so popular. We don't need these machines. Real couturiers sew everything by hand. I've been doing some asking around," Laura whispered. "We can get jobs in the city."

The city.

Whenever Enza heard those words, she was filled with a sense of possibility.

Laura had been born in New Jersey, but she longed for New York. She knew the names of the families who built mansions on Fifth Avenue, where to find the best cannoli in Little Italy, where the best pickles were brined on the Lower East Side, and the times of the marionette shows in the Swedish Cottage in Central Park. But Laura also knew her rights on the job, and how to ask for a raise. Laura Heery thought like a man in a man's world.

"Do you really think we can get jobs?" Enza asked nervously.

"We'll take any job until we can get a job sewing. You could be a secretary, and I could be a maid. Can you imagine working in an atelier on Fifth Avenue?"

"I almost can," Enza says excitedly. Talking to Laura was like opening a treasure chest.

"Well, dream big!" Laura had been waiting for a partner to help her make the crossing to Manhattan. Her family swore they'd disown her if she ventured into the city alone, but now that Enza was game, they could make the leap.

"Where will we live?" Enza's mind raced.

"We'll figure that out. There are hotels for women. We could share a room."

"I'd like that." Enza had visited Laura's family in Englewood Cliffs. They were a big family, living in a small, clean house filled with Laura's nieces and nephews.

Most weekends, Laura hopped on the ferry to window-shop in Manhattan. She was inspired by the windows on Madison Avenue, filled with crystal flasks of perfume, leather satchels, and hand-tooled silver pens. She imagined owning fine things and taking care of them. She stopped and admired the shiny motorcars that seemed as long as a city block, the society ladies in hats and gloves who got in and out of them with the help of a chauffeur. She looked up at their windows and imagined living inside spacious rooms with billowing draperies and paintings framed in gold leaf.

Whenever she heard Laura describe New York City and all it had to offer, it made Enza want to be a part of it too. No matter what happened at work, Laura was upbeat and positive; she lifted Enza's spirits, bolstered her courage, and looked out for her in every way. Laura was a shot of emerald green in a gray world.

"We just have to pull the money together," Laura said. "I have some savings. Do you think you could put some money aside?"

"I'll add a shift and do more piecework. And I'll write to Mama and tell her not to expect most of my check until I get a new job."

"Good." Laura looked at Enza, who had a look of doubt and fear on her face. "Don't be afraid. We'll figure it out."

When the night shift was over and they'd clocked out, Enza and Laura often left the factory through the second-story fire escape so they might watch the sun come up behind the island of Manhattan. The soft silence was broken by the rhythmic chuff of early-morning trains behind them, while in the distance, the Hudson River's placid surface shimmered like a mirror. Beyond the river, in the first rays of sunrise, Manhattan seemed dipped in silver.

The city, their destination and dreamscape, was made of glass and stone. Would those windows be filled with kind faces? Behind those doors, would they find jobs? And somewhere along the wide avenues and side streets, or tucked in the gnarl of winding lanes in Greenwich Village, would they find a place to live?

Laura encouraged Enza to imagine a new life, to create what she hoped for in her mind's eye. Enza reserved her dreams for her family and hadn't ever thought to a picture a better life for herself. Now, with Laura's encouragement, she would. One day, Enza would know her dream when she held it. Every detail would be recognizable, and the future would fall into place, like the stitches on a hem, one leading to the next.

They dreamed of one room, one window, two beds, a chair, a burner to cook on, and a lamp to read by, the simplest of requirements; just a place of their own, a place to call home.

14

A ROPE OF TINSEL
Una Cordia di Orpello

Columbus Day in Little Italy was an extravaganza. The streetlamps were adorned with ropes of red, white, and green tinsel. Italian flags, resplendent silk squares of bright red, emerald green, and pristine white, rustled on poles over storefronts and houses. Small paper versions of the flag were tucked into lapels on the men, and tastefully into the bands on women's hats. Children held small flags mounted on sticks, stuffing them into their back pockets like bandanas. The autumn air felt as fresh as peppermint, and the sun flickered in the distance like a knot of gold.

"It's velvet time," Enza said. "Just cold enough to wear my favorite fabric."

"Velvet is boiled wool with money," said Laura.

Laura and Enza spent every weekend afternoon they could spare in New York City, applying for jobs. They were on waiting lists for a room at the Rosemary House, the Convent of Saint Mary, and the Evangeline Residence.

They had also applied for jobs all over the city, as nurse's aides at the Foundling Hospital, as cooks and waitresses at social clubs on the Upper East Side, and as private maids in the mansions on Park Avenue. They applied at several tailoring shops, and at a milliner's showroom.

Now that they had made the decision to leave the Meta Walker factory, their new lives could not come fast enough. Laura rushed home every day, hoping the mail would bring them good news. Enza had nothing sent to Adams Street, as she knew the ruckus that would ensue if Anna Buffa thought that her personal maid might leave her.

Today, however, was not a day for filling out forms or checking vacancies in boardinghouses; it was a day of celebration. Every street in the neighborhood between lower Broadway and the Bowery was filled with proud Italian immigrants in their best clothing, proper gloves, and hats, parading in from every borough of the city, along with the crowds who had come to sample the delicacies of southern Italy and celebrate Columbus Day.

Enza and Laura walked across Grand Street, turning heads, in Laura's case because of her pale beauty and her height, and in Enza's because of her dark beauty and trim figure. They wore their own creations; for Enza, a skirt of brushed gray velvet with a fawn-colored jacket trimmed in lavender, while Laura wore a green silk skirt and a matching brocade coat, belted with wide gold cording. Enza's hat was woven of gray and beige satin, while Laura's was a wide-brimmed gold felt. They looked every bit as stylish as the women who had their clothing made in the ateliers on Fifth Avenue.

The girls joined the throngs in the crowded streets, who came for the food, to celebrate their ties to home, and to revel in the camaraderie of being with their own people. Vendors set up simple stands along the avenue, tall whitewashed poles suspending canvas awnings over slim plank counters notched to the poles.

Customers were served every Neapolitan treat imaginable, prepared before their eyes, fresh, hot, sweet, and perfect. Bubbling vats of oil bobbed with puffy clouds of white dough that turned golden brown and would be drenched in sugar to become *zeppole*. Sweet squares of tomato pie resembling the red squares on the Italian flag, drizzled with olive oil and decorated with fresh basil, were placed in waxed paper sleeves and sold one by one.

A booth of fresh pastries featured trays of cannoli shells filled with fresh cream and dipped in chocolate shavings; *sfogliatelle*, pastry seashells filled with ricotta; biscotti rolled with pignoli nuts; *millefoglie*, thin sheets of pastry interlayered with strawberry cream and dusted in powdered sugar; and every kind of gelato and granita. Hazelnut braids hung down from the canopy, to be sold by the foot. A giant slab of *torrone* made of honey, almonds, and egg whites was hoisted above a marble-topped table suspended overhead on rope as though it had been lifted out of a mine. The purveyor hacked away, selling generous hunks of the taffy to the hungry crowd.

"Signora Buffa loves *torrone*." Enza stopped at the stand.

"You're going to buy that witch candy?" Laura asked.

"I keep hoping she'll change," Enza said.

"Go ahead then. Buy it. I hope she breaks a tooth."

"You know what? I'm not going to bring her anything," Enza said.

"Now, that's more like it. Do not wilt in the face of the oppressor!"

The young women wondered which delicacy to sample first. Enza steered them toward the sausage and pepper stand. They watched as the cooks tossed glistening slices of green peppers and ribbons of onions on a griddle while fragrant hot sausage, splitting its skin over the open flames, was placed in fresh, crusty rolls.

Laura took a bite. "*Delizioso!*" she exclaimed.

"Delicious," Enza said in English.

"Nice. But it's only appropriate that we speak your native language. Everything is Italian today, including me!"

A young man handed them each a flyer and disappeared into the crowd to dispense the rest. Enza saw that there was a political cartoon on the front and a caption about the evils of Germany. The Great War, as it was known, was burning through Europe; it was just beginning to touch the lives of these proud immigrants. Italy had joined the war, and talk was that the United States was next. Enza worried about her brothers, and Laura about her nephews, who longed to be soldiers.

Enza tucked the flyer into her purse to read later. She knew how poor the people of her village were. They couldn't survive a long war, which would only make matters worse.

But today, talk of war was minimal. The Italians thriving in America didn't have time for politics. They were hard at work, many on double shifts, making American money. They kept their eyes focused on the bobbins of sewing machines, used their might on construction sites, laid railroad tracks and built bridges, factories, and homes, and took to the sky, balancing on beams high above the city as they built skyscrapers. Here, too, war would be an unwelcome interruption.

"A lot of handsome men in Little Italy," Laura said.

"A few."

"That's why you get the attention. You could care less." Laura laughed. "I remember last summer in Atlantic City. You had a three-hour conversation with that fella from Metuchen. Whatever happened to him?"

"It was just a conversation." Enza shrugged.

"They passed envelopes for Mary Carroll, Bernadette Malady, and the Lindas in finishing, Linda Patzelt, and Linda Faria. Everybody's getting married. Some diamond mine in Africa has just been sucked dry, and I'm gonna go broke celebrating other girls and their happiness. When are we gonna get ours?"

"We will. You'll be first. And I hope you don't settle."

"Are you kidding me? *Never.* I want a man with a bright future. And you don't have to wait for that guy back home, you know. You need to live *now.*" Laura smiled back at a handsome young man who tipped his hat to her.

"I'm not waiting for anyone."

"You are pining for that grave digger. Ciro, right?"

"I wonder about him. But I don't pine for him."

"Okay." Laura wasn't buying it. "Do you write to him?"

"No."

"Letters to Italy go two ways, Enza."

"He isn't in Italy. He's here."

"In America?"

Enza nodded. "In Little Italy."

"You've been holding out on me!" Laura shrieked. "Do you know his address?"

"He was a shoemaker's apprentice on Mulberry Street. But that was so long ago."

"He could be one block from where you're standing, and you're eating a sausage and pepper sandwich! I don't believe it."

"Who knows where he is? It's been six years! He had a girlfriend."

"So? You were teenagers. I think we should have a stroll on Mulberry Street."

"He probably went back to Italy. " Enza shrugged. "I don't care. He never tried to find me."

"Maybe you ought to try and find him."

"Maybe I don't want to find him."

"The *maybe* means that you do," Laura insisted. "You're never going to look prettier than you do today, so you might as well let the man see what he is missing."

"I didn't dress for him!"

"A girl never knows when fate is going to give her a tumble. Look at me. I'm always prepared." Laura pulled a small sterling silver atomizer from her pocket. "A little mister in case I meet my future mister." Laura spritzed the perfume on her neck. "Want some?"

"All right. But just a little. I don't want you to waste it on me. If he's not there, what's the point?" Enza closed her eyes, letting a cloud of cedar and jasmine settle over her.

As the girls made the turn onto Mulberry Street, they were stunned by the size of the crowd. The street was filled with revelers, but so were the sidewalks, the stoops, and the roofs. There was barely any room to move. Enza took in a short breath as her heart beat faster.

"Do you remember the address?" Laura asked.

"Not exactly."

"Come on. You've memorized every detail of every person you have ever met. Think."

Enza surrendered. "He works for the Zanetti Shoe Shop."

Laura squinted down the block. "There it is!" They saw the awning in the middle of the block, the name of the shop emblazoned upon it. Laura took Enza by the arm. "Come on."

Enza had little faith in Laura's plan, but before she could protest, Laura had grabbed her hand and pulled her headlong through the crowd until they reached the shop.

"Wait!" Enza's intuition told her that she would not like what she found behind the door. But it was too late—a determined Laura was unstoppable, on the factory floor or the streets of Little Italy.

"Leave this to me. I'll do the talking." Laura climbed up the steps and poked her head inside.

Enza followed with a combination of dread and curiosity. Her thoughts raced, placing Ciro at the center of every possible scenario, with or without her. Ciro was probably married by now; after all, he was twenty-two, and he seemed hardworking and ambitious. Enza would be cordial and get out of there fast. That's all. She smoothed the front of her skirt before entering the shop after Laura.

Carla Zanetti stood behind the counter. She handed money to a young boy as he placed a large cookie tray on the counter. "I included your tip," Carla said to the boy as he went.

"Hello. My name is Laura Heery, and this is my friend Enza Ravanelli. We're looking for a young man, the apprentice here . . . ," Laura began. "Ciro Lazzari."

"He's out."

"Oh," Laura said, taken aback by the gruff manner of the old gatekeeper. "Enza knew Signor Lazzari from their province in Italy."

"We're from the same mountain," Enza said quietly.

Carla waved her hands. "You see those crowds out there? We're all from the same place. I could call any *jadrool* on the street a blood relative if I wanted to. But I don't want to"—she peered over her reading glasses—"so I don't."

"But this is different. Ciro and Enza really do know one another from some cliff in the old country," Laura insisted.

"We've met, Signora." Enza stepped in, before Laura could do further damage. "I met you, with your husband and Ciro, on my first day in New York, at Saint Vincent's Hospital. I was with my father."

Carla looked at Enza, taking her in. She studied the details of Enza's clothes and hat, deciding that this young woman was a lady.

"The day Ciro cut his hand," Carla remembered.

"Yes, Signora."

"How's your father?"

"He took a position in the mines, but now he's building roads in California."

"Rough work."

"Better than the coal mine."

"We work in a blouse factory in Hoboken," Laura said with a smile. "We'd love to bring you one some time."

"That's very kind of you." Carla smiled. "But I can't be bribed. Ciro has many girlfriends, most of whom I do not approve of—the ones I know about, anyway."

Enza exhaled. She hadn't realized she'd been holding her breath. Ciro was not married.

Carla continued, "Girls nowadays are so fresh. They don't wait for proper courting. They just show up and come right out with their demands. They line up at this counter to look at Ciro Lazzari like they're buying cheese."

"I'm not here to buy cheese, Signora. I was looking for an old friend, just wondering how he was getting along." She was relieved that Ciro was not there. She didn't know if she could have borne it if he hadn't remembered her. "Thank you, Signora. I hope you and Signor Zanetti have a lovely holiday."

Enza and Laura turned to go.

The door of the shop opened wide, the bells on the hook jingling loudly. Signor Zanetti entered first, followed by a couple, Luigi Latini and his girlfriend, Pappina, a delicate brunette with a pink porcelain complexion. She was followed by Felicitá Cassio in a wide-brimmed red hat and matching suit. Finally Ciro Lazzari, in a fetching navy blue three-piece suit with an elegant blue-green silk tie, the exact color of his eyes, entered, carrying two bottles of cold champagne. Suddenly the room was full of people.

Enza turned away, wishing she had never set foot in this shop.

"Which one of you handsome gentlemen is Ciro Lazzari?" Laura asked.

Signor Zanetti blushed at the forward young American.

"Well, you know it's not the old one, he's mine," Carla said.

"Don't look at me. I'm Luigi Latini. I'm neither handsome"—he looked at Remo—"nor old."

"I'm Ciro. What can I do for you?" Ciro asked.

"My friend is an old acquaintance of yours," Laura said. "From the Alps."

"If I'm lucky, it's Sister Teresa from the convent kitchen of San Nicola," Ciro joked.

"This young lady hasn't taken the veil." Laura pulled on her gloves.

"Not yet, anyway. Hello, Ciro," Enza said quietly.

"Enza!" Ciro took her hands into his as he looked at her. The pretty girl from the mountain had become a beauty. Her figure was shapely and trim; in her gray and beige day suit, she looked like a sleek sparrow.

Felicitá crossed her arms across her chest as she checked her face in the mirror behind the cash register.

"Enza, this is Felicitá Cassio," Ciro hastily introduced them. He kept his eyes on Enza, his expression one of wonder. He had so many thoughts. He was struck by how sophisticated she seemed. How far she had come in the six years since he saw her at Saint Vincent's! Only another immigrant would understand what it took to come here so young, and grow up in a place that was so different from home. Clearly, Enza had thrived under the challenge. Ciro was impressed, and his heart was beating fast.

"Felicitá was the May Queen at Our Lady of Pompeii, six years ago," Carla said in a tone that implied Felicitá was no longer at the peak of her desirability.

"I've never met a real queen before," said Laura.

"Oh, I don't rule a country or anything. I just crowned the Blessed Lady."

Laura shot Enza a look.

"Well, they made a lovely choice," Enza said generously. She looked to the door, wanting to escape this awkward situation. She was really going to let Laura Heery have it when they got back on the street.

Ciro stepped forward. "Remo, this is Enza. Remember? You met her at the hospital when I cut my hand."

"This can't be the same girl." Remo sized her up. "Che bella."

"I was very sick when you saw me," Enza said.

"Hoboken agrees with you," said Remo.

"Yeah. It's the beauty capital of the world," Laura said, causing everyone to laugh, especially Carla.

"Carla, did you offer them a drink?" Remo asked.

"I was about to take the trays to the roof. There are fireworks." Carla turned to Laura and Enza. "Would you like to join us?"

Enza looked at Ciro, who had not taken his eyes off her. "We can't. I need to go home."

"No, you don't," said Laura. "Enough with the Cinderella routine. You work hard enough over there. This is your day to celebrate. Count us in, Signora Zanetti. And thank you. Happy Columbus Day!" She clapped her hands together.

"This is great. What a surprise." Ciro picked up the tray for Carla. "I want to hear all about Cinderella."

"I'll bet you do," Felicitá said as she adjusted her hat. "He loves a fairy tale, this one."

* * *

The Zanettis' roof on Mulberry Street was modest. Covered in tar paper, it had a low bench, a few straight-backed wooden chairs, distressed from rain, and a string of lights with fat clear bulbs strung across the chimney wall.

The rooftops of Little Italy were a village unto themselves, a few stories off the ground, but so close, the children could easily hop from one building to another. Most rooftops were decorated simply; some had tomato plants and herb gardens, others flowerpots and small grills for cooking. But tonight they were filled, like a choir loft, high above the action, with revelers waiting for the fireworks.

Carla balanced a cookie tray on the chimney ledge, while Remo opened a bottle of champagne. Carla handed out glasses as Remo poured.

"To Cristoforo Colombo!" Remo toasted.

Enza took a seat on the bench next to Pappina. She felt an instant affinity for the petite brunette with the sparkling black eyes. Pappina had a warm smile, and her curls reminded Enza of Stella. "You seem so familiar to me. Where are you from?"

"Brescia."

"I'm from the north too. Schilpario."

"Way up on the mountain," Pappina said.

"Almost as high as you can go."

"Not too many of us from the north," Pappina said. She patted Enza's hand. "We have to be friends."

"I'd like that."

Enza watched Ciro laugh and talk with Luigi and Remo. She could spend the entire night observing him, and she just might. His strong hands held the glass almost delicately. Happiness animated his entire body, as he threw his shoulders back, feet planted on the ground, and laughed. How lucky the girl who marries Ciro Lazzari, she thought.

Ciro excused himself from the men and joined Pappina and Enza on the bench. Pappina soon excused herself in turn and joined the girls at the edge of the roof. Shrewd Laura had Felicitá deeply engaged in conversation.

"I can't believe you're here," Ciro said.

"This was all Laura's idea," Enza confessed.

"I find that hard to believe. You're a born leader. I remember a girl who lifted cemetery rocks like she was picking up spare change."

"I was a sturdy mountain girl then."

"I like the new version," Ciro said.

"You haven't changed a bit," Enza said drily. "You flirt with your girlfriend ten feet from you—on a roof, no less. Don't you worry she'll hear you and throw you off?"

"If she did, you'd catch me, wouldn't you?"

Enza laughed, but couldn't imagine why. She felt like crying. Maybe it was the cookies and the champagne, but she was filled with both hunger and regret. So much time had passed since she had seen Ciro, and every moment of it felt wasted.

"I miss the mountain this time of year," he said. "Do you?"

"Stream Vò turns silvery gray, and the cliffs turn from bright green to nutmeg."

"Do you think anyone but us thinks of Stream Vò?"

"They think the Hudson River is glorious. It's only beautiful if you've never seen the rivers on the mountain. I can't help it, I compare everything to home."

"How's your family?"

"Still on the mountain. Papa took a job in California. How's your brother?"

"He's in the seminary in Rome."

"A priest in the family. You're blessed."

"You think so? I'd rather have him here in America with me. But I also know that he is doing what he loves, so I accept it."

Enza looked off over the rooftops. She was so happy on this old bench in this moment. Ciro was sitting next to her. After years of wondering what that would feel like again, now she knew. She wished the moment could last her whole life long.

It was as if Ciro could sense what she was feeling. "The world just got smaller, didn't it? You found me again," he whispered.

"It wasn't hard. I walked down Mulberry Street."

"I know, I know, it was an accident. But really, are there accidents? Or does fate determine time and place and opportunity?"

"I don't know—for a shoemaker's apprentice you sound like Plutarch."

"I don't know him. I read Cellini."

"Benvenuto Cellini's autobiography?" Enza asked.

"You know it?"

"I read it on the mountain. My teacher gave it to me. He thought I would grow up to be an artist."

"And have you?"

"I don't know. A lot of artists work in factories." Enza smiled. "And some even make shoes."

"I'm not nearly the artist he was," Ciro said shyly.

"But I bet you're a better man. Cellini was horrible to his wife and children. He was jealous, he maimed and murdered, he practically invented the vendetta. So you'd better stop talking to me and pay some attention to the May Queen, or we'll see some old Sicilian curses thrown around here like party streamers."

Ciro laughed. "I like your hat."

"You would."

Soon the fireworks filled the sky over Little Italy as swizzles of blue, yellow, and pink exploded on a swath of purple. Ciro and Enza joined the other guests. Enza drank champagne and nibbled on the biscotti with the women, while Ciro smoked with Remo and Luigi as they watched the colors ricochet overhead, an explosion of colored stars as far as their eyes could see.

Enza glanced up at the fireworks, but kept looking at Ciro, as if to memorize every detail of him. What a beautiful man he had grown up to be. No wonder the girls of Little Italy hoped to marry him. The fireworks ended with more colors and more cannon fire, the loud booms rattling Little Italy.

"That's the show," Carla said, throwing back the final slug of her champagne.

Enza went to the hosts. "Thank you for a wonderful night," she said to Remo and Carla. She said her good-byes to Felicitá, Pappina, and Luigi.

Enza remembered that it was important to know when to leave a party; it was as gracious as arriving on time. Enza seized the right moment to depart, before it got awkward, before the lines were drawn among the guests and decisions were made: who left with whom. There wasn't much to clean up on the roof, the glasses cluttered the tray, and the cookies had been eaten. It was time to go.

"I'll walk you ladies out," Ciro said, following Enza and Laura down the stairs, through the dark apartment and through the shop. As they reached the door, Enza turned and asked Ciro, "Where do you stay?"

"I'll show you."

"I'll wait here." Laura innocently searched through her purse for her gloves.

Ciro took Enza by the hand to the back of the store. He pulled back the curtain and showed her his cot, sink, mirror, and chair, his neat and clean corner of the world.

"It's immaculate. The nuns would be proud of you," Enza said.

"You haven't seen the best part," he said, pushing the drapery aside and opening the door to the garden. Enza followed him outside.

An accordion played in the distance, underscoring peals of laughter and the low drone of scattered conversation from the porches and yards close by. The cool night air had the scent of buttery caramel and cigar smoke. Rolling gray clouds from the last of the fireworks hung over the jagged rooftops of Little Italy as the moon, full and blue, pushed through the haze to illuminate the garden.

"You have a tree!" Enza exclaimed.

"How many trees did we have on the mountain?" Ciro asked. He put his hands in his pockets and stood back from her, observing her delight.

"A million."

"More," Ciro remembered. "And here, all I have is this one tree, and it's more precious to me than all the forests below Pizzo Camino. Who would have thought that one tree could bring me so much joy? I'm almost ashamed."

"I understand. Any small thing that reminds me of home is a treasure. Sometimes it's small—a bowl of soup that makes me think of my mother—or it's a color. I saw a blue parasol in the crowd this afternoon that reminded me of the lake by the waterwheel in Schilpario. It's the kind of thing that catches you unaware and fills you with a deep longing for everything you once knew. Don't apologize for loving this tree. If I had a tree, I'd feel the same."

Ciro wished he had more time to talk with her.

"We should go," Enza said, as she went through the door and back into the shop.

Ciro walked Laura and Enza out onto Mulberry Street, strewn with bits of confetti, twists of crepe paper, and pieces of ribbon. A few stragglers had found their way down to the corner of Grand Street, where a street band played into the night. Laura walked ahead, just far enough to allow Enza some privacy.

"I should say good-bye," Enza said, even though she didn't want to. "And you should get back to your girlfriend."

"She's just an old friend, I've known her since I came to Mulberry Street," Ciro said. "We just have fun, Enza. We laugh. We have a good time. It's nothing serious."

"It's not a romance?"

"It can't be," he said honestly. "She's been betrothed since she was twelve years old."

"Did someone remember to tell her that?" Enza laughed.

For a moment, Enza had to think about what he was saying. Fun was so low on Enza's list of priorities, she'd practically forgotten it existed.

"You should be having fun, of course," she said. "You work hard, it makes sense. Don't pay any attention to me. I'm too serious. I wear my responsibilities like an old saddle on an old horse."

Ciro took her hand. "Don't make excuses for the way you are. You're working to take care of your family, and there's no higher purpose than that."

"Sometimes I'd like to be young too." Enza spoke without thinking. She was surprised to realize that she felt this way. She never thought about what she wanted, only what was best for those she loved. And as far as her own heart was concerned, she hoped she would do the choosing.

Enza saw how it went with the girls at the mill. Some young women had been betrothed by their parents to young men who were chosen for them, making a match that served both families, pooling their meager assets to benefit both. Others chose for themselves, lucky enough to properly court and fall in love. Still others were forced to marry quickly, when they had not followed the rules of the church. When the banns of marriage went unannounced, the bride and groom were relegated to a private ceremony, deprived of a high mass and reception, taking their vows quietly behind the doors of the sacristy, hidden away in a shame that lasted a lifetime. Maybe this was why it was so hard for Enza to be young. It wasn't just the money that had to be earned, and the house in Schilpario that needed building, there was danger in youth.

Ciro took her hands. "I don't want you to be like them."

"Who?"

"The girls on Mulberry Street. They just want to get married because it's time. I want more."

"And what is *more* to you, Ciro?"

"Someone I can talk to."

"And when did you decide that was important?"

"I think just now." He laughed. After a moment, he took her face in his hands. "You're different, Enza."

"Signora says you see a lot of girls." She removed his hands from her face and held them.

"She exaggerates. But she would. Signora is worried I'll take off after my heart's desire and leave her with a crate of shoe tacks, and a line of angry customers."

"And will you?"

He didn't answer. And just as it had on the mountain, the moon shifted, its beam seeming to single out Ciro, like light through a stained-glass window in a dark chapel. It was as if her world had changed in that moment, had tilted on its axis just enough to give Enza the view she had longed for. He leaned down to her. She felt safe in his shadow, and as his lips grazed her cheek, he took in the scent of her skin, which was at once familiar and right.

Enza knew that in that moment a thousand good men could not compare to Ciro Lazzari. He was the one who owned her heart. She had known it since that night on the mountain. But thoughts of Felicitá intruded, and she wondered how she would ever know whether he truly felt the same about her. In this regard, she would not settle. Better to carry the cross of unrequited love than squander herself on someone whose heart was divided. His tender, delicate kiss emboldened her to tell him what she knew.

She took a step back, letting go of his hand. "I won't come after you again, Ciro. I've had enough of chasing the things I want in this world. It's too difficult. I've learned that it's fine to have expectations, and dreams are wonderful, but once in a while, it would be good to have something come my way without having to fight for it. If you want to be friends, that's your choice. I have nothing to offer you but understanding. And I won't chase you down in every borough of this city to convince you that what I have to give has value to you. I think I understand what makes you who you are, what you want out of life, and I know for sure where you come from. These often aren't the gifts a man is looking for in a woman, but it's what I'm looking for in a man. And if you would like to be that man, it's up to you."

"Where do you live?"

"Three-one-eight Adams Street."

"May I call on you?"

"Yes, you may."

"I've promised Remo to run the repair cart out to Queens. We have new business there with the road. I may not be able to come to see you for a few weeks. Is that all right?"

Enza smiled. "Of course." She had waited all her life for him. A few more weeks would just make their next meeting sweeter.

15

A YELLOW DIAMOND
Un Brillante Giallo

The Zanetti shoe repair cart served Carla Zanetti's goal of keeping Ciro under her roof while turning a greater profit for her business. Ciro paraded their wares through the five boroughs, making repairs and selling new boots to the hundreds of workers recruited for the enormous construction projects—to erect bridges, train stations, and buildings.

Remo hitched the repair cart to his carriage, driving Ciro and Luigi to Astoria, Queens, before dawn. The streets of Manhattan were quiet, except for the clinking of the glass bottles on the carts delivering milk.

Ciro had to pay off Paboo, the local padrone, to park the cart on Steinway Plaza, but it was worth the freight. There was a perfect spot on the plaza for the cart, as it was a busy thoroughfare at the foot of the Hell's Gate Bridge.

Luigi lifted the window flaps on the cart, while Ciro set up the repair table inside. The cart was painted forest green, with "Zanetti Shoe Repair" emblazoned across the side in white letters. Luigi opened the storage drawers under the counter and lifted out dozens of pairs of boots, repaired and tagged with customers' names.

"Know where I can buy a diamond?" Luigi asked Ciro.

"What for?"

"What do you think, what for? For an engagement ring."

"You're gonna get married?"

"I'm older than you."

"By a year," Ciro said.

"It's a long year."

"*Va bene.*" Ciro laid his tools out on the repair table. "You go to Mingione's in the diamond district in the Bowery."

"How do you know?"

"Felicitá," Ciro explained. "If there's a diamond for sale in Manhattan, she's tried it on."

"Maybe they'll sell us a couple of stones. We'll have a double wedding. Pappina is a simple girl with simple tastes. Felicitá will probably want a big diamond."

"She'd like one the size of a slab of *torrone*. But I'm not going to marry Felicitá."

"Why not?"

"She wants to do better than a shoemaker," Ciro said as he pulled a sole from a vamp to resew it.

"She's got some crust. Her father sells grapes on a cart."

"He sells a lot of grapes, Luigi. He's a wealthy man."

"He spits out the pits just like you and me."

"A woman chooses a man she thinks she deserves. And then she sets out to change him to suit herself. I'm not enough for Felicitá. But," he said, his face breaking into a wide grin, "she's not enough for me, either."

"I don't know how you do it," Luigi said. "I am lucky to have found one sweet girl who likes this face. You have found so many."

Ciro thought of the girls he had known. It didn't feel as though he had had an abundance of experiences. In fact, he worried that he had been too guarded with his feelings. He wondered if he would ever know what it was to be truly devoted to one woman. "What did you think of Enza?"

"The girl from the roof? She was nice."

"Beautiful?"

"I'm not allowed to look," Luigi said. "But when I did, I thought she was."

"We're here to pick up our boots." A sturdily built Irishman leaned on the counter. "John Cassidy."

"And I'm Kirk Johannsen." A muscular blond, around Ciro's age, joined him. "I got the retreads."

Ciro looked through the finished bundles, finding the boots.

Cassidy examined his boots, impressed. "They look new."

"Mine too," Kirk said. "Not that I'll be needing them."

The men reached into their pockets to pay.

"Are you quitting the bridge?" Ciro asked.

"I joined the army," Kirk said. "Gonna do my bit."

Ciro and Luigi looked at one another. They would join if they could, but they weren't American citizens. "Put your money away. This one is on us," Ciro said.

"Thanks," Kirk said. "You guys with accents can get in, too. If you sign up and serve, you get your citizenship when you return. Automatic. The army needs ten thousand recruits a week. Right now, they're getting most of them from Puerto Rico."

"We know we can lick the Germans in France," John Cassidy added. "If I were young, you'd find me in the trenches of Cambrai. I'd be itching to go."

John Cassidy looked at Ciro and then Luigi. It was as if his observation was a challenge to the young men to step up and engage in defense of the country that was doing so well by them. It was a look Ciro had seen before, established American to tender immigrant, like the passing glance from a government worker processing the permit for the cart, or the expression of the woman who sold him a standing-room ticket to the opera. There was a fleeting cold front, the slight judgment that said immigrants were a necessary fact of life, one that must be tolerated but never truly accepted. The only way to ever become a permanent part of America's greatness would be to defend it.

Cassidy and Johannsen took their boots and climbed the hill to the bridge, joining the workers who poured on to the plaza from the train platform below.

"Did you mean it?" Luigi asked.

"I've been lucky here," Ciro said.

"So have I."

"Do you believe in signs?" Ciro asked him.

"That depends. Does it require my own bloodshed?"

"Maybe." Ciro looked at Luigi. "We're pretty strong, we're tough." He shrugged. "We could take the Germans."

*   *   *

The night sky over Astoria was speckled with a few small yellow stars that looked like chips of citrine. Luigi was fast asleep in his sleep roll, next to the cart. Ciro finished the last of the sweet sausage calzone packed in the food tin by Signora Zanetti. The boys planned to stay two weeks in Queens before Remo returned to take them back to Mulberry Street, hauling the cart behind them like plows on a tractor.

Ciro and Luigi closed down the cart after nightfall, when the final shift of the last crew from the bridge had departed for home. Ciro hooked the flaps shut and locked the entrance door; Luigi went to sleep as soon as he finished his supper.

Ciro leaned against the cart and wrote a letter. Writing did not come easily to him, perhaps because he did so little of it. Because Eduardo had been such a good student and a beautiful writer, both in penmanship and content, he'd handled any correspondence the boys had to do. Ciro had difficulty finding the right words.

Ciro was writing to Enza Ravanelli on Adams Street to explain that he wouldn't be able to see her as soon as he had hoped. There was his obligation to the Zanettis, of course, his tireless work with the cart to earn his freedom from apprenticeship. But there were other concerns, as well, before Ciro could offer Enza what she needed. He still saw Felicitá, and they both had found it difficult to end what they had started.

There was also the war, the urge to finish what the English and French had begun and take back Europe for the good people, including his own on the mountaintops of northern Italy. Thoughts of becoming a soldier were never far from a young man's mind. Luigi and Ciro wanted to "do their bit," but they also wanted to stand up for something and flex their might.

Ciro didn't know how to begin to tell Enza he was about to join the army. She had made her feelings regarding Ciro absolutely clear. When he went to her, it must be to surrender his heart, to pledge himself to her in total. By writing this letter, he had hoped to simply buy time. He was sure that with a few months at his disposal, the mist would lift, the road would become clear, and he would be able to offer to walk it with Enza.

·   ·   ·

The early December snow over Hoboken was not of the storybook kind, but rather big wet flakes that melted and caused leaks in roofs, improperly patched and hardly built to withstand the harsh winters. Enza placed buckets under the leaks on the top-floor storage room of the Meta Walker factory. She looked up, finding more rusty circles overhead. *There aren't enough buckets in Hoboken*, she told herself as she took the metal stairs down to the main floor of the factory. If the water leak hit the electrical system where the girls worked, someone could be badly hurt.

Enza had been pulling double shifts since Laura and she decided to get out of Hoboken. When Enza was this exhausted, she felt the withering despair of defeat down to her bones. She was so depleted, she was beginning to doubt Laura's grand schemes.

Perhaps it was the letter she'd received from Ciro Lazzari that contributed to her black mood. He was making excuses not to see her. He said his work would keep him in Queens for longer than he expected; it might be Christmas before he could visit. Their kiss on Columbus Day had meant something to her, but the meaning for him was not the same. Perhaps she had been too direct, a fault that had been brought to her attention before.

A letter from her father told her he would not see her this Christmas either. Marco was working on a highway crew in California, and could pick up overtime working through the holiday. Everything they did, every penny they saved for their future, was to be reunited with their family on their mountain. But at moments like these, Enza wondered if the time would ever come when the Ravanellis would be together again.

The weathered row houses of Hoboken, built of plywood covered with cheap tin roofs, leaked in the rain and were hot in the sun. Winters meant furnaces that didn't work, frozen pipes, and the kind of conditions that forced people to give up before they even got started. Enza hiked to work through drifts of snow, because nobody bothered to shovel and plow tenement streets.

Year round, small packs of hungry children were left to wander the streets and beg. Occasionally, during school months, a truant officer would knock on doors and admonish parents that they were required by law to educate their children. But there was rarely a follow-up. The poor were left to fend for themselves.

The air over Hoboken was choked with clouds of heavy smoke from the factories, and the constant stoking of ovens burning cheap wood for heat. Enza longed to see the sky in the daytime, but the clutter of roofs and the low-hanging industrial smoke created a dismal canopy. At night the stars were obscured by the same haze, making it impossible for Enza to follow the patterns of the night sky as she had in Schilpario.

Sometimes Enza broke down as black thoughts consumed her, worries about her father, anxieties about her job, and fear for how she would ever survive the trip home to Italy. She tried to pray through the despair but found no peace, not even in church, which had always given her comfort. This wasn't how it used to be.

The only joy Enza knew was her paycheck, the portion saved to make the move into Manhattan, and the satisfaction that came from the money order sent to Mama in the envelope each week. She still relished the return letters each week confirming the arrival of the money, and filled with news written by each of her brothers and sisters:

I am taking care of your garden. Love, Alma.
I have fallen in love with Pietro Calva. Love, Eliana.
Don't believe Eliana. Pietro Calva doesn't love Eliana. Love, Alma.
We bought a new horse. We named him Enzo after you. Your brother, Battista.
I found the most truffles on the cliff. Battista took one to Bergamo. It brought 200 lire! I miss you, your brother Vittorio.

The small bits of news were like spoonfuls of honey for her hungry heart.

We cleared stones from the land. Everyone helped. Battista and Vittorio cut down a birch tree and made planks for the

windowsills. Eliana sewed the curtains. Alma helped me dig the
garden. I am watching every lira. I love you, Mama.

Enza could withstand anything, knowing that she was making her
mother's life easier. She was thinking of her when she climbed the
ladder to the supply room above the machines. She was busy loading
her apron with spools of tickets to pin to the finished blouses when she
felt hands against her back. She was thrown against the wall, her hands
pinned behind her.

Enza cried out for help, but the drone of the sewing machines below
drowned out her calls. Feeling a man's hands moving up her legs and
under her skirt, she tried to kick from behind, but lost her footing. She
landed on the floor, her face hitting the uneven planks of wood. She felt
the warm ooze of blood down her face.

"Dago bitch. Now you'll talk to me," she heard Joe Neal growl in her
ear. Enza pulled her hands out of Neal's grasp, flipped herself over, and
buckled her knees, kicking him. He lunged at her and, as she rolled over
to crawl to the ladder, pinned her again.

"*Mai!*" she shouted in Italian. "Never!" she repeated in English.

Months of being ridiculed, shamed, and humiliated by Joe Neal created a fury within her, and with the full force of her body, she threw him
off. She saw the momentary flash of anger in his eyes before he threw
himself back on top of her. His full weight crushed her, and the feel of
his body against her own disgusted her. Enza heard her underskirt rip
as she twisted to get away, but she could not.

"Let her go, Joe Neal!" a voice thundered from behind.

Enza saw Laura on the top rung of the ladder, brandishing a large
pair of scissors from the cutting-room table. "I said, let her go. I'll plunge
these scissors into your back. Move away from her!"

He rolled off.

"Keep your distance. Stay over there." Laura pointed with the blades
of the scissors as he cowered in the corner.

"Come on, Enza. Come down the ladder. You stay there, Joe. And I
mean, stay there," Laura said to him.

Enza stood, reeling from the assault. She took the hem of her apron
and held it to the cut on her face. She made it to the ladder, where she

fell into Laura's arms. Laura helped her down the ladder, step by step, to the waiting arms of her fellow operators, who had gathered at the foot of the ladder.

"Come down out of there, Joe," Laura demanded.

He climbed down the ladder.

"Now get out of here."

The operators protected Enza and hissed as he passed.

*   *   *

Laura stood in the break room. The young women of the night shift filled the room and spilled out into the factory.

"Can everyone hear me?" Laura raised her voice. "Keep your work scissors in your apron pocket. From now on, you travel in pairs to the ladies' room, and take your lunch in groups of three or more. If you are threatened, you must speak up. We all tolerate the comments and whistles, but if anyone puts their hands on you—you are within your rights to strike back. We let them know we have the scissors, and we let them know we will use them."

The operators, most of them teenagers, all foreign born, often didn't speak English. They fared better at this factory than most because of the sheer numbers of Italians, Yugoslavs, Czechs, Greeks, and Jewish girls who had learned to watch out for one another. They trusted Laura to protect them, and to do right by them.

Each poor immigrant girl had a plan in place to survive. Some had brothers or fathers for protection, others, young husbands; but for all of them, the first line of defense was their scissors. The girls gathered and talked strategy: Imogene May Haegelin drafted a letter to management explaining the perils of the night shift; Patte Rackliffe vowed to bring her fiancé and his friends to the factory; Alanna Murphy's brother knew "some people"; Julia Rachel's father was a boxer; Lena Gjonaj's brother-in-law was a cop; and Orea Koontz was a good shot, who owned a pistol and vowed to use it on Joe Neal or any other man who approached her with evil intent.

The operators were bound together by what they were running from—poverty in all its forms, despair, hunger, decimated families—as well as what they hoped to gain. Their imaginations were filled with American treasures: painted houses, boxes of chocolates, bottles of soda pop, white sand beaches, Ferris wheels, rumble seats, silk stockings, and the words *a better life*.

Better meant American. *Better* meant safe, clean, honest, and true. Dreams of every size and description lulled them into restful sleep at night and fueled them through their backbreaking days.

At the end of their shifts, the girls took magnets and pulled stickpins from the cracks in the factory floor, saving every pin, and therefore every penny, for management. Sometimes the silver pins shimmered in the cracks like buried treasure, and the girls imagined there might be something more beneath the wide planks of old wood, something more just for them.

.   .   .

The cut over Enza's eye was not deep, but it angled above her eyebrow like an apostrophe. Laura entered with the first-aid kit from the office.

"That's it. I had the office send for Mr. Walker. He's on his way. They told him everything." Laura threw open the metal kit and poured rubbing alcohol on a square of gauze.

"Was he angry?" Enza asked.

"It's the middle of the night. He wasn't happy." Laura reached over the sink to swab Enza's wound. "This is going to hurt."

"I'll do it." Enza said. She took the gauze and dabbed the cut.

"Why don't you cry? You'll feel better."

"I'm not sad."

"But he hurt you."

"No, you came in time. He's been after me for months. I'm lucky you were there," Enza said, but there was no mistaking the anger in her voice. "How soon can we get out of here?"

"We can leave right now, if you have enough money saved. Do you think you can get by? Because if you can, now is the moment. We just got paid, so I'm flush. I'll resign the minute Mr. Walker gets here. I'll need an hour or so to go home and pack. We can get a short-term room at the Y and hunt for jobs from there. We'll split everything right down the middle, fair and square," Laura promised. "Go home and pack. I'll meet you on the sidewalk in front of three-eighteen Adams Street by eleven a.m. Does that give you enough time?"

"Yes!" Tears sprang to Enza's eyes.

"*Now* you cry?" Laura said in disbelief.

"Happy tears," Enza said, wiping them on her handkerchief. She decided, for the first time in six years, to take her last paycheck from the factory to provide a foothold for her new life instead of sending it home to the mountain. This was the day she had learned her value. She would be worth nothing if she continued to take the abuse in the factory and on Adams Street. The old ways were finished, and not for one moment would she miss them.

As Enza walked back to Adams Street, the haze over Hoboken hung like a bolt of thick charcoal wool in the early light of morning. She saw a group of street urchins, hungry, barefoot, covered in the ash-gray desperation of poverty, playing in the streets with an old rusty tin drum, which they rolled down the street with sticks.

There were times when she stopped and bought bread for the children, or sweet rolls, or hot pretzels. This morning, Enza stopped at the corner and bought a large sack of oranges. They were expensive, but Enza wanted to do something special, since she wouldn't be here on Christmas. Enza waved to the children. They ran to her, gathering around her like pigeons pecking for crumbs, extending their open hands.

On this gray winter morning, on the brown street, the only flashes of color came from the oranges, bright and full like the sun itself.

As she handed out the fruit, Enza imagined that these young faces were her own brothers and sisters. She saw Eliana in a girl with a torn brown apron, Vittorio in the tallest boy of the group, who went barefoot even in the cold, and finally Stella, in the little girl with the black curly hair, left in her sister's care, although the older girl couldn't be more than eight years old. Enza fought back tears when she thought about her baby sister, and how the little girls who wandered the streets of Hoboken were reminiscent of Stella's spirit. They were unlucky, and so was Stella.

One by one, she placed an orange in every outstretched pair of hands, a small sign of hope in a place where there had been none for so long, the children couldn't remember what it felt like to receive a treat. Elated, the children shouted, "*Grazie mille,*" a million thanks, for one small thing, one bright, sweet orange apiece. They would eat the pulp, the juice, and the peel.

. . . .

As she packed, Enza felt the full weight of having spent an irreplaceable stretch of her youth in a place undeserving of it. The bandage over her eye tugged at her skin, but she was already thinking of the scar she'd carry, the marker that signaled the end of her old life and the start of a new one. Enza refolded her clothes neatly, arranging them in her satchel. She flipped the top of the duffel and buttoned it, pulled on her sweater and then her coat.

The basement door swung open, surprising Enza and filling her with a dread she knew she had felt for the last time. She smiled to herself.

Signora Buffa stood at the top of the stairs. "What do you think you're doing?"

"I'm leaving your house, Signora." Enza climbed the stairs and pushed past her.

"No, you're not! You can't!" Signora barked.

"My debt to you is paid in full. I prepared every meal, scrubbed every dish, washed, hung, pressed, and folded every article of clothing for three households and for you for six years," Enza said calmly.

"Make my lunch," Signora sneered.

"Make your own lunch, Signora."

"Enza, I am warning you, I will report you!"

"I already have my papers. You can't compromise them."

"You ungrateful girl—"

"Maybe. But there's plenty of that to go around here." Enza went through the kitchen to the living room, buttoning her coat with one hand as she went.

"What do you mean? Answer me!" Signora sounded weak and pathetic. "I said, answer me."

Enza realized her father was right: a bully backs down when you stand up to her.

Enza heard the footsteps of Dora, Jenny, and Gina on the stairs behind her. They lined up like train cars, Gina carrying her infant, Dora balancing her toddler on her hip, Jenny tightening the belt on her robe, long past the appropriate hour to be wearing one.

"She's leaving us!" Anna moaned.

"You can't go!" Dora sneered.

"The diapers!" Gina groused. "Who will do the diapers?"

"You were to bake bread today," Gina complained. "Where are you going?"

"None of your business." Enza turned to Anna. "Signora, you live in a tenement, and yet you behave like the entitled rich. You have airs of privilege without the pedigree or education that define them. You've indulged your sons, and to your surprise, they married shrews—"

Gina lunged forward. "Who are you calling names?"

Enza held up her hand, and Gina stepped back. Enza continued, leveling her gaze upon Anna: "You've earned an old age of misery. Your daughters-in-law are lazy." She turned to the women of the house. "You breed children in this house like animals, and expect me to cook, clean, and pick up after all of them. Now it's your turn," she said as she pushed the front door open.

"You get back here right now, Enza," Signora Buffa shouted.

Enza walked through the door. "You're a drunk, and it's no wonder your husband stays in West Virginia."

"He's working! You ungrateful girl!"

"You kick a dog long enough, and eventually it will bite. I would say thank you, but for all these years I have never heard you utter the words. So let me say this to you for the last time, Signora: 'Stupid girl. Stupid, stupid girl.' How does that make you feel, Signora? Ah. Now you know." Enza looked up at the others. "Now you *all* know."

Enza walked out on to the porch, leaving her life of indentured servitude behind, the awful women, the howling babies, the filthy cribs, the stagnant baby bottles, mounds of dirty diapers, the dank, dark basement, and the broken cot.

Laura Heery beamed as Enza skimmed down the stairs with her duffel. Soon the porch behind her filled with the Buffa women, who called out to Enza and over one another in high-pitched squawks:

Puttana!

Strega!

Pazza!

Porca i miserable!

Doors opened up and down Adams Street as prying eyes peeked

out. Neighbor women hung out the windows, turning toward the cater-
wauling at number 318. Still others took seats on their stoops, ingesting
the theatrics with relish, happy for once that the misery visited upon
this street was not their own.

Enza felt the first delicious rush of freedom. Good, kind Laura
looped her arm through Enza's, carrying her suitcase and hatbox with
the other.

The Buffa women continued to call the girls names from the porch
as the two friends walked proudly together up the block in lockstep.
As the neighbors joined in the taunts, Enza and Laura deflected their
curses. They held their heads high, and kept moving, as the insults fell
around them like grounded arrows, missing their marks.

As they made the turn off Adams Street onto the Grand Concourse,
finally free, they smiled, broke into a run, and didn't stop until they had
reached the ferry landing and boarded the boat for the quick ride across
the river to Manhattan.

A CHOCOLATE TRUFFLE
Un Tartufo di Cioccolata

There was no place more serene on Christmas morning than New York City; the streets were so quiet, it was as if they were carpeted in velvet.

Ciro maneuvered the repair cart into the carriage house on Hester Street. He removed his sleep roll, lunch tin, and a box of chocolate truffles he'd purchased in Astoria before he headed back to Mulberry Street.

Carla and Remo attended Christmas mass at the church of Saint Francis Xavier, after which they took the train to visit Signora's cousins in Brooklyn.

Ciro unlocked the door of the shop and went to his room. He laid out his best shirt, pants, socks, and underwear on the cot and removed his signet ring, placing it on the nightstand. He took a fresh towel and went upstairs, to the alcove off the kitchen. As the water filled in the four-legged tub, he shaved, careful not to nick himself. He brushed his teeth with a paste of baking soda and salt, rinsing thoroughly. He took off his clothes, stacked them in a neat pile, climbed into the tub, and, beginning with his face, neck, and hair, lathered up and scrubbed down his body, careful to take the small brush and clean under his nails, down to his feet, where he spent extra time on his heels. Proper fitting shoes had changed his feet—no calluses or blisters, even though he was on his feet thirteen hours a day. If Ciro had learned anything, proper fitting shoes, made with good leather, could change a man's life, or at least his ability to withstand long hours on his feet.

He emptied the tub and scrubbed it down, leaving it spotless and dry, as though he hadn't bathed in it. This was a habit from the convent. Wherever Ciro went, including the cart with his sleep roll, he neatened up after himself, leaving the premises better than he'd found them. This was also the mark of the orphan, who never wanted to appear to use anything beyond the portion assigned, including bathwater.

Ciro picked up his clothes, wrapped the towel around his waist, and went quickly back down the stairs to his room, where he dressed, careful to lay the collar flat on his shirt and make the knot in his silk tie square. He placed his gold signet ring back on his finger. He pulled on his jacket, then his coat. Finally, he grabbed the chocolates.

On the ferry to New Jersey, he sat back on the bench and took in the Hudson River. This morning, the foamy white waves of the water matched the overhead sky. He remembered how Stream Vò had poured in a waterfall over the mountain, then thinned out in the distant valley, flat and gray, like the scribble of a lead pencil. He wondered if anyone had thought to make cleansing mud to wash down the church statues with ingredients dug from the bottom of the Hudson River. Memories of Iggy, his short cigarettes and happy laughter, made him smile.

The streets of Hoboken were filled with people on the move this Christmas morning. Freshly scrubbed, his clothes neatly pressed, Ciro stood out, looking robust and healthy in a neighborhood where the people were anything but. He moved through the crowd, checking the numbers on every building until he found 318 Adams Street. He climbed the steps and rang the bell.

A woman came to the door. She looked at Ciro through the screen, which was odd, as it was winter, and the screen door had not yet been taken down. There must not be a man on the premises to do the chores, he thought.

"*Ciao*, Signora."

Anna Buffa smiled at him. Her shirtwaist skirt and blouse looked as though she had slept in them. He noticed that she was missing two teeth from the side of her mouth. Ciro could see she once had been attractive, but no more. "*Buon Natale*."

"*Buon Natale*, Signora. I am looking for Enza Ravanelli." When Ciro said her name aloud, his voice caught. Weeks of preparation had brought him to her doorstep. He had broken off his relationship with Felicitá, put money in the bank, and was ready to court her with the dream of marriage, when and if that was her desire. He'd thought of every conversation they had, and reread the letter she had written to him in response to his, in which he had begged her to be patient. Now it was he who couldn't wait to see her and tell her his feelings.

"Who are you looking for?" Signora Buffa asked.

"Enza Ravanelli." Ciro repeated her name loudly. "Is she here?"

Anna's smile faded. "She doesn't live here."

"I'm sorry, I must have the wrong house."

"You have the right house."

"*Va bene.* Do you know where she is?"

"I don't know who you are."

"I'm Ciro Lazzari."

"She never mentioned you."

"Could you tell me where she's gone?"

"She went back to Italy."

"Italy?" Ciro's eyes widened in disbelief.

"Packed up and left. Just like that. She owes me rent too." Signora Buffa eyed the box of candy.

"When did she leave?"

"Weeks and weeks ago. It was such a scene. I don't remember. She screamed at me, upset my daughters-in-law. Disrespectful. An awful, awful girl. She had been stealing from me for months. I was glad to see her go."

"That doesn't sound like Enza."

"You don't know her like I do. I had to throw her out. She had men in this house at all hours. A real *puttana*. A disgusting pig of a girl, really."

Fury rose within Ciro to hear Enza described in that way, but he could see that the old woman was drunk, and no protest on his part would have even registered. Besides, he was too devastated to think of anything but the love he had lost because he hadn't expressed it in time. He had missed his moment with Enza, and there was no retrieving it. She had made her demands clear, but he was too late.

Ciro turned to go down the steps.

"You want a drink?"

"Excuse me?"

"Come in for a drink." She opened the door wide. "It's Christmas." Inside, the house was a disheveled mess. She ran her hand down her thigh and lifted the hem of her skirt to show her leg.

Ciro leaped down the stairs and onto the street. He didn't look back at the strange woman in the yellow house; instead he looked around to see if there was anyone who might know what had happened to Enza Ravanelli. He approached a neighbor, who turned away, and another who did the same. He stood there for a long time, until the beggar children surrounded him.

"*Dolci! Dolci!*" they cried when they saw the blue box covered in foil. More children gathered around, until they had encircled Ciro. He opened the box of chocolates, and one by one he placed a chocolate candy, wrapped in paper, in each outstretched hand, until he had given away every single sweet.

A girl with wide-set brown eyes looked up at Ciro, holding her chocolate. "Are you Santa Claus?" she asked before running off with the candy.

Ciro buried his hands in his pockets and made his way back to the ferry. If Enza had fled Signora Buffa's house, why hadn't she come to Mulberry Street? Had she returned to the mountain without him?

*   *   *

Laura pushed through the glass doors of the Horn & Hardart's Automat on Thirty-eighth and Broadway, scanning the bustling eatery for Enza.

Enza and Laura were regulars at the Automat, centrally located in midtown, convenient for most of the random jobs they'd been picking up through leads, tips, and advertisements in the paper.

"It's brutal out there." Laura sat down next to Enza, peeling off her gloves and coat. "It's freezing. Nice new year so far. Nineteen seventeen, the year of the tundra."

"Anything from the agency?" Enza asked. The girls had registered with Renee M. Dandrow Associates before Christmas, looking for work.

"How do you feel about scullery work?"

"When you taught me English, you never once said the word *scullery*."

Laura laughed. "I didn't teach you *old* English. Scullery is kitchen work. Not rolling dough and making soup, but the rough stuff. Scrubbing pots, mopping, that sort of thing."

"I can do that," Enza said.

"Good, because we're booked to work through the weekend at a private home on Carnegie Hill on the Upper East Side." Laura spread the newspaper want ads on the table.

"What are they paying?"

"Fifty cents per shift," Laura replied. "And we're lucky it came through, since rent is due on Friday. You want to split a slice of pie? That's always in the budget."

"Would you like coffee with it?"

"Please," Laura said without taking her eyes off the newspaper.

The scent of chicory, cinnamon, and cocoa gave the bright, shiny eatery a feeling of home. The coffee was a nickel, the pie was ten cents, and the girls left full. There were no waitresses at the Automat, which was self-serve.

Enza paid for the pie and coffee, scooped up four nickels from the bin, and placed two in the glass slot outside the serving wall. The serving wall was filled with single portions of everything from macaroni and cheese to a single black-and-white-iced cookie. The customer chose his portion, dropped the nickels in, and took the serving out himself. She grabbed two forks, took them with the pie over to their table, and returned to pour the coffee. The white ceramic cups and saucers with their gay green borders always managed to lift her spirits. She balanced the cups on saucers, black for Laura, with cream in her own.

"We're doing fine, Enza," Laura said when Enza served her coffee. "We've got a room at the Y, and we're working."

Enza was worried that she wouldn't be able to send money home if they didn't get permanent jobs. "Any sewing jobs?"

"I have a feeling Marcia Guzzi is going to come through at Matera Tailoring."

"And I put our names in at Samantha Gabriela Brown," Enza said. "They make children's clothes."

"Yeah, but they don't pay. We can't do day shifts for fifty cents. And they don't give piecework until you've been there six months."

"Maybe we could talk to the desk manager at the Y and get the room fee down," Enza said.

"I know the Y isn't plush, but it's better than the basement on Adams Street. Or my four-to-a-room bedroom in Jersey."

"I don't mean to sound ungrateful," Enza said softly.

"We're wait-listed at the good boardinghouses—something will come through. Let's look at this as an adventure instead of a chore. All of it. Being poor, looking for work, being scared, and going hungry is all part of the adventure. We've never been scullery, and now we have the opportunity. This will be educational. We'll turn hell into *swell*." Laura laughed.

* * *

Enza and Laura left the Y in midtown, bundled in scarves, gloves, coats, and wool cloche hats pulled low, and headed up Fifth Avenue on foot.

The mansions on Fifth Avenue looked like a row of top hats, as the kerosene streetlamps lit by the doormen threw shadows on their facades. Enza and Laura walked in and out of the pools of light under the entrance awnings, feeling a blast of warmth from the small portable coal ovens positioned to keep the wealthy warm as they walked through the polished brass entrance doors and into the motorcars waiting to take them out on the town.

Enza and Laura observed the shift change in the mansions, as black maids left through the service entrance and the night staff entered, replacing them. Irish maids made their way east to the el train for their commute home. The wind was bitterly cold, whistling through the city blocks, creating errant gusts that hit Enza and Laura like the crack of a whip as they crossed the streets.

Enza and Laura found 7 East Ninety-first Street easily. Lit from within, the Italian Renaissance mansion dazzled as torches lit the street, throwing golden light on to the entrance. The elegant home had a particular Roman opulence, and yet, like most of the new buildings born of the latest architecture trends in the city, it seemed courant and fresh, or maybe it was the people who lived inside that imbued the homes with those qualities. Semicircular arched windows were embedded in the eggshell-colored limestone like jewels. Thick mahogany castle doors, arched and set with iron bindings, were thrown open, festooned with garlands of fresh cedar and bunches of cranberries and walnuts. Enza marveled that simple fruit and nuts, available for free everywhere on her mountain, became embellishments for the gentry of New York City. She would remember to write to her mother about the decorations.

"This is it. The James Burden mansion." Laura scanned the notes she had made for them. "We are to enter from the carriage drop door in the back and ask for Helen Fay. She's in charge of the house."

"This is not a house. It's a palazzo," Enza said, taking it in.

"It's a palazzo with a kitchen. Let's go."

Enza followed Laura through the service entrance. Laura asked the butler for directions, and he sent them through a small hallway. No sooner were they in the service hallway when the girls were forced to back against the wall to make room for a team of waiters, who passed by carrying enormous flower arrangements, Tuscan urns stuffed with fuchsia peonies, red roses, and green apples. Laura and Enza looked at one another in disbelief.

As the butler opened the doors to the rotunda, the girls looked inside. The opulent foyer, the granite floor, the limestone walls, and even the stairs were pearl white, set off by a grand staircase that resembled ivory keys on a piano. The wide Hauteville marble steps twirled in an S shape up to a landing with an ornate gold-leafed railing. The banister railing was lined with black velvet; Enza imagined it would be like holding a gloved hand for guests making their way to the party upstairs.

The urns were placed on pedestals throughout the atrium, vibrant shots of color against the pale marble. Crystal hurricane sleeves covered white pillar candles made of beeswax that threw warm, fractured light onto the marble, making the atrium glow.

"Where do they get peonies in winter?" Laura whispered as they proceeded to the kitchen.

The kitchen was as wide and deep as the main factory floor at Meta Walker. Long aluminum tables inset with wooden chopping blocks were situated down the center of the room like a racetrack. Sleek pots and pans hung overhead. The long wall was a series of smooth griddles attended by a staff in white, headed by a chef who wore a toque. Beyond the kitchen was an assembly room, where trays of fine china waited to be filled before serving. Off the assembly room, the work doors were propped open to reveal a courtyard, where a Negro attendant in a white apron and wool hat hand-cranked ice cream in an aged wooden barrel. His warm breath exhaled in the cold looked like puffs of smoke as he operated the crank.

The kitchen ran like the greased gears of a sewing machine, one operation leading to the next without a glitch. The workers spoke little, coordinating their work via a series of hand signals.

The first person Enza and Laura met was Emma Fogarty, a no-nonsense young woman around their age with light brown braids twisted up on her head, bright blue eyes, and a nondescript figure hidden behind a brown cotton smock, with wooden clogs on her feet and red woolen knee socks on her legs. She wrote on a blackboard visible throughout the kitchen.

"We've been sent from the Dandrow agency," Laura said.

"Both of ye?"

"Yes, ma'am."

"You're slop and wash. I'll show you."

"We're supposed to report to Helen Fay."

"You'll never lay eyes on Helen Fay. She's upstairs, fanning the napkins."

"I'm Laura Heery, and this is Enza Ravanelli."

"Emma Fogarty. I'm the kitchen captain."

Emma pointed to a coat closet, and the girls took off their outer clothes. She handed them each a smock like the one she wore, which they pulled on as they followed Emma through the catacombs of the kitchen. Along a long hallway, floor-to-ceiling closets with small windows revealed stacks of dishes, cups, tureens, bowls, and glassware.

Emma led the girls down a dark flight of wooden steps to a dimly lit room, in which a large wooden table was surrounded by stools. On the far wall, the mouth of a dumbwaiter sat open, stacked with empty trays. Under the dumbwaiter was a metal trough with a shaft leading into a hole in the floor for scraps. A series of deep sinks with movable nozzles attached to the faucets created an L shape beyond the trough. Wooden dowels, on which dishes could drain before they were dried, separated the sinks.

"This is a real affair tonight. Two hundred people. You gotta move fast, and you gotta be careful. We're using the china from Russia, some czar sent it when the Burdens got hitched." She held up her hand. "Don't ask. It's got gold leafing. Helen Fay will check for scratches, and she'll do a count tomorrow when the shelves are refilled. So don't break any. You two do the slopping—that's cleaning the dishes before washing—then you're gonna wash them—if you run out of hot water, you let me know; sometimes we do—and then you let 'em dry and then buff with cotton rags, they're on the shelf over there. Then you're going to put them in chamois sleeves—never, ever stack the plates without the chamois, or they'll throw me in the furnace. When the party's over, we'll run 'em up the dumbwaiter to the storage closets."

Enza's head swam. Emma spoke as fast as the click of typewriter keys. Enza barely understood anything she said.

"Got it?" Emma asked.

"Yes, absolutely," said Laura.

"I'll be up in the kitchen if you need me. It's dead right now, but the action will start in about an hour, when cocktails are served. Just keep the dumbwaiter moving. Don't hold it down here. The last dishwasher almost got shot by the butler, he got so mad when he couldn't send glasses down. Backup is the enemy here, girls." Emma went to the dumbwaiter and yanked the pulley. The gold trays ascended smoothly in the hand-operated elevator.

"Thank you," Laura and Enza said.

"Don't thank me. You'll hate me with a divine fury when you see the dishes you have to do. But that's what this is. The rich enjoy life, and we clean up after 'em. Just the luck of the draw, I guess."

As the dirty dishes descended, Laura and Enza quickly created their own system to move things along. Just as they had in the factory, they figured out a way to make the most of their time. Laura cleared the food with one hand, giving the plate to Enza, who put it in soapy water, scrubbed, and then to another sink for rinse, then dry.

In between courses, they were able to keep up because of the time allotted the guests to eat. The trick, the girls learned, was to let the dishes stay on the drying racks until they could get to them. The time came when one course was served and the other was bussed down the dumbwaiter.

As hard as the work was, Enza and Laura did not complain. They had both seen worse, and there was something about working in a mansion that made the work seem more pleasant. Maybe it was just the opulence of the candlelit rotunda, the weightless beauty of hand-painted Russian china, or the idea of sharing a space with peonies in winter that elevated their moods. They couldn't be sure. All they knew is that they were together; they could talk, scheme, and dream as they worked through the scullery chores.

Enza dried the dinner plates carefully, then slid them into their blue chamois sleeves and stacked them. She made a note of how many plates were in the stack. A tray cluttered with dessert plates was lowered in the dumbwaiter, and she reached in to remove the tray. She stopped when she heard singing, a rich tenor voice, with a full timbre. The notes sailed down the dumbwaiter as though they had been wrapped in velvet: the lyrics of *Tosca* in the language of her birth.

Amaro o sol per te m'erail morire

"That's Mr. Puccini, playing for the singers," Emma Fogarty said from behind her. Laura lifted the tray out of the dumbwaiter.

"He's at the party?"

"You just washed his dish," Emma said. "He's playing on a Steinway baby grand in the music room. Alessia Frangela and Alfonso Mancuso are singing duets under the Bonanno mural. Maria Martucci is playing the harp. The guests are gathered around them like they're singing around a campfire."

"My old boss used to play Caruso singing *Tosca*."

"I can't send you up. You're scullery," Emma said. "But you know what? If you go upstairs to the dish closets, I'll open the flaps on the dumbwaiter, and you'll be right under the music."

The girls loaded up trays with china and went up the small staircase. Emma led them to the dish closets. She put down the dishes and opened the latch on the wooden cubby.

"Go ahead, lean in. That's how I eavesdrop on the Burdens."

Enza put her head into the dumbwaiter, resting her hands on the trim. Puccini's crystal clear notes sailed down. This time it was like being in the room; the volume was perfect.

Laura sorted the dishes on the shelves as Puccini and his singers serenaded the crowd. She watched as Enza listened. Her head bowed reverently, Enza took in the notes, the chords, the sweep of the music. It was as if the sound filled her up and her body floated overhead, as light as meringue.

Enza couldn't wait to write to Mama and tell her of her stroke of luck.

This is my Italy, she thought. The power and beauty of the antiquities, the detailed frescoes, the imposing statuaries carved of milk white granite, Don Martinelli's hammered gold chalice, the glorious tones of the music, the Italy of Puccini and Verdi, Caruso and Toscanini, not the Italy of the shattered spirits in Hoboken and the drunken, desperate Anna Buffa. This was the Italy that fed her soul, where hope was restored and broken hearts were mended in the hands of great artists.

For the first time since she had come to America, Enza felt at home. In that moment, she suddenly realized how to marry American ambition to Italian artistry. Both had nurtured her and helped her grow. That night, Puccini's music stoked the fire of her ambition, and she felt her determination rise anew.

When Puccini finished the aria, the crowd erupted in applause. Enza put her hands in the dumbwaiter and applauded as well.

"He can't hear you," Emma Fogarty said.

"But I have to honor him." Enza turned and faced Laura and Emma.

"Send up the dumbwaiter," Emma said.

Enza cranked the chain, and the tray rose to the upper floor.

"Wash and dry the crystal for the digestifs, and you girls can call it a night." Emma checked her pocket watch. "Or morning, as it will be shortly. Once the guests leave, and I lock down the kitchen, I got a hot bath calling my name."

"You have a bathtub?" Laura marveled.

"I live at the Katharine House in the Village. We have tubs. And a library. I like to read. And two meals a day. I like to eat."

Enza and Laura looked at one another. "How did you get in?"

"Like everything else in this city. I got the lowdown on the crosstown bus."

"Which line?" Enza asked.

"Any. Just look for girls our age. It's a circuit."

"We applied to the Katharine House, but no cigar," Laura told her. "We're at the Y."

"You'll get in somewhere. You'll just have to wait for the vacancies every spring," Emma told them. "Wedding fever hits, and the mighty fall. Come April the girls dump out of the boardinghouses like cold bathwater. Rooms galore. You'll get your pick. What are you here to do?"

"To make a living," Enza said.

"No, I mean your dream scheme. What do you really want to be?"

"We're seamstresses."

"Then you need an arty boardinghouse. I'd try for the Milbank. They take the playwrights, the dancers, the actresses, and the designers. You know, the crafty girls. You want me to put in a good word for you?"

"Really?" Laura said. "You can you help us get into the Milbank?"

"Sure. I'll talk to the house mother."

Emma paid them cash, a dollar each instead of the fifty cents they had been promised, which she dutifully recorded in the kitchen log. They were paid extra because they hadn't broken any dishes and got the work done without annoying the butler. The girls couldn't believe the windfall.

The scent of beeswax, fresh from the extinguished candles, filled the service entrance as Enza and Laura made their way to the street, buttoning their coats and pulling on their gloves. They ignored their aching necks, shoulders, and feet, floating home instead on the notion of their own dreams.

As they walked down Fifth Avenue, they said not a word. They walked for blocks and blocks in the quiet knowledge that something had shifted that evening; a scullery job had proved to be a turning point.

As the sun pulled up behind Fifth Avenue, the girls were warmed by the idea of it but not by its rays; the air around them was still freezing cold. Shimmering icicles clung to the barren trees that lined the avenue, looking like silver lamé evening gloves. The sidewalks, treacherous with ice, now looked as though they were sprinkled with diamond dust, and the plowed drifts of dingy gray snow took on a lavender tint in the early light.

"Automat?" Laura said as they reached Thirty-eighth Street.

"Pie?" Enza asked.

"Two slices this morning. We can afford it."

"And we deserve it," Enza agreed.

17

A SEWING NEEDLE

Un Ago da Cucire

Trumpet vines cascaded down the drainpipe in shots of bold orange and soft green like fine silk tassels against the freshly pointed coral bricks. Purple hyacinths spilled out of antique white marble Roman urns on either side of the black-lacquered double entrance doors of the Milbank House at 11 West Tenth Street in Greenwich Village.

The floor-to-ceiling formal windows off the entrance stairs were appropriately festooned in layers of white silk sheers, the pale gold jacquard draperies drawn back to let in the soft light of the tree-lined street. There was not a card, a sign, a communal mail slot, or any other indication that the Milbank House was anything but an elegant brownstone owned by a single family of incredible wealth.

Tucked in the middle of a wide, tree-lined block of opulent homes, anchored by a lavish Episcopal church on the corner of Fifth Avenue and the charming Patchin Place houses across Sixth Avenue on the other, this block had character and whimsy, a rare combination in New York City at the turn of the progressive century.

The Milbank House was a double brownstone with twenty-six bedrooms, fourteen bathrooms, a formal library, a dining room, a deep garden, an enormous basement kitchen with dumbwaiter, and a beau parlor. It was owned and operated by the Ladies' Christian Union, who provided young women without family or connections in New York City with room and board for a reasonable fee.

Emma Fogarty had stopped by and bragged to the house mother about her talented, hardworking friends, one an Italian immigrant, the other a feisty Irish girl, both of whom needed a proper address to pursue their dreams as seamstresses to the upper class, along the park on Fifth Avenue, and in the theatrical houses of Broadway.

Breakfast and dinner were included in the weekly rent, and there was a wringer washing machine as well as drying racks in the basement. But more important than all these lovely features of gracious living was the camaraderie of the young residents, who aspired to better lives on the wings of their talent and creativity. Finally, Laura and Enza were with like-minded peers, who understood their feelings and drive.

Miss Caroline DeCoursey, the house mother, was an elegant white-haired lady, petite and well bred, who took an instant liking to Laura Heery; Miss DeCoursey's mother was Irish, and from the same county as the Heery family.

Enza and Laura were led to the fourth floor, where the wide hallway was lit by a skylight. A series of closets lined the wall, each with a simple brass handle. Miss DeCoursey opened one of the closets. Inside was a long, deep storage shelf at the top for hats, a hanging rod with empty wooden hangers, and enough floor space for shoes and storage of suitcases and duffels.

"You take this one, Miss Ravanelli," Miss DeCoursey said. "And this one is yours, Miss Heery," she said, opening another set of doors.

The girls looked at one another, unable to believe their good fortune. Closets! Enza had lived out of her duffel since leaving Italy, while Laura shared a cupboard and hooks with her sisters and cousins in her family home.

"Follow me," Miss DeCoursey said, unlocking a door in an alcove nearest the closets. She pushed the door open, and there was the most beautiful room Enza had ever seen. The ceiling sloped under the dormer, and a fireplace and mirror occupied the center of the room. Light poured in the window, reflecting off the buffed walnut floors.

Two plump beds were made up with soft cotton coverlets, a night-stand set between them with a reading lamp. A desk under the window and another by the door would give each girl plenty of room. The calm simplicity of the decoration, the scent of lemon wax, and the fresh breeze coming in off the garden through the open window made the room seem like home.

"I thought two seamstresses might like a room with good light, even though it's on the fourth floor. Most of the girls prefer being on the second floor—"

"No, no, it's the most beautiful room I've ever seen," Enza insisted.

"We'll never be able to thank you enough!" Laura added.

"Keep your rooms neat, and don't dry your stockings in the common bath." Miss DeCoursey handed them each a key. "We'll see you at dinner, then," she said, closing the door behind her.

Laura threw herself onto one bed, and Enza did the same on the other. "Did you hear that?" Laura asked.

"What?"

"That was the sound of the dinner bell . . . and our luck changing." Laura laughed.

* * *

Ciro figured Luigi could handle the shoe repair cart alone for a few hours. Business was brisk but in no way overwhelming by the docks of lower Manhattan, where the construction workers took lunch by the pier.

Ciro decided to walk back to Little Italy through Greenwich Village. He liked to walk through the winding streets in the warmth of spring, taking in the Georgian-style homes on Jane Street, with their double set of stairs, and the Renaissance town houses on Charles Street, with their wrought-iron balconies and small private parks behind airy gates filled with urns of yellow daffodils and purple iris.

Beautiful homes soothed him. Maybe it was the connection to his days as a handyman, when he'd painted and planted at San Nicola, but whatever the reason, manicured gardens and well-tended homes reassured him, giving him a sense of order in a world where there was little.

As Ciro passed Our Lady of Pompeii Church, a wedding party spilled out onto the sidewalk. A dazzling brand-new Nash Roadster was parked in front, with a bouquet of white roses nestled in tulle and streaming with satin ribbons anchored to the hood ornament.

Ciro stopped to take in the convertible, midnight blue with a red leather interior. The sleek lines of the polished wood and gold brass buttons were enough to make any young man swoon. The car was almost as gorgeous as the most beautiful woman he had ever seen.

As the organist played the recessional, the guests poured out of the church onto the sidewalk. A lovely collection of bridesmaids, carrying long stalks of calla lilies, wearing wide silk headbands peppered with crystals and floor-length gowns in soft pink chiffon, lined up on the stairs.

Ciro took in their faces, recognizing them from the neighborhood— southern Italian girls with dark eyes, their hair worn in elaborate upsweeps of serpentine braids. Their figures, delicate and curved, were as smooth as porcelain teacups. They reminded him of Enza Ravanelli and how she looked on the roof at Mulberry Street. He put her out of his mind as quickly as he'd conjured her; he was not a man who longed for what he could not have, or specifically, what he had lost.

The bride and groom emerged from the top of the stairs, showered by rice and confetti. Ciro was astonished to see Felicitá Cassio, her veil of tulle trailing behind her, in a gown of palest white. As ethereal as smoke, she looked out over the crowd and smiled at the guests. He had not seen her since last Christmas, before he'd traveled to Hoboken, when he told her they had to end their easygoing relationship once and for all.

Felicitá had just married an attractive, compact, dark Sicilian, who left his bride with a quick kiss on the cheek to have his picture taken with his parents.

Ciro turned to go, but it was too late. Felicitá had locked eyes with him, an expression of shock crossing her face, which she quickly masked with a warm bridal smile. She waved to Ciro. His fine manners and good convent training, ingrained so deeply, wouldn't allow him to walk away without paying his respects.

Felicitá handed off her bouquet to her maid of honor like a necessary nuisance. Ciro looked down at his coveralls, smudged with smears of oil and chalk from his work. He was hardly properly dressed to greet his old girlfriend in her wedding gown. Felicitá's satin gown, cut on the bias, skimmed the sleek lines of her body. As she moved, the sheen of the satin hugged her curves. Ciro was hit with a powerful wave of desire.

"You just got off work," she murmured, knowing the effect her sultry voice had always had on him.

"I was down on the pier. Congratulations," Ciro said. "I didn't know."

"They announced the banns several weeks ago. Since you never go to church . . ." She allowed her voice to trail off flirtatiously. "I meant to write and tell you," she added.

"You like to write about as much as I do. It doesn't matter. I'm happy for you. You're a beautiful bride. Is he the match?"

She looked down at her satin shoes, trimmed in marabou. "Yeah. He owns half of Palermo."

"Ah, a Sicilian prince. It may take you a year or two, but I think you can turn him into a king."

"My mother did it for my father, so I guess I can too," she said, not looking forward to the task that lay ahead.

Ciro had turned to go when Felicitá stopped him. "You gonna give that girl from the Alps that ring I always wanted?"

"Pray for me, will you?" Ciro smiled.

* * *

The library at the Milbank House was a beautifully appointed room in the English style, decorated in shades of sage green and coral with glass-fronted barrister bookshelves and a grand piano, angled between the front windows.

Eileen Parrelli, an eighteen-year-old prodigy from Connecticut, ran scales on the piano and sang. Her red curls and freckles indicated her mother's Irish lineage, but her voice was pure operatic Italian, from her father's side.

Enza sat down on a chair with a notebook and pen, listening while Eileen practiced. She could not believe how much her life had changed in a few short weeks.

No one, except Laura and maybe the other girls who occupied these rooms, would ever understand what admittance to the boardinghouse meant to her. The last thing that Enza wanted was to lose her room at the Milbank House. Laura and she needed jobs, and not just any temporary position. They needed jobs that would assure them a steady salary.

As Eileen finished her exercises, Enza went to the secretary. She placed paper and envelopes on the desk; then she pulled two square swatches out of a muslin pouch, one of black velvet embroidered in gold, the other, double-backed pink silk in a fleur-de-lis design of seed pearls and small crystals. Enza checked out the spelling in the library dictionary as she went.

> *To Whom It May Concern:*
>
> *Enclosed please find two sewing samples for your perusal. Enza Ravanelli and Laura Heery are experienced machine operators, but also pattern makers, seamstresses, and most excellent trim and beading specialists.*
>
> *We have extensive knowledge of the stories of the opera, plots, and characters, due to repeated exposure to the phonograph records of Signor Enrico Caruso.*
>
> *If you would like to meet with us regarding potential positions with your organization, please write to us at the Milbank House, 11 West Tenth Street, New York City.*
>
> *Thank you.*
>
> *Very sincerely yours,*
> *Enza Ravanelli and Laura Heery*

* * *

Ciro made a decision in the spring of 1917, no different from other Italians on long-term work visas. He decided to go to war. Without a sweetheart to keep him stateside, he decided to see the world and do his bit.

The U.S. Army recruitment office on West Twentieth Street was a temporary storefront with an American flag in the dusty window. Inside, a makeshift office operation with temporary desks and rolling stools made up one of the hundreds of official recruitment offices, compliments of the passage of the Selective Service Act.

Ciro met Luigi outside before they entered. A long line of young men snaked around the block, most of them dark-haired like Luigi.

"I didn't tell Pappina," Luigi said.

"Why not?"

"She doesn't want me to go. She thinks I'm slow on my feet and will get my head blown off."

"She's probably right."

"But I want to fight for this country. I want to get my citizenship, and then Pappina will have hers."

"Are you going to marry before we go?"

"Yeah. Will you be my best man?"

"I've never been asked a question with more enthusiasm."

"Sorry. I have a lot on my mind. I don't like doctors." He whispered, "They squeeze the *noci*."

"I know all about it."

"It's barbaric, that's what it is."

Ciro chuckled. If Luigi thought the physical was barbaric, what would he think of war itself? Once inside, the men's applications were taken, and they lined up to go inside to see the doctor. Luigi and Ciro undressed down to their undershorts and waited in line. More than a few young men were asked to leave, when an infirmity was diagnosed that prevented them from serving. Some of the boys were belligerent when asked to leave, while others were clearly relieved.

"You ever held a gun?" Luigi asked.

"No. How about you?"

"I used to shoot birds in Foggia," Luigi admitted.

Luigi went behind a screen with the doctor. Ciro stood and waited his turn for what seemed like a long time.

Luigi pushed the curtain aside and shook his head. "I have a bad ear. They won't take me."

"Oh, pal, I'm sorry."

Fifteen minutes later, Ciro joined Luigi on the sidewalk outside. Ciro carried the paperwork to report to New Haven, Connecticut, on July 1. He folded the paper and stuffed it in his pocket.

"You got in?" Luigi asked.

"Yeah."

Ciro was gratified that the army had accepted him, knowing that it was the fastest route to earning his citizenship. But there was also a sadness, a gnawing anxiety that he was running from something he couldn't name. It was in moments like this that he thought of Enza and wondered about the different path his life might have taken had she been waiting for him on Adams Street.

"I wanted to go fight." Luigi kicked a pebble off the sidewalk into the gutter. "Maybe I ought to take Pappina and go home to Italy."

"And what will you do there?" Ciro asked.

"I don't know. I got no place to go. When the U.S. Army doesn't want you, you don't have a lot of choices."

"You keep working on Mulberry Street. By the time I get back, you'll be a master."

"Signora takes all our profits. You'd think she'd cut us in. You invented the cart, after all."

"Remo taught me a trade. I owe him," Ciro said firmly. "But I think we have generously paid off the marker. We need our own company, Luigi. And I'm going to count on you to pull all the pieces together while I'm overseas."

Ciro's wise offer seemed to assuage Luigi's feelings of failure at the recruitment office. For young fellows like them, the war was a chance to become men, to see the world and save it and return home as American citizens. It didn't occur to either of them that lives would be lost, that the world they were to defend would shift under their feet and never be the same again. They only dreamed of the adventure.

A flower cart parked on the corner of Fifth Avenue and Fourteenth Street overflowed with bouquets of white lilies and pots of pink hyacinths tied with gold bows. Glassy, bright green boxwood hemmed in the front gardens of brownstones. Windowboxes sprouted with purple and pink bachelor buttons, red impatiens, and bright yellow marigolds. Enza breathed deeply as she walked to Tenth Street. As she climbed the steps to the entrance of the Milbank House, Miss DeCoursey was sorting the mail in the vestibule. She handed Enza an envelope. The return address read: The Metropolitan Opera House. Enza sprinted up four flights of stairs to open it with Laura.

"It came," Enza said. Laura pulled a hairpin from her chignon and handed it to Enza, who carefully opened the envelope.

Dear Miss Ravanelli,

Miss Serafina Ramunni would like to meet with you and Miss Laura Heery on April 29, 1917, at ten o'clock in the morning. Please bring your sewing kits and further samples of your workmanship, in particular with foil paillettes, silk trims, and crystal beading.

Very truly yours,
Miss Kimberly Meier
Company Manager

The girls immediately ran to the church of Saint Francis Xavier and lit every candle at the foot of Saint Lucy, the patron saint of seamstresses. The girls needed this job. The temporary kitchen work was not enough, and they were one week away from losing their room at the Milbank.

The morning of their interview, they ate a hearty Milbank breakfast of scrambled eggs, coffee, and toast before loading their sewing kits and samples into their purses for the walk from Tenth Street, thirty blocks uptown, to meet Serafina Ramunni, the head seamstress of the costume shop. Enza and Laura wore their best skirts and blouses. Enza wore a Venetian gondolier's straw hat with a bright red band, while Laura wore a straw picture hat with a cluster of silk cherries for adornment.

The girls spent the night developing a strategy for the interview. If Miss Ramunni liked one of them and not the other, the one offered the job should take it. If there were no immediate openings for seamstresses, they agreed to take whatever starting positions were available. They both dreamed of working in the costume shop eventually, but they knew it could take years to earn a spot there, *if* they were lucky enough to be hired in the first place.

The Metropolitan Opera House, built of native yellow stone hauled from the valleys of upstate New York, took up a full city block on West Thirty-ninth Street. Its architectural grandeur was evident in its details—ornate doors, embellished cornices, and Palladian arches. The opera house had the massive dimensions of a train station.

On the ground level, a series of doors capped by brass scrollwork emptied the theater in minutes. The wide carriage circle accommodated every mode of transportation on wheels: motorcars, cabs, and horse carriages had plenty of space for dropoffs before curtain and pickups after the final ovation.

The main entrance doors, attended by footmen, were hemmed by velvet ropes. Enza and Laura entered through the lobby, where a handyman buffed the white marble floor with a motorized brush machine.

A swirling staircase rose before them, carpeted in ruby red, with a high polished brass railing. A crystal chandelier, dripping in shimmering glass daggers in the shape of a wedding cake, had been lowered on delicate wires to eye level for cleaning, and a maid dusted the crystal drops gently with flannel mitts.

The box office door was propped open. Inside, the ticket sellers were smoking and taking a coffee break. Laura walked up to the window. "We're looking for Serafina Ramunni. We have an appointment."

A young man in shirtsleeves and brown tie ashed his cigarette and nodded. "She's onstage."

Laura and Enza passed a series of Renaissance paintings framed in gold leaf in the inner lobby. They pushed the doors open, entering the dark theater, an enormous jewelry box trimmed in gold. The scents of fresh paint, linseed oil, and the lingering gardenia of expensive perfumes created a heady mix. Rows of seats swathed in red velvet tilted toward the downstage lip of the cavernous stage like rose blooms. Enza thought that church was the only other place where such hushed reverence was required.

The stage floor was lacquered black, with white lines indicating where scenery should be placed. A series of small X's were painted strategically across the downstage lip, where solos were performed. From the highest tier of the theater, the follow spotlights were angled at these marks like cannons.

The ring of private viewing boxes, dubbed the "diamond horseshoe" by Cholly Knickerbocker and other society writers, was reserved for the wealthiest subscribers. These theatrical boxes were suspended over the orchestra seats, like delicate gold carriages, decorated with ornate medallions. Red damask draperies hung behind the seats, softening any sound from the stairways and grand aisles. Faceted glass sconces shaped like tiaras softly illuminated each level.

The girls walked down the vom and turned to look up into the upper mezzanine, empty seats that extended as high and far as the eye could see. The theater could hold 4,000 people, with 224 standing-room tickets sold for a lesser price, but never a lesser performance.

The grandeur of the opera house thrilled Laura too. It took thousands of employees to keep such a vast place running. There were hundreds of artists involved behind the scenes—stagehands, electricians, set builders, property masters, costumers, dressers, wigmakers, and milliners.

There is a beehive under every pot of honey on the island of Manhattan, thought Enza.

Where Laura was galvanized by the possibilities of working at the Met, Enza was nervous. Enza worried about her English, fretted about the skirt and blouse she'd chosen to wear. The Met was a long way from the traveling troupes that pitched tents in the fields of Schilpario or the vaudeville theaters that Laura remembered from her own childhood on the Jersey shore.

Serafina Ramunni stood with a fabric peddler on the bare stage. The head of the costume department was in her thirties, a handsome woman with strong features and a slim shape, accentuated by a belted-waist suit jacket and a long skirt with a kick pleat. She wore brown calfskin boots, and a black velvet hairband in her shiny brown hair. She chose fabrics from the bolts on display, marking the ones she would purchase with a stickpin. Angelic chiffons, sturdy velvets, and liquid satins were unfurled like flags for her perusal. She looked over at the girls, feeling their stares. "You are?"

"Laura Heery, and this is Enza Ravanelli."

"You're here for the seamstress jobs?"

They nodded in unison.

"I'm Miss Ramunni. Follow me to the workroom," she said, walking upstage.

The girls looked up at her, unsure where to go.

"You can come onstage. The steps are over there."

Enza followed Laura up the steps to the stage, feeling unworthy to step out onto it. It was like approaching a tabernacle in a cathedral. She peered down into the orchestra pit, lit by dim worklights. Black lacquer music stands were cluttered with white sheet music, like the open pages of a book.

Laura followed Miss Ramunni backstage and down the stairs to the basement, but Enza took a moment to turn centerstage and look out into the opera house before following. The upper levels of the theater looked like a massive field of poppies.

"Who wrote the letter?" Serafina asked.

"I did," Enza said shyly.

"I passed it around the office."

Laura looked at Enza and smiled. Good sign.

"We got a kick out of it. No one ever applied for a job here using listening to Caruso records as a skill."

"I hope I didn't do anything wrong," Enza said.

"Your sewing samples saved you." Serafina smiled, ushering the girls into a lift to the basement. "I don't usually appreciate humor, intended or not, in query letters."

The costume shop in the basement of the Met was a cavernous space that extended the full length of the building. From cutting tables, to a series of fitting rooms, through a hall of mirrors where the actor could see himself from every angle, past the machines, and through to finishing, where the costumes were steamed, pressed, and hung, it was a wonderland unlike anything either of the girls had ever seen. All weaves and textures of fabric—bolts of cream-colored duchesse satin, wheels of jewel-toned cotton, soft sheets of silver faille and shards of powder blue organza—lay neatly on worktables, stood upright in bolts, or were bundled in bins or jigsawed on the pattern table, waiting to be sewn.

Dress mannequins were staggered around the room, bearing garments in various states of construction. On the walls, a peek into the gallant characters of pending productions—watercolor sketches of Tristan, Leonora, Mandrake, and Romeo—hung like saints in the portrait gallery of the Vatican.

Twenty sleek, top-of-the-line black-lacquered Singer sewing machines outfitted with bright work lamps and attended by short-backed padded stools were lined up like tanks on the cusp of battle on the far side of the room. A three-way mirror and a circular platform for fittings were set off to the side with a rod and privacy curtain. Three long worktables, enough to accommodate fifty seamstresses, split the center of the room, with walking aisles in between.

A worker pressed muslin on the ironing board; another, at a sewing machine, did not lift her head from her task; still others, in the next room, operated the wringer washing machines, hanging voluminous petticoats on drying racks.

Laura and Enza took in all of it and fell instantly, immediately, and irrevocably in love. They wanted to work here more than they wished to live.

"You, over here." Serafina pointed to Enza. "And you"—she pointed to Laura—"there."

Serafina handed them each a square of fabric and a bin of crystals. She placed thread, scissors, and needles before them. She opened a sketchbook to a page featuring a copy of a harlequin beading design made famous by Vionnet.

"Reproduce the fan design," Serafina directed. "Show me what you can do."

The girls measured the triangles across the fabric, marking them with chalk. Laura picked up a needle and threaded it. Enza fished through the bin to find the right beads. She collected them and brought them to Laura, who handed her the needle, then threaded a second one for herself. Without a word between them, they made fast work of attaching the crystals, quickly and with dexterity.

"I assume you can fine-embroider from your samples," Serafina said.

"We can do anything. By hand, by machine," Laura assured her.

"Can you make patterns from a beading design on a sketch?"

"I can do that, Miss Ramunni," Enza assured her. "I can take any sketch from a designer and break it down for production."

"I know my way around beads," Laura volunteered.

"And I'm an excellent fitter," Enza said.

"You know the opera is more than Signor Caruso. But he is the king around here. We put on the operas he wants to sing, and we cast the sopranos of his choosing. He's in London until next month, at Covent Garden with Antonio Scotti."

"The baritone," Enza remembered. "He appeared with Caruso in *Tosca* in 1903 here at the Met."

"You do know your opera."

"She listened to Puccini through a dumbwaiter," Laura volunteered. "We were working scullery at a fancy party, and he was there."

"I wasn't aware Signor Puccini was renting himself out for parties."

"Oh, he wasn't. It was in his honor," Enza said. "He played several arias from *Tosca*."

"Your passion and curiosity will hold you in good stead around here," Serafina said to Enza. She turned to Laura. "And how about you?"

"I'm a Gerry flapper," Laura said. "You know, the Irish and all."

"Geraldine Farrar is our best soprano. But know your place here. You are on the costume crew. You are not fans. No ogling, no joking, no familiarity, even when the performers are familiar with you. Treat every singer like your boss. If there's a problem, you go to your crew captain."

"Who is she?" Laura asked.

"Me. But first, we have a problem. I only have the money in the budget to hire one of you. Who wants the job more?"

Enza and Laura looked at one another sadly. The fantasy of being hired together had been dashed. "She may have the job," they said in unison.

"No, no, no," Laura said, shaking her head. "It's Enza's dream to work here. Please hire her."

"But it's your dream too." Enza looked up at Serafina. "Laura and I met in a factory in Hoboken. She taught me English, and I'm trying to teach her Italian. She looked out for me there, and we moved into the city and took any jobs we could get. But our dream was to work together here at the Metropolitan Opera House."

"Why?"

"Because it's the best," Enza said. "And we believe our skills are excellent, and we belong in a place where our talents are used."

"Not that we don't have a lot to learn. We do," Laura added.

"Well—" Serafina ran her hands over the beadwork swatches. "My parents came from Calabria. And I was trained by Joanne Luiso, she was a great seamstress. She was patient with me, taught me about fabrics, drape, and line. I wouldn't be here without her. I was given a break."

"It's only right to give the position to Enza," Laura said.

"But I was hired by an Irish woman named Elizabeth Parent." She glanced at Laura and smiled. "I'm going to take you both, though they'll have my head upstairs. I'll have to blame the budget overrun on Caruso, but God knows it's happened often enough before."

Laura and Enza were elated. They hugged one another, then looked to Miss Ramunni.

"You'll start at one dollar a week. I don't like clock watchers or break takers. I like a girl who sits down at the machine and sews straight through. If you're actually as good as you say you are, you may eventually graduate to fittings and costuming the chorus. But first, you do the assembly work. Sometimes we work all night. No overtime."

"We're really hired?" Laura asked. "Both of us?"

With a curt nod, Serafina Ramunni said the sweetest words in the English language: "You have the job." And then she turned to Enza. "And you have the job. Welcome to the Met."

After they had completed their training, Enza chose the sewing machine at the end of the line in the costume shop, just as she had at the factory. Laura sat down next to her, tossing a brown-bag lunch into the drawer. Behind them, a dozen military jackets for the chorus had to be deconstructed, epaulets replaced, buttons redone, new collars and lapels inserted, for a special show the opera company was putting on for a bond drive for the American troops off to fight in the Great War.

The show was planned for the last day of June, so there were only a few weeks to design, mount, and produce the show, a pastiche of great arias and chorus anthems put together for the sole purpose of rallying the crowd to buy bonds to support the U.S. government.

With a sketch of a military uniform pinned to the wall before them, the girls began to rip out the old elements of the costumes, used in a production of *Don Giovanni*, careful to save the frog enclosures, brass buttons, and metal studs. Every clasp, trim, and embellishment in the shop was reimagined and used repeatedly. A button was never wasted.

"I think I've found my future husband," Laura said.

"Where?"

"In the lobby this morning."

"Not the door attendant."

"No, he's entirely too short for me. I found a tall one. His name is Colin Chapin. He works in accounting."

"How do you know?"

"I asked him."

"You just walked up to him and started talking?"

"I had to. I felt the tug of destiny. I'm not like you. I don't have to be dragged into love by my braids. He's going to take me to the show. He likes westerns, especially Tom Mix."

"I didn't know you liked westerns."

"I don't," Laura said, "but I like him. He seems wise. Colin is ten years older than me."

"You just came out and asked him how old he was?"

"No." Laura laughed. "I have some couth! I asked Janet Megdadi in the office."

"You are thorough."

"Gotta be. Plus, I found out he's a widower."

Enza shook her head, amused. Laura Heery was, above all things, thorough.

"Enza, you know what my dream is for you? I want you to stop living like you did in Hoboken. You're free now. Nobody's gonna take away your happiness ever again."

Freedom came naturally to Laura. Enza wished it came more naturally to her. Laura had a way of bringing out the best in Enza, and Enza was masterful at keeping Laura focused.

Enza laid a particularly ornate chorus jacket out on the worktable. She scribbled chalk marks across the lapels and down the sleeves.

"This one was a general," she said. She took her small work scissors and began to disassemble the hardware on the face of the jacket. She attacked the small stitches, pulling out the threads quickly.

"Did you know him personally?"

Enza ceased her ripping and looked up.

"He'd rather have taken a bullet, the way you're ripping out that lining," a man said, in a deep voice with honey edges. Enza looked up into the stranger's blue eyes. He ran his hand through his straight black hair and smiled. This is a handsome man, Enza thought. He must be a baritone, from the timbre of his speaking voice.

The angles of this man were all sharp. Square shoulders, a firm jaw, and a straight nose, but a beautiful mouth, with full lips over straight white teeth. His suit, perfectly cut for his lean body, was navy blue with a light blue pinstripe. His starched collar was snapped with a gold cross bar. His fitted vest was fastened with ivory buttons. Enza also noticed that the sleeves of his jacket broke perfectly at the wrist, revealing the crisp shirt cuffs underneath. His cuff links were deep blue lapis lazuli squares set in gold. He had beautiful hands.

"I'm Vito Blazek," he said.

"Are you one of the singers?" Enza asked.

"Publicity. Best job in the building. All I have to do is let the papers know that Signor Caruso is singing, and four thousand tickets are sold that minute. Sometimes I like to come and watch the *real* work of the opera taking place."

"I have an extra pair of scissors for you," Enza joked.

Unfolding his arms, he leaned across the table. His skin had the clean scent of cedar and lime. "I'm tempted," he said with a grin.

"I bet you are," Laura said. "I'm her best friend, Laura Heery, and if you want to flirt with her, you need my approval."

"What do I have to do to impress you?"

"I'm thinking." Laura squinted at him.

"You ladies have discernment." He smiled. "I'm afraid I haven't gotten your names yet."

"Enza Ravanelli."

"Sounds like an opera. Ravanelli? Northern Italy?" he said. "I'm Hungarian and Czech, born in New York City. Makes for an interesting stew."

"I'll bet," Laura said, still giving him the once-over. "Nobody knows about stews like the Irish."

"Hey, Veets, we gotta blow," a young man said from the doorway.

"On my way," Vito called over his shoulder, then added, "I hope I see you later."

"We'll be here, sewing our little hearts out," Laura said as they watched him go.

"This job has perks." Laura whistled. "If you decide to go out on a date with Mr. Blazek, I'm going to make you a new hat."

Enza chalked the inseam of the coat. "I like blue," Enza said. "Something bright—peacock blue."

Laura smiled, pulling stitches out of another jacket.

Serafina pushed the door open to the workshop and placed a stack of files on the worktable. She surveyed the work of the seamstresses down the line. She lifted the finished chorus jacket, nodding her head in approval. "I have a job for you, Enza. Signor Caruso is back in the morning. His costumes are ready, but they need some adjustments. I'd like you to assist me."

"I'd be honored to attend to Signore," Enza said, trying to mask her surprise. After Serafina disappeared, taking the finished jacket with her, the girls on the machines congratulated Enza. Laura was so thrilled for her friend, she let out a whoop.

Enza took a deep breath. She knew this was the most important moment in her professional life thus far—the moment she was chosen and singled out for her talent. She had worked since she was fourteen years old for this opportunity. Her skills, nurtured in Mrs. Sabatino's dress shop on the mountain and perfected by rote in the factory, had finally been revealed in full. Her talent was no longer a private matter; it was on display for all to see and appreciate on the stage of the Metropolitan Opera. And now, she would hem the garments of The Great Voice. She could scarcely believe it. If only Anna Buffa could see her now.

18

A CHAMPAGNE FLUTE
Un Bicchiere da Spumante

Enrico Caruso stood on the fitting stool in his spacious dressing room in the Metropolitan Opera House, puffing a cigar.

Hoping to please their star, the set decorator had poached the best ideas from interior designer Elsie de Wolfe, creating a lair for the singer inspired by the colors of the Mediterranean on the southern coast of Italy, where Caruso was born. The decor was all sun, sea foam, and sand.

A seven-foot sofa, covered in turquoise chenille and studded with large coral buttons, conjured the waters of the port of Sorrento. The lamps were milk-glass globes topped with tangerine shades. Overhead, the light fixture was a brass sunburst with round white bulbs on the tips. An Italian summer was tucked away behind the scenery, costumes, and props.

"I live in a seashell," Caruso remarked. "I'm a real *scungeel*."

Enrico's makeup table was oversize, painted white, with large light-bulbs encircling an enormous round mirror. On the table, laid out with the precision of surgical equipment on pristine starched cotton towels, were vanity tools, brushes, powders, black kohl pencils, and tins of hair pomade. A small tin of glue for hairpieces, mustaches, and beards was open on the table. A low gilded stool covered in coral-and-white-striped fabric was tucked under the table.

"I have a *bagno* like the pope," Caruso said as he stood on the fitting stool. "Have you met him, Vincenza?"

"No, Signore." Enza smiled at the thought of ever meeting a pope, as she pinned the darts in the back of the costume.

"I have the same bathroom," Caruso said. "But where I have silver fixtures, he has gold."

Caruso was five foot ten. He had a thick waist and a barrel chest that could expand four inches when his lungs were inflated with enough air for the trademark power of his tenor. His legs were powerful, with muscular calves and substantial thighs, like the men who hauled marble and lifted granite in the villages of southern Italy. Expressive hands, muscular biceps, and slim forearms were grace notes on his physique. He acted with the dimensions of his body, just as he sang through them.

The most memorable feature of the Great Caruso's face were his eyes, large, dark brown, dramatic, and expressive. His gaze was so penetrating, the whites of his eyes could be seen clearly from the mezzanine, as if the beams of the spotlights originated within him, instead of simply illuminating him from the rafters above. The intelligence behind his eyes made Caruso an artist of emotional scope and power, and a brilliant actor as well as the greatest opera singer of his time.

Caruso knew what the audience wanted: they wanted to *feel* something, and they wanted him to take them there, so he gave of himself from the depths of his talent, from a bottomless well of sound, willingly and generously. He was the first opera singer to make phonograph records and sell them in the millions. He saw art as a gift to the masses, not simply a diversion for the upper classes. Giulio Gatti-Casazza, the general manager of the Met during Caruso's reign, marveled at Caruso's ability to fill every seat and satisfy every customer. It would have been difficult to find anyone who didn't love Caruso, and he liked it that way.

Caruso could move an audience with a simple gesture, a wink, or a single tear. The occasional improvisation was not beyond him, as his good friend Antonio Scotti had experienced onstage with the master. Once Scotti had entered a scene early; instead of being thrown off, the master went to Scotti, embraced him, and invented an a cappella greeting that Scotti sang back to him. The audience went wild.

"I demanded an Italian girl." Caruso blew a cloud of gray smoke up to the ceiling as he stood in a pair of navy military pants with runners of ruby red satin down the sides. Enza marked the hems with chalk.

"There are lots of us in the workroom, Signor Caruso," Enza said.

"But Serafina tells me you're the best."

"That's very kind of her, sir."

"You like the opera, Vincenza?"

"Very much, sir. I used to work for a woman in Hoboken who played your records. Sometimes she played them so much, the neighbors would all shout, '*Basta!*' until she was forced to stop."

Caruso laughed heartily. "You mean every house in Hoboken isn't filled with fans of the Great Caruso? You have a musical soul, Vincenza. You know how I can tell? Your eyebrows. They're like D minor notes. They shoot up high, and drop low on the staff. Do you cook?"

"Yes, sir."

"What can you make?"

"Macaroni."

"Be more specific."

"Gnocchi."

"Ah, peasant food to survive a long winter. Good. You make it with potatoes?"

"Of course."

"What sauce?"

"Butter and sage are my favorites. And I use a pinch of cinnamon sometimes."

"Very good! You will make gnocchi for the cast!" he exclaimed.

"For everyone?" Enza put her hands on her face.

"Yes. Antonio, Gerry. The chorus. They sing. They need to eat."

"But where will I cook?"

"Do you have a kitchen?"

"I live in a boardinghouse."

"And I live in the Knickerbocker Hotel, which is getting to be like a boardinghouse. All the grandeur has left this city."

"I still think it's grand."

"I'm spoiled, Vincenza. It's a terrible thing to be old and spoiled."

"You're not old, sir."

"I'm bald."

"Young men go bald too."

"It's hitting the high notes—I blow the hair off my head when I hit them."

Enza smiled.

"See there, you can smile. You're too serious, Vincenza. We're in show business. This is smoke, mirrors, rouge, and girdles. I wear one of those, too, you know."

"Not if I'm tailoring your costumes," Enza promised him.

"Really?"

"Really, sir. All it takes is proportion. If I build your smock for *Tosca*, I raise the shoulder, drop the sleeve, nip the waist in the back, pipe it boldly, and use double-size buttons. You will shrink underneath it. If I make the pants the same fabric as the smock, and give you a shoe with a pointed toe, it will slim you out even more."

"Ah, *la bella figura*, Caruso style! I need to be slimmed out, but I don't want to give up the gnocchi."

"You don't have to. I will achieve everything you hope for with illusion."

"Jesus. Tell the old man whatever he wants to hear." Geraldine Farrar stood in the doorway, puffing a cigarette.

Geraldine wore a long muslin skirt for rehearsal. Her light brown hair, braided like a milkmaid's, lay on her chest on a white cotton blouse, over which she had tied the sleeves of a black cashmere shrug. Enza had never seen a woman so beautiful, and yet so completely unaware of it. Her style was casual, thrown on like an old sweater. Geraldine had the coloring of a gold pearl: tawny skin, offset by pale blue eyes. She possessed the ready and wide smile of an American girl.

"Get out, Gerry," Caruso said.

"I'm looking for some amusement." She rifled through the button box on the table.

"You won't find it here."

"No kidding."

"Vincenza is going to make us gnocchi."

"You're supposed to drink warm tea and eat lettuce. The doctor has you on a diet," Geraldine reminded him.

"Vincenza is going to make me magic costumes. I will look thinner from the mezzanine."

"An elephant looks thinner from the mezzanine," Geraldine reminded him. She scooted up on to the worktable. "What am I wearing for this shindig?"

"Crimson satin."

"I'd rather wear blue. Cornflower blue. Who do I tell?"

"Miss Ramunni."

"That old battle-ax?"

"You're exactly one year younger than me, Miss Farrar," Serafina Ramunni said from the doorway.

"Oh, you got me." Geraldine fell back against the pattern table as though she had been shot.

"And you're not wearing crimson or blue, you're wearing green," Serafina announced. "The set is raspberry red, and I won't have the soprano looking like a cheap blue horn against the damask. Green will pop."

"Ugh. For once, let me wear what I want!" Geraldine carped.

"She's so dramatic," Caruso said to Enza. "Demanding too."

"Hey, watch it. I don't need the criticism. I'm doing you a favor with this benefit," Gerry said. "You owe me."

"May I remind you, I'm Italian, and I'm doing this for the American soldiers. This is an act of generosity on my part. *You* owe *me.* "

"Last time I checked, you Italians were on our side in the war," Gerry said.

"So I'm killing two birds with two stones."

"Two birds with *one* stone! God, I hate it when you people don't learn the idioms."

"I try to teach the Great Caruso, but the Great Caruso doesn't want to learn," Serafina said.

"At least she calls me the Great Caruso." He winked at Vincenza. "When they start calling me Enrico, I worry."

*   *   *

Enza stood in front of Geraldine Farrar's dress dummy, over which was draped an A-line gown of emerald green satin, with pale green satin lining.

A series of small X's across the bodice indicated where the paillettes would be sewn; a triangle, a drop crystal. Enza had been sewing the beadwork for two days, hoping to finish by the end of this long night. She picked up a needle and began to attach the delicate embellishments.

She would sew each sequin on with precision, looping it twice through, to make sure Geraldine Farrar sparkled from the mezzanine as the lights danced off the surface of the beads.

Enza did some of her best thinking when she did detail work. Giacomina had taught her daughter that you must dig constantly for meaning in the sorrow of this life, and that this sorrow must galvanize you, not define you. During her years with the Buffa family, Enza had tried to find some meaning in her mistreatment, but she never could.

But now, as she sewed the crystals on, she saw her mother's wisdom at long last. Signora Buffa had played opera on her phonograph records constantly. The Great Caruso had accompanied all of Enza's suffering on Adams Street—every wring of the laundry, every buff of the moppeen on the linoleum floor, the chop of every tomato, and each careful pressing of every ribbon of pasta.

As Enza labored on Adams Street, she had learned the stories of the operas—*Fra Angelico*, *Pagliacci*, *Carmen*, and *La Bohème*. She had heard the master sing the great arias of Verdi, Puccini, and Wagner. The music had become a part of her. It had earned her a place at the Metropolitan Opera House.

Enza slipped out of her skirt and unbuttoned her blouse. She unzipped the mannequin's green gown and slid into it. Lifting the hem, she hiked up onto the fitting stool and examined the gown from all angles in the three-way mirror. The drape of the green satin suggested gentle waves on a summer lake, an effect Enza had achieved by making tiny tucks along the bodice and lowering the waistline in the back. The crystal swag along the low back of the gown lay straight, and with slight movement, it threw off light that gave the silk a watery effect along the seam. Enza checked the bodice and waist, the armhole and sleeve. She bowed deeply from the waist, and slowly stood to check the drape of the skirt.

Bellissima, she thought.

Ciro sat under the old elm behind the shop on Mulberry Street and took a smooth, cool drag off his cigarette. The moon was silver, like a grommet punched into black leather. He leaned back and studied the

sky with new interest. Perhaps he would read about astronomy on his
way to France, so he might learn how to follow the stars. He imagined
he would need the skill in an unfamiliar place; the only markers that
would stay fixed would be overhead. He would not know the villages,
fields, and hills of France.

Signora Zanetti washed, pressed, and hung Ciro's uniform, an in-
distinct mud brown, in preparation for his departure later that week.
In trench warfare, the soldiers must match the color of the earth. The
field jacket fit well when belted, and the pants had too much room in
the thigh, but the length was right. His height served him well, in life
and in uniforms.

Remo had bought Ciro extra socks and double-lined cotton undershorts, knowing that the nights in France could be cold. Pappina
had pressed handkerchiefs, and Luigi had given him a new fountain
pen. Ciro smiled at the gift; both he and Luigi knew it was unlikely
that any letters would cross the Atlantic, from Ciro's end, anyway. His
duffel was not packed much differently from the one he had carried
from the convent when he was fifteen. A lot had changed, but not his
basic needs.

Ciro imagined his mother, and wondered what she would think
about the war, and about her son the soldier. She wouldn't like the lack-
luster uniform, he imagined. Eduardo, a peacemaker, would be support-
ive, but would not want his brother to lose his life for anything but
the honor and glory of God. Even Ciro could see that this venture had
nothing to do with God. It was about obligation, and the repayment of
a debt.

When Ciro thought about his father, he wept for all he had missed.
His father would have known what to say and how to prepare him for
the worst. A father is the person who teaches a son to be brave, to do the
right thing, and to defend the weak. Ciro extinguished his cigarette and
put his face in his hands, leaning forward under the leafy canopy of the
tree. His tears flowed and turned to sobs, and soon his heart felt leaden
in his chest, aching with the sadness of all he had lost.

When he had dried his tears on his sleeve, Ciro sat back in the
chair, feeling no better for his outburst—a lame catharsis, he thought.
He looked up at the sky. The moon was brighter now, but its glow

diminished the stars, which looked like the heads of pins stuck in a great map, a plan for war.

. . .

There was no window in the kitchenette of Enrico Caruso's hotel suite.

Enza rolled the dough to make gnocchi on the table, just as her mother had taught her. Peeling and boiling the sack of potatoes was a real chore in the efficiency kitchen, but she arrived early and took her time gently mashing the boiled potatoes, and now, as she added eggs and flour, the pasta took shape beautifully, just as it had on the old farm table in Schilpario.

"How's it going?" Laura asked, placing bags of fresh greens on the counter.

Laura was followed by Colin Chapin, the cultivated, erudite thirty-five-year-old opera accountant who'd caught Laura's eye in the first month on the job. Tonight he wore an elegant suit, vest, and tie. He had neatly combed blond hair and clear gray eyes, and his thick horn-rimmed glasses gave him the appearance of a studious professor.

"We went to Veniero's for the bread." Colin opened the brown sack and showed Enza the loaves.

"Perfect."

"And we got sage at the Cassio market," Laura added. "Funny, I never see Felicitá slinging basil there."

"You won't, either," Enza said.

"You know the Fruit Cassios?" Colin asked.

"If they are the Fruit Cassios, then I'm a Cotton Heery, and Enza is a Burlap Ravanelli." Laura laughed.

"I'm a little fancier than burlap." Enza wiped her hands on her apron. She poured salt into the large pot of boiling water on the stove.

The doorbell rang. Colin went to answer it. A hotel butler pushed a rolling bar cart, filled with bottles of fine wine, cut-glass bottles of hard liquor, crystal stemware, sleek champagne flutes, and an ornate silver ice bucket. He placed it in the suite by the sofa.

"It's the booze cart," Colin called out happily as Laura peered ador-ingly at him through the pantry doors.

"You're in love," Enza said with a smile.

"Falling like a sack of buttons," Laura said dreamily.

"I'm not going to need a single at the Milbank House, am I? When is he going to introduce you to his sons?"

"Hopefully soon, but don't go roommate-shopping just yet."

Enza rolled the last of the gnocchi, cut it into pieces, and made an impression with the fork in each doughy puff, while Laura washed and sorted the fresh greens in the sink.

Enza prepared the sauce, cleaning the sage and placing it on the stove in a pan with olive oil and garlic. She turned on a low flame and slowly added butter to the mixture. The suite filled with the scent of an Italian farmhouse at suppertime.

"You girls all right?" Colin asked.

"We have everything, I think," Laura said, looking around the kitchen, taking a quick inventory.

"I'm going to blow," Colin said.

"Thank you," Enza said. "You were a big help."

"My pleasure." He winked at Laura, took his hat, and went.

"That man is *not* going to fit in with my family in New Jersey. He went to boarding school at Phillips Exeter, graduated from Amherst, and he's captained a ship in a regatta somewhere off the coast of Rhode Island. His mother descended from people that have been here so long, they had mailboxes at the Jamestown settlement. I am out of my league. I am in over my head. And I am completely besotted. Trust me, when he meets my family and finds out we brew our own beer, he'll never ask me out again."

"So bring them to Manhattan to meet him."

"All seventy thousand of them? I'll need a barge, not a ferry. No, thank you, I'm keeping my family under wraps. If he gets a load of them, he'll run."

"The entire population of Ireland won't bother him if he loves you."

"That's where you're naive," Laura sighed. "When it comes to high society, the only things they mix are their drinks."

The door to the suite blew open, bringing the best voices of the Metropolitan Opera into the room.

The suite was decorated in white damask silk with accents of black velvet, a color scheme borrowed from Caruso's sheet music. The furniture had sleek lines and curves, like musical instruments. A pair of deep-cushioned English sofas in white chenille faced one another, separated by an upholstered ottoman with pearl buttons. The only color in the room was a large silver vase filled with blood red roses nestled in waxy green leaves.

The table in the alcove was set for dinner, with the hotel's fine bone china, edged in silver, and sterling silver serving pieces. Water glasses were filled, and wineglasses were empty, ready for the Chianti.

"I am in heaven!" Enrico Caruso said from the foyer. "Sage! Garlic! *Burro!*"

"They're early!" Laura said, stirring the sauce. "We have so much left to do!"

"Stay calm," Enza told her.

"This better be good, Erri," Geraldine said, throwing off her sweater and reaching into the pocket of her skirt for her cigarettes.

"I need a glass of wine," Antonio Scotti said to the host, removing his hat. Scotti was of medium height, with classic southern Italian features—a nose that extended far like an alpine road, lovely lips, and small brown eyes like a bird's.

"I'll pour," Caruso said, uncorking a bottle.

Caruso poured the wine, including a glass for himself, and joined the girls in the kitchen. Enza dropped the puffs of gnocchi into the boiling water.

"At last, I eat like the peasant I am!" Caruso said.

Antonio joined them. "Where did you find the cook?"

"At the sewing machine."

"That doesn't bode well," Antonio said.

"Women have more than one skill, Antonio. And if you're lucky, they have two. They can make both gnocchi . . . and meatballs."

"Watch it, boys. You're in the presence of a lady or three." Gerry sipped her wine. "What are you making?"

"Gnocchi with sage," Enza said.

Caruso dipped his fingers in the bowl of freshly shaved Parmesan cheese. "I travel with a wheel of my own cheese."

"Better than a wife," Geraldine said.

"Weighs more," said Caruso. "My little Doro prefers to stay in Italy. She's painting the villa."

"We work, and your Doro redecorates." Antonio shrugged.

"You need a wife, Antonio," Caruso said.

"Never. I'll paint my own villa."

"Women give a life shape and purpose," Caruso said.

"You should know. You're never without one," Antonio remarked.

Enza ladled the steaming puffs of pasta into a serving bowl, as Laura slowly stirred the sauce. Laura gave the spoon to Enza, who added a cup of cream to the pan, then wrapped the dish towel around the handle and ladled the sauce over the steaming gnocchi.

"Italians always wind up in the kitchen," Antonio said. "It's our destiny."

The doorbell rang. "I'll get it—it may be my true love calling," Geraldine said as she pushed through the saloon style doors.

"Unlikely," Antonio said drily. "He's in Italy with his wife."

Laura kept her head down, like a proper Irish scullery maid, and pretended not to take in the gossip as she tossed the salad.

"Please everyone, to the dining table," said Enza.

Enza and Laura made fast work of grating fresh Parmesan cheese over the gnocchi, sprinkling it with lacy branches of browned sage.

"I'll serve, you pick up the dishes," Enza said.

"Happy to. But save some for us," Laura whispered. "This smells heavenly!"

When Enrico Caruso had invited Enza to make him "a dish of macaroni," Enza went to Serafina immediately. At first, Serafina had been against the idea. But when Caruso mentioned it to Serafina himself, she knew she had to allow Enza to prepare the meal. Caruso was never to be denied any request, great or small, by the staff of the Metropolitan Opera. Serafina reminded Enza to remember her place, to serve the maestro and his friends but not to join them at the table, or assume that to be Caruso's intent.

Enza stopped short when she saw Vito Blazek sitting to Caruso's right, across from Geraldine. Antonio sat at the head of the table, opposite Caruso. Vito looked up and winked at Enza. She blushed.

"*Delizioso*, Enza!" Caruso said, when Enza brought the salad plates to the server.

Enza quickly served the meal and went back into the kitchen. "Did you see?" She placed the dishes in the sink.

Laura peered out the door. "Vito Blazek. Publicity. He's everywhere. But I guess that's the point."

"He'll think I'm scullery," Enza said, disappointed.

"You *are* scullery. And so am I, for that matter."

"Is he dating Geraldine?" Enza asked.

"I doubt it. Signor Scotti said she had a lover in Italy. Don't you listen?"

"I try not to."

Laura poured Enza a glass of wine, and they listened to the conversation beyond the kitchen doors. Antonio talked about the changes in England since they'd entered the war, and how the audiences craved music now more than ever. Caruso said that war was good for nothing except the arts that flourished in bleak times. Geraldine spoke up about her concerns for Italy. Laura and Enza looked at one another, taking in the dinner conversation. Laura got the giggles when she realized that they had just made gnocchi in a kitchenette for the biggest musical star in the world, and last winter, they had been running through the streets of Hoboken in boiled wool, wearing bad hats. Enza shushed her, so she could continue to eavesdrop.

Caruso waved a dumpling of gnocchi on the end of his fork.

"My good friend Otto Kahn cannot sit in a viewing box because he's a Jew. And yet he paid for everything you see, including the box, the draperies, the set, the costumes, and the singers. Without him, no grand opera."

"Why does he give the money to the Met when he's treated that way?" Vito asked.

"Love." Caruso smiled. "He loves art like I love life."

"You mean he loves art like you love women," Antonio said.

"Women *are* life, Antonio." Caruso laughed.

"Mr. Kahn said that a piano in every apartment would do more to prevent crime than a policeman on every corner," Vito said.

"And he's the man to buy those pianos. Believe me. I'd like to be Mrs. Kahn, but he already has a wife. A beauty named Addie. As usual, I'm a day late and an aria short." Geraldine toasted herself with her wine.

"Poor Gerry," Enrico said, not meaning it.

Enza and Laura prepared a dish of gnocchi to share. They sat at the kitchen table. Laura reached for a dumpling and tasted it. "This is divine!" Laura whispered.

The girls ate their meal slowly, savoring every bite.

"Well, hello. I didn't realize *you* were the Italian girl making dinner for Caruso when he invited me." Vito stood in the doorway. He placed his arms casually over the saloon doors of the kitchen. "That was the best meal I ever had."

"She may leave the sewing needle behind and take up the spatula," Laura said.

"Never," said Enza.

"Whatever man is lucky enough to marry you will eat well for a lifetime."

"And any man that marries me . . . will have a clean sink," Laura said.

"What are you doing after dinner?" Vito asked.

"I'm busy," Laura joked.

"Are you busy too, Enza?" Vito wanted to know.

Enza smiled but did not answer him. Maybe Laura was right. Vito Blazek showed up wherever Enza happened to be, whether it was backstage, in the workroom, or up in the mezzanine. Enza had never been so ardently pursued, and she liked it. Vito was polished, beautifully groomed, and handsome, but even more alluring to Enza, he was persistent. This quality she understood and appreciated.

Laura nudged Enza. "Answer the man. He just asked you out for a date."

"I'm not busy later, Mr. Blazek."

"Wonderful." He smiled.

As Enza and Laura straightened the kitchen, the scent of cigarette smoke and freshly brewed espresso wafted through the suite. Enza was thinking about Anna Buffa's kitchen, and how the meals she prepared there had never been appreciated, only criticized. Enza realized that a grateful person was a happy one.

Signor Caruso asked Enza to prepare him a dish of macaroni on many more occasions, and the girls found themselves making spaghetti in unlikely places—the cafeteria of the Met, or on a hot plate in Caruso's dressing room. Many nights, Enza prepared a dish for Signore to carry with him back to the hotel after rehearsal. The great stars, out of touch with people except for those moments when they were onstage, reaching out to the audience in their velvet seats, longed for home when they couldn't have it. Caruso was always thinking of Italy's warm sun and soft golden Caravaggio moons, and he was just a little closer to them when the seamstress made macaroni.

. . .

Once she agreed to date him, Vito Blazek pursued Enza relentlessly, as if she were a good story that would make hot copy. He gave her the best of Manhattan, as though it was a crystal flute overflowing with champagne, never in need of a refill. He had tickets to opening nights on Broadway, invitations to posh parties in penthouses, and box seats for concerts at Carnegie Hall. They spent long hours at the Automat, talking into the night about art. He gave her books to read, and took her to the Bronx Zoo and for long walks down Fifth Avenue. Enza was being properly courted, and she enjoyed every second of it.

Vito handed Enza a box of popcorn as he took his seat on the aisle next to her at the Fountain Theatre on West Forty-fifth Street. This movie house had shows around the clock; the best times to go were afternoons, when you could stay to watch the movie a second time, because most of the world was at work. The late shows were convenient for the artisans who worked at the Met, as their hours were long, and fittings and rehearsals could run late. Vito stole Enza away for the midnight show, knowing that he'd have to keep her out all night, because the doors of the Milbank were locked until breakfast. Vito managed to fill the wee hours of the morning with wonderful excursions. Enza could not believe the places Vito had taken her. She'd had no idea such fun existed when she was indentured to the Buffas in Hoboken. There was nothing like this on the mountain. It was all new; at long last Enza could be young, on the arm of a gentleman who knew how to live. He relished showing her his world, and it delighted him to know she enjoyed it.

"I hope you like the show," Vito whispered.

"It's my first," Enza admitted.

"You haven't been to the movies?"

"I saw some shorts with Laura in Atlantic City. But never a whole movie." She smiled.

"Charlie Chaplin is my religion," he said. "He makes me laugh almost as much as you do."

Enza smiled to herself. It seemed that she could never find a pious man. Maybe, she decided, she wasn't supposed to.

An attendant in a burgundy uniform pulled the curtain weights. As the massive gold draperies moved aside, an enormous silver screen was revealed behind it. Enza felt her heart beat faster, with the same thrilling sense of anticipation that turning the first page of a new book can bring. The screen read:

The Immigrant
A film by Charlie Chaplin

The screen filled with the image of a steamship as it sailed across the Atlantic, plowing through turbulent whitecaps. The deck of the ship was revealed; Chaplin, dressed as the little Tramp, cavorted with the poor immigrants, who wore the same kind of clothing Enza's fellow passengers had worn on her passage aboard the *Rochambeau*. When the audience roared with laughter at the image of a fish Chaplin caught and tossed onto a sleeping immigrant, whose nose it bit, Enza didn't find it funny. Soon the image of the rocking ship brought back the spinning, tossing, and delirium she had endured. Afraid she might faint, she pulled on her gloves and buried her hands in her coat pockets. Eventually, she excused herself and ran from the theater into the lobby.

"Enza." Vito joined her. "What's the matter?"

"I can't watch it—I'm so sorry."

Vito put his arms around Enza. "No, I'm sorry. I'm an idiot. You came over on a ship like that, didn't you?"

"I don't remember much of it. I got very sick."

"I should have asked. Come on. You need air."

Vito led Enza outside, putting his arm around her shoulder. The cool summer night air revived her, and as it did, she became ashamed of herself. "I'm so embarrassed," she said. "You must think I'm silly."

"No, I don't at all. I'd like to know why you had such a strong reaction in there."

"I came here to make money to build a house on our mountain. We weren't going to be here very long. And here we are, seven years later, and my papa is still on a road crew. But the house is almost finished, and then he'll go home."

"Will you go with him?"

"I was told I could never cross the ocean again." Enza didn't talk about that much. She was always busy earning money to stay afloat, sending most of it home. For the first time, she faced the fact that she might not make it back to the mountain. But she still wanted a happy life.

"I guess I'll have to make you happy here. I'll have to make you so happy you won't miss your mountain."

"Do you think one person can make another happy?"

"I know I said Charlie Chaplin was my religion, but really, *love* is. I lead a good life, but it can be frivolous. I'm a town crier. I talk to the press and try to fill seats at the Met. Sometimes men envy me. I know starlets and dancers and sopranos. But the truth is, it would only take one seamstress who can cook to make me happy." Vito put his arms around Enza.

"You sound so sure," Enza said.

"It only takes one special girl to love." He placed his hands on her face.

"You believe in love like I believe in the saints."

"What else do you believe in?" Vito hoped Enza believed in him.

"Family."

"No, you. Just you. Apart from your family."

Enza had to think. Her first thought was always of her family, her mother's needs and her father's health. She worried about her brothers and sisters, their welfare and future. She had lived so long for them, she didn't know how to live without them. She had crossed the ocean to give them security. If she would do that, she would do anything for them. They had always been her purpose.

Vito took this in. "You should think about what *you* want, Enza. What do you want from your life? Besides sewing Signor Caruso's costumes, and letting them out because you make him too much macaroni?"

"No one has ever asked me that."

"Maybe no one ever loved you enough to put you first," Vito said.

"Maybe not. You take me to all these exciting places, but you also push me to think. That's just as important."

"You're important," Vito assured her. "To me."

On the corner of Forty-sixth Street and Fifth Avenue, he stopped and kissed her. Enza didn't know where this would lead, and for once, she didn't question it. She just kissed him and lived.

19

A CALLING CARD

Un Biglietto da Visita

Garlands of purple wisteria were draped along the velvet ropes at the entrance of the Metropolitan Opera House, bringing to mind a grape trellis in a Tuscan garden.

As the society ladies took their places in line to enter, their brooches of emeralds and sapphires, their platinum tiaras shimmering with diamonds and pearls, created the impression of an enchanted forest, filled with wingless fairies under a night sky.

Inside, orderly pandemonium ensued as the costume crew handed off last-minute fixes to the dressing crew, who ran the costumes through the catacombs and up to the actors, who reviewed their sheet music and ran scales before the performance.

Signor Caruso was nervous.

The United States had entered World War I, and Caruso wanted to show his appreciation. Antonio Scotti and Caruso had put the show together, using arias from their favorite operas, enlisting the help of the Met chorus and friends like Geraldine Farrar. Even Elia Palma had arrived from the Philadelphia Opera House, with his favorite sopranos in tow, to be part of the star-studded evening. Every friend Caruso had would either appear onstage or play in the orchestra pit. No one would ever deny a request from the Great Caruso.

Caruso enjoyed playing several parts in one evening, but it was something he did in private homes or performing at smaller gatherings. His costumes hung on a free-standing rolling rack. He sat in his white cotton undershorts and shirt, beige silk dress socks and braces, smoking a cigar, checking the show order, a handwritten list of numbers he was to sing. Caruso's secretary, Bruno Zirato, took notes to deliver to the conductor.

The orchestra seats were a sea of crisp brown uniforms, as soldiers shipping off to Europe were given priority, with complimentary tickets to the show. They poured into the rows with military precision, as if they were running a maneuver.

The diamond horseshoe overflowed with members of New York society, their elaborate evening gowns of coral, turquoise, and grass green tulle gave the effect of opulent windowboxes in full bloom.

Calling cards, hand-printed on linen paper, were placed on a round table in the vestibule outside the boxed seats. The names written in midnight blue calligraphy included royalty and the political and military elite, as well as the families who had built the city and sustained its culture: Vanderbilt, Cushing, Ellsworth, Whitney, Cravath, Steele, and Greenough. They slipped into their box seats, were served champagne and strawberries, and waited for the curtain to lift with the same giddy anticipation felt by the working people who'd bought single tickets to stand in the back of the theater to hear the Great Voice.

Geraldine Farrar slipped into her satin gown, wriggling her hips, then pulling the bodice over her bosom.

"I don't miss the blue," she said. "Serafina, you were right."

"Thank you." Serafina crossed her arms and nodded appreciatively at Geraldine.

The dresser adjusted the mirrors so Geraldine might see the gown from the rear. She nodded, pleased with the results, as the dresser handed her a pair of diamond drop earrings, which she clipped onto her ears as if she were fastening the snaps of a work smock.

Antonio Scotti, in full tuxedo, placed a clean moppeen over his shirt and cummerbund and slowly sipped warm chicken consommé from a cup as he flipped through the sheet music for his selections, stopping to ponder a particular chord.

Enza and Laura lifted the hems of their evening gowns and ran at full speed through the catacombs beneath the stage. Enza wore a pink drop-waist satin gown, cut on the bias, while Laura wore a structured yellow silk skirt, tied at the waist with an enormous bow made of lilac tulle and topped with a white silk blouse with covered buttons.

"Let's go, butterflies," Colin hollered from the end of the catacomb. The girls reached him, laughing.

"Vito's waiting for us in the light lift."

Enza and Laura followed Colin through the hidden passages, up the stairs, until they were behind the diamond horseshoe. They could hear the heavy footfall of evening shoes above them from the balcony, as the patrons took their seats for the show.

Colin guided them up a small ladder at the upper tier of the mezzanine. The girls hiked their skirts before climbing up into the light booth, past the row of spotlights, which tonight, looked like a string of lucky full moons.

Vito, in a tuxedo with tails, extended his hand to help Enza up into the booth and gave her a kiss on the cheek. "You look beautiful," he told her.

"So do you," she said.

"You're not even panting from the climb," Vito marveled.

"She's part alpine goat, remember?" Laura said from her place on the ladder. "We Irish girls run on flat land, and never far, only door to door for a cup of sugar for tea."

Colin pushed Laura up into the booth by her hips to join Enza and Vito.

"Do I get a warm welcome too?" Laura asked Vito as she flounced her skirt back into place.

"No, you get warm champagne."

"Great. Worth the hike."

Vito popped the cork and handed out paper cups. As the timpani sounded in the orchestra pit like a warning gong over an ancient valley, they sat on work stools and watched as the grand curtain parted, and a blue spotlight bathed Enrico Caruso in a single diamond-cut beam.

The audience rose to its feet. Caruso stood in the blue light, his eyes shining like black diamonds, and grinned with the delight of a man who loved what he did for a living. The violins crescendoed, and the first note of the evening, a solid A above middle C, sailed out over the crowd like a clean, clear cannon shot.

Enza took Vito's hand and held it tight.

Vito left the light booth before the final curtain to accompany the press to Caruso's dressing room. The standing ovation from the soldiers lasted for six minutes, until Caruso bade them good night, laughing that they would surely lose the war if he continued to sing and they remained in their seats.

Laura and Colin made their way to the box office, where Colin would collect the proceeds of the night, run a tally, and deliver the bags of cash to the company manager. The money would go to buy bonds for the families of the soldiers. Laura would sit with him as Colin ran the adding machine; as she said to Enza, "I'd watch the man break matchsticks in two for hours on end."

Vito was going to be busy for a few hours with publicity, so he arranged a carriage ride home for Enza, but the weather was so balmy, she decided to walk. As she moved through the crowd of soldiers to make her way to Fifth Avenue and home, she pulled her pink satin shrug over her shoulders against the night air.

"Enza!" She heard her name called. She looked around, but did not recognize any of the faces in the crowd. This happened to her often in the city. She imagined it was thoughts of her mother that brought on these moments, some deep longing that somehow manifested itself as her name in the din of a crowd.

"Enza!" She heard her name again, and this time, she stopped and waited. She felt a hand upon her forearm, and looked up into the bluegreen eyes of Ciro Lazzari, who, in the brown uniform of the American army regiment, looked like a giant, taller than he ever had on the mountain or on Mulberry Street. She was shocked to see him.

"What are you doing here?" Ciro asked, looking at her, taking in her hair, her face, and her gown. He had thought about her so much, he wondered if the moment was real. He had dreaded going off to France without ever seeing her again, and now it seemed that fate was on his side.

"You joined up," Enza said, taking in his uniform, his short haircut, and the boots that laced up to his knees. He was the picture of the perfect soldier, but she didn't want to admit it. She didn't want to feel anything for him; that part of her life was over. He hadn't chosen her; he hadn't come to Hoboken, as his letter had promised, and despite her growing feelings for Vito, that fact was still painful for her.

"I thought it was the right and honorable thing to do." Ciro was filled with too many complicated feelings to sort out qiuckly: apprehension about the war, equal parts admiration and desire for this lovely young woman standing before him, surprise that she was here, and not in Italy as he had been told, and confusion over what her feelings for him might be. His thoughts tumbled over one another, until he felt unable to speak or think clearly. But he knew he had to talk to her—tonight, before he reported for duty—and tell her everything he was feeling and thinking. "Where are you going?" She looked so lovely and soft, he could barely resist reaching out to touch her. More than anything, he wished he could hold her.

"Home," she said. "Tenth Street."

"May I take you for a cup of coffee?"

Her instinct told her to say no. After all, she was seeing Vito Blazek on a regular basis; they were sweethearts. She had embraced a new life, and it was working. Why would she rip out the hem of a garment she was building on the chance of a better offer from Ciro? But Ciro was going off to war, and she wanted to leave nothing left unsaid between them. "Okay, yes, let's go for coffee."

The Automat was full of soldiers on their last night before they shipped out. Ciro explained his orders on the way to the restaurant. He was to take the train to New Haven in the morning, where they would board the USS *Olympic* to England, and then take a ferry to France. His unit would proceed to the north of France on foot.

Enza poured the coffee, while Ciro bought Enza a plain doughnut from one window, and a slice of coconut cream pie for himself. He sat down at their table, shifting his chair to cross his long legs in the bit of room left between their table and the next one over.

"I want you to know, I went to see you on Adams Street. Last Christmas. Signora Buffa told me you went home to Italy."

"Well, I didn't." Enza forced a smile, her heart filling with regret. She couldn't help but think that any plans regarding Ciro were doomed. She was weary of the back-and-forth; her unrequited longing for him was exhausting. And now Ciro had joined the army. Not only would she be required to pine for him for an undetermined length of time, maybe years; she might lose him altogether. The thought was too painful for her to bear. She just needed to let him go.

"No, you didn't." He smiled weakly, his mind reeling at the amount of time he could have spent with her.

"When did you sign up?"

"A few months ago. Do you remember my friend Luigi? He tried to enlist, too, but he has bad hearing, so I'll be going to fight alone."

"Oh. They only take you if you're perfect?"

"We know I'm not perfect." Ciro took a deep breath. "May I write to you?"

Despite herself, Enza smiled, then reached for a pen inside her evening purse, but she hesitated before handing it to him. "Maybe you shouldn't write to me, Ciro. I don't want you to feel obligated to write to me."

"But I want to write to you. Please, give me your address?"

"But what if I give you my address, and you never write? I would worry that something happened. Or, I would wonder if it was something I had said or done to offend you. Maybe I spilled your coffee, or maybe you don't like girls who wear pink—"

"I like pink," he said softly.

"You always like everything about me, until I'm gone. And then you forget me. We have this way with each other"—Enza's eyes misted—"that's . . ."

"*Difficile.*"

"*Difficile,*" she agreed. "You don't owe me anything just because we come from the same place. It's just a thread, Ciro. I could snap the bond with my teeth."

"I wouldn't want you to."

"It's as if you seek me out because you buried my sister."

"Stella isn't the only thread between us," Ciro insisted.

"You remember her name."

"I would never forget it." He folded his hands in his lap and looked at her.

"I feel like I've waited my whole life for you, only to be disappointed."

"I'm here now." Ciro reached out to take her hand.

"But tomorrow you'll be gone."

"We have a history."

"No, we don't. We have moments."

"Moments *are* history. If you have enough of them, they become a story. I kissed you on the mountain when we were fifteen," he said. "And I've never stopped thinking about you."

"And Ciro, I remember every word you ever said to me. I could tell you what you were wearing that night on the Passo Presolana and in the chapel at Saint Vincent's, and on the roof of the Zanetti Shoe Shop. How could you not know what I was feeling? I thought I made it plain that night on Mulberry Street." Enza looked away, thinking the Automat was so crowded, it would take her a few minutes to navigate her way out onto the street should she cry. She didn't want to cry in front of him.

"You did—I know that. And I wrote you that letter. I said I would come in a few weeks, and I came—I was there, Enza! But Signora Buffa lied to me."

Enza pulled her hand from his and placed it on her lap. "No, Ciro! Listen. A man who wants a woman will do anything it takes to win her. If you thought I went back to Schilpario, why wouldn't you write? Why wouldn't you move heaven and earth to find me? No ocean, no obstacle, no excuse could have kept us apart had you wanted me."

"That's true." His heart grew heavy as he realized she was right. He knew how single-minded he could be when he pursued a woman he desired; why had he avoided pursuing Enza?

"But there wasn't an ocean. There wasn't even a *mile* separating us. I've seen you with other women, Ciro. I've seen you when you're happy. Then you run into me—"

"That's fate—"

"Or just an accident!" Enza replied. "I remember the look on your face when you came into the shoe shop with Felicitá. You were blissful. You had champagne and a beautiful girl on your arm, and you were happy. You took one look at me, and you were instantly uncomfortable."

"No, I was happy to see you there!"

"Well, it didn't seem so, Ciro. It's not wrong of you to choose women who make you happy. You should have that."

"You're encouraging me to go with other women?" Ciro felt himself losing patience. "That's rare in a girl."

Enza persisted. "I remind you, I imagine, of things you'd rather not think about."

"You know what I'm thinking?"

"I can only trust what people *do* in this world, not what they say. You say all the right things, and then you disappear," Enza said quietly. "When I was ready for you, I couldn't find you."

"What if I told you that I want you now?" Ciro leaned toward her.

She smiled. "I would think that you're a courageous soldier going off to war, who wouldn't mind leaving a nice girl behind to pray for him. I remind you of what you come from. Don't mistake that for love. It's a deep connection, but it isn't what you think." Enza released her hands from his grip, put them in her lap, and leaned back.

Ciro walked Enza home to Greenwich Village that night. She shared stories about the opera. She mimicked Enrico Caruso, Geraldine Farrar, and Antonio Scotti and made Ciro laugh. He told Enza about the repair cart and his plans for the business when he returned from the war. He marveled again at how easy it was to talk to Enza, and how honest and open he was when he was with her.

They held one another close on the stoop of the Milbank House. Ciro wanted to kiss her good-bye, but she kissed his cheek instead. And that night, she remembered him in her prayers, but she did not pine for him.

20

A HATBOX

Una Cappelliera

November 22, 1917
Cambrai, France
Dear Eduardo,

I hope this letter reaches you, as it's the only one I have written in my time at the front. You know, above all others, how difficult it is for me to describe the world in words, but I will try.

From the first moment of my service, the days have rolled out with such uncertainty that I was unable to describe them. We sailed to England on July 1 on the USS *Olympic*. There were two thousand of us on the ship, though no one counted. I am in the regiment of General Finn "Landing" Taylor. His daughter Nancy Finn Webster made sure every new recruit had a new pair of socks for our tour of duty. Each of us received a pair when we boarded the ship. It reminded me of Sister Domenica and her knitting needles, clicking for hours on end, making us socks and sweaters.

We ran drills on the deck during the day. We proceeded to Tours, France, by ferry. From there, we walked for hundreds of miles, pitching camp, digging trenches, and when we did not dig trenches, we jumped into the ones that had been dug by the soldiers before us. You couldn't help asking yourself, "What happened to those men?"

I have been lucky to make some good friends. Juan Torres grew up in Puerto Rico, but lives in New York City, 116th Street. He introduces himself as the proud son of Andres Corsino Torres whenever he meets someone new. He is thirty-two years old, with six children and a wife, and is very devout to Our Lady of Guadalupe. When I told him my only brother was a priest, he went down on one knee and kissed my hand. So please, remember him in your prayers.

I cannot believe what I see here. We spend as much time burying the dead as we do fighting the enemy. We came upon a field, and we could not even see the earth beneath the dead. The wise soldier hardens his heart against all he sees, but I have not mastered that skill. I don't think I can, brother.

The land is badly scarred, forests have been torched, and the rivers are so full of slag from the fighting that the water has slowed to a trickle. Sometimes we happen upon a small blue lake or a pristine corner of a forest, and I can see that France was once beautiful. Not anymore.

We were told that our regiment was hit with mustard gas. On that morning, I was dreaming, asleep in the trench, sitting in my helmet (yes, better than the mud!), and I thought we were back in the convent with Sister Teresa when she made the aioli bread. But that scent of garlic was not the herb, but the poison of the gas. We were assured by our commander that very little of it blew across our area, but the soldiers think differently. I don't feel any effects of it yet, and this is good. I don't smoke too many cigarettes, so I am able to feel my lungs.

I hope to see you in Rome for your final vows in the spring. I think of you every day and send you my love,

Ciro

It seemed to Ciro that there were two ways a soldier tried to survive the war. He had examples of both in his regiment.

There was Private Joseph DeDia, who kept his gun cocked, his helmet straight, his eyes on the middle distance, as if his very gaze would send a message to the enemy. Order and skill would save him.

On the other hand, there was Major Douglas Leihbacher, who patrolled the trenches like a lowly private, making them laugh, conversing with them through the cold French nights. If Major Leihbacher could shore up the spirit, he could guide his men to win the war. A clear goal would save him.

Ciro was a good soldier—he obeyed orders, stayed alert, and performed every duty asked of him—but he remained skeptical of the politics behind the decisions made in the field. The men were often moved from place to place without preparation, and there seemed to be no apparent master plan. Ciro anticipated the worst, coming up with his own contingency plans because he had no confidence in the leaders.

While Ciro was aware of the sacrifice he and the others were making, he had not fully contemplated his own mortality, even as the bullets rained down around him. Every soldier comes to this, a moment when he acknowledges how he will meet his fate. Ciro listened to the voice within and remained focused. He saw the terrible waste of lives across the bloody fields of France. He thought of all those men might have accomplished in their lives. He decided that he would defend his life and the life of his fellow soldiers at all costs. But he would not seek to kill the enemy for the sake of winning the war. He would only kill to defend.

Most of the victories in battle seemed almost accidental. As they covered ground, the regiment came upon an arms storage unit in the barn of an old farm, and later a tank factory where lace was once made. But no intelligence guided them; it was simply vast numbers of men, in regiments that were numbered but not named, that canvassed the small villages of France, in search of whatever they might find, seize, or hold.

There would be entire days when Ciro would think the war was over, with not a single shot fired, or any sign of movement in the distance. And then battle would begin anew. It always began in the same way; faint sounds would grow louder, and within hours, the world around them would explode in a hailstorm of shells and bullets. The tanks sounded like pile drivers that crushed stone in the Alps. Their treads flattened anything in the tank's path. Ciro, who loved machinery and its design, thought the tanks were ugly. What beauty could be found in something that was created with the sole purpose of destruction?

Once Ciro's regiment made it to the trenches of Cambrai, they stayed. Sometimes he thought he would go out of his mind from the tedium, the long stretches when there was nothing to do but worry about when the next assault would come.

The nuns of San Nicola had taught him that no major decisions should be made in a state of exhaustion. But it seemed every decision in the trenches was made by men who were bone-tired, hungry, wet, and cold. There was no rest.

There was no peace to be made with death. Conversations steered around it. Some men asked their fellow soldiers to shoot them if they were left without limbs. Others vowed to turn their guns on themselves if captured. It seemed every soldier had his own ideas about how to control the outcome of war, knowing he was powerless to change what fate had in store for him.

Death was dodged, shirked, and outwitted daily. And still, death found them.

Ciro understood why they needed ten thousand men a day shipped from America to do battle on the fields of France. They were determined to win by sheer numbers, with or without a solid plan for victory. Some men, without a plan in place, began to cling to their dreams. Others began to see death as a way out of the horror of what they were living through. But not Ciro; he endured the cold fever of fear because he knew he must go home again.

Enza tucked the gold-filigreed invitation into her evening bag. She looked in the mirror, taking in her pearl gray brocade gown with a critical eye. Its columnar shape, with one shoulder exposed, was dramatic, even in the eyes of the woman who had created it.

Enza wore her long black hair in an upsweep. She pulled on silver satin evening gloves that stretched over her elbows, the contrast of the fabric leading the eye to the delicate blush of her bare shoulder. The effect was sophisticated and daring.

Dawn Gepfert had hosted a party every fall for the entire staff of the

Met, including the board of directors, crew, actors, and designers. It was the only time every department at the Met came together socially, and everyone who worked for the opera considered this party the ultimate perk.

Mrs. Gepfert had a twenty-room duplex on Park Avenue, with windows the size of doors and vaulted ceilings so high, they reminded Enza of a cathedral. Rooms were decorated in cheery English chintz, the walls papered in rosebuds climbing trompe-l'oeil trellises, and thick wool rugs and low lamps made the apartment seem cozy, despite its size.

The party was at its peak—a string quartet played music, there was lots of laughter and party chatter, most of the rooms were filled with guests—but Enza, Colin, Laura, and Vito had found a quiet spot.

Enza sank into a pale green velvet slipper chair facing the fireplace in the library as Vito added a log to the fire. The French doors leading to the wraparound terrace were open, and awnings had been unfurled, with small heaters placed along the perimeter. The evening hovered on the line between fall and winter; the night air had a nip to it, but it was still warm enough to be outside with a light wrap. Colin brought Laura a drink.

"This is living," Laura said.

"Great friends and good wine," Colin agreed.

Vito settled on the arm of Enza's chair. She held a glass of champagne, and he picked up his glass. "To us," he said.

Colin, Laura, and Enza raised their glasses.

"I wish this night would never end." Enza sighed. Sometimes she was so deeply in the moment of the present, Enza forgot the pain of the past and was free to enjoy herself without guilt. The scaffolding of her new life was sturdy, but she wanted the contents to be light, just like the colors of Dawn Gepfert's apartment.

"It doesn't have to," Laura said.

"I like where this is going." Colin pulled Laura close.

"Me too." Vito put his arm around Enza.

"I propped the Milbank's basement door open with an old shoe." Laura toasted herself and took a sip of wine. "Now we can stay out as late as we want without having to wait on the front steps in the morning like we're on a first-name basis with the milkman."

"I go with the smartest girl on earth." Colin laughed.

"And don't forget it."

This had been a good week for Laura. At long last she had met Colin's sons, and she found them as rambunctious as the brothers she helped raise. They went to Central Park where Laura proved herself to them. She thew a baseball, ran fast, and played hard, which engaged the boys and impressed Colin. Laura approached her love life just as she did her sewing. She was careful in the pattern stage, so there were no surprises later. But she would have to be flexible if she married Colin and became an instant mother to his boys because that family plan was already well in place.

Enza settled back into the chair, resting her head against Vito. She was overwhelmed with a feeling of contentment, attending their party in the clouds, the glittering city at her feet, with her friends who she had come to rely upon and treasure.

"Did you tell Vito what Signor Caruso said about you?" Laura nudged Enza.

"No," Enza said softly.

"What did he say?" Vito asked.

"He asked Enza when she was going to design costumes instead of just sewing them."

"He did?" Vito was impressed.

"He thinks I have a good eye," Enza said with a shy smile.

"Come up with some sketches," Vito said.

"She already has two hatboxes full at the Milbank," Laura said.

"And that's where they will stay." Enza sipped her champagne.

"All of a sudden, the tireless Italian girl is shy about her work. I don't believe it." Vito shook his head.

"I still have a lot to learn," Enza said.

They heard applause and cheers from the living room.

"He's here," Vito said. Enza, Colin, and Laura followed him out to the living room, carrying their drinks.

The living room of the Gepfert home was filled like a church on a feast day. The revelers faced Enrico Caruso, who stood under a chandelier, taking in their love like sweet cream in his coffee. Vito pulled Enza close in the doorway as Colin and Laura sneaked through the crowd to get closer to him.

"You know how much affection I have for each and every one of you. I want to thank you for all the hard work you did on *Lodoletta*. Gerry and I are grateful for your dedication."

Geraldine Farrar held up her glass. "Thank you all for making us look so good. And I would also like to thank the United States Army, who is making fast work of putting the Germans in their place—"

The revelers cheered loudly.

"We look forward to having the heat back on in the opera house. It'll be a long winter without it. We're doing our bit and keeping the furnace on low, to send our coal to the front for a good cause. But there's only so many times I can embrace Enrico Caruso onstage and pretend it's a love scene. Frankly, I needed his body heat to keep me from frostbite."

Caruso made his way through the crowd, shaking hands, embracing his dresser, bowing deeply to the hostess in gratitude. As he passed Vito, Vito leaned in and whispered in Caruso's ear, "Don't forget your seamstresses."

"My Vincenza and my Laura," he said, embracing them both at once. "You have been so kind to me. I will remember your invisible stitches on my hems and your macaroni."

"It was an honor to work for you, Signore," Enza said.

"We'll never forget it," Laura assured him.

Caruso reached into his pocket and placed a gold coin in each of their hands. "Don't tell anybody," he whispered, and moved through the crowd.

Enza looked down at the coin. It was a solid gold disc with Caruso's profile etched on it.

"It's real," Laura whispered. "I'm gonna buy myself a mink."

"I'll never spend it," Enza whispered back.

And that was a promise Enza Ravanelli kept her whole life long.

*   *   *

Ciro found a small room available at the Tiziano Hotel, close to the Campo de' Fiori, where the peddlers sold blood oranges, fresh fish, herbs, and bread. He had only the uniform on his back, a change of underclothes in his knapsack, a document guaranteeing him free passage home on any ship departing from Naples, and his final paycheck from the U.S. Army. The war had officially ended a few weeks ago, and after all he had withstood, he was eager to return to his life on Mulberry Street. But first, he had to find his brother.

The last letter he had received from Eduardo explained that he was scheduled to be ordained as a priest into the Franciscan order in Saint Peter's Basilica at the end of November.

If Ciro thought the U.S. Army had layers of bureaucracy, he knew now that they had nothing on the Roman Catholic Church. No information was available regarding the ordination ceremonies. When Ciro went through the proper channels to obtain details, he was turned away, or the response was vague and veiled in secrecy.

Ciro knew, when his brother left for the seminary so many years ago, that they would have little contact, but they both had hoped that would change when Eduardo became a priest.

On the advice of a Vatican secretary, who by chance had ties to Bergamo and took pity on him, Ciro addressed letters to every deacon, priest, and prelate in the general directory, hoping to find someone who had information regarding his brother's final orders.

Ciro was careful not to smudge the ink as he addressed the last envelope. He laid the sealed letters in the bright sunshine of the hotel windowsill so they might dry as he dressed. As he pulled on his boots, he saw a split in the seam where the upper met the sole. He examined it, then looked around the room for supplies to fix it. He pulled scissors and a large sewing needle from his backpack. The last time he'd used either was to dress a wound incurred by his friend Juan when he stepped on a spike of barbed wire buried in a trench's mud.

The surgical thread wouldn't hold the leather, so Ciro looked around the room for string with heft that might work. He was prepared to take the pull string from his windowshade when his eyes fell on his knapsack. Instead, he clipped a six-inch portion of the pull cord from the knapsack, knotting the end. Then he threaded the cord through the needle and sewed his torn shoe together, deftly securing the thinning leather to the sole. He tidied up the end, looping it through the upper so it might hold.

Ciro slipped into his boot, pleased with his temporary fix. The patch job should last until he was back on the machines at the Zanetti Shoe Shop. He gathered up his letters and left the hotel.

The side streets of Rome were packed with foreigners who had been siphoned through Italy on their way home from France. Ciro saw an occasional American soldier, who would nod at him, but for the most part, the men wearing uniforms were with the Italian army.

Wherever there were soldiers, there were the parasol girls, like the redhead who had greeted Ciro when he first arrived in New York. He looked at those girls differently now, understanding that they needed work, just as he did. There seemed to be so many more of them on the streets of Rome than there had been in New York.

Ciro was comfortable as he walked the streets of the city, not because he was a native Italian, but because the noise reminded him of Manhattan. He found himself looking into the faces of those he passed, hoping he might recognize a priest or a nun who might be able to help him find his brother.

The addresses on the envelopes took him to various parts of the city, requiring a good deal of walking to deliver them. He had one to deliver to the center of the city, and one a mile away, at the basilica within the gardens of Montecatini. He learned that he must hike up beyond Viterbo to the small chapel on the hillside outside of Rome, where the Franciscans stayed when they traveled through. Having delivered the last letter, Ciro lingered outside the chapel until nightfall, hoping that his brother might miraculously pass through on his way to the Vatican. But with hundreds of priests and seminarians in Rome at any given time, Ciro knew his chances of getting to Eduardo were slipping through his fingers with each passing day.

Ciro walked back toward the city, stopping at a crowded restaurant, a simple open-walled structure with a loggia shaded with olive branches. Jugs of homemade wine were filled to the top, splashing purple tears onto the white tablecloths as the waitresses set them out for customers. There was much chatter and laughter as hearty bowls of risotto speckled with mushrooms and chestnuts, with a side of hot, crusty bread, were served to the locals, farmers, construction workers, and day laborers. Ciro was the only soldier in the restaurant. His uniform drew some curious stares.

Ciro tore into the feast hungrily, having spent the day on foot, unable to stop to eat, because he wanted to deliver every last envelope to the correct address. He hoped the meal would fill him up, and even ease the heavy burden he felt in his heart. He had all but given up hope that he would see Eduardo again. He sipped the wine, which soothed him as the warmth of the smoky grapes spread through his body. He knew that when he sailed back to America, it would be many years before he would return to Italy.

The waitress placed a bowl of fresh figs on the table. Ciro looked up at her. He guessed her to be around forty. Her black hair was streaked with white, pulled off her face in a low chignon. She wore a linen apron over a black muslin skirt and red blouse. She had an attractive face, with black Roman eyes. She smiled at Ciro, and he nodded respectfully. He sipped his espresso, and remembered a time before he was a soldier when he would have smiled back at her, prolonged her stay at his table, suggested they steal away for a few minutes later in the evening. Ciro shook his head. It seemed that everything about him had changed; his reaction to the world and the things that went on in it was as unpredictable as the moods of a Vatican secretary.

＊   ＊   ＊

Ciro stood at the front desk of the Tiziano Hotel, looking at the mail cubbies behind it. Most were stuffed with letters and newspapers, but when he gave the attendant his room number, there was nothing. Not a single response to any of the letters he had delivered.

Ciro climbed the steps to his room. Once inside, he sat and unbuckled his boots. He slipped them off and leaned back on the bed. What a fool's errand this trip to Rome had been! Ciro's face flushed with embarrassment when he thought about the long story he'd told the attendant at the Vatican rectory, dropping in the names of priests and the orders of nuns that he knew from his days in the convent. It had been a disingenuous exercise, a waste; no soldier in mended boots could possibly impress any watchman to the pope. Ciro chided himself for forgetting to bribe them with money—that might have worked.

There was a soft knock at the door. Ciro got up to answer, expecting the night maid. Instead, his heart filled with joy as he looked into tender brown eyes he had not seen in seven years. "Brother!" Ciro shouted.

Eduardo embraced Ciro and slipped into the room. Ciro closed the door behind him and looked at his brother, who wore the mud brown robes of the Franciscans. A belt of white hemp rope was knotted around his waist. Upon his feet, he wore sandals with three bands of plain brown leather across the top of his foot. Eduardo threw the hood off his head; his black hair was cropped short. The glasses once used only for reading were perched on his nose. The round lenses trimmed in gold gave Eduardo a sober, professorial look.

"I've been looking for you everywhere," Ciro said. "I left letters in every rectory in Rome."

"I've heard," Eduardo said. He sized up his brother and couldn't believe what he saw. Ciro was terribly thin, and his thick hair was shorn, but more shocking to Eduardo were the dark circles under Ciro's eyes, the hollow spaces where there once had been robust, full cheeks. "You look terrible."

"I know. I don't make a very handsome soldier." Ciro looked around the room. "I have nothing to offer you."

"That's all right. I'm not even supposed to be here. If the monsignor finds out, they'll kick me out of the order. This visit is not allowed, and I must hurry, and be back at the rectory before they realize I'm gone."

"You're not allowed to spend time with your only brother?" Ciro said. "Do they know you're all I have in the world?"

"I don't expect you to understand, but there's a reason for it. To become a priest, I have to separate from all I love in the world, and sadly, that includes you. I have something to occupy my heart in a wholly different way now, but I understand that you don't. If you love me, pray for me. Because I pray for you, Ciro. Always."

"Any racket but the Holy Roman Church. You could have had any career in the world. Writer. Printer. We could've bought the old press and bound books and sold them like the Montinis. But you had to put on the robes. Why, Eduardo? I would have been happy had you been a tax collector—anything but the priesthood." Ciro fell back on the bed.

Eduardo laughed. "It's not a career, it's a life."

"Some life. Cloistered away. Vows of silence. I could never shut you up. How can you live that way?"

"I've changed," Eduardo said. "But I see you haven't. And I'm glad."

"You just can't see it. But I'm different now," Ciro said. "I don't know how I could be the same after what I've seen." He sat down next to Eduardo. "Sometimes I get a good night's sleep, and I wake up and think, *Anything is possible. You're not in the trenches. You don't have a gun. Your time is your own again.* But there's a heaviness inside me. I don't trust that the world is better now. And why else would we have gone to war? What reason could there possibly be to behave like a bunch of animals? I'll never know the answer."

"You're an American now," Eduardo said.

"True—I will be a full citizen soon. And at least I was on the side of the mighty. I wish you could come with me and live in America."

"You'll have to be in the world for me, Ciro."

"I wonder if I still know how to do that."

"I hope you will have a wife and a family, the way you always dreamed of. Give them the childhood you always wanted. Be the father we didn't have. There has to be a special girl. You wrote to me about the May Queen at your church."

"I only wrote about Felicitá to impress you. I wanted you to think that I'd found religion through a pious princess. I found a lot, but not God. She married a nice Sicilian."

"I'm sorry. Is there anyone else?"

"No," Ciro replied, but even as he spoke, an image of Enza Ravanelli appeared in his mind's eye, and his body filled with a sad ache.

"I don't believe it. No one loves women more than you do."

"Is that an achievement?"

"You had a knack for it. There was never any question that marriage would be your calling. It's not really that different from my own calling. We both reached out for what we needed. Whether it's spiritual or emotional sustenance, we both went looking for our heart's fulfillment."

"Except you have to live in a cell."

"I am leading a good life in that cell."

"What about Mama? Have you learned anything else since you wrote to me?"

Eduardo reached into his pocket. "The sisters at San Nicola forwarded this letter to me."

"What does it say?"

Eduardo unfolded the letter. "She's had a hard time, Ciro."

Ciro's heart was pierced with pain at the thought of his mother suffering.

"All I ever wanted was for the three of us to be together again. Papa was taken from us, but you and me and Mama, that could have been." Ciro wiped the tears from his eyes.

"I pray every day for Papa's soul, Ciro. We can't forget all the effort that went into securing our happiness and safety. Mama tried her best to protect us. No matter what happened, we have to be grateful to her for knowing what was best for us."

"I wanted *her*," Ciro cried. "And even now, she doesn't want us to know where she is. Why?"

"She tries to answer that in the letter. She was ill when she left the mountain, and she thought she would return."

"But she didn't," Ciro said. "We lost Papa, then we lost Mama. And tomorrow I'm going to lose you."

"You will never lose me, Ciro. I risked my ordination to come to you tonight. I came to tell you to be strong. Don't be afraid. You're my brother, and you will always be the most important person in my life. As soon as I'm ordained, I will find Mama, and I'll keep her safe until you can see her again. It's all I can do."

"Do you really want this life?"

"I want to be useful. To use my mind. To pray. To know God."

"What do you get out of it?"

"To know God makes sense of life, I don't know how else to say it. Come to my ordination tomorrow, Ciro. I want you to be there. Ten o'clock at St. Peter's Basilica."

Eduardo stood and opened his arms to Ciro. Ciro remembered scrubbing the statue of Saint Francis, and how careful he had been with the folds of the robe, where the artist had carefully drawn slim lines and painted them with gold leaf. Now, standing before him, was his humble brother, the finest man he would ever know in the same brown robes of the Franciscan order. Ciro embraced him, and felt the billowing sleeves of Eduardo's robes enfold him like wings.

Eduardo lifted the hood of his robe and placed it on his head. He opened the door, then turned back to Ciro. "I'll write to you as soon as I know where they're sending me. If you ever need me, I will come to you, regardless of what the church says."

"And I'll come to you, regardless of what the church says." Ciro smiled. "That would be my pleasure."

"I knew that." Eduardo slipped out the door, closing it softly behind him. Ciro sat down on the bed and unfolded the letter from his mother.

> Dear Eduardo and Ciro,
>
> I am so proud of my boys. You have become a shoemaker, and Eduardo, a priest. A mother wants her children to be happy, and please know that's all I ever wanted for you.
>
> When I left you and Eduardo at the convent, I had planned to return that summer. But my health took a terrible turn, and I was unable to return to Vilminore. The sisters were good about sending your marks and updates about your life in the convent. I was happy to know that there was never a time that a single hearth was not prepared to be lit. The sisters said they had never known what it was like to have the fireplaces roaring at once, keeping the convent warm. I am so proud of you. I hope to be well enough to see you someday, and your brother too. Your mama loves you.

.   .   .

The charcoal clouds hung low over the Piazza di San Pietro as rain fell onto the cobblestones like silver stickpins. The piazza outside the Vatican was empty as the crowds sought shelter under the colonnade from the downpour, including a cluster of pigeons lined up on the joice overhead, perched like a row of musical notes.

Ciro stood by a red obelisk in his brown uniform as the rain jingled against his tin helmet. He took a final drag off his cigarette, tossed it away, and walked to the entrance of the church as a slew of black-and-white nuns, moving in an orderly cluster, entered the Basilica. Ciro took off his hat, bowed his head to the nuns, and walked with them as they entered the church. He smiled when he thought of Sister Teresa, who had advised him to look for the black-and-whites when he was unknown in a city. Ciro Lazzari felt unknown everywhere he went now.

He knelt in a pew behind the nuns. They bowed their heads in prayer, but Ciro looked around, taking in the architecture of the Basilica as though it were the church of San Nicola and he was assessing it for a spring cleaning. Even though his brother's life was about to change forever, penitents and tourists meandered through the massive portals, stopping to pray at the sepulchers and shrines in a most ordinary way. There was not the feeling of something special in the air.

A group of African priests in gold robes walked up the left transept and disappeared into a chapel behind the main altar. The Vatican, Ciro thought, was like a train station, disparate groups peeling off from one another to go to various destinations, under one roof, *leading where?* he wondered.

The aisle soon filled with what seemed like hundreds of priests in the brown robes of the Franciscans, tied with white rope belts. Ciro watched the ordained priests glide by silently.

Following the brown robes, a choir of altar boys carried the brass-trimmed candles of acolytes. The candidates followed them, in starched white robes, in two long lines. They filed by the Chapel of the Blessed Sacrament in the right transept, hands buried deep in their billowing white sleeves, heads bowed reverently.

Ciro had moved behind a rope attended by Vatican guards to get a better look at the seminarians' faces. He made note of every face, one after another, until finally he found Eduardo, resplendent in white.

Ciro reached across the rope to touch his brother's arm. Eduardo smiled at Ciro before two Vatican guards took Ciro by the arm, pulled him to a side aisle, then removed him to the back of the church. It wouldn't matter if the guards had dumped Ciro in the Tiber; he had seen Eduardo on the most important day of his life. That was all that mattered.

Ciro whispered to the guards, explaining that his brother was receiving holy orders. They took pity on the soldier and allowed him to watch from the back of the pews.

Eduardo lay on the cold marble floor, arms outstretched in the shape of a cross, face to the floor, as the cardinal in his ruby red zucchetto leaned over him to administer chrism and holy oil. Tears sprang to Ciro's eyes as his brother rose to his feet to receive his blessing. He had lost Eduardo for good as the sign of the cross was placed upon his brother's forehead.

Ciro stayed in the Basilica long after the ceremony, hoping that his brother would make his way from the sacristy out into the church, as he had on so many mornings at San Nicola, to set out the Holy Book and the chalice and light the candles for mass.

But the Holy Roman Church had other ideas. As soon as Eduardo was made a priest, he was shuttled away swiftly. Eduardo was on his way to his assignment, and that could be anywhere! Sicily, or Africa, or as close as the gardens of Montecatini in the center of Rome. Near or far, it didn't matter. Eduardo was gone. It was finished.

The arrangements made by the U.S. Army to return Ciro home to America were through the port of Naples. Ciro bought a one-way train ticket to Naples at the station.

As he stood on the platform, waiting for the train, Ciro imagined what it would be like to take the old Roman road, Via Tiberius, out of the city and up to Bologna to catch the train to Bergamo. He imagined taking the Passo Presolana up the mountain by carriage and looking down into the gorge, finding the brown brambles of late autumn every bit as beautiful as the spring flowers. Ciro imagined that he would appreciate everything about where he came from now, but the ache in his heart wasn't about missing a particular place; it was about something else entirely. He knew he must return to America to put that ache to rest.

Enza turned the work light off on her sewing machine. She rose from her work stool and stretched her back.

"Hey, you." Vito poked his head into the costume shop. "How about dinner?"

"How about yes?" Enza pulled on her coat and grabbed her purse.

"Where's Laura?" Vito asked.

"Colin took her to see the boys tonight."

With a twinkle in his eye, Vito hummed the wedding march. *"Bum, bum, bum, bum . . ."*

"Where are we going?" Enza pulled her coat from the closet. "Do I need gloves?"

"And a hat."

"Fancy?"

"Maybe."

"I'm a very fancy girl," Enza said.

"When did this happen?"

"There's a gentleman who keeps taking me places. And now I can't drink out of anything but Bavarian crystal, and if the caviar isn't cold, I can't eat it."

"Poor you."

"I'm afraid I'll never see Hoboken again."

"You can wave to it from the first-class cabin of the *Queen Mary.*"

Vito took Enza's hand as they left the Met. He guided her west; Enza figured they were going to one of Vito's favorite bistros in the theater district, intimate rooms with glazed brick walls, low lighting, and rare steaks on the table. Instead, he kept walking, taking her to the west-side docks at Thirty-eighth Street.

A massive construction site greeted them, a surface of gravel plowed smooth over river silt and mud. Dump trucks were parked by the river's edge, while a cement mixer was angled near the street. There were stacks of steel beams, enormous wheels of tubing, bins of picks, and large shovels resting in wheelbarrows.

Enza waited on the ramp outside the construction booth while Vito ducked inside. Enza chuckled to herself. Vito was always planning an adventure. If he wasn't renting out the Ferris wheel at Coney Island just for the two of them, he was taking her to speakeasies where the jazz was as smooth as the gin. Vito was a man who knew how to live, and he wanted everyone in his life to live it up. After a moment, Vito emerged with two tin hard hats. He handed her one.

She removed her hat and put on the hard hat. "You said it was fancy."

"You wait," he said.

Vito helped Enza into the outdoor elevator. He snapped the gate and pressed the button that would lift them to the top of the construction site. Enza held her heart as the elevator ascended up into the night sky. She felt as if she was flying, though Vito had a firm grip on her. Soon the panorama at her feet changed, and she looked out over New York City at night, rolled out beneath them like a bolt of midnight blue silk moire staggered with crystals.

"What do you think?" Vito asked.

"I think you're a magician. You pull things from the ordinary and turn them into magic."

"There's something I want to give you."

"I think this view is plenty."

"No, it's not enough. I want to give you everything. I want to give you the world."

"You already have." Enza rested her head on his shoulder. "You've given me confidence and adventure. You've given me a new way of being."

"And I want to give you more—" Vito pulled her close. "Everything I am. Everything I dream. And everything you could imagine. It would be my purpose and joy to make you happy. Will you marry me, Vincenza Ravanelli?"

Enza looked out over the shimmering lights of Manhattan. She couldn't believe she had come this far, and climbed this high. She thought of a thousand reasons to say yes, but she only needed one. Vito Blazek would make sure she had fun. Life would be a party. After years of taking care of everyone else, Vito vowed to take care of her. Enza had worked hard, and now she was ready to experience life with a man who knew how to live.

"What do you say, Enza?"

"Yes! I say yes!"

Vito kissed her, her face, then her ear, then her neck.

He placed a round ruby surrounded by diamond chips on her hand. "The ruby is my heart, and the diamonds are you—you're my life, Enza." He kissed her, and she felt her body weaken in his arms. "I would make love to you right here, if you'd let me," he whispered in her ear.

"I'm afraid of heights, Vito."

"Will you change your mind on the ground?" he teased.

"Let's get married first." Enza had traveled far from home, but her parents' hopes lived within her. She was a proper young woman, raised in a religious home by pious parents. She would continue to follow their rules, even though she had earned the right to make her own decisions long ago. Enza believed there was a beauty in the sacraments that brought grace to living. She wanted a life of refinement and serenity, and certainly Vito, with his grand vision of the future, understood that. He believed Enza deserved the best because she was, without a name, education, or position, the embodiment of true elegance. Her natural grace had been born in her. It could not have been manufactured or bought. It simply was.

The crisp autumn air was cold and sweet, like vanilla smoke. High above the city, Enza was no longer the Hoboken factory girl, but a hard-working American woman of Italian birth who had risen to a new station in life, a climb not to the second floor on the service stairs but to the penthouse via the elevator.

Enza would marry Vito Blazek.

As a team, these two young professionals, one an artisan, the other a liaison to the talent, would continue to work at the Metropolitan Opera House, eat breakfast at the Plaza Hotel, and dance at the Sutton Place Mews. They had fine friends; they wore silk, drank champagne, and knew where to buy peonies in the winter. They were on their way up.

21

A GOLD BRAID
Una Treccia d'Oro

As Ciro stood on the deck of the SS *Caserta*, the Atlantic Ocean was the color of green carnival glass. In the distance the depths turned a charcoal gray as the waves ruffled the surface in iridescent silver.

This was an entirely different view than it had been upon his passage from New Haven almost two years ago. Ciro was now twenty-four years old, a veteran of the Great War. The family he once knew was gone, the mother he longed for still absent, and his only brother, his last connection to Vilminore di Scalve and his dream of a house on the mountain, had left the comfort of the ordinary world and become a priest.

Ciro's desire to remain a lifelong confidant to Eduardo and an uncle to his brother's unborn children had disappeared into the air like puffs of smoke from the urn of burning incense with which the cardinal blessed the seminarians, who were turned into men of God with a drop of holy oil.

Eduardo was a far better person than any of the priests that Ciro knew. Eduardo was generous where Don Martinelli was stingy and chaste where Don Gregorio was not. Eduardo had the best heart that Ciro had ever known—man or woman—fair, competent, and contemplative. The seeds of wisdom were planted deep within Eduardo, just as an appetite for life—good food and beautiful women—was planted deep in Ciro.

Ciro mourned Eduardo's new life, because it meant that he had lost his brother for good. Perhaps they would see each other a few times in the decades to come. There would be letters, but they would be infrequent. For two boys who had been inseparable, two brothers who were completely simpatico, to lead such separate lives was a terrible sacrifice. Ciro couldn't help but feel cheated by the church; after all, with the recommendation of Don Gregorio, it had broken up two brothers who were the only living family each had. So much for the healing love of the Sacred Heart.

Eduardo's devotion to Ciro would now be given instead to the priests of the order of Saint Francis of Assisi, and whatever was left beyond that would go to the Holy Church of Rome. Eduardo had given up any possibility of finding a wife and making a family when he became a priest. Ciro had wanted so much more for his brother. He wished that Eduardo could know the comfort, ease, and abiding serenity that came from the company of a good woman, and how the appetite for love and its simple but glorious connections made a man seek more in the world, not less.

Ciro imagined that Eduardo would try to save the world one soul at a time, but why would he want to?

Before the war, Ciro had thought he too was capable of great things. But now, with the landscape of France carved up and scarred forever by the trenches, filled with the broken dead, Ciro wanted no part of government and the men who ran it. Rome had been a great disappointment to him. The Italians were losing their way, he thought. There was something fragile about his Italy now. The Italian people had been poor for so long, they no longer believed they had any power to change the country they lived in. Even in the wake of victory, they couldn't see better times. They no longer believed these were possible. They would grasp the next ideology that came along, just as a drowning man grabs at any sliver of wood. Anything is better than nothing, the Italians would shrug, an attitude that cleared the way for despots and their reigns of cruelty, for wars and their blighted landscapes.

Ciro had learned that life was never better after a war, just different.

He would always long for the Italy he knew before the war. The borders were soft; Italians traveled to France without papers, Germans to Spain, Greeks to Italy. Nationalism had now replaced neighborliness.

As a soldier, Ciro had learned that good men can't fix what evil men are intent on destroying. He had learned to choose what was worth holding on to, and what was worth fighting for. Every man had to decide that for himself, and some never did. He had not survived the Great War to return home the same man.

Ciro had faced death. This was when a man was most likely to turn to the angels for intercession. Instead, Ciro had turned inward. He'd endured moments of paralyzing fear. He'd felt dread deep in his bones when the scent of the mustard gas permeated the fields in the distance, a pungent blend of bleach and ammonia that at first note seemed like something decent and familiar, the garlic herb simmering in Sister Teresa's kitchen pot, rather than a death warrant as the cloud of gas snaked its way to the trenches that formed a border across France.

He remembered diluting bleach and cleaning the crevices of old marble with a small brush to remove stains from the stone. That same scent, stronger and more pungent, would linger over the battlefield with a thick stillness. Sometimes Ciro would be relieved when the wind carried the poison away from the front instead of toward it. But he also learned that a soldier could not count on anything—his commanding officer, his fellow infantrymen, his country, or the weather. He only had luck, or didn't.

Ciro had discovered that he could go for days without much food; he'd learned to erase the image of a rare steak and potato, a glass of wine with purses of gnocchi and fresh butter, from his mind. Hunger too, it seemed had little to do with the body, but everything to do with the mind.

He didn't imagine gathering eggs, as he had as a boy back at the convent, or the egg gently whisked in the cup with sugar and cream in Sister Teresa's kitchen. He tried not to think of Sister Teresa, or write to her to pray for him. He was so hungry he did not want to imagine her in her apron, kneading sweet dough or chopping vegetables for stew. There was no comfort in happy memories; they just made it all seem worse.

Ciro had also thought every day at the front about women. What had soothed him in the past comforted him even more during the war. He remembered Sister Teresa in the convent kitchen at San Nicola, how she fed him and listened to him. He thought about Felicitá's soft skin, the rhythm of her breath, the sleepy satisfaction that enveloped them after making love. He remembered women he had not met but had only seen on Mulberry Street. One girl, eighteen years old in a straw hat, had worn a red cotton skirt with buttons down the back from waist to hem. He thought about the curve of her calf and her beautiful feet, in flat sandals with one strap of pale blue leather between the toes, as she walked past the shoe shop. He imagined, over and over again, the power of a kiss, and he thought that if he made it out of these trenches, he would never take a single kiss for granted. A woman's hand in his was a treasure; if he held one again, he would pay attention and relish the warm security of a gentle touch.

When his fellow soldiers visited a village known for their *belles femmes*, he'd made love to a girl with golden hair braided to her waist. Afterward, she had loosened her long braid and let him brush her hair. The image of her head bowed as he stroked her hair would stay with him for the rest of his life.

His moment of greatest clarity had come on the day he was certain he would die. Word had reached his platoon that the Germans were bombing with mustard gas, and their intention was to leave not one man, woman, or child alive in France. Their goal was total annihilation, soldier and civilian. In what the men believed were their final moments on earth, many prayed; some wrote letters to their wives, tucking them carefully next to their field orders and identification, hoping that their allies would deliver the message after burying their bodies. Young men wept openly at the knowledge that they would never see their mothers' faces again.

But to Ciro, it seemed disingenuous to ask God to save him, when so many soldiers deserved life more—men with children, wives, families, lives. Let them pray. They had someone at home waiting for them.

Ciro hoped his mother, Caterina, was safe somewhere.

The red robes of Rome would protect Eduardo; Ciro was certain his brother would be all right.

There was only one other face that he pictured. He remembered her at fifteen in a work smock, at sixteen in traveling clothes, and at twenty-two years old, in a pink gossamer dress. He imagined her at fifty, gray, yet still strong and sturdy, with grandchildren. *His* grandchildren.

Ciro knew in that instant that there was only one thing worth dying for, only one person for whom he would lay down his life. Enza Ravanelli. She had owned his heart all along.

How ironic that Enza had told him not to write and not to think about her. Ciro could not stop thinking about her. If he were lucky enough to live through this carnage and chaos, the love of one good woman would be all he needed to sustain him. Starving, wasting away, falling sick and dying, fighting fevers and fending off lice and rats, filth and dysentery, all the guarantees of war—all of it was worth it if he could live out the rest of his days with Enza.

It had always been Enza. Life without her would be as grim as the trenches he'd called home during the war, where a piece of bread was like a diamond, and a cup of clean water, a dream fulfilled. In that instant he knew that nothing—not even the acid scent of mustard gas in the air or the decay of the dead around him—could keep him from going home to the woman he loved. And as he stood on the deck of the SS *Caserta*, he knew how lucky he was to have survived, and he hoped to take the gift of his great fortune and pledge his life to a deserving woman. He could only hope that she had waited for him.

. . .

Laura helped Enza make her wedding suit. She had chosen a Tintoretto-inspired cinnamon brown wool, piped with black velvet and finished with black buttons. The earthy red-brown tone of the bouclé wool was the exact hue of the earth on the Passo Presolana. Enza thought about her mother, and how many times she had made her tell the story of her wedding day. Now it was Enza's turn. How she wished her mother could be here! She would have appreciated every detail. Enza built a hat of matching brown felt with a wide brim, tucked with a black satin knot and set with a black pearl.

Vito wrote to Marco in California and Giacomina in Schilpario for permission to marry their eldest daughter. He wrote pages about why she was a wonderful girl, and described the life he hoped to give her.

When Giacomina read the letter from Vito, she wept. She knew this meant that Enza would never return to live on the mountain. Her beloved daughter had a new life. Giacomina prayed to be happy for the girl who had worked for so many years to make their lives secure. She did not worry about Enza, because she believed she would make the best choice in a husband. But she did worry about the Ravenellis, who would not be as strong without Enza's leadership.

When Marco received his letter from Vito, he also cried. Longing to return to his family, he had hoped Enza would go with him despite her terrible ordeal on the passage over. He had spent seven years in America working to make enough money to build their home. The house was finished, and when Marco returned, he would sit before the fire in the house his sacrifices and those of his daughter Enza had made possible. It was a bittersweet realization that Enza would never share the family hearth with him.

Choosing to marry Vito meant that Enza accepted that she would never go home again. She had put her illness out of her mind, but now she admitted to herself that she would never be able to show her husband or her future children with him the frescoes in Clusone or the fields above Schilpario; nor would they ever hear the orchestra in Azzone. Vito had brought her to the best doctors, who made it clear there was no cure for her particular motion sickness. They would have to learn about her family through her, and it would be her responsibility to keep them close in her heart despite the distance.

The sun was pink that November morning, embedded deep in a pale blue sky. Enza thought it odd, but didn't take it as a sign. Her mother always checked the sky over Schilpario and took every movement and color change as an omen. There would be none of that today. Enza had a calm sense about her, a serenity Laura noticed that morning when they dressed at the Milbank House.

"You're so quiet," Laura said.

"I'm about to change everything about my life," Enza said, pulling on her gloves. "I'm sad to leave you. Our room. I'll never be a young unmarried woman again."

"You knew we had to grow up and fall in love and marry," Laura said. "It's a natural progression. And you're happy with Vito, aren't you?"

"Of course." Enza smiled. "It's just a shame that whenever life is good, things can't stay the way they are. Every decision leads you forward, like when I used to step across the stones to cross streams in the Alps. I'd take a step, and another, and another, and soon I'd be safely across."

"As it should be."

"But there were times when I took a step and there was no stone to step onto. And the water was so cold. "

"You'll get through the bad times," Laura assured her.

"Because we know they'll come."

"For all of us." Laura smiled. "This is not a day to be solemn. It's a day to celebrate. Leave serious Enza right here in this room. You're a beautiful bride, and this is your moment."

Enza and Laura said good-bye to the girls of the Milbank House, who gathered on the front steps to wish Enza well. The future dancers, playwrights, and actresses were enthusiastic about Enza's new life, an affirmation that all the stories told on the stage with happy endings were somehow true. Enza was a walking symbol of success to them that morning. They were giddy with delight for her.

Enza and Laura traveled the few blocks to Our Lady of Pompeii from the Milbank House on foot. Vito and Colin Chapin, his best man, would meet them in the sacristy. The small ceremony would take place with Father Sebastianelli officiating at the Shrine of the Blessed Lady.

Enza and Laura walked past the fruit vendors, the street sweeper, the men in felt hats on their way to work. Everything in Greenwich Village was in its place, as it was every morning, reliable and predictable. The only people for whom this day was special were Enza and Vito. The world outside was spinning as it always had, and two lovers exchanging rings was not going to change it.

"You wait here." Laura gave Enza a hug. "I'll go inside and make sure everything is ready for you."

"Thank you, Laura." She gave Laura a warm embrace. "Always be my best friend."

"Always." Laura smiled and went into the church.

Enza stood on Carmine Street. She remembered Signora Buffa, and how hard her first months in America had been, how those months had turned into years, and how homesick she had been. She looked back and remembered her room at Saint Vincent's Hospital, just a few blocks from where she stood. She reviewed the forward movement of each year of her life since, the decisions made and steps taken, sewn like small stitches with care and consistency. Enza could step back to see, at long last, a finished garment. Her life was something beautiful to behold, and she had built it herself.

"Enza," a voice said from behind her. She smiled and turned, thinking it was Vito, with her flowers.

"Enza," Ciro Lazzari said again. He wore the dull brown uniform of the doughboys, the belt notched tight, the knee boots laced with precision, though Enza could see where the laces had been knotted together several times to make them long enough. Every hem on his uniform was ragged, each cuff turned from wear. He was thin, his face etched with exhaustion and worry, but he was clean, his thick hair cut short, and his eyes were more blue than the sky that morning. He held a bouquet of violets in his right hand, his helmet in his left. He gave her the flowers.

"Ciro, what are you doing here?"

"I made it." He managed a smile, knowing he was not too late. The girls at the Milbank had filled him in. "I went to the Milbank House. They said you'd be here. You're always in church. Is it a Holy Day of Obligation?" He asked knowing for sure her purpose in attending church that morning.

She shook her head that it wasn't.

He saw the worry in her eyes. "You're so beautiful." Ciro leaned forward to embrace her, and she stepped back.

"I'm getting married," she said.

"I know."

"I should go inside," Enza said. "The priest is waiting."

"Padre can wait. He has nowhere else to go. It's a Monday. Who gets married on a Monday?"

"There's no opera tonight," she explained. "We . . ." Enza stopped herself. *We* suddenly sounded selfish, as if to exclude Ciro.

They stood and looked at one another. Laura pushed the church door open, but they didn't hear it. Enza didn't hear Laura when she whispered her name. Ciro took his hand out of his pocket and motioned for her to close the church door. Laura slipped back inside and quietly pulled the door behind her.

"You can't do this," Ciro said.

"I most certainly can. I'm getting married."

"He's not the right man for you, Enza. You know it."

"I made a decision, and I'm going through with it," she said firmly.

"You make it sound like you're taking a punishment."

"I don't mean it to sound that way. It's a sacrament. It requires thought and reverence." Enza wanted to walk away, but she couldn't. "I have to go." She checked her wrist. She had forgotten to wear her watch. Ciro reached into his pocket and opened his watch. He showed her the time. "There's no rush," he said calmly.

"I don't want to be late."

"You won't be," he promised. "Let him go."

"I can't," Enza replied, but she couldn't look at Ciro when she said it.

"I said, *let him go.*"

"I made a promise."

"Break it."

"What am I to you, if I break my word to him?"

"You would be mine."

"But I'm his." Enza looked to the door. Where was Laura? Why didn't she come outside and take her into the church, where she belonged? "I belong to him."

"Don't say it again. It's not true."

"This ring says I'm his." She showed him her hand, the ruby and diamond ring sparkled in the sunlight.

"Take it off. You don't have to marry me, but you can't marry him."

"Why not?" Her voice cracked beneath the strain of emotion.

"Because I love you. And I *know* you. The man in that church knows the American Enza, not the Italian girl who could hitch a horse and drive a carriage. Does he know the girl who sat by her sister's grave and covered it with juniper branches? I know that girl. And she's mine."

Enza thought of Vito, and wondered why she'd never told him about her sister Stella. Vito only knew the seamstress to Caruso; he didn't know the Hoboken machine operator or the eldest in a poor family who made it through the winter eating chestnuts, praying they would last until the spring came. She hadn't told Vito any of her secrets, and because she hadn't, Vito was not really a part of her story. Perhaps she had never wanted Vito to know that girl.

"You can't come back here and say these things to me." Enza's eyes filled with tears. "I have a life. A good life. I'm happy. I love what I do. My friends. My world."

"What world do you want, Enza?" Ciro said softly.

Enza could not fight the past. Life is a series of choices, made with the best of intentions, often with hope. But she knew in this moment that *life*, the life she'd always dreamed of, was about the family, not just two people in love. It was a fresco, not a painting, filled with details that required years of collaboration to create.

A life with Ciro would be about family; a life with Vito would be about her. She would have the apartment with the view of the river, a motorcar to take her places, beautiful gowns to wear, and aisle seats to every show. There would be such ease to life with Vito! But was she a woman meant for that life? Or was she meant to be with a man who understood her, down to her bones?

For a fleeting instant, her heart filled with affection for the girl she had once been. The girl who'd left her village, and worked hard, and week after week faithfully sent the largest portion of her pay to her mother, enough money, over time, to build the family home, a gift in honor of the gift of her very own life. And she would do it all over again. Didn't she deserve a prize for it? Wasn't the prize a New York City life with all its sophistication and shine, on the arm of a man who loved her?

Why couldn't she marry Vito Blazek? *He was a good man.*

Enza realized that she was meant to be married; it wasn't her fate to be alone, she wasn't like Gloria Berardino or Mia Grace Lisi or Alexis Rae Bernard or any of the girls who worked in the costume shop at the Met. She was not to grow old over a sewing machine, making costumes for fantasy characters, building capes, fastening collars, and gluing wings, nor was she meant to live with her mother until the day she died, in service to the family, devoted to the whole instead of her own piece of it.

Enza would not be the meticulous aunt, steam-pressing dollar bills with starch to place inside greeting cards for baptisms, missalettes for first communions and confirmations. She would never sign a card, "With love, Zia Enza." She was not destined to wear the small, simple hat or the gold knot pin, the marker of the single woman, the spinster, the unadorned and the unloved, good enough for the gold but not the diamond chip.

Enza lived to love.

But she hadn't known it until she saw Ciro Lazzari again.

Enza was meant to carve out her own way, and be with a man who loved her. She thought it was Vito, with his kind heart and good taste. Vito would give her a proper address, friends of his social standing, and a view from the heights. Until this moment, she'd thought every need she had was met, and all roads to possible happiness had been mapped out; all she had to do was put on her best shoes and follow him.

Vito would not count on her to have children, or fill his world with anything but the joy that comes from two careers, quiet breakfasts in the morning, dinner on the town at night, and glorious Mondays, when the doors of the Metropolitan Opera House would be closed, the stage would be dark, and they could walk in the park and have a late dinner in one of those glazed brick rooms lit by candlelight, its shadows punctured by the scarlet tips of cigarettes.

That was meant to be her life, the sole focus of a man who adored her, in a city that celebrated the best life had to offer. Why would she leave the stability of the world Vito had created for her, to go back in time to the man who'd claimed her heart before he even knew her? What did Ciro Lazzari know about the woman she was now? It seemed reckless to believe Ciro all over again, foolish to consider his pleas, and ill-advised to do as he wished.

But Enza thought that was the nature of love, to catch you unaware and play the notes of your past in a haunting melody over and over again, until you believe it is your aria, your future, too.

But how could she break Vito Blazek's heart?

And yet she knew that the only thing that had got her this far was listening carefully to her own heart and keeping her own counsel in every situation. When Enza dug deep within herself, she always found the truth. So, as if it were a rope slipped off its mooring, dropping without a sound into the water, setting the boat free, Enza quietly took off Vito Blazek's engagement ring. She held it between her fingers and looked down at the blood red ruby as it gleamed in the morning light.

The truth was, Enza had never stopped loving Ciro Lazzari from the first moment she saw him, surrounded by four walls of earth in the cemetery at Sant'Antonio. She'd let him go and mourned him when he loved other girls, thinking he wanted something altogether different, and who was she to present herself as an alternative? Enza had grieved for what might have been, and turned away from the pain of it by inventing a new self.

New York City, the enchantments of the opera, the friendships she made, the homes she was welcomed into—why would she ever leave the satisfying and wide-open world Vito had shown her to fall into the arms of Ciro Lazzari? This poor, penniless, motherless soldier, with nothing to recommend him but his words—why would she ever gamble her future on Ciro Lazzari? What thinking woman would?

Enza looked down at the ring in her hand.

Ciro took Enza's face in his hands. "I have loved you all of my life. I was a boy who knew nothing, but when I met you, somehow I understood everything. I remember your shoes, your hair, the way you crossed your arms over your chest and stood with one foot pointed right and the other left like a dancer. I remember your face over the pit of your sister's grave. I remember that your skin had the scent of lemon water and roses and that you gave me a peppermint from a dish on the table in your mother's house after your sister's funeral. I remember that you laughed at a silly joke I made about kissing you without asking. I remember when you received communion at Stella's funeral mass and how you cried because you missed her already.

"I took in every detail of you, Enza. I know I disappointed you when I didn't come for you, but it wasn't because I didn't love you, it's because I didn't know it yet. I never once forgot you. Not for a single day. Wherever I went, I hoped to find you. I've looked for you in every village, train station, and church. I once followed a girl in Ypres because she wore her braids like you. When I sleep, I imagine you there, beside me. And if I was ever with another, the purpose wasn't to love her, but to remember you.

"I could have gone home to Vilminore after the war. I stood on the road outside Rome and thought about going home, but I couldn't bear the idea of the mountain without you.

"I don't know what to say to make you believe me. I don't believe in God so much. The saints have long ago left me. And the Blessed Mother forgot all about me, just as my own mother did, but none of them could give me what one thought of you could do. But if you come away with me, I promise to love you all my life. That's all I have to offer you."

Enza was so moved by his words, she couldn't speak. She knew that a woman can only know two things when she falls in love: what she sees in the man, and what she believes he will become in the light of her care. But never once in the months of her betrothal had Enza felt for Vito what she felt when she looked at Ciro. Ciro's height and strength reminded her of the mountain; she felt protected when she stood with him. Her body rose to meet his, and her spirit followed.

A group of children played stickball on Carmine Street. They chased the ball down the sidewalk in front of the church. They saw Ciro's soldier uniform and gathered around. They inspected his helmet, his boots, and his backpack.

Enza's desire for Ciro was so overwhelming, she put her head down so no one could read her thoughts. Her need to feel his body next to hers was so intense, it almost shamed her.

Enza knew that if she married Vito, she would lose *her* Italy forever. Even if she could have braved the ocean, Vito would hope to show her the island of Capri, the antiquities of Rome, and the enchantments of Firenze, not the mountains, lakes, and rivers of the north. She was from the land of the mandolin; the exquisite violins of La Scala were not hers to claim.

If Enza was going to create a new life, she had to build it with conviction, on her own truthful terms, with a man who could take her home again, even if that meant a new home of their own invention and not the mountain. Ciro had her heart; he was her portion of the mountain.

For Ciro, Enza would sacrifice, fight to put food on the table, worry and fret over babies, and live life in full. She had only one life to share, and one heart to give the man who most deserved it. If she took Ciro on, she was in for a struggle compared to her life with Vito, but the love of all loves was worth it.

Ciro pulled Enza close and kissed her. The children whistled and teased and fell away like sound across water. The taste of his lips was just as she remembered. His face against her own was warm; the touch of his skin healed her.

She would go to the ends of the earth for Ciro Lazzari, and she always knew it. Her wedding suit would become traveling clothes. It always seemed that her costumes were built for different intentions. The cinnamon suit was no different. She stuffed the violets Ciro had brought her into the waist of her suit jacket. They fit perfectly, as if the suit had been awaiting their finishing touch.

"I belong to you, Ciro," she said. And with those words, Enza left one life behind to start a new one.

PART THREE

minnesota

22

A BUNCH OF VIOLETS
Un Mazzolino di Viole

A ribbon of light cut through the darkness into Laura and Enza's bedroom window in the Milbank House. Enza, in her nightgown, shifted in her bed. "My mother said it was bad luck to sleep in the moonlight."

"Too late for that," Laura said, kneeling before the fireplace. "Luck took a powder today." Laura stoked the fire with a poker, the small orange embers on the floor of the grid bursting into flames. She threw another log on the fire and climbed into bed. "This time last night, we were hemming the skirt on your wedding suit." Laura lay back on her pillow. "So much for me coming home to a single. What in the Sam Hill were you thinking?"

"I'm sorry." Enza moved the violets on her nightstand so their small velvet petals faced her.

"It's Vito that deserves an apology," Laura said.

"He'll never forgive me, and he shouldn't," Enza said as she leaned back on the pillow. She couldn't believe that she had made Vito so unhappy, when all she had done her whole life was put others' happiness before her own. But something had shifted within her in a profound way. When a devout girl is about to make an irreversible, lifelong vow, she must be honest. When Enza searched her heart, she knew that she could only marry for love, and that meant choosing Ciro.

"Vito left Our Lady of Pompeii like it was on fire. Ran out of there like a shot."

" . . . After he let me have it. Did you hear what he said?"

"The doors of the sacristy at Our Lady of Pompeii aren't very thick. But I couldn't blame him for being angry."

"Neither could I. Then, it was so strange, he got very quiet and sat down. And then he said, 'I never really had you. And I knew it.' "

"This is so unlike you, Enza. You're not impulsive. This is the act of a flighty girl."

"But I've loved Ciro since I was fifteen years old. He's had my heart all along. I tried to create a kind of happiness with Vito by putting Ciro out of my mind. But he came for me, Laura. Today, *he came for me*. He chose me."

"But *you* have a choice in the matter."

"You know, back on our mountain they have tried to build dams to harness the power of the waterfalls. But sooner or later, there's always a leak or a flood or something else to make the structure come crashing down. The water seems to have a will of its own. The engineers can't figure out a way to stop nature. That's exactly what it was like when I saw Ciro this morning. I can't fight the power of it."

"And you don't want to try." Laura sighed. "What was wrong with the life Vito offered you?" she asked as she sat up and pulled the blanket around her.

"Nothing," Enza said quietly.

"Then why would you throw it away? Are you sure about Ciro? When we were working in Hoboken, you talked about him. And when we saw him on Columbus Day so many years ago, you told him your feelings, and he never came for you. I remember how miserable you were for months after that. I thought he was a heel. Doesn't that worry you? Is he reliable?"

Enza sat up in her bed. "He has a plan."

"Oh joy," Laura said, lying back on her pillow. The tone of her voice made Enza laugh for the first time that day.

"Ciro is ambitious," Enza continued. "He talks about opening his own shop someday. He'd like to learn how to make women's shoes. But he's not just a shoemaker, Laura. Spending time with him today, I realized he has an artist's view of the world."

"So do *you*! Does he have any idea of what you can do? Has he ever seen your work up close, like I have, or from a distance, from the diamond horseshoe, like a society matron? You're a masterful seamstress. You make the rest of us in the costume shop look like a pack of amateurs. Signor Caruso may like the way you boil macaroni, but that's not why you were chosen to work for him. He saw how you built a costume, and that's why he selected you to head up his crew. You're inventive. *You're* the artist! You took scraps from the floor during the war rationing and made them into glorious capes and suits for Caruso! Does Ciro know who you are and how far you've come since he left you on the roof?" Laura pummeled her pillow into a fluffy circle and rolled onto her side to face Enza.

"I'm not going to stop working," Enza vowed.

"I hope you like making shoes."

"I'll help him, and he'll help me."

"Really. A man is going to put *your* work on a par with *his*? I can't believe what I'm hearing!"

"I have hope, Laura."

"Yeah. Hope is wonderful thing. It has no memory. It fills you with possibility. Whatever your imagination can conjure, hope will design and deliver."

"You just don't like him," Enza said.

"I don't *know* him. But it's not about liking Ciro. It's about loving my friend and wanting the best for her. You have no idea what you're getting into. You'll be living on Mulberry Street, doing his boss's laundry. I don't know how he convinced you to change your life, one that you created over years, in a matter of minutes. He must have made some pretty big promises."

"He promised to love me. And for once in my life, I'm going to do the impractical, unwise, ill-advised thing. I'm going to make a decision based upon the feeling I have in my heart, and not what looks good on paper or makes anyone else happy. I'm going to do something for me, and I'll live with whatever Ciro brings into my life and be happy that I did."

Laura sighed. "You've gone over the cliff. He's got you. I have to hand it to him. For a woman, love is the highest dream, and if a man promises to build a ladder tall enough to reach it, she believes him, hikes up her skirt, and follows him to the stars. Now it's my turn to hope. I'm going to hope Signor Lazzari doesn't disappoint you."

Laura rolled over in her bed, pulling the blanket up to her chin.

Enza didn't sleep that night. She spent the late night hours thinking about Vito and Ciro and the life she had chosen.

The fire threw a soft glow onto the walls, illuminating the cracks in the old paint. There were no shapes or strange shadows to portend Enza's future, no signs whatsoever. On what should have been the happiest day of her life, Enza cried silent tears so as not to wake Laura.

* * *

Ciro stretched out on his cot at the Zanetti Shoe Shop. He crossed his arms and stared up at the squares of the tin ceiling, as he had done for many nights before he left for the war.

Remo and Carla had gone to bed after a supper of steak and onions, fresh bread, coffee, and cake. Ciro talked for hours about the war and his travels to Rome. He thought about telling them about Enza, but decided not to, as Carla seemed to expect him to get back to work immediately. Her bank purse was never so thick as when Ciro made excellent-quality work boots at the pace of a machine. Signora wanted the old profits back, the sooner the better.

Ciro heard a key turn in the front door of the shop. He stood and looked out from behind the curtain.

"Don't shoot," Luigi said, holding up the key. He looked at Ciro. "My God, you're thin," he said as he embraced his friend.

"You're not. How's married life?"

"Pappina is expecting."

"*Auguri!*"

"*Grazie. Grazie.* We're living on Hester Street."

"How is it?"

"It's no good. It's noisy. There's no garden. I want to get Pappina out of here."

"Where would you go?"

"We thought about going home to Italy, but there's no work there. The war made it worse." He lowered his voice. "And I'm tired of making money for them." He pointed upstairs. "I work seven days a week, and she pays me for five."

"Signora wants me back on the machines in the morning—at the same salary. Says times are tough."

"For us. Not for her," Luigi said. "She couldn't wait for you to return. I'm surprised she didn't rent a mule and do a search for you in the fields of France. Did she make you steak?"

Ciro nodded.

"That's how she keeps us under her thumb." He patted his stomach. "When she expects double time at the same rate, you get tenderloin. We need to make a break."

"Remo says he wants to go home to Italy."

"And you think they'll sell us the business? It will never happen. Signora loves the cash too much. She'll work him to death and then spend the rest of her time counting the money."

"I've thought about opening our own shop," Ciro said. "What do you think?"

"We work well together. I'd love it."

"Where should we go? Brooklyn? New Jersey?"

"I want to get as far from the city as possible," Luigi insisted. "I want land. Fresh air. Don't you?"

Ciro had given a lot of thought about where to live during his endless nights in France. When Enza embraced him that afternoon, she had no idea the gift she had given him. Ciro was ready to make a life for her that he had never dared imagine alone. With Luigi as a partner, they could go anywhere. "How about California?"

"Half of Calabria is in California. There are more shoemakers than feet out west."

Ciro nodded. "There are mines in Kentucky and West Virginia. Maybe they need shoemakers," he offered.

"I don't want to go south," Luigi said. "I'm from southern Italy, and I've had enough heat and humidity to last me a lifetime."

"We could go north. I'd love a place like Vilminore. Someplace green, where there are lakes."

"There are plenty of lakes in Minnesota."

"That's where my father went to work," Ciro said quietly, an expression of unresolved pain crossing his face. "And he never came back to us."

"What happened?" Luigi asked gently.

"We don't know. And you know what, Luigi? I don't want to know. They say he died in a mine, but all we know is that he never came home. It broke up our family, ruined my mother's health, and split up my brother and me."

"All right. We'll never go to Minnesota."

"No, no, we should consider every possibility," Ciro said slowly. Minnesota had always had a mythical quality to him. It was the place that had swallowed up his father without apology. Yet it held a certain fascination for Ciro because his father had chosen it. Would it be fate or sheer folly to offer up another Lazzari to the Iron Range? Choosing Minnesota might tempt fate—or maybe it could redeem the loss of his father.

"I heard some men talking at Puglia's," Luigi continued, oblivious to Ciro's internal struggle. "The iron ore mines operate around the clock. Lots of guys are heading up there. We should think about it. The mines employ thousands, and somebody's got to build the boots and repair them. We could make a good living. And you'd certainly have your lakes."

Perhaps it was the memory of all the places Ciro had been during and after the war—the romantic hills of England, the pristine vineyards of France, and the stately antiquities of Rome—that gave him the desire to leave New York City. Or maybe it was sleeping in the same cot behind a thin privacy curtain, as he had done since he was a teenager, that made him long for a home of his own. Suddenly the old ways, the way things had always been, were not enough. He intended to give Enza a good life and a home of her own. He needed to be bold in his thinking, open to new ideas; and he hoped she, too, might think beyond the borders of Manhattan Island. He shook his head at the odds of his plan succeeding. "Enza will never leave New York City," he said finally.

"Who?"

"Enza Ravanelli," Ciro announced. "I'm going to marry her."

"Marry her?" Luigi was stunned. "Enza . . ." He remembered. "The nice girl from the Alps? I can't believe it. She's a glove-and-hat girl. She's not like any of the girls you used to see."

"That's the point."

"You're like every other doughboy home from the front. You turned in your rifle and went shopping for wedding rings. How did you pull this off so fast?"

"I don't know," Ciro lied. He had planned to return to New York and win Enza's heart from the first moment his boots hit the ground in France. The complete chaos of war had helped him think clearly and to define life for himself in a plain way. It was either yes or no, life or death, love or loneliness. War had taught him that everything was absolute. So he too began to think like a general, even when it came to his own heart. He had nothing to gain by taking more time to make what was, for him, an obvious decision. "She wants to be with me," Ciro said.

"So does every other girl between here and Bushwick. But you never gave Enza a tumble. Why now?"

"I've changed, Luigi."

"I'll say. Did you get hit on the head in France? You're the man who always got the girl. *Any* girl. All of them," Luigi marveled.

"There's only one girl for me. And that's Enza."

"A masher no more. *Va bene.* I hope you know what you're giving up. When you were gone, there wasn't a day in this shop when the bells on the door didn't jingle and some *ragazza* come to the front desk and ask where to write to you."

"I didn't get a single letter," Ciro said with false indignation.

"That's because Signora told them you were in Tangiers."

"I never went to Tangiers." Ciro threw his hands in the air. "I doubt I could find it on a map."

"Yeah, well, there's some tent in Tangiers filled with love letters to Ciro Lazzari drenched in rosewater that will never see the light of day. What a shame."

Later that night, after Luigi left, Ciro lit a cigarette under the old elm in the courtyard. He propped his feet on the trunk of the tree and leaned back in the chair just as he had done every night before he left for the war. He had always enjoyed a hard day's work in the shoe shop, followed by a smooth, sweet cigarette under the tree after supper. But since he returned, it wasn't the same. It seemed to Ciro that everything had changed in Little Italy while he was away, including the tree. The old bark on the trunk had begun to peel away, revealing a layer of gray underneath with deep rivulets in the surface that looked like old candle wax. The autumn leaves had skipped their brilliant golden phase; instead they'd turned a dingy brown and fallen to the ground, leaving barren, dry branches.

Ciro acknowledged how important this old tree had been to him; it had given him a cover of green in a city of stone, a place to prop his boots and have a smoke, but now he knew it had never been beautiful in its own right. It had only given him pleasure because he leaned against it to remind him of home.

In the time it took to smoke one cigarette, Ciro realized that he wanted to take Enza to live and work in a new place that would be wholly their own. They needed land and sky and lakes. Fertile earth can produce many crops. If a man walks in beauty, he will create, and when he creates, he prospers. He and Enza did not belong on Mulberry Street. He could not offer her a grand apartment on the Upper East Side, as Vito Blazek might have, and he did not want to join the Italians in Brooklyn and Queens. Nor could he picture them in New Jersey, Rhode Island, or New Haven, Connecticut, all filled with every manner of Italian craftsmen. The best Ciro could hope for would be to work for one of the many established shoemakers in one of those places. But why trade a position at Zanetti's for a similar one? Besides, it was the city life that Ciro wanted to leave behind. One tree in a concrete courtyard would not satisfy him any longer, and he hoped Enza felt the same.

He wondered what she would say about giving up her position at the Metropolitan Opera, and he had doubts about asking her to do so. But he also knew that if he could make a success of himself in a place that needed his services, they would have the freedom to decide where they would live in the years to come. He would be able to return to Italy and offer her life on the mountain once his pockets were full of American dollars. It was time for Ciro to become a padrone; nothing less would do, and there was not enough he could do for Enza.

Thoughts of the Iron Range played through his mind. *Minnesota* was like the title of an unread book he knew he would eventually pick up and devour by lamplight. Here in America, his father had died. The fortunes of his family had been changed by events in that distant state. Perhaps it was time he finally cleaned the wound of his father's death. Perhaps he would find peace if he walked in his father's steps along the shorelines of Minnesota's crystal lakes. Maybe that's where he belonged, where they could be happy.

As Ciro put out the cigarette, he thought of Eduardo. His brother would see to it that their mother was taken care of. What Ciro needed to do was simple: make a good living to take care of his wife and their future children. For him, that meant embracing a new chapter, while filling the void the absence of his father had made. It meant Minnesota.

Laura, dressed and ready for work, joined Enza at the breakfast table in the dining room of the Milbank House. Enza had woken early, bathed, and dressed before Laura had risen. Enza was having her third cup of coffee when Laura joined her.

"I think we should post a summons on the bulletin board regarding your wedding. There's more whispering going on around here than there was when housekeeper Emmerson took a drunken tumble down the front stairs last New Year's Eve."

"You don't have to answer for me," Enza assured her.

"I don't? Isn't that what best friends are for?"

Enza put down her coffee cup and looked up at Laura. Laura had slept soundly through the night; she always did whenever she had been honest and cleared her conscience. Enza, however, was the opposite; she spent many nights wrestling with decisions, last night among the most difficult. She needed Laura and couldn't imagine her life without her. "Are we still best friends?" Enza asked. She had hoped that Laura would not make her choose between her lifelong friendship and her lifelong love.

"Yes." Laura sat down. "I'm just wondering what you're going to tell your father when he gets here this afternoon. You've swapped out one groom for another. And that might make your dear old dad dizzy."

"I'll do what I've done my whole life. I'll tell him the truth."

"I've got to get to work. Anything you want me to say to the girls? They think you're on your honeymoon."

"Just tell them that I'm happy."

"Can do." Laura stood and drank the last sip of her coffee. She pulled on her gloves. "Should I tell Serafina that you'll be back sooner than you had planned?"

"Don't let her assign my machine to anyone else," Enza said.

"Hallelujah!" Laura clapped her gloved hands together.

. . .

The clock over the mantel in the beau parlor at the Milbank House ticked loudly as Enza prepared a tray with tea. She folded the linen napkins, angled the china platter filled with delicate cookies and small sandwiches. She checked the sugar bowl and the cream pitcher. She lifted the silver tea ball out of the pot and placed it on the silver coaster.

The bell rang. Miss DeCoursey answered the door. Enza didn't wait for her father; she sprang off the sofa and ran to him. Father and daughter held one another a long time.

Marco took a good look at Enza, and then stepped back to look at her surroundings. The Milbank House was beautifully appointed. Behind Enza in the foyer, the wide staircase that curved over the second floor had a polished mahogany railing and balusters. The pocket doors were open to the entrance to the living room and beau parlor. The library, with its lavish black marble fireplace and mantel, was lush by any standards. He had not seen opulence like this since he dropped a package at the cardinal's residence in Brescia many years ago. It comforted him to know that his daughter lived in this stately brownstone.

Marco also noticed that his daughter had acquired a worldly sophistication since he left her with the Buffa family eight years ago. He wondered if that didn't have something to do with her recent change of heart.

"Why did you call off your wedding? What did he do?" Marco asked, and made a fist. "I'll take care of him if he hurt you."

"No, Papa, I hurt him."

"What happened?"

Marco was now in his late forties. He was not the robust man Enza remembered. He had the stoop of a stonecutter and the bronze skin that came from doing hard labor outdoors in a place where there was summer year-round. Now, at long last, the house in Schilpario had been built. He had fulfilled his contract to the California Department of Highways and was ready to return to the mountain for the rest of his life. Any spring in his step and smile upon his face were in anticipation of returning home to his wife and children; they no longer came from ambition, drive, or exuberance, but from the desire to see his home again.

"Papa, come and sit with me." Enza led him into the beau parlor and motioned for him to sit on the chair before the game table in the window.

Marco took her hands into his. "Tell me everything."

"Eliana wrote a long letter about the house. Vittorio painted it yellow like the sunflowers. He put in cabinets, and the doors are thick. There are many windows. The root cellar is filled with sweet potatoes and chestnuts. Mama put up peppers and cherries for the winter."

"Enza, did you know that Battista made a deal with the Ardingos? He bartered free carriage rides down the mountain for all the prosciutto and sausage our family could eat."

"Battista was always a schemer." Enza laughed.

"And he always will be. I can't wait to see my children. But mostly, I can't wait to see your mother again," Marco said. "Do you want to brave the ocean with me now that you're not getting married?"

"I wish I could, Papa."

"The old mountain can't compete with Caruso's opera house."

"It's not that." Enza looked down at her hands, unsure of what to say.

"Are you going to give Signor Blazek another chance?"

"No. It's done."

"Then you'll come home with me," Marco said quietly.

"Papa, you know it's not possible."

Marco took his daughter's hand. " I know you got very ill on the way over," he began.

"Papa, I almost died," she said softly. The only person on earth who understood what had happened to her on the crossing would also understand why she could never make that trip again.

"We'll go right to the doctor and make sure he can help before the ship ever leaves the harbor," Marco said.

"And what if he can't help, Papa? What if I get so sick I don't make it across? I want you to go home and be with Mama and our family and revel in every corner of that house. I want you to throw open the windows and light the fire, and plant the garden and fill it with love. *That* will make me happy."

"But that house belongs to you too. You worked harder than I did to build it. I don't want to believe you won't ever live in it."

"But it's my choice, Papa. I'm going to stay here. And it's more than my job. Do you remember a boy named Lazzari? He was sent from Vilminore to dig Stella's grave. I brought him home to meet you?"

"I don't remember much about that time, Enza."

"And you met him again at Saint Vincent's Hospital in the chapel when I was ill. Ciro is from a good family. His brother has become a priest. They lived at San Nicola when they were boys."

"The Lazzaris of Vilminore." Marco pondered the name. "I once drove a widow Lazzari down to Bergamo. I remember it was snowing. She had sons, and she had taken them to the convent. I remember that. And the nuns paid me three lire. It was a fortune then."

Enza took in a breath. The threads that connected her to Ciro were so strong, it seemed inevitable that they would have found one another again and after so long. "Another sign that we are meant to be together."

"What makes you think that this young man knows how to treat you? Just because he's from the mountain doesn't mean he's good enough for you. He was raised in a convent. That's not his doing, but how would he know how to take care of a family if he's never been a part of one? How can you be sure that he won't leave you, as his mother left him?"

"I'm very sure of him, Papa."

"But can he be a good husband?"

Marco knew his daughter. She'd had a mind of her own since she was a girl, and she had always honored her own heart. Marco stood and went to the window. He surveyed the street below, buying time to find the right words to say to his daughter. She was at a turning point in her life, and needed her mother's wisdom, but she was not there to provide it. Marco would have to do his best.

Ciro, polished and neat, wearing a suit, was bounding up the front stairs to the entrance door of the boardinghouse. "Is this Lazzari coming to meet me?"

"Yes, Papa."

"You have chosen a tall one, haven't you?"

Miss DeCoursey brought Ciro into the beau parlor. He wore a navy blue suit, white shirt, vest, and tie. His oxblood shoes were laced in navy. Marco turned to meet his future son-in-law, and they shook hands. "It's good to see you again, Signore."

"Enza, I'd like to speak privately with Signor Lazzari," Marco said.

Enza deferred to her father and left the room, closing the door behind her.

"Lazzari," Marco said aloud.

"Yes, Signore."

"What did your father do?"

"He was a miner. He worked in the marble mines in Foggia, and then went up the mountain to work in the iron ore mines in the Alps."

"What happened to him?"

"He came to America almost twenty years ago to find work. I was told he died in an iron ore mine in Minnesota."

"And your mother?"

"The Montinis."

"The printers?"

"Yes, Signore."

"They made the missals for Holy Week," Marco remembered.

"For all the churches on the mountain, and in Bergamo and *Citta Alta*."

"Why aren't you a printmaker?"

Ciro looked down at his big hands, not exactly the best tools for pen-and-ink calligraphy. "I'm not *delicato*, sir."

Marco took a seat and motioned for Ciro to join him. "How do you earn your living?" Marco asked.

"I apprenticed to Signor Zanetti on Mulberry Street. I'm a shoemaker."

"Are you a master?"

"Yes. I've completed my apprenticeship to Signor Zanetti. My debt to him is paid, and I'm ready to go into business for myself."

"A lot of competition in this city. They say you can throw a rock in Brooklyn and you'll hit a shoemaker."

"I know, Signore. I have a partner, Luigi Latini, and we're looking to get a loan and start a business where shoemakers are needed."

"You need a partner?"

"I prefer it, Signore. I grew up with a brother to whom I was devoted. And when I went to enlist in the Great War, I made good friends. One in particular, Signor Juan Torres, looked out for me, and I did the same for him. Sadly, he didn't come home, but that does not lessen the bond I have to him. I've made my way alone for a very long time and it comes naturally for me to seek a partner. Luigi Latini is a good man, and I work well with him. I think we could build a good business together."

Marco took this in and reflected upon his own experience since he'd come to America. It had been a long and lonely slog. A partner in business was a sounding board, the work was cut in half, and life was less isolated. Ciro made sense.

Marco leaned over the chair and looked at Ciro critically. Ciro's size and strength designated him as a natural leader. He was an attractive young man, probably popular with the ladies. "Have you had many girlfriends?"

"A few, sir."

"My daughter was engaged to Vito Blazek."

"I know. I must have had an angel with me that morning. I got to the church moments before she went inside."

"When Signor Blazek wrote to me for Enza's hand, I was impressed with him," Marco said. "He wrote a very moving letter."

"It's better we meet in person, sir. I couldn't begin to impress you on paper, and I probably wouldn't try. I used to count on my brother Eduardo to do the writing in the family." Ciro smiled.

Marco sat back in his chair and took Ciro in. "I can see what kind of a man you are, Ciro."

"I hope you will trust me with Enza."

Marco looked down at his hands. The strings within his heart tightened. He did not want to let Enza go, and yet he trusted her judgment. He wondered if Ciro Lazzari had any idea how strong his eldest was. "My daughter is independent. She has made her own decisions for a long time now."

"I love her because she is so strong. It's one of the things I most admire about her. When I think of marriage and a long life ahead, I want to know that my wife could take care of my family if something happened to me."

Marco smiled. He thought of his own Giacomina, who had taken care of the family while he and Enza lived in America. So he said, "We work hard in my family. Do you?"

"Yes, sir."

"We're people of faith. Are you?"

Ciro swallowed hard. He didn't want to lie, but he didn't want to mislead his future father-in-law either. "I try, sir."

"Try harder," Marco admonished.

"I will, Signore."

"We're also loyal. I've been away from my wife for more than a few years now, and I haven't been with another woman. Would such devotion to my daughter be possible under similar circumstances?"

"Yes, Signore." Ciro began to sweat.

"May I have your word?"

"You have my word, sir." Ciro's voice broke.

"There is one more thing I need to know before I would agree to entrust my daughter to you."

"Anything, sir." A sliver of panic sliced through Ciro's chest. Could he have come this far, only to have Enza's father reject him?

"I want to know why you love my daughter."

Ciro leaned forward in his chair. He had to think about *why* he loved Enza because he hadn't questioned it. Ciro knew that there was a correct answer. He knew that men learned how to love; they weren't born with that capacity. He knew the qualities of a good man included all the aspects that concerned Marco: loyalty, fidelity, ambition, and gentleness. As a man, Ciro had been shaped by the loss of his father, the absence of his mother, the ordination of his brother, and his decision to volunteer to fight in the Great War. Each of Ciro's choices had changed the landscape of his heart and his ability to love. In many ways, he felt lucky he still could.

As a boy, Ciro had learned how to give of himself generously in the convent. He knew how to be loyal because he had grown up with Eduardo, who taught him the nuances of what it meant to be a loving brother. Ciro had given up searching for love, hoping it would fill that deep well of regret that he still carried at having been abandoned by his mother, but he was wise enough to know that you can't always blame your parents for your sadness. After so much rejection, and periods of emotional drift and loneliness, Ciro had finally found what was missing. He didn't want Marco to think that he'd chosen Enza to save himself, but deep down, he believed it was true. Ciro loved Enza, but was that enough for Marco, who had put everything he was into his family? There was no building, bridge, ocean liner, or shoe with Marco Ravanelli's name on it, just the quiet and exemplary life of a good man who lived in service to the family he created. Ciro hesitated to tell Marco what was in his heart, because he knew more than Ciro ever would about what it takes to love one woman and build a life with her.

So Ciro said, "I traveled far, Signor Ravanelli. I have never met a woman like Enza. She's intelligent without being condescending. She's beautiful without vanity. And she's funny when she isn't trying to be. I love her and will give her a good life. Your daughter encourages the best in me. When I'm with her, I'm in the presence of grace, and she makes me aspire to it."

Marco took a moment to think about Ciro's words. He saw that an honest young man sat before him. If Marco were completely honest, he would admit that he saw also a sadness in Ciro, one that he could not name. Marco didn't know if that meant Ciro hadn't made peace with the past, or if it might portend something grave in the future. He knew there was a certain seriousness about Ciro, born of a life experience that Marco himself had not endured. On the surface of things, it appeared to Marco that this was a solid match, and one that Giacomina would endorse. Ciro was from the mountain, and he knew Enza's dialect and way of life. That accounted for something on this unexpected morning. He would find comfort in the knowledge that his daughter would marry a man who understood what she came from, and for Marco Ravanelli, this tipped his decision in Ciro's favor.

Ciro still sat on the edge of the chair. His future and the fulfillment of all his dreams were at the mercy of another.

Marco slowly reached into his pocket and removed an envelope. He placed the envelope on the table and rested his hand upon it. He looked at Ciro. "For Enza."

"This is not necessary," Ciro said.

"It is to me. I am giving you permission to marry my firstborn daughter. Men hope for sons, but I will tell you that there was never a son who brought a father more joy than my Enza did for me. There are daughters and daughters, but there is only one Enza. I entrust you with my own flesh and blood. I expect you to honor that trust."

"I will, sir."

"Our home on the mountain was completed nearly one year ago. I could have gone home then. Instead, I stayed on to make this purse for my daughter's dowry. It brings me contentment to know that this small sacrifice will make it easier for my daughter as she starts her new life. One year of my forty-six on this earth is a pittance compared to what she means to me."

"I thank you, Signore. And I won't forget how hard you worked to provide this for Enza."

Marco rose from his chair. Ciro stood. Enza pushed the door open and peeked into the room.

"It's all settled, Enza," Marco said.

Enza ran to her father and put her arms around him. "Your happiness is mine," he whispered in his daughter's ear. "Be happy, Enza."

Later that same night, Enza slipped down to the library in the Milbank House, striking a match to light a small work lamp on the writing table. She pulled a clean sheet of linen paper out of the desk drawer, along with a fountain pen.

November 30, 1918
Dear Signora Ramunni,

It is with a heavy heart that I resign my position as seamstress in the costume shop of the Metropolitan Opera House. I have loved every moment of my job, even when the hours were long and it seemed we might not finish a project in time for the opening night curtain. I will never forget the privilege of standing in the wings and watching as costumes we created by the labor of our own hands delight the audience through color, line, shape, drape, and form, the essential elements you taught me.

Laura and I often reminisce about the day you hired us. We thought then, as we do today, that no greater lady ever graced the opera. In every way, you made our work sing, which was always the point.

> *As I leave you, the staff, my coworkers, and the great singers,*
> *please know you will always be in my heart, and when I think of*
> *you, I will say a prayer of gratitude. I wish you the best in all as-*
> *pects of your life, as I know no one is more deserving of happiness*
> *than you. Your generosity to me will hopefully be repaid tenfold*
> *in the years to come. Mille grazie, Signora. Auguri! Auguri!*
>
> > *Sincerely yours,*
> > *Enza Ravanelli*
> > *Station 3, Singer machine 17*

Enza carefully placed the letter on the blotter. As the ink dried, her eyes filled with tears. This was the true meaning of sacrifice. Ciro had made a plan to start their life together in Minnesota, and Enza had agreed. Ciro had laid out the plan like a cartographer, explaining where in Minnesota they would go, and how he and Luigi planned to start their business. Enza had liked Pappina from the first moment she met her at the Zanetti's shop so many years ago, so she knew that she would begin this journey with a good friend who would be there for her.

She had no regrets about her choice to go to Minnesota, or about marriage to Ciro, but she knew she would always pine for the Metropolitan Opera. Enza remembered sitting at this very desk and writing a letter seeking employment at the opera house. She smiled when she thought about the silly samples she had placed in the envelope, showing off her technique with beadwork and embroidery, along with Laura's effortless stitchwork. Serafina Ramunni had overlooked Enza's insouciance and hired them anyway. And what a glorious career path had ensued, in service to great singers and actors, who relied on the costumes they built to tell the timeless stories in song of the great operas. It was a small thing, Enza knew, and yet, it wasn't. Their garments were part of the spectacle, and the show had been spectacular.

Enza knew what it was to stand in the pale blue edge of the spotlight, to serve the Great Voice, and now, hopeful she had made the right decision, she was more than ready to serve another, this time around: the man she loved.

* * *

Ciro Augustus Lazzari and Vincenza Ravanelli were married at Holy Rosary Church on Pearl Street in lower Manhattan on December 7, 1918. Luigi Latini served as best man, while Laura Heery was maid of honor.

Colin Chapin read the scripture. Pappina Latini laid a bouquet at the feet of the shrine of the Blessed Lady, unable to walk behind the communion rail because she was with child. Enza wore blue and carried the black leather-bound prayer book that Eduardo had given to Ciro, over which she placed a bouquet of red roses.

After the ceremony, they brought Marco to Pier 43 to board the SS *Taormina* for Naples. After the nine-day crossing, he would take the train north to Bergamo, where he would be reunited with his wife and children, who could not wait to show him the house he and Enza had made possible.

Enza stood at the foot of the gangplank to say good-bye to her father. She pulled a red rose from her bouquet, snapped off the stem, and placed it in the buttonhole of her father's coat.

Marco remembered standing on this pier years ago, afraid that Enza had died and he would never see her again. He also remembered putting his hand in the pocket of his old boiled-wool coat and feeling a small patch of fine silk where Enza had lined the inside. This was a girl who sought in every way she could to make the world beautiful, to give comfort when it was least expected and joy where it was most needed. His heart was breaking that he could not take her home, but he knew that a good father would support her desire to build her own house and a new life with the man she loved. And so he did.

"Papa, write to me."

"I will. And you must write to me," he said through his tears.

"I will," she promised, reaching into her pocket for the wedding handkerchief that Laura had made, with her initials and Ciro's intertwined.

Marco put his arms around his daughter. She took in the scent of the tobacco and clean lemon that she had come to know as his, and held on just a moment longer until the horn sounded aboard the ship. Marco turned and went up the gangplank. As the aisle of metal was lifted and secured, Enza didn't move from her spot on the pier. She stood and searched the layers of the decks, until she found her father and the red rose. He took off his hat and waved it in her direction. She waved good-bye to him and smiled, and knew that from this great distance, he would not be able to see her tears. And she couldn't see his either, but she knew for sure he would not stop weeping for the loss of her for the rest of his life.

Enza joined her new husband and friends behind the fishing net that separated the pier from the docks. Ciro put his arms around Enza and held her for a long time. To her relief and delight, his embrace helped her endure what she had just lost.

Afterward, Laura, Colin, Luigi, Pappina, Enza, and Ciro celebrated their nuptials with a breakfast feast in the atrium of the Plaza Hotel under the Tiffany skylight. Ciro outlined his business plan, while Colin offered suggestions. Laura looked over at Enza, who smiled blissfully at the ring on her finger, a glistening gold signet ring with a *C* engraved upon it, which Ciro had worn since he was a boy.

There were many toasts at their table, wishes for long lives and many years of happiness. But there was one very special toast in honor of Enza's new citizenship. Ciro's citizenship had been awarded to him on the day he received his honorable discharge from the U.S. Army. Now, his legal wife shared in that gift. The sacrament, the vows, the ring, and the license made Enza an American at last.

The entrance to the Plaza Hotel was heated by small cast-iron ovens tucked discreetly behind velvet ropes along the red-carpeted stairs of the entry. A soft snow had begun to fall. Colin pulled Ciro, Luigi, and Pappina aside so Laura would be able to say good-bye to Enza.

"Are you happy?" Laura asked. "Don't answer that. You'd better be, and I know you are." Her voice broke.

"Please don't cry." Enza tried to reassure her. "I swear. This is not the end of anything."

"But we had our beginning together. And I can't imagine my life without you." Laura fished in her purse for her handkerchief. "I don't want you to go. It's so selfish of me."

"There is no way I could ever thank you for all you've done for me. You made me the most beautiful hats I'll ever wear. You always split your pie with me at the Automat, even when you were very hungry. You almost killed a man for my honor with a pair of factory scissors. You gave me words. I couldn't read or write English until I met you."

"And I wouldn't have been able to speak to Enrico Caruso without the Italian you taught me. So you see, we're even."

"Are we?" Enza cried.

"All right, maybe I pictured us together forever, and maybe someday, we will be. But I want you to know, if you need me, any time, you write to me and I'll run to Minnesota. On foot. You understand?"

"And the same goes for me. I'll come back when you need me," Enza promised.

"And start writing me a letter first thing in the morning on the train. You can mail it in Chicago."

"Come on, girls, we have to make the train," Colin said. He loaded everyone into his Ardsley. There were a lot of laughs in the ride between Fifty-ninth Street and Penn Station—not enough to last a lifetime, but enough to have made this wedding-day departure end on a joyous and gay note.

At three o'clock that afternoon under a gray sky the color of old velvet, the Latinis and the Lazzaris arrived at Penn Station, bought four one-way tickets on the Broadway Limited, and boarded the train for Chicago, where they would transfer trains to take them to Minneapolis, Minnesota. Colin and Laura saw them off, watching until the silver train disappeared like a sewing needle into thick wool.

Ciro and Luigi were business partners. They would make shoes and repair them, just as they had on Mulberry Street, except this time, the purse would be theirs to keep.

The Caterina Shoe Company was born.

* * *

The dining car on the Broadway Limited was elegant, with polished walnut walls and leather banquettes, like a sophisticated Manhattan restaurant on wheels. The tables were dressed in starched white linen, crystal glasses, white china trimmed in green, and silverware buffed to a sparkling sheen.

Small vases with white roses were clipped to the window sashes. A series of eight booths, four on either side, with an aisle down the center, were connected to the kitchen car. The leather seats in the booths were forest green to match the china.

"I can barely fit in the booth," Pappina said, laughing. "How long is this ride?"

"Twenty hours," Luigi said as he adjusted the cushion on the seat to make his wife more comfortable.

Enza and Ciro slipped into the booth across from them.

"They just got married," Luigi said to the Negro waiter.

"Congratulations," the waiter said to Enza and Ciro. His crisp black uniform with a gold bar on the chest made him look like a general. "I'll see you have some cake."

Ciro kissed Enza on her cheek.

"Okay, boys. You've got us where you want us. We know what you're going to do in Minnesota, but what about us? You'll be busy very soon"— Enza smiled at Pappina, happy for the new baby—"but what am I going to do?"

"Be my wife," Ciro said.

"I like to work. There's no opera company in Hibbing, but I could sew for a living. After all, we've been living in New York City, and I could keep track of the latest fashions before they go west. I could sew some lovely dresses and coats with a Paris flair for the girls on the Iron Range."

"I sew a little," Pappina offered. "But nothing fancy."

"Well, we'll sew clothes, curtains, layettes—whatever they need, we'll make," Enza said warmly.

Ciro took Enza's hand and kissed it.

Enza was surprised that she was filled with anticipation for their new life together in a new place. New York City had meant everything to her. She had reveled in the excitement, glamour, and sophistication of the port city, and she couldn't, before Ciro returned, have imagined living anywhere else in the United States.

But she was beginning to understand that her great love for Ciro transcended every other desire. She had heard of the power of this kind of love, but was certain it would never happen to her. Now she understood why her father could leave the mountain and the woman he loved for so many years. It was only to serve her that he could leave her. And now Enza was in the same position. Building a new life meant sacrifice, but it also meant that fulfillment and surprise would be hers, and she would have a wonderful husband to share it with. She couldn't imagine a better reason to start over again.

Enza trusted Ciro with her future. This did not mean a vow of obedience like the one the priest intoned at their wedding. Enza had long ago rejected second-class status for women; she'd left those notions behind when she earned her first paycheck. Her plans for sewing on the Iron Range weren't about busywork, or keeping up with her craft, or earning pocket money. In fact, she intended to contribute to their home life and be a full and equal partner in the young marriage that they had yet to define.

Ciro had made a bet in proposing to her, and on that same day, Enza made a bet of her own. She was putting her money, effort, and future into a partnership that she believed could not fail. She was going to pour all of herself into her marriage: love would sustain them, and trust would see them through. That was her belief, and that's how she was raised. When she spun the gold ring on her finger, it was as though it was made for her, but it meant even more that her husband had worn it since he was a boy. She was a part of his history now.

Ciro held Enza in his arms in the top berth of the sleeping car. He pushed the curtains over the window aside. The countryside of Pennsylvania, with its low rolling hills, was purple in the moonlight as they sped through it.

Occasionally a flicker of light from the lamp of a distant barn or the glimmer from the flame of a candle in a window lit up the dark briefly like the dance of a firefly. But mostly, the world rolled away from them as they pressed forward to their future.

They had celebrated their wedding with cake and champagne, and a silver dish filled with small chocolates dusted in powdered sugar and dressed with small candy violets. They laughed and told stories in Italian, immersed in the rhythms of the language of their birth.

When they returned to the sleeping cars, Enza changed into a peignoir set that Laura had made for her, a floor-length white satin gown with a ruched bed jacket. Enza thought it too fancy for the train, but she knew Laura would be upset if she didn't wear it. Plus, she felt like Mae Murray in the arms of Rudolph Valentino.

The steady purr of the engine and the smooth coasting of the wheels made a kind of music as the train moved through the night. As they made love for the first time, Enza thought it was like flying, and love felt like a dream state, where she was safe, in a place and time she hoped never to leave. She understood at long last why this act, at once so natural and so universal, was also considered sacred.

Ciro was experienced in these matters, but he felt enveloped by Enza and treasured each of her kisses. Her expression of love for him meant even more in reality than it had in his imagination. His body wasn't his own anymore, but *hers*, and there was nothing he would deny her; whatever she wanted, whatever small happiness he could provide, he would search the world to bring it to her. Ciro knew Enza had sacrificed for him; she had given up a good life on the gamble that he could build one. He held her trust in the highest regard, and he knew it was on loan.

Enza responded to him without restraint. Her love filled the deepest places in his heart, healing the loneliness that had followed him since he left Eduardo at the train station in Bergamo. In Enza's arms, Ciro felt whole. He could feel the possibilities of what they could become together, the thing he had reached for, and hoped for, a family of his own.

La famiglia.

Ciro slid his hand up Enza's hip to her waist and pulled her close. "When you love someone, you think you know everything about them. Tell me one thing I don't know about you." Ciro kissed her neck.

"I have one hundred and six dollars in my purse."

Ciro laughed. "Good for you."

"It's yours to open the shoe shop."

"*Ours*, you mean," he corrected her.

"Ours." She laughed.

"Have I taken you away from a life you loved?" Ciro asked her.

"I'll miss Laura and the opera. And the candied peanuts on the corner of Fortieth Street and Broadway."

"I'll make sure you have your peanuts."

"Thank you, husband."

"How about Signor Caruso?"

"Yes, I'll miss him, too. But I guess I understood the words in the arias he sang. A happy life is about love—every note he sang reinforced it. I'll miss how he made every person he met feel special. He made us all laugh. I've come to appreciate a good joke and the conversation of intelligent people. But I have that with you."

"Are you afraid?"

"Why would I be afraid?"

"We might get to Hibbing, and you won't like it."

"Well, if I don't like it, we'll have to move."

Ciro laughed. "*Va bene.*"

"It wasn't at all like I thought it would be," Enza said.

"Getting married?"

"Making love. It's really a blessing, you know. To be that close. It has a certain beauty to it."

"Like you," he said. "You know, my father said something to my brother, and I never realized what it meant until now. He said, 'Beware the things of this world that can mean everything or nothing.' But now I know it's better when it means everything." Ciro kissed her. He traced the small scar over her eye. It was barely discernible, the width of a thread and as long as an eyelash. "Where did you get this scar?"

"In Hoboken."

"Did you fall?"

"Do you really want to know?"

"I want to know everything about you."

"Well, there was a man at the Meta Walker factory who was awful to all the girls, and one night, he grabbed me. After months of putting up with his slurs, I fought back. I was so angry, I thought I could take him. I went to kick him, but I fell against the wood planks of the floor, and I cut my eye on a nail. But Laura saved me. She threatened him with a pair of cutting shears."

"I would have killed him."

"She almost did." Enza smiled at Laura's bravery, the moment that had cemented their friendship. "I look at the scar every morning when I wash my face. It reminds me of how lucky I am. I don't think about the wrong that was done to me, I remember my friend and how brave she was. She taught me English, but I realize now, she taught me the words that I needed to know, not so much the ones I wanted to learn. Those would come later when she gave me *Jane Eyre*. She used to make me read it aloud to her. Sometimes she would make a comment when Rochester was surly, and we'd laugh about that. Like Jane, we had no connections, but Laura taught me to act like we did. Laura tapped my creative vein, pushing me to sew a straighter seam, choose a daring fabric, and to never be afraid of color. My world went from the hues and tones of our mountain to this great American palette, and I would have never had the guts to try if it weren't for Laura. I walk in the world with confidence today because of her."

"You must always stay close. And we'll visit them, and they'll come to our house."

"Of course, I would like that. But we'll be happy to write to one another, because that's how we learned to be friends, on the page, with words. I imagine that won't change."

Ciro kissed her. "I don't think a man could ever come between you. Or two, if you're counting Colin."

Enza looked through the window as Ciro fell asleep, his face nestled into her neck. She imagined there would be many nights like this ahead, just the two of them, holding tight in a world that was flying by.

Until she met Ciro, Enza had spent her spare time contemplating facts and figures, thinking up sensible solutions to her problems, estimating how many feet of fabric she needed for a particular garment or how to send a little extra money home to the mountain. Her dreams were about the safety and comfort of her family. This great romantic love shared with Ciro was mystical to her. He had finally made a dreamer of her, but at the same time, love felt as practical and durable as a sturdy velvet that only gets softer and lovelier with age. Without knowing the future, she was assured, in the deepest place in her heart, that this love would last.

There was something constant and reliable about Ciro Lazzari. He made her feel no harm would come to her as long as she loved him.

As Enza said her prayers that night, she pictured her father's safe passage on the steamship to Naples, and a speedy train ride from the south to Bergamo in the north. She imagined the entire family there to greet him by the garden of their new home, built by the labor of their own hands and lit by the light of the winter moon.

23

A LIBRARY CARD
Una Tessera della Biblioteca

Enza could barely make out the flats of the Iron Range under the snow from the window of the train as it pulled into the station at Hibbing. Low rolling hills covered in white drifts seemed untouched for miles. Close to the train tracks, there were gray zippers on the ground where flatbed and dump trucks had made impressions in the snow. Haulers and cranes were parked close by in an open field, plenty of equipment at the ready to plow, carve, and dig into the earth.

The mining operations were vast, decamped over two hundred miles of northern Minnesota terrain. The mouths of the mines were studded into the earth like nailheads along the range. Shifts went round the clock, as hundreds of miners extracted the ore with a mechanical vengeance. Iron ore, the key component in the manufacturing of steel, was valuable and in demand. Steel was the building block of the future, used to create motorcars, bridges, and airplanes. Iron ore fed the industrial boom, and the development of defense weaponry, tanks, and submarines. The range was split open wide and deep for the taking, the precious ore a lucrative business.

As the couples stepped off the platform at the Hibbing station, a bitter cold wind greeted them, nearly toppling Enza over. Ciro put his arm around his bride to guide her safely over the ice. Luigi followed with Pappina, worried that she might slip, and terrified that she and the baby would be injured. The air was so cold, they could barely catch their breath. The sky was saturated as blue as India ink, without a star in sight. Enza thought no place on earth could be colder than the Italian Alps, but now she knew she just had never been to Minnesota.

As they crossed Main Street, Enza could see that Hibbing was a city raised quickly on the outskirts of the mines. A collection of new buildings including a hospital, a school, a hotel, and a few stores stood away from the landscape like stakes plummeted into the flat earth. The architecture of the buildings was serviceable and plain, with thick windows, sturdy doors, and functional trim, including spikes attached to every roof to break the ice that inevitably formed during the long winters. There was nothing grand about Hibbing; it was built to withstand the harsh elements.

As they passed the Hibbing department store, Enza noticed that the mannequins in the window did not wear gowns of silk and brocade they might in B. Altman's in Manhattan; rather, they were outfitted in wool coats, boots, and scarves, the couture of subzero living.

Pappina took note of the construction of the buildings along Pine Street, where a red-brick schoolhouse faced the Carnegie Library. Scaffolds, ladders, and the open steel frames of unfinished buildings were set against the sky like pencil slashes. Hibbing was growing, and not even a Minnesota blizzard would halt the progress.

As a mother-to-be, Pappina's first concern was where her children would be educated. She also looked at the modest homes that lined the streets, full of children who would become potential playmates. She saw snow-covered lawns and sledding hills with sleek grooves carved into them. The town was tidy, sidewalks were shoveled, and the parking lots were scraped clean of snow. The stable lights glowed outside the barns off Main Street, indicating that while the area was industrial, they didn't have machines for everything just yet. A horse-drawn carriage was still a popular mode of transportation in this part of the world.

"Just a few more steps," Ciro shouted over the wind as he guided the group to the entrance of the Hotel Oliver. Ciro held the door open for Pappina and Enza, who were so thrilled to be inside in the warmth, they embraced.

Luigi followed them inside, carrying the bags like a good sherpa, handing Ciro's off to him. They peeled off their hats, coats, and gloves. The hostess sat them in a Victorian dining room, decorated with lace curtains and polished walnut tables with matching chairs. The crackling fire in the hearth warmed them immediately. The scent of the burning pine was sweetly fragrant and welcoming. Miner's lamps were used on every table instead of traditional candlelight. "We know who runs the town here," Luigi commented as he placed a napkin on his lap.

"They do it with a pick and shovel," Pappina said.

"Mr. Latini?" A sturdily built man around forty joined them at the table. He wore a wool suit and tie, and snow boots on his feet.

"You must be Mel Butorac," Luigi said as he stood and shook his hand. Luigi had sent a telegram from New York to Mel Butorac, a local businessman who leased real estate to entrepreneurs and helped them set up their businesses with the local banks.

"Ciro, this is the fellow who lured us up here to make boots." Ciro stood and shook Mel's hand. They introduced their wives and pulled up a chair so Mel might join them.

"How was your trip?" Mel seemed friendly and energetic.

"I think the trip across the ocean was faster." Pappina smiled.

"I wouldn't know." Mel smiled. "I've only been as far south as the Twin Cities. Someday I hope to visit my cousins in Croatia."

"Nothing like the Adriatic Sea in the summertime," Luigi said.

"I've heard," Mel agreed. "I'm here to help you make a smooth transition. The city government is here to provide whatever assistance you need. We want to make you feel at home."

"You said you had some real estate for us to look at," Luigi said.

"I do. But I wanted to offer up an idea. I know your plan was to open a shop together, but the truth is, we need a shoemaker in Hibbing, but there is also a need for one down the road in Chisholm. If you split up, you could open two shops and still have plenty of work."

Enza leaned back in her chair. They just dropped their luggage, and already the deal was no longer the deal as it had been presented to them in New York.

Ciro could see that Enza was concerned, so he said, "This isn't what you promised."

"Of course I will show you the real estate for the shop here in Hibbing as planned. All I ask is that you keep an open mind about Chisholm," Mel said in a tone that told Luigi and Ciro that he had given this speech before to other tradesmen lured to the Iron Range to serve the mining industry. "Hear me out. I didn't mean to mislead you in any way. The conditions on the Iron Range change daily. Mines open, we get an influx of new workers, and we have to meet their needs. Give me a chance to *show* you what I'm talking about. Have your dinner, get a good night's sleep, and I can show you both properties in the morning. I have a truck, and we can go over to Chisholm and you can take a look around. You may like what you see, and if you don't, we'll stick with the original plan. Fair enough?" Mel proposed.

Ciro and Luigi looked at one another. They did not expect that everything would go according to plan, but they had counted on the fact that they would face whatever came together. Still, they had come to Minnesota in the first place to make bold business choices. Ciro spoke for their partnership. "All right, Mel, we'll keep an open mind and we'll see you in the morning. Seven o'clock all right with you?"

"I'll be here in the lobby," Mel said. "We are happy to have you, and we look forward to introducing you to your fellow Italians here on the Iron Range." He shook hands with the men, bowed his head to the ladies, and went.

"I don't like the idea of splitting up. We just got here." Pappina smoothed the napkin on her lap.

"Neither do I," Luigi said. "Should I check the train schedules back to New York?"

"Let's decide in the morning," Ciro said as he took Enza's hand. "Let's take a look before we leave."

* * *

The next day, Enza stood on the corner of West Lake Street in Chisholm and looked across the bridge to Longyear Lake. It reminded her of Schilpario. The lake was deep and wide, making her think of the midnight blue waters of Lake Como and the windswept whitecaps on Lake Garda. To her astonishment, Chisholm felt like home.

Ciro put his arms around Enza. "Come inside."

The empty two-story red-brick saltbox had two workrooms on the first floor, separated by a service window. A small patch of yard for a garden was just a step off the back room, but it was covered in ice. Ciro and Enza joined Luigi and Pappina in the front room. They were chatting with Mel. "I'm going to leave you folks to talk things through. I'll be at Valentini's, having a cup of coffee." He put his hat on and left them alone.

"What do you think?" Luigi asked.

"I think Mel has a point. If we split up, we can serve two mining operations. I can handle the work from Buhl and Chisholm, and you can handle the Hibbing operation."

Luigi paced with his hands in his pockets as he considered their options. "It's true. When we had the cart, we made double the money for the Zanettis."

"Yeah, but was that us or Signora's bullwhip?"

"A little of both." Luigi smiled.

"Mel assured me we can get enough of a loan from the bank to open both shops," Ciro said. "The only problem is that we'll be separated, essentially starting a business single-handed, even if we're partners on paper. What do you think, Enza?"

"There's a hospital in Hibbing, and Pappina needs to be close to it when the baby comes. There's a trolley, so it isn't difficult to get from here to there. I think the more boots you can make, the better off all four of us will be. It's simple, really."

Ciro and Luigi took Enza's opinion seriously. She was experienced in weighing business propositions, first with her father, and later in the costume shop. Enza had learned that even the Great Caruso took extra jobs to fill his purse. He sang in the opera house, but he also performed private concerts for profit and made records of his arias. There was no such thing as a one-track career, and Enza knew the value of two men capitalizing on two towns that needed shoemakers.

"I liked Hibbing." Pappina smiled. "But I leave the shoemaking to the shoemakers, and the business to you, Enza. You know what you're talking about. I've only ever worked in my mother's home, so I don't know the first thing about ledgers, figures, and banks."

One thing was decided for certain that morning. They were not going to run back to New York City at the first bump in the road. They

were going to give the Iron Range a real shot. Luigi and Pappina left
to meet up with Mel and sign the lease for the shop in Hibbing. They
would also take the apartment above the shop, which was clean and
spacious. Ciro and Enza stayed behind and spent the afternoon looking
over the property at 5 West Lake Street.

A set of wide-plank wooden stairs, painted burgundy, led to the upstairs apartment. A large open living room with three windows overlooked the lake. A dining area connected to the kitchen. A hallway led
to three bedrooms and a landing porch outside the master bedroom
that overlooked the backyard. A small bathroom, one of the town's only
indoor facilities, was tiled in white, with white enamel fixtures.

Enza's heart leapt when she noticed that despite the dark sky on that
winter day, the apartment was filled with light because every room had
a skylight in the ceiling.

"What do you think?" Ciro asked when he joined Enza in the room
that would become their master bedroom. "The rent is three dollars a
month."

"Tell Mr. Butorac we will take it. You'll make shoes in the front workroom, and I'll sew in the back. We'll do just fine."

Ciro kissed his wife, certain that he was the luckiest man in the
world for having married her. Enza's practical nature was a tonic for the
emotions that had controlled him all of his life. In her presence, Ciro
forgot the isolation he'd felt as a child, and the injustice he'd endured
when he was exiled from his mountain. He even put the anguish of war
behind him. Ciro was in love with a good woman who had become his
full partner, and they were going to build a life together.

. . . .

Ciro unpacked the crates in his new workroom. He set up a pattern
table, with bright metal lamps suspended overhead. He had purchased
several planks of wood to build cubbies for storage, a top-of-the-line
saw to cut the patterns, a buffing machine with four brushes, a thread-
ing machine, and a rolling machine to prep the leather.

Ciro had also bought a Singer sewing machine for Enza, with enough
thread, needles, buttons, and trims to start her own business.

"*Buon giorno!* You look like you could use a hand," Emilio Uncini said as he entered the front door of the shop. He leaned on the table and smiled at his new neighbor. Emilio was in his middle forties, with a thick thatch of gray hair, a small black mustache, and a winning smile. He placed his hands on his hips. "What is the wood for?" he continued in his rapid-fire dialect.

"I'm going to build shelves. I'm Ciro—"

"Lazzari. I heard all about you. Our prayers have been answered. We need a shoemaker."

"What do you do?"

"I'm a stonemason. I live one street over. I built the fieldstone wall around the library."

"Very nice. So tell me about your town." Ciro lifted the wood onto the pattern table, and Emilio helped him stack it.

"It's a nice place. But watch your business. The Chisholm bank is solid, but avoid the third window and Mrs. Kripnick. She repeats figures at the bar at Tiburzi's after work on Fridays, so if you don't want everyone to know what you have, don't let her see your deposits."

"*Va bene.*" Ciro laughed.

Emilio continued, "The winters are harsh, but the spring and summer more than make up for it. You will love the cool breezes off the lakes when the weather turns warm. There are lots of italians here. *Molte famiglie* . . . we have the Maturi, Costanzi, Bonato, Falcone, Giaordanino, Enrico, Silvestri, Bonicelli, Valentini, Ongaro, oh, and the Falcone, Sentieri, and Sartori families. I don't like to leave anyone out because they mind if I do! We also have Austrians from Trentino, who are as Italian as you and me."

"I know all about them. I spent a few years on Mulberry Street in Little Italy."

"So you know about the rest of the Middle Europeans. We have the Czechs, Hungarians, Romanians, Polish, Yugoslavians, Serbians, and Croatians. They just got here too. The Finlanders, the Scandinavians, this is *their* town. They got here first, and they act like it. They still are frosty with outsiders, but that's because they opened the first iron ore mine and became the padrones. But most are nice, if you're polite to them."

"I build boots for all feet, including Finlanders," Ciro assured him.

"Have you made a friend?" Enza asked from the doorway. Ciro introduced his wife to Emilio.

"My wife, Ida, will be happy to show you around," Emilio told Enza.

"I'd like that. *Grazie*. Ciro, we need some things for the apartment. I'll be back shortly." Enza waved good-bye. Ciro had used Marco's dowry to put a down payment on 5 West Lake Street. Enza had kept a firm hand on her savings and was happy to spend it on things that would bring the newlyweds comfort. She also liked the feeling of not having to ask her husband for money; it was that sense of independence that attracted Ciro, and it gave Enza a certain self-confidence.

Enza made her way up West Lake Street, taking in the storefronts. Chisholm was a prim, small town compared to New York City, but when she thought of Schilpario, Chisholm was a big city by comparison. It was interesting that her new married life had landed her somewhere in the middle, between the small alpine village of her childhood and the international city of her young adulthood.

Enza peered into the glass window of Leibovitz Jewelry and admired the pearls resting on a velvet display. She was mesmerized by the beautiful gold rings studded with clear blue aquamarines and diamond chips, the slim platinum chains dripping on velvet, and the enameled cuff bracelets stacked on a Lucite dowel. A town that had beautiful jewelry for sale must have a clientele that required them. This boded well for her custom clothing business. Enza passed the Valentini Supper Club, the Five and Dime, and several bars (the staple business of all mining towns), including the bustling Tiburzi's, until she reached Raatamas Department Store.

The department store was owned by a Finnish couple who had lived in Chisholm all their lives. It was an enormous single-story room with a tin ceiling painted pale blue and the clean lines of Scandinavian design. The walls were painted oyster white, a cool backdrop for the variety of merchandise.

Unlike the chic stores in New York City, each filled with merchandise over several floors connected by escalators, Raatamas displayed all their goods on one level. The sections were cordoned off with sheer linen curtains. There was a fabric and notions section, another for furniture, and yet another with housewares. Glass cases were filled with gloves, purses, hats, and scarves. Enza walked up and down the aisles, surveying the inventory.

"May I help you?" The salesgirl was a young Nordic beauty, around sixteen years old, with a small nose and large blue eyes.

"I'm a new bride." Enza smiled. "And we just moved to Chisholm."

The salesgirl followed Enza as she chose a mattress and box spring, two lamps with yellow ceramic bowl bases, a white lacquered table with four chairs, and two comfortable reading chairs, covered in soft sage green chenille. Enza remembered the sage green and coral used for the interior decoration of the Milbank House, and chose the same colors for her new home, reminding her of happy times with Laura.

Enza intended to splurge on the best items she could afford. She had American money in her purse, but she had the Italian determination to purchase things that would last. She had a good head start, as she and Laura had packed a trunk with the basics for any proper home, including linens, sheets, towels, moppeens, napkins, and tablecloths, made in the costume shop of the Met. They filled another trunk with fabric—yardage of wool, silk, cotton, and corduroy—knowing that there were things that Enza might need once she arrived, and she would already have the material to sew whatever she needed.

In the furniture department, along the wall, were three models of phonograph players in wooden cabinets. Enza ran her hands over a mahogany model with brass bindings. She lifted the lid and spun the turntable with her gloved hand.

"I'd also like to buy this record player. Could you deliver it to Five West Lake Street?"

"Of course." The girl smiled, knowing that her mother and father, the owners, would be thrilled with the sale. "Would you like to see the records?" she asked Enza. "They're over here in this cabinet." The salesgirl opened a wooden cabinet filled with phonograph records, arranged in alphabetical order.

Enza looked through the selections until she found the recordings of Enrico Caruso. She was pleased to find compilations that included duets with Geraldine Farrar and Antonio Scotti. Their faces adorned the cardboard sleeve, their profiles drawn inside large silver stars with their names emblazoned in clouds underneath their images. Enza bought the scores to *La Traviata*, *Aida*, and *Cavalleria Rusticana*. She decided not to have the records delivered; she would carry those herself.

She held the brown paper package close to her, and somehow it made her feel connected to her days at the opera.

Enza walked to the top of the hill, the end of West Lake Street. The snow had begun to fall again, throwing a glittery gauze over the town. Enza imagined this was Chisholm's way of asking her to fall in love with it. She crossed the street to enter the building that had most intrigued her when they drove past the first time in Mel Butorac's truck, and walked up the wide half-moon steps into the Chisholm Public Library, a regal red-brick building in the Georgian style, angled artfully on the block in the shape of a half moon.

Enza treasured the public library. She'd first gone with Laura, at the behest of Signora Ramunni, who sent them to the New York Public Library to research fabrics for historically accurate costumes when she worked at the Met. Laura had insisted that Enza get a library card, and until she became a citizen, it had been Enza's main source of identification.

As she pushed open the front door, she was met with the familiar scent of books, leather, and lemon polish. Enza took in the main room, with its cozy reading alcoves, a picture window revealing a garden in winter across the back wall, long walnut study tables outfitted with low lamps, and the floor-to-ceiling stacks, filled with cloth-bound books in shades of deep green, blue, and red. As she went to the front desk, Enza imagined she would spend many happy hours here.

"Good afternoon"—Enza looked at the librarian's name tag, reading it aloud—"Mrs. Selby."

The portly, white-haired lady wore a simple serge day dress and hand-knit white wool sweater. She did not bother to look up at Enza, especially after she heard her Italian accent. "I have no books in Italian. If you want them, I have to special order them from the Twin Cities."

In an instant, Enza was back in Hoboken, where Italian immigrants received little respect and it was assumed that they were illiterate and therefore unintelligent. She took a deep breath. "I would like to sign up for a library card," Enza told the librarian firmly but politely.

Mrs. Selby finally looked up, taking in Enza's proper hat, well-structured wool coat, and gloves.

"You do have library cards, don't you?" Enza asked.

"Yes, of course." Mrs. Selby sniffed.

Enza filled out the application as Mrs. Selby watched her out of the corner of her eye. When she was finished, Enza placed it on the desk blotter.

"I'm afraid the card itself won't be ready until tomorrow," Mrs. Selby said, clearly taking pleasure in the delay.

"It's no problem for me to come back," Enza said. "You see, I love to read, and I can tell that you have a lot of books here that will keep me busy on these long winter nights. You'll be seeing a lot of me." Enza flashed her most dazzling smile and turned on her heel before the lady could respond.

Enza walked out of the library, relieved to be outside in the fresh air. She realized that life might be difficult in a new place, in a part of the country that she did not know. She decided to bring Mrs. Selby an embroidered handkerchief on her next visit to the library. Winning a stranger over with kindness was a tactic Enza had used in Schilpario, and was certain it would work in Chisholm.

·   ·   ·

Enza and Ciro had been in Chisholm a couple of weeks when they were invited to a party. The Knezovichs lived across Longyear Lake in an old farmhouse with red cotton curtains in the windows, trimmed in white rickrack. Inside, Ana, the mistress of the house, had had her husband, Peter, paint every piece of the simple furniture a lacquered candy apple red. On the floor, he stenciled black and white squares on the wood, an artful contrast to the red. Enza remembered when the scene designer would have a crew paint the floor at the Met, and how dramatic the pattern would look from the mezzanine.

Enza couldn't wait to write to Laura about the Serbian style. Every detail was bright and polished, like the jewels in the Leibovitz window. Enza had been to many fancy parties in New York, but none could top the theatrics of the Slava.

While the Roman Catholics honored the feast days of their saints quietly with a visit to church or early morning mass, the Serbs threw an all-day, through-the-night party, serving homemade plum brandy and robust cherry wine, glasses refilled without request.

The house was so full that the guests spilled out into the cold winter night, where firepits had been lit in the fields, and an open tent had been raised for dancing.

The Serbian women wore full silk skirts in jewel tones and white blouses trimmed in lace, topped with fitted velvet vests secured with gold silk buttons. The men wore traditional high-waisted wool pants and hand-embroidered shirts with billowing sleeves. The clothing they wore served the same purpose as theatrical costumes: they served a theme, were colorful, and moved to accommodate the dance.

Long tables filled with Serbian delicacies were placed under the tent and inside the house, as a loyal band of women kept the platters filled to overflowing, while their daughters bused dishes and washed and dried them for the next shift of revelers.

The Serbian dishes were prepared with fragrant spices, including sage, cinnamon, and turmeric. The festival bread *kolach* was hearty and delicious, with its thick buttery crust and soft doughy center. They ate it with *sarma*, a fragrant meat mixture of bacon, onions, rice, and fresh eggs wrapped in *kupus*, tangy cabbage leaves that had been pickled in a crock. *Burek*, a meat strudel with a tender buttery crust, was cut into squares and served with roasted potatoes. The dessert table was a wonderland of pastries filled with fruit, dusted in sugar, and glazed with butter. Small ginger cookies and bar cookies made with candied dates were dipped in strong coffee and savored. *Kronfe*, round doughnuts dusted with cinnamon sugar, were passed in baskets piping hot from the fryer. *Povitica*, layers of thin pastry dough filled with walnuts, brown sugar, butter, and raisins, rolled carefully, layer over layer, baked, and sliced thin, was served on a platter in neat slices resembling pinwheels.

Emilio and Ida Uncini joined Ciro and Enza by the dessert table. Ida, a petite brunette in her forties, wore a full turquoise skirt and a gold velvet jacket. For an Italian, she was throwing herself into the Serbian *festa* like one of their own. In the short time Enza had been in Chisholm, Ida had been steadfast, showing up at the new building to help her wash floors, paint walls, and arrange the furniture. Ida had been through a big move herself years ago, so she understood how important it was to make a home comfortable as soon as possible.

"I'm going to ask Ana to teach Enza how to make *povitica*," Ciro said, taking a bite.

"She has enough to do," Ida chided him. "She has curtains to make, and a sewing machine to assemble. And I know, because I promised to help her."

"And I need your help," Enza said.

"This is some party," Ciro said. "Is everyone in Chisholm here?"

"Just about. But let me warn you. This is nothing. Wait until you go to Serbian Days in July. Every Serb from here to Dbrovnik shows up to sing," Emilio promised them.

"My husband loves that celebration the most because the girls have a dance competition. Baltic beauties, each more stunning than the one before, line up to tap, kick, and sashay," Ida assured them.

"I like the dancing for the art of it, Ida." Emilio winked.

"Now he's a patron of the fine arts." Ida shrugged.

"How long have you and Emilio been in Chisholm?" Enza asked.

"Since 1904," said Ida.

"We were here for the Burt-Sellers mining disaster in Hibbing," Emilio said. "It was quite a welcome to life on the Iron Range. Hundreds of men died underground. Such a tragedy."

Enza looked at Ciro, who looked away. An expression of hollow grief crossed his face. He forced a smile. "Emilio, want to join me for a smoke?"

Emilio followed Ciro to the outside of the tent. "Did Emilio say something wrong?" Ida asked.

"Ciro's father died in a mining accident in 1904 in Hibbing."

"How awful. I'm sure Emilio didn't know."

"He wouldn't. Ciro never talks about it. It's such a terrible part of his past, and his mother, poor thing, didn't handle it very well. She ran out of money, had no family to turn to, and finally had to put her sons in a convent."

"Iron ore makes steel and widows," Ida remarked.

Ida showed Enza the wine barrels, set up at the far side of the tent, with easy access from either side. Enza helped herself to a glass and sipped the sweet wine, feeling her mood plummet at the thought of Ciro's unhappiness. She didn't know what to say or do; any mention of his father produced either a depressive silence or a quiet rage, never directed at her, but taken out on equipment, tough leather, and himself. She wished there was some way to heal his broken heart. Maybe moving to the place where his father died hadn't been the best idea.

Ida excused herself to join a group of ladies, leaving Enza to circulate through the tent alone. Suddenly the band began to play and men and women paired off, practically skipping onto the dance floor, planks of wood set into the ground for just that purpose. Enza looked around for Ciro, going up on her toes to look over the crowd. She saw him enter the tent alone and waved to him. He looked around but did not catch his wife's eye.

A comely young woman of twenty with a long, silky blond braid cascading down her back grabbed Ciro by the arm and pulled him on to the crowded dance floor.

"You better watch your husband," Ida said to Enza as she passed her on the way to join the cakewalk in the field.

Enza didn't need any reminders from Ida to look out for Ciro. Plus, Enza could find Ciro in any crowd easily because of his height. She tried to move onto the dance floor to join him, but the surrounding bystanders were too thick, and she couldn't push through.

She watched as Ciro put his arm around the waist of the Baltic beauty, who was eager to show him the steps of the dance. He laughed as she took his hands, and Enza flashed to Mulberry Street, when he'd entered the shop carrying two bottles of champagne in the delightful company of Felicitá so many years ago. Ciro had the same look on his face that he had then—not a care in the world, just a sense of unfettered joy. The girl was not that much younger than Enza, but suddenly Enza felt a hundred years older. The beauty leaned in and whispered something in Ciro's ear, and he whispered in hers. Enza felt a flash of pain in her chest, sudden and piercing.

Ciro's lean build and broad shoulders were an athletic counter to the willowy limbs of the girl, whose own green eyes shimmered like emeralds. At one point, the couples swayed toward the bystanders near Enza, and she tried again to wave to her husband. But he was no longer looking for her. He was laughing with abandon as the girl spun around him, pivoting back as she lifted the hem of her voluminous pale green velvet skirt, revealing her smooth calves and small ankles. Ciro drank the details of her in, and it made Enza's stomach churn.

"She seems to have no idea he's married," Ida said.

Ida's comment jolted Enza back into reality. "He doesn't wear a ring. I wear his ring." Enza twisted the signet ring on her finger.

"You should go out there and break it up right now," Ida insisted. "There were too many barrels of plum wine at this shindig, and they've all been emptied. Go. Go get him!"

If Laura were here, she would probably have said the same thing. But for some reason, Enza couldn't seem to make the move to claim her husband. Instead, she watched the scene unfold as though it was not her husband dancing with another woman, but a character in a novel she'd once read. This made what she witnessed less true, almost manageable. He didn't mean anything by his actions. He couldn't possibly. Wasn't the nature of trust to let go? Enza tried hard to remember how the novel ended, but for the life of her, she couldn't.

One of the Knezovich girls came by with a tray, and Enza placed her empty glass on it. When she looked up, she couldn't find her husband on the dance floor. She pushed her way into the crowd, but it quickly became a morass, and she had no choice but to let the crush of the bodies push her along. Eventually she was shoved to the spot where she had seen Ciro and the girl dancing, but they were gone.

Enza felt her face flush. She reminded herself that Ciro loved her, and that she trusted him, but a wrenching pain twisted in her gut, perhaps a premonition of some kind, the kind her mother used to have but which Enza had never experienced before now. She closed her eyes, telling herself that the sweet sugar fermented in the wine had gone to her head.

Suddenly Enza was afraid. She felt so helpless, she almost began to cry. She shuddered at the thought that every decision she had made had been wrong; she was in a place that she did not choose, married to a man she could not find, and all she knew was that the nagging feelings of doubt within her had replaced reason in her mind.

Enza fought her way back through the crowd to reach Ida and Emilio, but they too had gone. Enza took a deep breath to calm herself. She told herself that she was just overtired, and not thinking straight. She told herself that her instincts were off, that her tears were simply a product of the gray smoke billowing from the firepits.

Enza walked out from under the tent. She couldn't discern how much time had passed. It seemed as though Ciro had been dancing with the girl for a very long time. She returned to the house, hoping to find Ciro there, and went through every room. The volume of the conversation, music, and laughter was deafening, but there was no sign of her husband.

The trays and serving plates that had been full earlier were now being consolidated down to a few. Ana, the hostess, checked the urn of coffee, a signal that the night would soon end. Enza thought to ask Ana if she had seen Ciro, but she didn't want her new neighbors to think that she was a flighty woman, or worse, a jealous one. She turned and went back outside.

Enza remembered what her father had taught her on the mountain: when you're lost, don't move, someone will find you. Enza wanted Ciro to find her. She stood and waited as the minutes stretched into an eternity. She stood on the cold field, by the edge of the tent, as the dance floor slowly emptied and the accordions eventually ceased.

Ciro had not come back for her. Ida and Emilio had left the party. Her new neighbors smiled as they piled into their wagons for the carriage ride home. Mrs. Selby, the librarian, waved the handkerchief Enza had made for her. The librarian offered Enza a ride, but she pretended that she didn't need one. She stood a few minutes longer, until anger rose within her and she could no longer contain her fury. She belted her red wool coat tightly around her, pulled a silk scarf from her pocket, and tied it around her head. She pulled on her gloves, snapped her collar up to protect herself from the cold, and walked back toward West Lake Street alone.

.   .   .

Enza lay alone in their new bed on sheets from her trousseau trunk, her head resting on one of the two feather pillows she had brought from New York. Laura had embroidered "Mrs." on one of the pillow shams, and "Mr." on the other. The scent of fresh paint wafted through the apartment. Everything, including her marriage, was new. Enza looked over at Ciro's side of the bed. It was four o'clock in the morning; she had arrived home at one.

The words of her father consumed her. Without the care of a mother and a father, and a solid example of marital love, what if Ciro did not know how to be a husband? He certainly didn't know how to be a good husband tonight. What if his womanizing ways had returned, his vow of fidelity a short-lived hope after the long war, but a promise he could never keep? She fell asleep as disturbing thoughts consumed her.

Later still, Ciro pushed open the front door of the shop. The bells on the door jingled, and he silenced them by reaching up and placing his hand over the ringer. He locked the door behind him. He climbed the stairs slowly, having had too much to drink and not enough to eat. He was a bit dizzy, and had no idea what time it was. He made his way down the hall and into their bedroom. He undressed slowly. He looked over at Enza, who was asleep. Ciro slipped into bed and pulled the covers over him. His head sank into the pillow, fragrant with lavender. The sheets were soft, the mattress firm. He smiled at the thought of having a wife who had made him a lovely home. He rolled over to kiss her sleeping cheek. She opened her eyes.

"You're home," Enza said.

"You're awake?" Ciro asked. "Why did you leave the party?"

"I couldn't find you."

"I was in the barn."

Enza's voice caught. "What were you doing there?"

"Playing cards with a man named Orlich, a Polish fellow named Milenski, an old man named Zahrajsek, and another man I can't remember."

"What about the girl?"

"What girl?"

"The dancing girl."

"I don't know who you mean," Ciro said. But he knew exactly who Enza was referring to. The girl had reminded him of the French girl he'd met during the war. She had the same gold braid and warm smile.

"I couldn't find you."

"I'm sorry. I should have told you I was going to play cards."

"Yes, you should have."

"I had too much to drink," Ciro said.

"Don't make excuses."

"But it's true," Ciro said, turning to face her in bed. "I drank too much, and nothing more."

"Do you want me to be honest with you?" she asked.

He nodded.

"When Ida mentioned 1904, you looked wounded."

"I don't want to talk about this." Ciro turned over in the bed, away from Enza. "What good would it do now?"

"If you accept what happened to your father, you'll find peace."

"I have peace," Ciro said defensively.

"Well, I don't. When you're troubled, you withdraw. I came home hoping to find you here. When you weren't, I had hours to think about what might have happened to you. I was afraid you went with the girl with the gold braid." Enza shuddered to admit that she'd felt abandoned, but this night had brought up every insecurity she had ever known.

"Why would I do that?" he asked softly.

"Because you could. You could disappear from my life, just as you did in the past. It made me wonder, what do I *really* know about you?"

"You know everything," Ciro assured her. Maybe it was his wife's brutal honesty and clear-eyed observations about his behavior, but it made Ciro think, and he had an epiphany. He not only appreciated Enza's point of view, it made him look at his own. The truth was, Ciro saw their romantic past as a series of near misses, the result of bad luck and poor timing. Once they were married, he forgot how close they had been to spending their lives without each other. Clearly, she hadn't. Enza was complex in ways he could not yet decipher. They were from the same mountain, but their insecurities created chasms that they couldn't fill.

Ciro turned over and placed his arm around Enza. "I'm sorry you couldn't find me. I danced with her without thinking of your feelings. I didn't know it would hurt you. It was just a dance. You're my *life*." He kissed her gently. He could feel the corner of her mouth turn into a smile as he kissed her.

"It can't happen again, Ciro," she said firmly.

"Please don't turn into the wife that chases her husband with a broom."

"I won't chase you with a broom." She returned his kiss with equal passion, then added, "I'll pick up a shovel."

Enza lay back and laced her fingers through his.

"We have a little money left over from my savings."

"You've done a wonderful job furnishing our home. Buy yourself a hat."

"I don't need a hat. But you need something."

"I have everything I want," Ciro assured her.

"You need a wedding band," Enza told him.

"Enza, I gave you the only ring I ever owned. It means everything to me to see you wear my mother's ring."

"And I'll always wear it because it says that I'm yours. Now you need to wear a ring that says that you're mine. Tomorrow we go to Leibovitz's. We're buying you a wedding ring. The thickest gold band I can find."

Ciro laughed. "I don't need a ring to prove that I'm yours. You have me, Enza."

"I know that. But I want the rest of the world to know it too."

Enza had done such a good job of decorating the Caterina Shoe Shop windows for Christmas that many women stopped in and asked to buy shoes. They were disappointed when they saw Ciro's industrial machines, the garish overhead lights, and the stacks of miner's work boots to be repaired. They realized it was a shop for men, with nothing to offer them, and they would depart as quickly as they had entered after Ciro apologized. Sometimes he would promise the ladies that one day, the window would be filled with fashionable shoes for them that he had designed and made. Then he'd send them up the street to Raatamas. He couldn't count how many times he threw the department store business.

Enza was in the back of the shop, sewing a satin blanket for Pappina's baby's layette, when she overheard a female customer talking with Ciro. She snipped the threads from the blanket, and when she heard the bells signaling that the woman had left, she joined Ciro in the front of the shop.

"Why don't we sell women's shoes?"

"Because I don't make them," Ciro said as he measured a sheet of leather.

"We don't have to make them," Enza said. "We could buy them from a middleman and sell them at a profit, just like any store in town. I could have Laura check with some suppliers in New York. There's enough room in the front of the shop. We could put in a couple of glass cabinets." Enza turned and imagined the perfect spot for the display cases.

"I don't have time to sell shoes," Ciro reminded her.

"But I *do*," Enza said. "We send more customers up the street than we keep. I won't bother you with any of it. I just need the space in the front of the shop."

"All right," Ciro said. "But when I start making women's shoes, you'll have to stop selling the ready-mades."

"You have a deal."

Enza took the trolley to Hibbing. She entered the Security State Bank of Hibbing on Howard Street in her best hat and gloves and went to the loan department to see Robert Renna.

"Mrs. Lazzari?" Mr. Renna looked up from his paperwork. He wore a suit with a vest and a plain navy tie. A pair of reading glasses was perched on the tip of his long nose. "How is everything working out?"

Enza smiled. The last time she was in the bank, she had cosigned Ciro's loans for the business and witnessed Luigi's paperwork. "Both shops are busy," she said as she took a seat.

"I'm happy to hear it. What can I do for you today?"

"We have a lot of ladies come through the shop. I'd like to sell ready-made shoes. But I need a loan to build the inventory."

"You have three stores in Chisholm that sell shoes."

"I know, but they don't sell the kind of shoes I would stock. I have a connection in New York City to bring real fashion to the ladies of the Iron Range. That is, of course, if you'll help me go into business."

"What does your husband think?"

"He has his hands full, so this would be my project."

Renna was used to widows coming into the bank for loans, but not married women. Usually their husbands handled the banking. Mrs. Lazzari was obviously an uncommon woman. "Let's take a look at your present loan." Mr. Renna went to the shelf and removed a ledger containing the pertinent information on all current loans. He opened the leather bound ledger and with a ruler, scanned the handwritten columns. "Here we are." He turned the page. "Your husband and his partner opened an account with a nice nest egg. You and Mrs. Latini co-signed the loan. They've borrowed against it at a reasonable rate. So I think there's some wiggle room here to help you out."

Mr. Renna went to the file desk and put together loan papers for Enza. She watched him as he handed the secretary some forms to type. A few minutes later, he returned with a contract.

"Take this home. Look it over. Talk it through with your husband, because I need his signature on the loan. And then let me know how much you need."

Enza smiled. "I can make a go of it, I know it!"

Renna showed Enza a ledger with a note in the margins. "Does your husband have a brother?"

"Yes. But he's in Italy."

"No, a brother here. There's a safety deposit box in the bank, it's under C. A. Lazzari."

"His father was Carlo Lazzari. He worked here about fourteen years ago."

"Would you like me to check?" Mr. Renna offered.

"Thank you."

Renna went to check on the information regarding Carlo Lazzari's accounts. Enza felt queasy, as she always did when the subject of Ciro's father came up. She thought of the Italian expression, "If you truly love someone, when he is cut, you bleed." Enza didn't know if it was simply her empathy for her husband that made her anxious about his father, or the unanswered questions that surrounded his disappearance and death. After a few minutes, Renna returned to his desk.

"Well, the accounts are closed," Renna explained. "But there's an unclaimed safety deposit box."

"I wouldn't know where to begin to look for a key," Enza said.

"We keep them here." Renna pulled a small silver key from his pocket and gave it to her. "I can show you to the vault."

"Should I wait for my husband?" Enza looked down at the key in her gloved hand.

"You're a signatory on all of your husband's accounts, including the business. You are authorized to open the box if you'd like."

Enza followed Mr. Renna through a steel gate to a large room with a marble floor. The walls were lined with small steel boxes, etched with numbers. Mr. Renna excused himself and went back out into the main floor of the bank.

Enza looked for Box 419. When she found it, she lifted the key to the lock. Her hand shook, though she hadn't thought she was nervous. She turned the key in the lock and looked inside. There was one sealed envelope inside. She removed it. It was a plain white business envelope, with neither an addressee nor a return address, slightly yellowed with age.

Enza removed a hairpin from her chignon, carefully opened the seal, and pulled out a document. It read:

> *Burt-Sellers Mining Corporation*
> *Hibbing, Minnesota*
> *100 shares of common stock*
> *Carlo A. Lazzari*

Enza folded the stock certificate and returned to Mr. Renna's desk. "I don't mean to bother you," she said, "but can you tell me what this is?"

Mr. Renna unfolded the stock certificate. His face broke into a wide grin. "Mrs. Lazzari, this is your lucky day. This stock is now worth a dollar a share. That is, if you sell it today. You can hold on to it, and watch it grow, if that's your preference."

"I don't understand."

"There are many safety deposit boxes in this bank with unclaimed stock certificates. After the mining disaster in 1904, Burt-Sellers almost went under. They couldn't afford to make a cash settlement to each family, but reparation was clearly required. So they issued stock. Some of the men that died left no survivors. Others had provided no information for contacting their survivors. But each of them had a box in this bank. It was lucky that we thought to check today. We didn't catch it when your husband and Mr. Latini came in for the loan. I guess you'd call this fate," Renna said kindly.

On the trolley ride back to Chisholm, Enza guardedly peeked into the envelope over and over again, scarcely able to take in this stroke of luck. When the trolley pulled into the station, she ran down West Lake Street and burst into the shop. Ciro was buffing a pair of work boots on the brushes. She ran to him and flipped the switch of the machine off.

"Ciro, you are not going to believe it. I went to talk to the bank about my shoe business, and Mr. Renna found a safety deposit box in your father's name. Since I'm a signatory, he let me open it. Look!" She handed Ciro the envelope. "Your father left you stock." He sat down on the work stool and opened it as she prattled on with the details. "Honey, it's worth a hundred dollars."

Ciro placed the stock certificate on the worktable. He stood, picked up the work boot he had been working on, flipped the switch on the brushing machine, and commenced polishing the boot. Enza was mystified, her excitement and impatience slowly giving way to anger. She went to the machine and turned it off. "What is wrong with you?"

"I don't want it."

"Why? It was your father's. You always tell me that you wished you had something of his. This stock was given as reparations for his death."

"And it wouldn't change a thing, now, would it, Enza?"

"He would want you to have it."

"Buy furniture with it. Or send it to my brother for the poor. That stock is blood money. It could have meant everything fourteen years ago, when my mother had to sell all our belongings to pay off our debts forcing her to leave Eduardo and me in the convent. But now she's gone, and my brother is a priest, and I don't need it." He put down the boot and looked up at the shelves he had built, loaded with boots, laces tied together, each pair affixed with a small tag showing the customer's name and a pick-up time. "This is my legacy. My hard work. You. Us. The rest of it doesn't matter. It's just money. And it isn't money that I earned. It will just remind me of all I lost and will never recover."

Enza stood for a moment, holding the certificate. She folded it and placed it in her pocket. She didn't bring up the subject again. Instead, she cashed the stock and opened a bank account in Chisholm in their names. Then, like Ciro, she put it out of her mind.

· · ·

Luigi opened the door of his apartment in Hibbing, festooned with fresh greens, tied with a bright blue bow. "*Buon Natale!*" Luigi embraced Enza and then Ciro. He helped Enza with the packages she carried.

Pappina had set their holiday table with candles and white china. The scent of butter and garlic simmering on the stove wafted through the three-room apartment. An empty bassinette in the corner was covered in small white ribbons. Pappina was in the kitchen, very pregnant and cheerful and delighted to see Enza and Ciro.

"What are you making?" Ciro asked.

"Escargot in butter and garlic."

"Did you put the nickel in?" Ciro asked.

"Go ahead," said Pappina.

Ciro fished in his pocket for a nickel and dropped it into the pan where the snails, in their copper-and-white shells, simmered.

After a few moments Pappina sifted out the nickel, still a shiny silver, returning it to Ciro. The Italians never eat escargot if the coin turns black. It means the snails are rotten. "They're good."

"They better be. We're starving," Enza said, pitching in to help Pappina with the pasta. Luigi poured Ciro a glass of wine in the living room, and they joined their wives in the kitchen.

"Ciro came to mass with me this morning."

"I don't believe it," said Luigi.

"We went to Saint Alphonse," Pappina said.

"We have to. If we want the baby baptized, we have to tithe," said Luigi.

"Oh, you make it sound like all the church wants is your money," Pappina said.

"They don't mind your money, but they'd prefer your soul," Ciro said.

"Your brother is a priest, and you talk like that?" Enza gently slapped her husband's cheek. "You know you enjoyed it—you liked the kyries and the hymns. Right?"

"I did. And looking at the statues brought me right back to San Nicola. It's funny how the things you do as a boy never leave you."

"I hope some of the things you did left you," Luigi joked.

"I'm a happy husband now. I only have eyes for Enza."

"Smart man." Pappina laughed.

"It's *difficile* for a statue to change its pose," Luigi said.

"I've changed for the better, brother." Ciro smiled.

"We'll take your word for it," Pappina said to Ciro. "Would you take the platter to the table? I need a strong man, I left the bones in the turkey."

Ciro lifted the platter and turned to take it to the living room. Enza watched him go. He seemed to get more handsome as time went on, and she imagined that when he was old, he would become even more attractive to her as his light brown hair turned white. She saw how other women looked at him, and knew that they were seeing on the surface what she had always known: there was no one else like him. She followed him into the dining room, where he placed the platter on the table. He stood up and rubbed his lower back with his hands.

"Honey, are you all right?" Enza asked as she massaged his lower back.

"He's got the shoemaker's stoop," Luigi said. "Put blocks under your cutting table to make it higher. A few inches will save your neck and shoulders. My back was killing me until I put down the blocks, and now I'm much better."

"I'll try it," Ciro said. "Can the blocks help me with my workload?"

"That they cannot do." Luigi laughed.

"Wooden blocks really work?" Pappina asked.

"Absolutely," Luigi said.

"Well, make me a pair of wooden shoes then." Pappina laughed. "I've had a sore back for seven months."

. . .

Enza went to early mass alone on Christmas Day. Ciro was tired from the long visit at the Latinis, and had made his once-a-year church appearance the previous evening. She let him sleep, leaving a note to tell him that she would be late coming home after mass.

Her Christmas gift to him was one she could not share until she was certain he would approve of it.

Enza tied the scarf around her neck and pulled her wool cloche over her ears. She set out on foot for Saint Joseph's Cemetery, about a mile outside Chisholm. She loved to walk, and whenever she went far, she remembered doing the same on the mountain trails above Schilpario. There were small reminders of the place she came from everywhere.

Her feet crunched the dusting of snow on the frozen ground as she walked. The clean air had the scent of pine and, occasionally, the smoke of a hearth fire from a farm off the main road. The winter in Chisholm had a palette of white and gray, like the feathers of a snowy owl, or the gray jays that would return once spring came. As Enza walked along the plowed road, she thought how much easier it was to walk in Chisholm. There were no steep trails to climb, just long black ribbons of road leading to new destinations.

The fir trees along the road were dense and tall, with trunks so thick, she wouldn't be able to put her arms around them. It was clear that this swath of forest had been untouched for a hundred years, just as they remained in the Italian Alps. She had seen the fields where the loggers had felled the forests along the road between Chisholm and Hibbing in the name of progress. It was only a matter of time before these old trees met the same fate. But this morning, they were all hers.

She pushed open the black wrought-iron gate to Saint Joseph's Cemetery. There were barren shade trees scattered about, a few statues of the Blessed Lady and kneeling angels, but mostly she saw tasteful polished marble markers embedded in the earth, with carved inscriptions. Unlike in Schilpario, there were no marble mausoleums with altars, colorful frescoes, or gilded gates to house the granite sepulchers. This cemetery was as plain in presentation as a farm field.

The priest had given her a map. In the center of the cemetery, under a grove of leafless trees, were the burial plots of men who had died in the mines. She began to dust the stones with her glove to reveal the names: Shubitz, Kalibabky, Paulucci, Perkovich. These men, she had been told, had worked in the Mahoning mine, the Stevenson mine at Stutz, Burt-Pool, Burt-Sellers, and the Hull mine. The Catholics among them had been transported from Hibbing on the Mesaba Railway, where they received a funeral mass and proper burial. Photographs had been taken and sent back to the families in Europe, although in some cases, nothing had been sent because the miner had not left any instructions or forwarding information.

They had not found the remains of Carlo Lazzari. He had burned in the fire.

Enza leaned down and cleared a headstone with her glove.

CARLO LAZZARI
1871–1904

She smiled. It was a smooth black granite stone with the engraving inset in gold. She made the sign of the cross.

"Enza!" Ciro said from the gate. He walked down the path to join her with a look of concern on his face. "You shouldn't be out in the cold. Monsignor Schiffer said I would find you here." He looked down at the gravestone and saw his father's name carved into the polished black granite. "What is this?" he asked, perplexed.

"I had it placed here. I bought it with a portion of the money from the stock. I felt it was the right thing to do, even though they never found him." Her voice broke, because she was afraid of his reaction. "I'm sorry. I didn't want to upset you any further, so I didn't tell you." Enza knelt next to the stone.

"Why would you place a gravestone when his body didn't survive the fire?"

"Because he lived. Because he was your father. I buried a box with a picture of you and Eduardo, a letter from me, and a lock of your hair. The priest blessed it, and they placed the stone here a couple days ago. It's the first time I've seen it."

Ciro's blue-green eyes stood out against the winter sky as Enza looked up at him. She realized she would never really know her husband; she was never sure what his reaction might be. He was a deeply emotional man, and his physical strength was in no way an indication of a strong resolve. He had lost so much in his life that he didn't know where to put the grief.

Ciro knelt next to her at his father's grave in the snow and began to cry like a boy of six. Enza leaned down and put her arms around her husband.

"All this time, I hoped it wasn't true."

"You had to hope," Enza said. "I would have."

"All my life I was told that I look like him and think like him—" Ciro's voice broke. "But I never knew him. I can remember small things about him, but I don't know if those are really my memories, or if Eduardo had told me the stories so often that I claimed them as my own. You would think a grown man wouldn't need his father or have to hold on to the idea of him. I know it was silly for me to pretend that my father might still be alive, but I wanted him to be. I needed him to be. To admit that he'll never see the man I've become or meet my wife or children . . . it's almost too much to bear."

Enza took a piece of pattern paper and a pencil out of her pocket. Asking Ciro to hold the paper against the stone, she rubbed the pencil against the engraving on the granite. Slowly, her father-in-law's name and years of birth and death appeared on the sheer white paper, a palimpsest, proof that he had received a proper burial. She folded the paper neatly in her pocket, then helped her husband stand. "Let's go home," she said.

They walked out of the cemetery and closed the gate. As they made their way back to West Lake Street, they clung together against the bitter winter wind. If a stranger had seen them walk past on that Christmas morning, he would find it hard to tell if the husband was holding up his wife, or if she was shoring him up.

Enza worried Pappina would go into labor and have the baby before Enza could arrive to help her. So Luigi paid a runner in advance to take the trolley from Hibbing to Chisholm at the first sign of labor, to let Enza know that it was time.

For the two weeks prior to Pappina's due date, not a flake of snow fell on the Iron Range. Though twenty-foot drifts remained from the January snows, the roads were icy, and the temperatures freezing, as long as the trolley tracks remained clear, Enza could be at Pappina's side in minutes.

Enza had helped her mother and the midwife in Schilpario when Stella was born. Enza hadn't been allowed to be with her mother for the birth of any of the other children, but by the time Stella came into their lives, Enza was like a second mother to her brothers and sisters.

She helped with the wash, the meals, and taught them how to read. Giacomina was so confident in Enza's abilities that she allowed her to watch the children when she left the house to run errands, or go up the mountain trails to gather herbs.

Giacomina had barely whimpered when Stella was born. In fact, Enza remembered that the room had been quiet and dark, and there was almost a sense of reverence to the way in which the baby slipped from her mother and into the arms of the midwife like a bouquet of flowers.

Enza held Pappina's hand as she hollered and struggled throughout her long labor, until the moment her son appeared, perfect, long, and squawking. The nurses in the Hibbing Hospital were accommodating, so Pappina was able to recover over the course of several days before going home to the apartment Enza had prepared for her.

Enza fell into the familiar routine of a new baby in the house. She set up the layette, made sure that Luigi had regular meals, kept up with the laundry, bathed and washed Pappina's hair, and made sure everything in the apartment was tidy. She made a large pot of soup, with tomatoes, root vegetables, orzo, and broth, that would help Pappina regain her strength. Enza felt a rush of giddiness, imagining that Pappina would do the same for her someday.

Enza took the trolley home to Chisholm after five days at Pappina's side. She smiled as she looked out the window, remembering that nothing made a woman more bone-tired than looking after a baby.

She pushed the shop door open and smiled. Ciro looked up and placed his lathe on the table. "How is young John Latini?"

"Almost ten pounds, and I have the sore neck to prove it." Enza laughed.

"A Valentine's Day baby." Ciro beamed.

"You should take the trolley over to see them." Enza turned to go upstairs, then remembered she had a message to deliver, "Luigi said to tell you that the baby had a small nose. He said you would understand."

"*Va bene*," Ciro said, bursting into laughter at the private joke.

"He's a healthy boy, small nose or not," Enza assured him.

"All that milk she drank was worth it."

"We'd better buy a cow," Enza said.

"Where would we put a cow? That patch of ground in the back will yield some tomatoes, and that's about it."

"It could be a small cow," Enza said softly, placing her hands on her hips and then the small of her back.

"Are you—" Ciro looked Enza up and down, in search of the lush fullness a woman carrying a baby would most certainly possess. She was as beautiful as ever; only her hand on her waist indicated a change.

Enza nodded that she was expecting a baby.

A honeymoon baby.

Their wedding-night baby.

Somewhere between Paoli, Pennsylvania, and Crestline, Ohio, on the path of the Broadway Limited to Chicago, Enza had conceived their child. Ciro went to her, lifted her up off the ground, and held her tight. "I thought I couldn't be any happier."

Ciro felt a joy within his heart that he could not describe, filling him up in a way he had never thought possible. It was instant, and would last for the rest of his life.

A baby of their own was his highest dream. Ciro remembered imagining his wife and children before he met them, and the house he would build in Vilminore for them. But all those dreams were beside the point, now that it was really happening. He had so much love for his wife and the baby within her that he felt a new fire within him, stoking a greater ambition to provide for them. All he hoped for in this moment was many children, and a long life to take care of them.

24

A TRAIN TICKET
Un Biglietto per il Treno

The Minnesota summer was as glorious as any Enza remembered as a girl in the Italian Alps. Longyear Lake dazzled like a sapphire, reflecting the cloudless sky that was saturated in deepest blue, like Marrakesh silk. The evergreen trees fringed the horizon, while low green thickets were speckled with the first buds of sweet blackberries. The loons wailed in the morning light, calling across the water.

Enza propped open every skylight in the house. In the final weeks of her pregnancy, she had nested with a vengeance; she had washed every window, scrubbed the floors, and perfected the details of the nursery. She had sewn a layette for the baby in snow white chamois and soft cotton. She trimmed the bunting in white grosgrain ribbon, and piped the hood in silk. Ciro had built a crib and painted it white. He stenciled the walls of the nursery in alternating stripes of cream and sandy beige, to give the effect of wallpaper—a trick Enza had learned watching Neil Mazzella as he directed the scenery load-ins at the Metropolitan Opera.

When the bells on the shop door jingled that morning, Ciro had looked up from his work. He was so surprised, he dropped his shears onto the table with a thud.

Laura Heery stood in the doorway, a suitcase in one hand and a hatbox in the other. She wore a navy crepe suit, a matching straw hat, and white gloves. "I couldn't very well let your girl have a baby without me." She grinned.

Ciro embraced her and called up the stairs to Enza. Laura removed her gloves and placed them in her purse. She walked the length of the main room, peering through the window to Enza's sewing room as Ciro ran up the stairs to bring Enza downstairs. Laura could hear them chatting in the stairwell, so she raced to the front of the shop. When Enza appeared in the doorway and saw Laura, she squealed with delight. Laura embraced her, and soon, both of them were weeping. Laura stood back and took in Enza's full and lush beauty.

A customer, a miner of around forty-five, pushed the door open, saw the women weeping, pivoted, and left.

"Girls, you're costing me business," Ciro joked. "How about we show Laura the apartment?" He picked up Laura's luggage.

"You must be exhausted," Enza said to Laura as they followed Ciro up the steps.

"No, I'm loaded with pep. I went stir-crazy on the train. I hope there's lots for me to do."

"You can put your feet up and rest, and maybe my wife will do the same," Ciro said.

"We have everything ready, and I'm glad. We can have a good visit before the baby comes," Enza said as she pushed the door to the guest room open. "Make yourself at home, I'll put on coffee."

"I'd like that," Laura said.

Enza closed the door behind her and stood in the hallway motionless, as if she was in a dream. Ciro put his arms around her.

"Did you know?" Enza asked him.

"I wouldn't have been able to keep it a secret." Ciro kissed her.

Enza took her handkerchief from her wrist, where she had tucked it in her sleeve, and dried her eyes. "As happy as I am about the baby, I was afraid of being alone. I am so happy Laura is here."

"Well, I may stay forever. I love my room!" Laura said as she joined them.

"I'm going to get back to work," Ciro said. "You girls let me know if you need anything."

"Let me show you the nursery," Enza said.

"The girls in the costume shop made some things for the baby. I'll get them." Laura went into her room and came out with a box. She followed Enza down to the nursery across from the master bedroom. Enza sat down in the rocking chair while Laura pulled up a stool, handing Enza the box.

Enza unfolded a satin baby blanket. There was a hand-knit cotton cap and baby mittens, and a black felt crib pillow shaped like a musical note. Laura had embroidered "From your friends at the Metropolitan Opera House" along the staff.

"How is Colin?" Enza asked.

"Who?" Laura pretended not to hear.

"What's wrong?"

"He hasn't asked me to marry him, and I don't think he will."

"Why?"

Laura shrugged. But then she tried not to cry. "I left without knowing why."

"You didn't talk to him about it?"

"It's very difficult to bring it up. Remember the girls who would issue ultimatums? They ended up with their ultimatums and not much else. Colin is wonderful to me at work. I thought I was good with his sons. I try to be. I take them to the park and the show. When they come to the Met, I clear a work space in the costume shop and help them do their homework while Colin is busy in the box office. I've really grown fond of them."

"So what's the matter?"

"It's his mother. She doesn't want her widowed son to marry a costume shop seamstress."

"That can't be," Enza said softly.

"Yes it can. I'm *shanty* Irish—and how do I know I am? I heard her say it to the help in the kitchen of her Long Island home. I was helping clear the dinner dishes, as a matter of fact, when I overheard it."

"Did you tell Colin?"

"I couldn't wait. I told him on the drive back into the city. And he made excuses for his mother. He said she was an Edith Wharton character. She had airs, and she always would. I shouldn't take it personally."

"You have to take it personally," Enza said.

"That's what I told him! There's no other way to take it. But I don't know what to do. I love him."

"And he loves you."

"But I'm without pedigree. I'm not a Vanderbilt or a Ford."

Enza couldn't help but think that Laura's work ethic had given her pedigree. After all, she had worked her way across the Hudson River to eventually gain a position at the Metropolitan Opera House. That had to account for something. So Enza said, "The Fords were Irish farmers, and the Vanderbilts were from Staten Island. They became wealthy because they worked hard in a country that let them. So you just tell Mrs. Chapin that the Heerys are on the way up, and you're taking them with you."

"His mother has another girl in mind for him," Laura said softly, "And Colin is taking her to a regatta in Newport this weekend."

"How do you know?"

"He told me. And that's when I decided to take my vacation days and come up and help you. There's nothing in New York for me. It's over."

That night, Enza made sure that Laura was comfortable in her room before she joined Ciro in their bedroom and climbed into bed. Ciro stacked the feather pillows around Enza like sandbags in a trench until she was comfortable. "Emilio and Ida offered to drive you and Laura to Lake Bemidji."

"I don't know if anything will lift Laura's spirits."

"I didn't know that Americans made matches like our people do back on the mountain."

"It's worse. You match up the ladder, never down. You not only have to be rich, you have to be educated. Laura is so smart, but she didn't go to finishing school. I guess that's a requirement, to marry a Chapin."

"I don't want you to have any anxiety."

"I can't help it. She's my best friend. And she's unhappy."

"So try and have some fun. You have time before the baby comes. There's Serbian Days, you can show her Canada, the lakes—there's lots to do." Ciro kissed Enza good night.

Enza leaned back on the pillows and stared at the ceiling. Laura was a few years older than she, and knew that her friend felt pressure to marry. Laura was not meant to be an old maid, but she already felt like one. The new baby would go a long way in helping Laura feel useful, but Enza wondered if it might also make her sad, knowing that her future with Colin was no longer a possibility.

. . .

Serbian Days was a celebration that filled the Mesabi Range with visitors from northern Minnesota, Wisconsin, and as far south as Chicago. Most families held their reunions and took their summer vacations during the festival week, and as a result, the range doubled its population. The stores on West Lake Street had sidewalk sales; eager to be a part of the action, Enza put out baby bibs, crib blankets, and flannel buntings she had made to sell. Laura marveled at the foot traffic, and promised Enza she would have the costume shop girls make all kinds of items to sell the following year.

Longyear Lake had a bandstand on the green, featuring a different group every night. There were fireworks over the lake, and shows that would highlight numbers from the dance contest that was held on the final night of the festival. Pappina and Luigi brought their son, John, who at five months old was already an active baby, a first class squirmer. Laura and Enza spread a blanket on the ground, while Ciro went for pierogies and soda.

"I could get used to this." Laura smiled. "The fresh air, the lake, good friends."

"Stay, then!" Pappina said.

"Do you know how hard it is to keep a room once you get it at the Milbank House?"

"It's like gold," Enza said.

"I was never a working girl, and I wish I could've been. But I went straight from my mother's house to an apartment with Luigi. What did I miss?"

"If you like not knowing where your next paycheck will come from, if you're able to make your own clothes from the ends in the factory, and if you like warm champagne in a paper cup on opening night at the opera, then the working-girl life is for you."

"I'll never know what it's like, but I sure love hearing all about it," Pappina said.

"It seems that girls always want what they don't have." Laura stretched her long legs out in front of her on the blanket, smoothing her skirt over them. "I wanted to be a petite brunette, and I'm built like a string of red licorice. I wouldn't mind having my own baby on my lap, but I'm unmarried, not by choice but circumstance. So you see, we don't necessarily get what we want, but we get *something*."

Enza laughed, as she always did when Laura was philosophical. She tried not to think about what it would be like when Laura went back to New York. It had been a wonderful two weeks, more of a vacation for Enza than for Laura, who had waited on her, anticipating her needs and encouraging her to rest.

Ciro placed a sack of pierogies and a box of cold sodas on the blankets. Enza, sitting on the blanket, felt a low, deep pain across her belly. She shifted on the blanket, thinking it was how she was sitting, until a few minutes later, the pain came again.

"Are you all right?" Laura asked Enza.

The band began to play, its brass section braying a patriotic march. Laura reached across the blanket to Ciro, nudging him. He turned and looked at Enza, his face turned ashen. "Is it time?" he said, though he didn't have to ask.

She nodded that it was. Laura handed baby John back to Pappina. Ciro helped Enza stand, and as the band played, he and Laura slowly walked Enza to the edge of the park, where he asked the policeman for a ride to the hospital. Luckily Officer Grosso played poker at the shoe shop when he was off duty, and was happy to give the anxious trio a lift up the hill to Chisholm Hospital.

. . .

Ciro pushed through the door of Enza's room at Chisholm Hospital. He stopped when he saw her, in a white chenille robe, holding a small blue bundle. Her beauty had taken on a new dimension now that she was the mother of his firstborn son. July 28, 1919, would be a date he would remember all his life, no matter what other details had slipped his mind. This was the day he and Enza became *una famiglia*.

Laura smiled and patted Ciro on the back as she left the room. Alone with their baby, Ciro went to Enza, slid his hand under the small of her back, wrapped the other around her and the baby, and pulled his small family together in a single embrace. His son had the scent of new skin and clean talc. He was long and pink, and his fingers poked the air as if he was trying to grab it.

When it came to naming their son, Enza had wanted to call him Ciro. Her husband had other ideas. He had thought to name the boy Carlo, after his father, or Marco after Enza's, or Ignazio, who had been good to him, or Giovanni, after Juan Torres, who had died in the trenches. But while all these men had shaped him, he decided to name his first son Antonio, after the patron saint of lost things.

He remembered the night he first met Enza, and as an orphan, he had always felt the vague rootlessness of abandonment, a quiet displacement that echoed loudly in the chambers of his growing heart. It was a hollow feeling of regret that he'd thought might never leave him. But after Enza's short labor, he had been found again. He was a father now.

Enza handed the baby to Ciro as if she were passing him a fine china teacup, fearful she might drop it.

"I am your father, Antonio. I will never leave you," he promised as he held his son. And as the words left his lips, which found themselves gently placed on the sweet, smooth cheek of his newborn son, he believed them and would do everything in his power to make certain they would always be true.

"He looks just like you," Enza said. "Imagine, two of you in the world."

Laura made a pot of vegetable soup with lots of diced potato, knowing it would give Enza strength. She had everything in the apartment ready, so when Ciro brought her home, all Enza had to do was nurse the baby and rest.

Laura sat with Enza as she nursed the first night, then took the baby and changed him, placing him in the bassinette, before she helped Enza across the hall to her bed. It was such an exciting time—Laura was such a good friend that any happiness Enza had, she felt doubly.

When the morning came for Laura to begin her journey back to New York, she packed slowly as Enza sat with the baby.

"Are you sure you don't want my sweater?" Laura offered her classic navy cardigan.

"Stop trying to give me things." Enza smiled.

"I don't know when I'll see you again." Laura sat on the edge of the bed.

"You can come back anytime."

"Maybe you can come to New York," Laura offered.

"Someday." Enza smiled. "What are you going to do when you get there?" she asked.

"Start over." Laura's eyes filled with tears. She wiped them away with her handkerchief. "I plan to leave my tears between here and Penn Station. Once I get off the train, I'll be fine."

Ciro appeared in the doorway.

"I know, I know, Ciro, I have to leave now or I'll miss my train." Laura stood and snapped the clasps on her suitcase. She lifted it off the bed.

"I think you may miss your train after all."

"Why? Has there been an accident?"

"No. There's a delay." Ciro leaned against the door frame.

"What do you mean?" Laura looked at her itinerary, as if it would hold a clue.

"There's someone here to see you," he said. "Will you girls come down to the shop, please?" He reached over and took the baby from Enza. "Follow me."

Laura was confused, and Enza didn't know what to say, so they followed Ciro down the stairs. Ciro went through the door first with the baby, followed by Enza. Laura came through the door last. Standing by the worktable was Colin Chapin, looking handsome but rumpled in a seersucker suit after the long journey. Seeing him, Laura was so stunned, it was as if she'd seen a ghost. She began to back out of the room toward the door.

"Where are you going?" Colin asked. "I came all this way for you."

Laura stopped. "Why?"

"Because I love you, and we're going to get married."

"We are?"

"If you'll have me." Colin smiled. "And my boys. They're part of the deal."

"What about your mother?"

"I reminded her that her own mother was a Fitzsimmons who worked in a glass factory."

"Your mother is lace curtain Irish?"

"The *laciest*." Colin laughed. "Don't make me beg. Will you marry me? The deal is on the table."

Ciro and Enza looked at one another, and then at Laura. Laura took a deep breath and said, "I'll take the deal."

Colin laughed, and soon Enza and Ciro joined in. But Laura began to cry. "You're all I ever wanted."

"Then why are you crying?" Colin went to her, pulled her close, and kissed her.

"Because I never get what I want."

"You can't say that anymore, Laura," Ciro said gently.

"Never again," Enza agreed.

Laura Maria Heery and Colin Cooper Chapin were married December 26, 1919, at the Chapel of the Blessed Lady at Saint Patrick's Cathedral on Fifth Avenue in New York City. Colin noted that it was Boxing Day, which meant they would either have lots of fights or none. They chose the day because the Met was dark through New Year's, and the boys were on school break; William was eleven, and Charles was twelve. The four of them went on a vacation to Miami Beach, which doubled as a honeymoon. Laura sent a postcard to Minnesota with three words written in her perfect Palmer penmanship: "Never been happier."

*   *   *

Enza kept a playpen next to her sewing machine in the workroom. There was no separation between work and home life; Enza and Ciro happily blurred the lines. The baby liked to take his bottle and watch the light dance through the shade tree and into the window, throwing petals of shadow on the old tin ceiling. While Antonio napped, Enza was able to help Ciro as he finished the work boots. Enza would buff the leather, and place a wooden rod inside the shoe to stretch the leather under the metal toecap.

Ciro often came from the front of the shop to play with Antonio, throw him in the air, or take him to the yard out back and let him crawl on the grass. They found their son endlessly fascinating. Now that Antonio was almost two years old, he had playmates who came by with their mothers. Enza's experience taking care of her brothers and sisters held her in good stead as a mother. There were many experienced parents around them. Ida Uncini, whose children were grown, made it a point to stop in and help out. Friends like Linda Nykaza Albanase would drop off a coffee cake and take Antonio for a ride in his pram.

Ciro's shop on West Lake Street continued to be a magnet for the miners who were looking for a card game after a long shift. Ciro would make sandwiches of mozzarella and tomato; he made the cheese himself, as he had back in his convent days. Enza made fresh bread twice a week, and made sure that Ciro had his friends over on baking day to take advantage of the fresh rolls.

Ciro and Enza took turns making lunch for one another. Ciro would flip the sign in the window, and for a half hour, they'd sit in the back under the shade tree, as their son played on a blanket close by. One warm August day, Enza joined her husband and son in the backyard with Ciro's favorite meal, eggs poached in fresh tomato sauce over dandelion salad. The mail was tucked under her arm, tied with a string.

"Here, Antonio. Catch." Ciro threw a ball to his son, who waited for it. Antonio reached up and grabbed the ball from the sky. "Big hands," Ciro said.

"Like his father."

"He is very quick."

"Every father thinks his son is a great athlete."

"Every father doesn't have a son like Antonio."

Enza handed the tray to her husband, who called Antonio to lunch. She gave her son a buttered roll, sat down on the bench, and sorted through the mail. "Bills," she said.

"Have your lunch, Enza."

She shuffled through the envelopes. "I will. After I read the letter from Laura." Enza took the barrette from her hair and opened the letter carefully with it.

August 2, 1921
Dear Enza,

It is with a heavy heart that I write to you on the death of Signor Enrico Caruso. I can hardly think of him without thinking of you. Remember how we made him macaroni? How about the

*time you pinned his hem and he jumped off the fitting stool and
the pins went into his calves and he jumped around like a kid?
You used to leave bowls of orange and lemon peels in his dressing
room to soak up the fumes from his cigars. Remember when he
called you Uno and me Due? "Always together, you two, like one
and two," he said.*

*What a gift he was to all of us. I will miss him terribly, but
will remember him the night of the bond benefit for the Great
War, when he stood on the opera stage, his arms outstretched,
and took in the love of five thousand fans on their feet, as if he
were gathering roses.*

*My heart breaks for you, as he was one of your own . . . a good
man, a great singer, and the ultimate pride of the Italian people.*

Sending you, Ciro, and Antonio my love,

Laura

P.S. Signore died in Italy, as was his wish.

Enza held Laura's letter as she sat on the bench and cried. Ciro took
the letter from Enza, read it quickly, and pulled Enza close. "I'm so
sorry," he said.

Enrico Caruso's death was the end of an era that had changed the
course of Enza's life. Her experience at the opera had brought rich
friendships into her life and transformed her from a poor immigrant
seamstress to a fine American artisan.

As Antonio played on the blanket at her feet, Enza took time to
remember the small details of the great singer. She recalled the way
he smoked a cigar, blowing the smoke in orderly puffs, like musical
notes. She remembered his strong calves and delicate feet, and how
she'd tried to lengthen his torso to slim him. She remembered the
night he'd put the gold coin into her silver glove, the last night she
would ever see him.

For the first time since they moved to Minnesota, Enza longed for
New York. Somehow, to be with Laura at the opera house, with the
machine operators in the costume shop, the footmen at the entrance,
the painters and scenic artists, the musicians and the actors, would be a

great comfort. Instead, she was here, with a family that barely knew the details of the life she'd had before she married.

Enza wept, too, for Caruso's Italy. They'd had long conversations in their native Italian about food—how to grow blood oranges; how to tear fresh basil, never cut it with a knife, to release the most fragrance; and how his mother sang all the verses of "Panis Angelicus" when she boiled pasta, and by the time she got to the last verse, she would lift it from the heat and it would be al dente, *perfetta*.

The world would miss Caruso's voice, and of course, Enza would too, but she would not think of his great artistry first and foremost; she would think of *him*. Caruso had known how to *live*; he extracted every drop of joy he could render from every hour of his life. He'd studied people, not to judge them, but to revel in their inimitable traits, and in so doing took in the best of them, only to give it right back when he performed.

Enza couldn't believe that Caruso was dead, because in so many ways he was life itself. He was breath and power, emotion and sound, with a laugh that was so loud, God Himself could hear it in heaven.

.   .   .

Pappina held her new baby in her arms. It was her fourth child, but for the first time, the bonnet was pink. Angela Latini was just two weeks old when Pappina brought her to the shop to introduce her to the Lazzaris.

Ciro and Enza were fussing over the baby when Antonio bounded into the shop.

"Look, you have a new honorary cousin," Enza said. "This is baby Angela."

"A girl?" Antonio sniffed. "What are we going to do with a girl?" Antonio was a lanky seven-year-old with long legs and jet black hair. Ciro thought he looked a great deal like his brother Eduardo. No one on Enza's side of the family was tall, but from the looks of her boy, he was going to be.

"Someday you'll find out, son," Ciro said.

Jenny Madich entered the shop with her young daughter Betsy in tow. Betsy went to school with Antonio, and from the first day, they had been sweethearts. Betsy was also tall for her age. Her white leather roller skates were knotted together and thrown over her shoulder. Her black hair, blue eyes, and small upturned nose gave way to a big smile that enchanted everyone she met.

"Wanna skate, Antonio?" Betsy asked.

"Can I, Mama?" Antonio looked up at Enza.

"Yes, but stay on the sidewalk, not in the street."

Betsy followed Antonio up the stairs.

Jenny Madich was around forty, a tall, slim, blue-eyed, raven-haired Serbian beauty with three daughters, one more beautiful than the next. She was known as the *povitica* queen on the Mesabi Range. Whenever she made a batch, she dropped one of the pastries off at the shop. Today, she'd brought two. "Did the shoes arrive?" she asked.

"I have them," Enza said. "They're beauties." She went behind the counter and gave the boxes to Jenny, who opened up the patent leather Mary Janes. The pair for her eldest daughter, who was sixteen, had a sleek, small heel. The others were classic with a stack heel. "Just like you ordered. They look like the ad in *Everybody's Magazine*. They were right next to the Edna Ferber short story."

"Are you selling shoes now, Enza?" Pappina asked.

"Special orders only."

"Enza saved my life with these shoes," Jenny admitted. "We take the train down to the cities before Easter and get our shoes there. I can never find black patent leather shoes for the girls. And they need them for the competition during Serbian Days."

"You go all the way to Minneapolis for shoes?" Pappina asked.

"What else can we do? It takes us months to make their costumes, and you don't want to finish off the look with a cheap shoe."

"See all you have to look forward to with a little girl?" Enza smiled at Pappina. Enza had been trying for a second child since Antonio turned two, but she hadn't had any luck. It seemed Pappina had babies one after the other with no problem. And now Enza's highest dream, a baby girl, had gone on to be realized by her dear friend. Enza reached out, and Pappina handed her the baby. Enza looked down at her and thought she had been given the perfect name; she was truly an angel.

Antonio and Betsy clomped down the stairs, ran through the shop, and went out the door. The bells clanged behind them. "Be careful!"

Jenny shouted after them. Then she looked back at Enza. "You know, I've been thinking. You could do pretty well selling the dance shoes. If I put an announcement in the Eastern Orthodox newsletter at our church, you'd have Yugos and Romanians and Serbs lined up out the door."

Enza looked at Ciro. "Honey, what do you think?"

"Whatever you want to do."

"Jenny, go ahead and put the ad in the bulletin. I can do special orders. And how about this: if I sell twenty-five pairs of shoes, your girls get theirs for free."

"You have a deal," Jenny said as she picked up her delivery box and headed out the door. "I'll grab Betsy on my way home."

Ciro carried a box from the back of the shop and placed it on the table.

"How's your back?"

"Soaking in the Epsom gave me some relief," Ciro said.

"You work too hard." Enza put her arms around Ciro.

"Do the camphor pack too, Ciro. I put one on Luigi, and it helps," Pappina offered.

"Let's face it. There are too many miners, and every single one of them has two feet. No wonder Luigi and I have sore backs."

*   *   *

Ciro propped open the front door of the shop to let the summer breeze through. Every window was open, and the pattern table had been cleared for a poker game. Ciro's friends, the two miners Orlich and Kostich, studied their cards. Emilio Uncini folded his hand into the pot on the table, reached for the grappa, and poured himself a slug. "I'm out," he said.

"Go help your wife with the purse," Orlich said, studying his cards. His fingernails were rimmed in black from the last shift at Burt-Sellers. Coal dust had settled in the fine lines of his face. With his sharp features and small mouth, he looked like a pen-and-ink drawing.

"I am not going near her," Emilio said.

Ciro had closed the door to the hallway, but through the transom, the men could hear the laughter and chatter of mothers and daughters, at least fifty of them, lined up on the stairs to go up to the apartment to pick up their patent leather dance shoes. Ida worked as Enza's secretary, while Enza took the measurements.

Enza had far exceeded her goal of selling twenty-five pairs of shoes; she had sold 76 pairs since the announcement was placed in the Eastern Orthodox church bulletin.

A stout woman in a straw hat entered the shop with her daughter. Ciro looked up from his cards.

"I'm looking for the shoemaker's wife," the lady said. "You don't look like Mrs. Lazzari."

Ciro pointed through the door and up the stairs in the direction of the noise. The lady left with her daughter, and when she was out of ear-shot, Ciro said, "And you, ma'am, do not look like a dancer."

25

A LUCKY CHARM

Un Ciondolo Portofortuna

Ciro followed his son up the hill on their way to see Doc Graham. Antonio skipped up the steep incline like a gazelle.

The sight of his son reminded Ciro of the days when he and Eduardo were boys, and Ciro had to run to keep up with his older brother. There were other reminders of the past in the present moment. Antonio had his uncle's dark good looks, his height, and dexterity.

At eleven years old, Antonio had grown to five foot nine, and showed no signs of stopping. Ciro shook his head and smiled as he watched Antonio, who had proven to be a prodigy in every sport he attempted, whether it was basketball, baseball, speed skating, or alpine skiing. Ciro remembered his strength as a young man, but it paled in comparison to his son's natural athletic ability.

"Come on, Papa, we'll be late," Antonio chided him from the top of the hill.

Ciro wondered why he was winded as he took the hill. He smoked infrequently now, only one cigarette when he played poker, but suddenly he felt the full brunt of his years. He was shocked that the physical changes he had always noticed in men twenty years his senior had come on so fast.

"Go ahead, son, I'll be right there," Ciro said.

Antonio pushed the door open to Doc Graham's office and took a seat in the waiting area. The nurse called for him. "Can you tell my father—," Antonio began.

"Of course, I'll let him know you're already in with Dr. Graham."

Antonio followed the nurse into the examination room. Antonio jumped on the scale, the needle of which finally came to rest at 152 pounds. When the nurse told him how tall he was, Antonio clapped his hands together triumphantly. Ciro joined them in the examination room, removing his hat.

"The doctor will be with you in a moment," the nurse said, taking Antonio's file.

"Papa, I'm almost five foot ten!"

"You're going to hit six feet soon," Ciro told him. "You'll be as tall as your Zio Eduardo. He's six foot three. I'm the short one at six foot two."

"I want to be taller than both of you." Antonio smiled. His resemblance to Eduardo was striking. The thick black hair, wide brown eyes, and straight nose were just the window dressing in their similarities. There was also the serene countenance, the sense of fair play, and the good heart. Ciro recognized that Antonio might have the name Lazzari on his file, but he was all Montini.

Doc Graham pushed the door open. At middle age, Doc had white hair and jet black eyebrows, and thin lips that parted to reveal a warm smile.

"So you want to play junior varsity basketball, Antonio?" Doc wanted to know.

"They say I'm good enough, even though I'm young."

"Coach Rukavina knows talent when he sees it," Doc Graham said as he took Antonio's blood pressure.

"*Dottore*, I worry he's growing too fast."

"No such thing if he wants to keep up with the Finns," Doc said.

The Scandinavian boys were known as power towers. Tall, strong, quick, and bright, they were stunning athletes. The sons of the local Italian immigrants had to work hard to compete with them.

Doc Graham checked Antonio's lymph glands in his neck, then peered down his throat, into his ears and eyes, and took his pulse. "I pronounce you perfectly healthy."

"I can play?"

"You can play."

Antonio thanked the doctor and pulled on his shirt. "I'll see you at home, Papa. I have practice." Antonio bounded out the door quickly. Ciro stood, placing his hands on his lower back.

"How's your back?" Doc Graham asked.

"Not any better than the last time," Ciro said. "I've done everything you've asked me to do. I take the aspirin, I lie on the floor with my legs in the air, and I soak in Epsom. I just don't get any better, and sometimes it's manageable, but the pain is always there."

"Let me take a look."

"*Grazie, Dottore.*" Ciro slipped back to his Italian, as he often did when a kindness was extended to him.

Doc Graham had Ciro remove his shirt. He pushed pressure points on Ciro's back. One, right above the kidneys, caused Ciro to cry out.

"How old are you, Ciro?"

"Thirty-five."

"Were you in the war?"

"Yes."

"Where?"

"Mostly in Cambrai."

"Were you hit with mustard gas?"

"It was not significant." Ciro straightened his back as best he could and pushed his shoulders back. He had long avoided discussing the war, and the last place he wanted to do it was in a doctor's office. "I saw the men badly burned from it. My platoon was not. We died in more traditional ways. Stray bullets and barbed wire."

Dr. Graham studied the skin on Ciro's back, and followed it with a small blue light. He stopped and asked Ciro to breathe. "Ciro, I want to send you down to Saint Mary's Hospital in Rochester. It's part of the Mayo Clinic. They're experts when it comes to health problems with veterans. I'll call them, and call my friend in the clinic. He'll see you right away."

Doc Graham ripped the sheet from his pad and handed it to Ciro:

Dr. Renfro, oncologist
Saint Mary's Hospital, the Mayo Clinic

*   *   *

Enza couldn't sleep the night before Ciro went for his tests in Rochester. She was nervous for so many reasons. Ciro had never complained of pain in his body, just the occasional ache that comes with hard, repetitive work. But lately he had been hurting. There was a night a month ago when she had to help him out of the bathtub. There was another time when he woke up in the middle of the night with shooting pains radiating down his leg. She didn't know if this was typical of growing older, though he was not yet forty, but all of it was of deep concern to her. She didn't know where to put her feelings and she didn't want to alarm her husband, so she wrote a letter to the doctor at the Mayo Clinic.

> *September 6, 1930*
> *Dear Dr. Renfro,*
>
> *Thank you for seeing my husband Ciro Lazzari. He will not give you much information, so my hope is that my letter might answer any questions you have. We have a young son and a shop to keep open, or I would have made the trip with my husband.*
>
> *He has been suffering from back pain since we were married in 1918. Over the past year or so, the pain has escalated. The old remedies of camphor packs and Epsom salt soaks no longer bring him much relief. He is a shoemaker, so he often works on his feet ten hours a day, and that may contribute to the problem.*
>
> *My husband is very intelligent. He will not, however, ask you important questions, nor will he inquire in any detail about how to follow whatever treatment you might prescribe. So please, if you don't mind, send him home with an explicit list of things, and I will make sure they are done properly.*
>
> *Sincerely yours,*
> *Mrs. Lazzari*

*   *   *

Rochester, Minnesota, was built on a raging river whose behavior was so precarious it took Franciscan nuns to defy the natural habitat and have the guts to build a hospital.

Saint Mary's Hospital, operated by the Mayo Clinic, had grown from a small operation into the best medical center in the Midwest by the time Ciro Lazzari entered its pristine lobby. The stately red-brick campus, with new additions hiding beneath wings of scaffolding, was filled with state-of-the-art labs and examination rooms and the most sought-after doctors in the country. It resembled a bustling honeycomb.

The nuns, their black-and-white habits so similar to those of the sisters of San Nicola, gave Ciro a feeling of familiarity that completely relaxed him and gave him confidence. He joked with the sisters as they put him through the arduous tests.

Ciro was handed a file, and throughout the day he was moved from one small examination room to another. X-rays were taken, dye was drunk, he was poked and prodded and placed on a gurney, blood was drawn, bones were scanned; there was not a cell in his body that the doctors did not examine or discuss, or at least it seemed that way to Ciro.

At the end of the day, he was brought into an office to meet with Dr. Renfro. When a young man of thirty came into the room, Ciro was surprised. He had been expecting an older man, like Doc Graham.

"You're a young man," Ciro said.

"Not in this job. You feel every day of your age."

"Why did Doc Graham send me here?"

"He saw a place on your back that concerned him. You'd never notice it yourself, but under your shoulder blades the texture of the skin is different from that of the surrounding area. Only a doctor who was looking for it would have seen it."

"See what exactly, *Dottore*?"

The doctor laid out the reports on the desk, flicked a light board, and put up X-rays of Ciro's spine. Ciro looked with wonder at the shadowy gray picture of the inside of his body, without any inkling of what the doctor was seeing.

"That is me?" Ciro asked.

"It's your spinal column." The gray shadows of Ciro's spine looked like a string of black pearls on the X-ray. The doctor pointed to the darker areas. "Here's your trouble." He circled a black area with the eraser of a pencil. "This black pool is a tumor. It's small, but it's cancerous."

Dr. Renfro pulled the shadowy images from the board and put up more. Ciro's lungs resembled the black leather bellows he used to use to make fire in the convent kitchen.

"Mr. Lazzari, as a veteran of the Great War, you were exposed to mustard gas."

"But I didn't burn like the other soldiers." Ciro's voice caught.

"No, but this particular kind of cancer is insidious. The mustard gas you inhaled has a long incubation period, usually ten to twelve years. The poison causes a slow cellular burn that alters the very nature of how the human body fends off disease. I can show you . . ."

"No—no, thank you, *Dottore*. I have seen enough." Ciro stood.

"We do have a few promising treatments," the young doctor said eagerly.

"How much time will your treatments give me?"

"It would be hard to say," Dr. Renfro said.

"Ten years?"

"No, no, not ten years."

"Ah, so I have very little time."

"I didn't say that. But the prognosis isn't good, Mr. Lazzari. I think you should try our course of treatment."

"Given all you know, from everything you took from my body today, do I have months?"

"A year," Dr. Renfro said quietly.

Ciro stood, pulled on his coat and then his hat. He extended his hand to Dr. Renfro, who took it. "Thank you, *Dottore*."

"I'll send your reports to Dr. Graham."

On the train north to Duluth, Ciro settled back in his seat. He watched the flats of southern Minnesota turn inky blue in the twilight. Somehow—Ciro thought this silly—as long as it was daylight, he could handle the bad news; somehow, the idea of knowing the truth in the dark made him panic. The train could not go fast enough. He wanted to get home, where life had order and made sense. He didn't know how to tell Enza, and certainly had no idea what to say to Antonio. It was as if an old enemy had shown up to ambush him. He thought he had buried all traces of the Great War and the horrors he had witnessed. He sensed that Dr. Renfro could have talked for hours on the subject, but

Ciro wasn't interested in the countless variations of being poisoned by mustard gas that the good doctor wanted to share. As in war itself, the outcome was the only thing that counted. It turned out Ciro had not survived the war, he had just been given a brief reprieve.

His soul had fended off the spiritual damage of war; the beauty of his life with Enza had erased the terrible images of loss. But his body had sustained the harm that Ciro believed he had spared his psyche. Ciro sighed. There was no winning. The pain of losing Enza and Antonio overwhelmed him.

As he took the stairs up to his home at 5 West Lake Street, Ciro loosened his tie and inhaled the scent of sage and butter. He saw a pool of light pouring from the kitchen, and heard his wife humming inside. He stopped on the landing and leaned against the wall, knowing that he was about to bring incalculable sadness to his wife and son. *Let them be happy a few moments longer,* he thought. He leaned against the wall, summoning his strength, before he went in to face them.

Ciro dropped his duffel at the top of the stairs.

"Ciro!" Enza called out. She came out of the kitchen, wiping her hands on a moppeen. She was wearing a new dress she had made, a simple navy-and-white polka-dot shirtwaist. She had done her hair, and her cheeks were pink with a sheen of rouge. She was more beautiful in this moment than she had been the moment that Ciro married her.

"What did the doctor say?" She smiled hopefully.

"I have cancer. They tell me I got it from the mustard gas in the Great War." As Ciro made the announcement, it was as if his very breath had been taken from him. He crumpled, gripping the back of the chair in the hallway.

Enza was stunned. The drastic news took her totally by surprise, as she had said her rosary throughout the day with a feeling of complete vindication that Dr. Graham's concerns were nothing to worry about. She put her arms around Ciro. He was sweating, and his skin was cold and clammy, as though he were facing the worst and there was no help on the way. "No," was all she could say, and then she cried. He held her a long time. He inhaled the scent of her hair, fresh and clean like hay, while she buried her face in his neck.

"Where's Antonio?" Ciro asked.

"He's at basketball practice."

"Should we tell him?"

Enza led Ciro into the kitchen. She poured him a glass of wine, and then one for herself. As in every crisis she had ever faced, Enza, practical and centered, dried her tears, owned the truth, and made a decision to be strong in the face of the challenge. Inside, her feelings tumbled over one another. She was at once desperate, fearful, and angry. She sat forward in the chair and gripped her knees.

"I thought we were the lucky ones, Ciro."

"We were. For a while."

"There has to be a doctor somewhere who can help you. I'll call Laura."

"No, honey, the doctors at the Mayo Clinic are the best in the world. People come from New York to see doctors there. And I know that for sure, because I spoke with some of them as I was waiting for my tests."

"You can't just give up," Enza cried as her mind reeled. All those backaches, for all these years—she should have known. She thought he was working too hard, and all he needed was rest. But she and Ciro never took the time to go on vacation; they were always worried about the mortgage, and then Antonio's schooling, and sports. They were running so fast they hadn't seen the signs. Or maybe they didn't want to see them. Maybe Ciro had suspected he was doomed all along and just wanted the peace of being left alone until he absolutely could not be. The time had come to be X-rayed, poked, prodded, blood drawn, veins in collapse at the prick of a needle—all of it was coming at them in a dizzy tornado of concerns, options, and treatments. She could not help but punish herself, admonish herself for not moving more swiftly. Why hadn't she sent him to Doc Graham sooner? Maybe he could have helped. She put her face in her hands.

"There's nothing you could have done," Ciro said, reading her. "Nothing."

"What do we tell Antonio?" Enza asked. "I will do whatever you want."

"We tell him everything. I have answered every question he has ever asked me honestly. He knows about my father and my mother, his uncle and the convent. He knows what I saw when I was banished from

Vilminore, and he knows why. I am not about to start to spin fables to my boy now. If I am going to die, I want him to know that I thought enough of him to share everything."

Enza wept. "Everything?"

"*Everything*," Ciro reiterated.

They heard the snap of the key in the lock of the front door opening downstairs. Enza looked at Ciro with desperation.

"Are you sure?"

Ciro didn't answer.

Antonio bounded into the living room, recounting the day's events as he dropped his gear. "Ma, I scored twelve points, and had four assists in practice. Coach says I'm first team JV. Isn't that great?" Antonio entered the kitchen. "Papa, you're home!" he said when he saw his parents sitting side by side at the small table.

Ciro extended his arms out to his son. They embraced.

"How did it go in Rochester?" Antonio went to the counter, took a heel of bread, slathered it with butter, and bit into it. Ciro smiled, remembering doing the same in the convent kitchen of San Nicola. It occurred to him that *this* is what he would miss when he died. His son as he ate bread.

"Want some?" He extended the bread to his father.

"No, Tony, I don't."

"So, what's the skinny?" Antonio looked at his mother, whose eyes filled with tears. The news had just taken root in her heart, and the pain overwhelmed her, more for her son than for her own broken heart.

"Mama. Papa. What is it?"

"Remember when I told you about the Great War?"

"You were in France, and you said the girls were pretty, but not as pretty as Mama." Antonio poured himself a tall glass of cold milk from the icebox.

"Yes, but I also told you about the weapons."

Enza took the glass of milk from Antonio and pulled out a chair. She indicated that he should sit.

"Listen to your father."

"I am. He just asked me about the weapons in the Great War. There were tanks, machine guns, barbed wire, and mustard gas."

"Well, I got hit with the mustard gas. So I have a little backache that comes and goes," Ciro explained.

"You look fine, Papa. Doc Graham can help you. He helps everybody. And when he can't, he sends you to Dr. McFarland."

"It's worse than that, son. I'm very sick. I know I look fine today, but as the days go by, I'm going to get worse. The mustard gas went through to my bones, and now I have the kind of cancer that it gives you. In a matter of time, I will die from it."

Antonio took in the words, but shook his head as though what he was hearing could not possibly be true. It was when he looked at his mother that he knew. Slowly, Antonio stood up and put his arms around his father. Ciro was shaking, but so was Antonio, who couldn't believe the terrible news. Enza got up from the table and put her arms around both of them. She wanted to say something to comfort Ciro, and something more to galvanize Antonio, but there were no words. They held one another and wept, and that night, there was no further conversation, or music on the phonograph, or even supper. The house was as quiet as it could be with a family living in it.

* * *

Later that night, Antonio buried his face in his pillow and wept. He had looked at a stack of his father's papers in the living room and seen the diagnosis. He had seen a sketch of his father's spine, and the strange circles with the words *tumor* and *metastasize* written next to them in ink.

Antonio had studied the Great War in school. He remembered a question on the quiz about mustard gas, and when he asked Ciro about it, he said it had the scent of ammonia and garlic. At the time, it hadn't registered with Antonio that if his father could identify the scent, he too had been hit with it. But now he knew it was true.

He rolled over and dried his eyes on his pajama sleeve and stared at the ceiling. His greatest fear had come true. He and his mother would be alone; how would they go on without his father?

Antonio had never argued with Ciro. Some said it was because Antonio was an only child, with little cause for conflict. Others said it was because Antonio was unusually serene, with no need to defy authority. But it was deeper than that. Antonio had visited the cemetery on every feast day and prayed near his grandfather's gravestone. He had stood beside his father as Ciro wept. Antonio had promised himself that he would never add to his father's sadness.

Antonio had heard the stories. He knew about his father's life in the convent without any parents. He knew that Zio Eduardo had been placed in the seminary, and Ciro had been forced to come to America when he was scarcely older than Antonio himself. The stories broke Antonio's heart, and they also made him realize that the last thing his father needed was a rebellious son. Enza was the disciplinarian, leaving Ciro free to love his son and coddle him in a way Ciro himself had never known. Antonio had always known he had a happy home. What would become of them now?

* * *

Silver moonlight poured through the skylight of Ciro and Enza's bedroom. The clean Minnesota breeze carried the pungent scent of spring. The wind off Longyear Lake was cool. It relieved them.

Ciro and Enza were entwined in one another, having made love. Their bodies were like two skeins of silk, woven together, inseparable. Ciro kissed his wife's neck, and closed his eyes to remember every detail of it.

"Should I draw the shade?" Ciro asked, and Enza knew he was thinking of the old wives' tale from the mountain.

"The bad luck is already here. The moon won't change it," Enza said.

"How do you think Antonio is doing?"

"He would never let you see how scared he is," Enza said. "It's good to keep his routine. We'll go to the games, and we'll be here when he comes home from practice. All we can do is be here for him."

"I wish he had a brother. Eduardo was always able to help me through things. I wish he had that."

"He is close to the Latini boys."

"Luigi and Pappina are going to tell the older boys, so that they can help Antonio. I didn't know what to say," Ciro said.

"I'm sure you said the right thing." Enza kissed him.

Pappina and Enza centered the navy-blue-and-white-striped tablecloth on the ground, anchoring the edge with a picnic basket on one side, the children's shoes along the other.

John Latini and Antonio were the same age, soon to turn twelve.

The Latini boys—Robert was ten, and Sebastian nine—waded in the lake, skimming stones and tossing a ball. The rose of the family, baby Angela, was now four. Angela had glossy black hair, wide brown eyes, and tiny rose-petal lips. In stark contrast to her rambunctious brothers, she played quietly on the edge of the cloth with her doll.

"What's it like to have a little girl?" Enza asked.

"She's my lucky charm. At least I can teach her my mother's recipes. Someone will know the old ways when they're grown." Pappina offered Angela a fresh peach. The little girl took it and then offered a bite to her doll.

Ciro and Luigi decided to walk along the shore of the lake. In the distance they looked like two old men, huddled close, talking as they went.

Enza unwrapped chicken cutlets, while Pappina sliced tomatoes from her garden, added fresh mozzarella, drizzled them in lemon, and shredded basil on top. They brought loaves of crusty bread, wine for the adults, and lemonade for the children. Pappina made a peach cobbler and a thermos of espresso.

"I talked to the boys. They know what to say to Tony," Pappina said.

"He'll need them. They're like brothers."

"They'll be there for him. And we'll be there for you."

"Pappina, I look at him and I can't believe he's sick. He eats well, he still works hard, he has some aches and pains, but nothing terrible yet. I keep hoping that the tests were wrong. I even went up to see Doc Graham, but he explained what's ahead for us. Pappina, I don't think I'll be able to get through it," Enza cried.

Pappina leaned over and comforted her. "That's when your friends will help you. I'm here for you."

"I know, and I appreciate it. I try not to cry in front of Ciro."

"You can cry to me anytime."

"I have so many regrets," Enza said.

"Why? You have a good marriage."

"I didn't have another baby."

"You tried." Pappina looked over at Angela, feeling sad that her dear friend could not know the joy of a daughter.

"Ciro wanted another child so much. It was his dream. And I just accepted that I couldn't. You know, I'm not one to pine for what I don't have. But my husband is."

"Remember something—children come into your life in many ways, all the days of your life. Antonio may be an only child today, but someday he'll marry and who knows? He may have a house full of children."

Luigi and Ciro made their way back from the shore of the lake. "Okay, girls, what did you make to eat?" Luigi asked. "I need to feed the beast."

"Your beast could do with a little less feeding," Pappina said as she prepared her husband a plate.

"Am I fat?" Luigi asked, patting his stomach.

"The third hole in your belt hasn't seen the prong in two years," Pappina said.

Ciro laughed.

"Not so funny." Luigi sat down on the tablecloth.

"Luigi and I were talking about the old days at Zanetti's."

"Signora could cook," Luigi said as he took a bite of a chicken. "Not as good as you, Enza, but pretty good."

"We'd like to be in the same shop again."

Enza and Pappina looked at one another.

"I like this town. Hibbing is getting too big. The boys like the lake, and they want to go to school with Antonio. They want to be Bluestreaks."

"Oh, the kids came up with this?" Enza asked.

"No, we came up with it on behalf of the kids."

"Well, Pappina and I would love nothing more than to be neighbors."

"That's true," Pappina agreed.

"So we'll close Caterina One and consolidate with Caterina Two," Ciro said.

Pappina handed her husband a cup of wine, and gave one to Ciro. She picked up her own cup, while Enza raised hers. "One God. One Man. One shoe shop," Pappina toasted.

Enza propped feather pillows around Ciro's back until he was comfortable. "You take good care of me." Ciro pulled Enza close and kissed her.

"Do you think I'm a dope?" Enza asked. "Consolidating the shop. Working under one roof. I understand what you're up to. You're shoring up the shop. You're putting a plan in place. A *man* in place."

"I'm being practical," Ciro said.

"I have a say in this. But you went ahead and made a plan without me. Luigi will keep things running, and you can die in peace, knowing there is someone to look after us."

"But I'm just trying to take care of you!" Ciro said, bewildered. "Why does this make you angry?"

"Because you've accepted your fate when you can change it! You're not going to die. But if you think you are, you will."

"Why do you insist every day that I have control over this?"

"Because you do! And you're just giving up! You're giving up on me, your son, and our family. I would never give up on you. Never."

"I wish things were different."

"If you want to bring Luigi here because it's good business, then do it. But don't bring him to take care of me. I won't have it. I can take care of myself. *I* can take care of our son." Enza began to cry.

"Come here," Ciro said softly.

"No. You come to me," she said to him.

Ciro went to his wife and put his arms around her. "I'm sorry. I want you to be secure. I didn't mean to insult you. Of course you can take care of yourself. You survived Hoboken without me."

"What would help you get better, Ciro?"

"A miracle," he said softly.

"I think I know of one."

"Monsignor Schiffer already dropped off a vial of holy water from Lourdes. Only a German priest would bring an Italian French holy water," Ciro joked.

"Not that kind of miracle in a bottle—the real thing. I want to take the money we've saved and send you to the mountain. You should go home and see your brother. Your friends. The convent. You should swim in the water of Stream Vò. It would heal you faster than the water from Lourdes."

"What are you talking about, Enza? My place is here with you and Antonio."

"No, Ciro, listen to me." She pulled Ciro close. "Remember the berries in late summer? The way the juniper trees had pale green shoots underneath the branches, and they'd turn velvety and dark as they grew closer to the sky? If anything can make you well, it's the place you come from and the people that loved you. Your friend Ziggy—"

"*Iggy*," he corrected her.

"Wouldn't you like to see him again?"

"He taught me to smoke."

"You have to thank him," Enza said wryly. "And the nuns—"

"My nuns." Ciro laughed. "I wonder who is left at the convent of San Nicola?"

"You must go and reclaim your home again. That mountain is as much yours as it is anyone's. That rotten priest banished you, and you never returned. It's not right."

"Is my beautiful wife at long last turning on the Church of Rome?"

"No. But a bad priest is a bad priest."

"I used to dream of building a home on the mountain like the one you helped your family build. I wanted a garden."

"Where was I in this picture?"

"You were always there. I just didn't know it yet. I didn't know the woman I would love all of my life was you."

"If you love me, you'll go back to the mountain and let it heal you."

         *   *   *

In the days that followed their conversation, Pappina and Luigi met with Ciro and Enza, and they agreed to consolidate the business. The Latinis would move to Chisholm that summer and rent a home on Willow Street. The men would pull together and build an inventory, making work boots and fur-trimmed winter boots for snowshoeing.

Enza took in alterations from the Blomquist's and Raatamas department stores, and Pappina helped in the shop when she could. Enza expanded the dance shoe business to provide the shoes year-round, not just by special order.

Ciro and Enza began to argue frequently about her desire to send him home to Italy. When Enza moved the tin money box from the kitchen to the dresser in the bedroom, Ciro would put it back in the cabinet. When she brought it down to the shop to leave it on the work-table, he would gently put it aside. When she left it on the kitchen table at breakfast, he ignored it.

Ciro told Enza that he would never go home, until one day, in the heat of the last day of August, a letter came from Eduardo.

> *My Dear Brother,*
> *I said a mass for you this morning.*
> *After a long search, more prayers have been answered on our behalf.*
> *I have found our mother. She is safe, but I fear she is beaten down from years in a convent with terrible conditions. She would like to see you, and so would I. Perhaps a trip could be arranged?*
> *My love to you, E.*

At first, Ciro didn't tell Enza about the letter. He kept it in his pocket, and in stolen moments would reread it as though there was a line in it that would help change his mind. He was relieved that his mother was alive, and soon after the relief subsided like the waves on Long-year Lake, the pain came through anew, and his broken heart filled him with a deeper and more profound regret. He wished to be angry at Caterina and abandon her, the way she had abandoned them. But his heart, having grown in the tender care of Enza, would have none of it. He loved Caterina and wanted to see her again. He needed his mother now more than ever.

Ciro agreed, at long last, to go home to the mountain. He wanted to see his family before he died.

When Ciro told Enza he had made the decision, she leaped out of her chair and threw her arms around him. "How will we pay for the trip?" Ciro asked her.

"Remember the Burt-Sellers stock money? You wanted no part of it. But I've saved it. Your father is paying for your passage home." Enza beamed.

Ciro had been stalwart in the face of every decision regarding his health. The idea, that his father, who had died so young and failed to provide for his family, would in fact, with his death benefit, pay to reunite his wife and sons was almost too much for Ciro to bear. He collapsed in Enza's arms.

"All those years ago, you told me to spend the money on hats. And I'm so glad I'm not vain about hats."

That afternoon, Enza stood in the telegraph office and dictated a telegram to Laura H. Chapin of 256 Park Avenue, New York City:

> BOOKED ROUND-TRIP PASSAGE TO ITALY FOR CIRO. LETTER
> FOLLOWS TO EXPLAIN. I WILL BRING HIM TO NEW YORK TO
> SEE HIM OFF. MAY WE STAY WITH YOU BEFORE DEPARTURE?
> E.R.L.

The train from Minneapolis to New York City sped through the night as Enza and Ciro sat in the reading car. She read *The Sheik* by Edith M. Hull as Ciro smoked a cigarette and watched her as her eyes scanned over the words.

Enza pulled the blue wool wrap she wore over her suit tightly, without taking her eyes off the page. Ciro took delight in watching Enza when she read; it was as if she were consumed by the words, and the world outside the one on the pages ceased to exist.

"You're staring at me," Enza said without looking up.

"Are you imagining Rudolph Valentino as you're reading?"

"No."

"John Gilbert?"

"No."

"Who, then?"

She put down the book. "If you must know, whenever I read a character described as a handsome man, I think of you."

"Then why don't you stop reading and join me in the sleeping car?"

Ciro closed the door softly and joined Enza in the berth. The reverence of their wedding night was long gone, and had been replaced with the glorious familiarity that came from years of marriage. They knew everything about one another, and each surprise revealed along the way had only served to make them closer.

Pappina and Luigi had taken Antonio until Enza could return home. This gave her peace of mind, as she knew that her son would be happy with his friends, who were nearly brothers to him.

As Ciro kissed his wife, he remembered the train ride from New York after they were married, and the memory of it gave him a feeling of peace, the first he'd had since he went to the Mayo Clinic. He was enthralled by Enza all over again when he thought back to the night they first made love. But soon the dull ache in his stomach returned, and the feeling of doom that accompanied the knowledge of his fate. He put those thoughts out of his mind, though, and kissed his wife, and made love to her as he had so many years before, when they were young and everything was new.

26

A CARRIAGE RIDE
Un Giro in Carrozza

Colin Chapin greeted Enza and Ciro on the platform of the train at Grand Central Station. Colin's hair was completely gray now, and his suits were Savile Row, but his smile was as open as it always had been. *He is a solid white brick of a man,* Enza thought. Colin was the general manager of the Metropolitan Opera, and with the job had come speaking engagements and lucrative coproductions with opera companies around the world. Colin and Laura were in the top tier of high society in New York, but Enza wouldn't have known it when he threw his arms around them. He acted like he was still the office runner in accounting that he had been when they first met.

Colin took their bags and led them to his car, a midnight blue and maroon Packard, custom made and the height of chic opulence. As he turned onto Fifth Avenue and Seventy-ninth Street, Enza saw Laura waiting in the lobby of the apartment building. Colin pulled up to the awning and Enza jumped out of the car and into the arms of her best friend.

"Autumn in New York," Laura said.

"Our favorite time of year!" Enza took in her friend, who opened her velvet opera coat to reveal a pregnancy so advanced, it appeared the baby could be born that same evening.

"You're having a baby!" Enza threw her arms around Laura. "And soon!"

"I know. Forgive me, Enza, I wanted to tell you. But it's been a very difficult pregnancy. The last week things have been so much better, but we've been on guard the whole time. The doctor said I would never have a baby, but here we are. It was a shock to Colin, to me, to the doctor, to the entire medical community as it stands in New York City. But it's true, and we're thrilled."

"I have sons in college, and soon we'll have a baby in the crib. We don't know whether to be thrilled or . . . cry," Colin teased.

Laura was at the peak of her beauty, the contrast of her pale skin and red hair were now softly dramatic. Her lovely profile had taken on the lines of aristocracy, and the sharp angles of her youth were gone.

"You should be on bed rest," Enza told her.

"How could I rest? My best friend was on her way."

Ciro and Colin joined them, and Laura embraced Ciro. "All right, all right, upstairs with you," Colin said. Ciro reached to help Colin with the luggage, but a bellman whisked it away. Ciro turned to see a valet drive the Chapin Packard to the parking lot. Ciro shook his head. They were a long way from Chisholm.

The elevator opened into the foyer of the penthouse apartment. Laura had decorated the apartment in soft greens and yellow, obeying the rule Mrs. DeCoursey always proclaimed back at Milbank House: paint your rooms the colors you look best in.

The spacious rooms were well appointed with polished Chippendale furniture, Aubusson rugs, crystal sconces, milk-glass chandeliers, and oil paintings of pastoral settings, including the farm fields of Ireland, the black rage of the North Sea tossing a boat in its milky foam, and tasteful miniatures of single flowers, a daisy, a hydrangea, and a gardenia.

"You're a long way from Hoboken," Enza said.

Ciro and Colin had gone out on the terrace. "Back in bed, Mama," Colin called out.

"I am!" Laura hollered back. She showed Enza the guest room, a cheery room with a canopied bed covered in chintz. "Come with me." Enza followed Laura to the master bedroom, a cool blue room with trellis-patterned wallpaper and a satin-covered bed. Laura pulled off her cape, revealing a nightgown underneath. She climbed back into bed.

"When are you due?" Enza fluffed the pillows.

"Any minute."

"Where's the nursery?"

"I haven't put it together."

Enza sat on the bed. "Superstitious?"

"The doctor is concerned." Laura wiped tears from her eyes. "And I'm scared." Laura cried because at long last, in the arms of her longtime and best friend, she could be honest.

"Before I had Antonio, I had terrible feelings of doom. I'm sure your baby is fine."

"Do you think so?"

"I've learned one important lesson in my life, and I'm going to share it with you. Don't worry about bad things that haven't happened yet. It will save you a lot of anxiety."

Colin brought a tray of tea in for the ladies. "You girls catch up, but as soon as you do, it's bedtime for the little mother here."

"He's so bossy," Enza teased as Colin went. "So what's the gossip? You said you had a lot."

"Vito Blazek left the Met, and now he works at Radio City Music Hall. He's on his third divorce. "

"Can't be!"

Laura nodded solemnly. "The three stages of romantic love for a flack: marry a showgirl, divorce her, marry the daughter of a producer, divorce her, marry a younger showgirl, and divorce her once you've come to your senses."

"How awful." Enza sipped her tea.

"Don't you want to know how he looks?"

"Every detail," Enza said.

"Gorgeous."

Enza laughed. "That figures."

"He's no Ciro Lazzari. Honey, in the sweepstakes of the acquisition of handsome men, you got the golden ticket. The man you married is one in a million. But you know that."

"And I'm going to lose him, Laura."

"He looks well," Laura said hopefully.

"I pray for him. I keep hoping that maybe the whole thing is a mistake. And when I say to that Ciro, he looks at me like I'm crazy. He knows the truth, and he's accepting it. He's never been a religious man, but he has an inner strength that defies faith itself."

"Maybe the trip will cure him," Laura said gently.

"That's what I tell him. And I'm going to say the same thing to you. Your baby is fine. Believe it, and all will be well."

Colin woke early to go to the Met for an early call. New scenery for the production of *La Bohème* was being delivered. Ciro left Enza and Laura after breakfast and went for a walk. His plan was to walk through Central Park, but he found himself walking south, down Fifth Avenue toward Little Italy. He thought about taking the trolley, but he felt good, and decided to see how the city had changed in the twelve years since he left.

Broadway widened out in lower Manhattan. The sidewalks were full of fruit vendors, flower carts, and newsstands. When he reached Grand Street and took the turn into Little Italy, he remembered the buildings, and was surprised that while upper Manhattan seemed to change, his old neighborhood had stayed the same.

He found his way easily to 36 Mulberry Street. The Zanetti Shoe Shop sign was gone, as was the Italian flag. The storefront was empty, with a sign that said, "For Rent." Ciro stood back and took in the place where he'd worked when he first came to America. He moved closer and looked through the window. The same bowed floors and tin ceiling remained, and he could see the place where his cot used to be. The privacy curtain was gone. The door to the back garden was open wide. Ciro peered through. The old elm that he loved had been chopped down. The tree that had given him comfort and hope was gone, and with that, Ciro left the past and returned to the present. He took the tree and its absence as an omen, and with a heavy heart, turned to walk back to the Chapins'.

Laura was taking a nap. Enza sat and waited for Ciro to return. When he came through the door, her heart leaped in her chest as it always had. Now, though, that joy was soon crushed by a feeling of impending doom. She went to his side and took his hands in hers. "I have a surprise for you," she said. "Are you tired?"

"Not at all," he said.

Enza grabbed her hat, coat, and gloves and pushed Ciro out the door.

Many nights when Ciro couldn't sleep, Enza would tell him stories of her days at the Metropolitan Opera House. He had only been twice; once for a concert when he was young, and the second time when he saw Enza before he left for the Great War. Both visits burned in his memory, and for him, there was no greater thrill than to see those of wealth and privilege stand in awe of the Great Caruso, a poor Italian boy who'd made good.

Enza took Ciro's hand as they climbed the steps into the entrance foyer of the Metropolitan Opera. Years later, she remembered in vivid detail what she and Laura had been wearing the day they came for their interviews. She remembered what she'd had for breakfast, and what it had been like when they walked into the theater together for the first time.

Enza took the same steps on this day with her husband. And when they entered the dark opera house, the lingering scents of expensive perfume, grease paint, lemon oil, and fresh lilies filled the air, just as they had the first time she set foot inside. She led her husband down the aisle and up to the stage, where the ghost lights glowed along the up-stage brick wall. The scenery, delivered in bundles, was stacked against it like giant envelopes waiting for the mailman.

Ciro turned and looked out at the red velvet seats and up into the mezzanine. Enza took him center stage. Ciro stood on the exact spot where the Great Caruso had sung the night before Ciro left for New Haven. He closed his eyes and imagined the send-off all over again.

Enza led him backstage and down the stairs to the costume shop, which buzzed with activity. No one noticed them as they walked through. Enza stopped to point out the places she remembered. The fitting room where Geraldine Farrar had tried on the first gown Enza ever made, the ironing boards where she and Laura would gossip long into the night, and finally, her sewing machine, the sleek ebony Singer with the silver wheel and the gold trim. A young seamstress was busy sewing a hem at Station 3, Singer machine 17. She might have been twenty years old; watching her, Enza was a girl again. She saw herself on the work stool. When she looked up at Ciro, she was certain he did too.

. . .

After a few days of visiting their old haunts, including having pie and coffee at the Automat, Ciro was packed and ready to depart for Italy. His suitcase rested by Laura's front door. Ciro was asleep, but Enza could not bear to close her eyes. She felt the great ticking of the clock: every moment that she slept was one less awake with Ciro.

If she could just delay the worst, if she could savor these moments, when Ciro still felt good enough to walk to Little Italy and back, and enjoy a meal, and smoke a cigarette, she believed it would be all right. She didn't want to imagine what it would be like when he couldn't do the things he wanted to do. That was why the trip to Italy was urgent. Enza believed that it would change the course of Ciro's life, just as it had changed his life to leave it. It might not save his life, but it would shore up his soul.

Sometimes Enza tried to imagine what life would be without Ciro, believing it would help her accept it when the time came, but she couldn't. The well of pain was too deep to imagine. There was a rap on the door, an urgent one that woke Ciro. Enza went to the door and opened it.

"It's Laura." Colin entered the bedroom. "She's in labor."

"Call the doctor," Enza told Colin calmly. "Tell him to come here."

"She should go to the hospital," Colin said in a panic.

"Send him here."

Enza abided with her best friend and gently coached her through the labor pains. Soon the doctor arrived, with a nurse assistant, who took one look at the space and began to transform it into a birthing room.

The doctor asked Enza to wait outside, but Laura cried out for her to stay. Enza took a seat next to Laura and gripped her hand, just as she had her own mother's on the night that Stella was born. The memory of her baby sister's birth came flooding back with every grip, heave, and sigh that Laura endured. Tears began to flow freely down Enza's face as she stayed in the moment while holding the memory of what she remembered from the mountain.

Laura's body soon opened up, and her son slipped into the hands of the doctor, who skillfully cut the umbilical cord, followed by the nurse, who took the baby to clean and swaddle him.

"You have a son, Laura. A son!" Enza told her joyfully.

She heard the nurse speaking with the doctor. The nurse left the room with the baby, and Laura cried out to her to bring her son back. The doctor went to Laura's side. "We're taking the baby to the hospital."

"What's wrong with the baby?" Laura cried out, and as she did, Colin came into the room.

"They have to take him, Laura. He's having trouble breathing."

"Go with them, Colin," Laura cried.

Enza could see Ciro behind Colin in the hallway. "Go with him, Ciro. I'll stay with Laura," Enza said.

Ciro followed Colin out the door as Laura leaned against Enza and wept, then, depleted from the birth, fell asleep. Enza straightened the room, changed the sheets, bathed Laura, dressed her, and covered her in warm blankets. She lowered the lights, pulled up a chair, and sat by her bed. Enza began to pray the rosary. She held Laura's hand, and soon she found herself on her knees, begging God again to change the course of events for someone she loved. Every prayer was a plea to bring good news by morning.

*   *   *

Henry Heery Chapin was placed in an incubator at Lenox Hill Hospital as soon as Colin arrived at the hospital with him. Through the muslin, Colin could touch his son's pink fingers and brush his cheek. At five pounds, Henry was big enough, but his lungs weren't clearing as he breathed. The doctor had suctioned his tiny lungs. Soon, they were working on their way to full capacity. It seemed to Colin that the baby was getting better as the hours passed.

When dawn came, the doctor checked the baby, and told Colin that the worst was over. They would keep the baby for a few days, to make certain that he was well enough to go home. Ciro stayed with the baby so Colin could go home with the news. The hospital was close to their apartment, but he stopped at the nurse's station and called. Enza woke Laura up to tell her. She shed tears of joy at the news of her baby's health. Enza tucked her rosary into her suit pocket, a believer once more.

The ship was leaving the port in lower Manhattan late that afternoon. Ciro thought about canceling his trip, but now that Henry was better, he felt he should go.

Ciro had watched baby Henry through the night, and as he watched the nurses in the hospital tend to him in his tiny, well-lit tent, and as he observed Colin, a new father again, yet alert to every detail of the infant's progress, Ciro decided that life would go on. The baby, Henry, had survived. Maybe it was a sign.

That afternoon, when Ciro said good-bye to Enza on the sidewalk on Fifth Avenue, before going to the pier to board the ocean liner for Italy, they held one another a long time.

"I want you to sleep on the boat. Take the fresh air and eat. Promise me you'll eat," Enza pleaded with him.

"And I'll drink whiskey and smoke." He laughed.

"You can have anything you want but the dance-hall girls."

"But they're so much fun," he teased, pulling her close. "And they like me."

"You don't have to tell me." She laughed. "Now, I want you to memorize every detail of my mother's house. I want you to visit Stella's grave and kiss the blue angel for me. Can you do that?"

"Of course," Ciro promised.

"And will you look up at Pizzo Camino? I've forgotten it, and I want you to see it for me."

"I'll be your eyes and ears and heart in Schilpario. Take care of Laura, she needs you. Make the nursery. Help her with the baby. And don't worry. Our mountain is a miracle," Ciro said as he kissed her good-bye.

* * *

Ciro practically spent the entire voyage on a chaise longue on the second-class deck of the SS *Augustus*. At any other time, he would consider it lucky that his middle name was the same as the ship's. But not this time. Whenever he heard the horns blow at sea, he remembered shoveling coal in the belly of the SS *Chicago*. He remembered meeting Luigi, and how no matter how much he scrubbed, his skin was gray from the coal dust after a week in the pit.

Now, he was an older man, and he led the life of one who has earned his way out of steerage. Ciro was not in first class, where the passengers were pampered, but his room in second class was comfortable, and the windows were above the waterline. He smiled to himself when he went to sleep the first night. He had never traveled across the ocean above the waterline.

Every moment of the journey brought back memories. When he heard his native Italian as the ship docked in the port of Naples, he was surprised to find that it moved him so deeply that he wept. When he boarded the train to go north, he couldn't get enough of the people; he took in every detail of them and remembered when he too was Italian. He realized he had missed them, and his heart ached with the knowledge that he would not die in the country where he was born. Now he was neither Italian nor American; he was a dying man on a mission to make whole what never had been, and to heal a wound for which there was no salve or balm.

Ciro decided to climb the last bit of the Passo Presolana on foot. He sent his duffel ahead on the carriage to the convent of San Nicola, where the nuns had prepared the guest room for him.

Ciro buttoned his coat as he hiked up the hill to the entrance of Vilminore. He stopped at the top of a cliff and looked down into the gorge, where the green leaves of late summer had fallen away, leaving behind a tangle of gray. From his vantage point, the branches looked like a mass of childhood scribbles, a charcoal nest of intersecting lines and curves, made when a boy was just learning to write.

Ciro smiled when he remembered the girls he would woo to walk with him along the cliffs, and how it was the perfect excuse to hold a girl's hand where the road narrowed. He remembered the day Iggy had brought Eduardo and him down the mountain, how they didn't say much, but Iggy let him smoke a cigarette. Ciro had been fifteen when he was sent away. One transgression against the priest in the Church of Rome had changed the course of his life.

As he walked in the grooves of the cinnamon-colored earth, he thought of Enza, and the life they would have had on the mountain. Maybe she would have been able to have more children here, away from the pressures of making a living. Maybe he would have built the house on the hill that he had imagined in his dreams.

It had been twenty years since Ciro stood in the piazza of Vilminore. As he surveyed the colonnade, he realized that not much about it had changed. Some of the shops had been handed down to the sons, but mostly the village was just as he left it, houses of stucco surrounding the San Nicola church and rectory, and anchored across the way by the convent. The chain of command appeared to be what it always had been; the feeling of the place was familiar.

Ciro rapped on the convent door, then pulled the chain to ring the bell. When the door opened, Sister Teresa gently took Ciro's face in her hands. She still had the face she had twenty years ago; only a small web of lines around her eyes like spider silk betrayed her age.

"Ciro Lazzari!" she exclaimed. "My boy!" She threw her arms around him.

"I'm an old man now. I'm thirty-six years old," he told her. "Look at my fingers. See the scars from the lathe? I'm a shoemaker."

"Good for you. Enza wrote to me. She told me if she waited for you to write a letter, I would be waiting until Judgment Day."

"That's my wife."

"You're a lucky man." She folded her hands into the sleeves of her habit. Ciro thought he was anything but lucky. Couldn't Sister Teresa see that he was running out of time? The nun took him by the hand into the convent.

"Did you make me pastina?"

"Of course. But you know, I work in the office now. Sister Bernarda is the new cook. They brought her up from Foggia. You never met her— she came a couple years ago. She knows her way around a tomato. And she is so much better with the baking than I ever was."

"You were a good baker!"

"No, I was good at the *pot de crème* and the tapioca—but when it came to cakes, they were like fieldstones."

The nuns had gathered in the foyer. The young faces of the novitiates were new to him, but a few of the nuns who had been young when he was a boy were still there. Sister Anna Isabelle was now the Mother Superior, Sister Teresa her second in command.

Sister Domenica had died soon after Ciro left, and Sister Ercolina recently. The black-and-whites were family to him—a crew of dotty aunts, some funny, most well-read, some brilliantly intelligent, others survivors like him, who used their wits, their quick humor, or their stubborn natures, but all of them, unlike him, when they knelt before the altar, were pious. In hindsight, Ciro could appreciate their goodness and their choices. When he was a boy, he had been confounded why any woman would choose the veil over the expanse of the wide world, a hus- band, children, and a family of her own. But in fact they were making a family inside the walls of the convent; he just hadn't recognized it for what it was when he was young.

"*Ciao*, Mother Anna Isabelle," Ciro said, taking her hands and bowing to her. "*Grazie mille* for Remo and Carla Zanetti."

"They said wonderful things about you. You worked very hard for them. They moved back to their village and had a happy retirement before they died."

"That was Remo's dream."

Sister Teresa took Ciro down the long hallway to the garden and the kitchen beyond. Ciro remembered every polished tile in the floor and every groove in the walnut doors. The garden was covered in burlap for winter, the grapes having been harvested. When he looked ahead to the kitchen door, propped open with the same old can, he laughed.

"I know. We change very little here. We don't have to."

Sister Teresa took her place behind the worktable and threw on an apron. Ciro pulled up a work stool and sat. She reached into the bread bin and brought out a baguette, slathered it in fresh butter, and gave it to him. Instead of pouring a glass of milk, she poured him a glass of wine.

"Tell me why you're here."

"My wife didn't say in the letter?"

"She said you needed to come home. Why now?"

"I'm dying." Ciro's voice broke. "Now I know in a convent, that's good news, because you ladies have the key to eternal life. But for me, the skeptic, it's the worst news. I try to pretend that the moment won't come, and it buys me time. But then the clock ticks, and I remember what's true, and I panic. I don't pray, Sister, I panic."

Sister Teresa's expression changed, her face filled with a deep sadness. "Ciro, of all the people I have known and prayed for, of all of them, I hoped for you to have a long life. You earned it. And you always knew how to be happy, so it isn't a waste for you to be gifted a long life. You would spend the time wisely." And then, like the good nun she was, she wrapped the sad news in her beliefs like a warm blanket. Sister wanted to assure Ciro of the promise of eternal life. She wanted him to believe, hoping that faith would change his prognosis. "You must pray."

"No, Sister." Ciro smiled weakly. "I'm not a good Catholic."

"Well, Ciro, you're a good man, and that's more important."

"Don't let the priest hear you."

She smiled. "Don't worry. We have Father D'Alessandro from Calabria. He is nearly deaf."

"What happened to Don Gregorio?"

"He went to Sicily."

"Not Elba? He wasn't banished like Napoleon?"

"He's a secretary to the provost of the regional bishops."

"His cunning got him far."

"I think so." Sister poured herself a cup of water. "Do you want to know what happened to Concetta Martocci?"

Ciro smiled. "Is it a happy story?"

"She married Antonio Baratta, who is now a doctor. They live in Bergamo and have four sons together."

Ciro looked off and thought about how life had changed for him and those he knew. Even Concetta Martocci had found a way to redeem the worst thing that had happened to her. This made Ciro smile.

"Concetta Martocci *still* makes you smile." Sister laughed.

"Not so much, Sister. There are other things. I am anxious to see my brother. My heart fills at the thought of seeing my mother. I want to visit my wife's family. I promised Enza I would go up the pass to Schilpario. Has much changed on the mountain?"

"Not much. Come with me," Sister said. "I want to prove to you how well I keep a promise."

Ciro followed Sister Teresa behind the kitchen to the convent cemetery. She stopped at a small headstone near the end of the gate.

"Poor Spruzzo," Ciro said. "He wandered these trails like an orphan, until he found an orphan."

"No, not poor Spruzzo. He had a happy life. He ate better than the priest. I gave him the best cuts of meat."

"Saint Francis would approve." Ciro smiled.

. . .

The convent had finally been given the old carriage when the priest graduated to having a motorcar. The current horse, Rollatini, was donated by a local farmer. Ciro hitched the horse and thought of his wife, who would do a better job with the harness, hitch, and reins than he could ever do.

He climbed up into the seat and took the Passo up the mountain to Schilpario. He remembered the first time he'd kissed his wife, when she was just a girl and he a boy. He took in every daisy, cliff, and stream, as though they were precious gems in a velvet case that only he could open. How he wished Enza could be on the mountain with him!

It was a relief to be in a horse-drawn cart after days on the open sea, and after the long train ride north from Naples. A cart and horse had a certain rhythm, and there was something soothing about the company of a horse. Ciro felt less alone.

Enza had told Ciro where the new house had been built, and to look for the color yellow.

As he made his way along the main street past the spot where he'd first kissed Enza, a flood of memories washed over him. He remembered Via Scalina as he passed it, and the stable where Enza had hitched the horse to take him home the night he buried Stella. The wooden window shutters on the stable were closed.

Ciro proceeded up the road slowly, as the hill grew increasingly steep. He spotted the yellow house on Via Mai, standing out against the mountain like a leather-bound book. A feeling of complete recognition pealed through his body; the house before him was the same house he had seen in his mind's eye as a boy, and had hoped to build for the woman of his dreams. How ironic, now, that the house Enza had worked to build for her family was the very one that had occupied the deepest wells of his imagination as a boy! It was almost detail for detail the house of his dreams. He couldn't wait to tell Enza how magnificent the Ravanelli homestead she had helped build was in completion.

Ciro guided the horse to the side of the house. The barren garden, surrounded by fieldstones, looked like an abandoned campfire when the wood had burned to ash. Ciro followed the stone path up to the front door. Before he could knock, the door swung open, and Enza's family moved toward him to greet him.

Enza's mother Giacomina, nearing sixty, was plump, her gray hair worn in a long braid. Ciro could see Enza's fine bone structure in her mother's face, and certain of her mannerisms were instantly familiar. Giacomina embraced her son-in-law. "Ciro, welcome home."

"This kiss is from Enza. She is well. She is in New York, helping Laura Heery with her new baby."

Marco stood up in his chair. He was now more robust than Ciro remembered; returning to the mountain had been a tonic for him. Ciro embraced him, too. "Enza sends her love to you too, Papa."

As Giacomina introduced each of her children, Ciro took careful note of any news that he could share with Enza. The boys, now men, were running a carriage service, now with a motorcar, and business was booming.

Eliana was close to thirty-five, expecting her fourth baby. Her straight brown hair was worn loose down her back, and she wore a work smock, skirt, and brown boots. She introduced her sons—Marco, eleven years old, Pietro, nine, and Sandro, five. Her husband, she explained, worked in Bergamo at the water plant, and was sorry he could not be there.

Vittorio was married to a local girl, Arabella Arduini, cousin to the town padrone.

Alma was twenty-six, and hoped to go to university. She wanted to become a painter, as she had a talent for fine art; she had painted a gorgeous fresco of sunflowers on the garden wall. She took Ciro's hands into hers. "Please tell my sister that I thank her for everything she did for us. Because of her, I can go to university."

The door pushed open, and Battista entered. Lanky, dark, and sinewy, he was thirty-six years old, had yet to marry, and showed no signs of interest in it. He had a sullen expression, and Ciro noticed that he seemed resentful of the family, and that his presence caused tension in the room. Ciro embraced him anyway, and called him *fratello*.

Eliana, who lived down the hill now, showed Ciro the house. It was not grand, but it was exactly enough for the family—five bedrooms, a loft, the kitchen, and the living room. Four windows along the front of the house gave beautiful light within. Ciro remembered the windows he'd wanted in the house of his dreams, and here they were, letting in the pale blue light of the Italian afternoon.

Vittorio and Marco showed Ciro the smokehouse, built of fieldstone and set into the side of the mountain. Another small structure served as a spring house; fresh, cold water from the mountain stream pulsed through it through two open troughs into a pool lined with stones.

Giacomina prepared a meal just like one Enza would serve: soup, followed by gnocchi, with a dish of greens and cake and espresso for afterward.

Eliana poured her brother-in-law a cup of espresso.

"Alma, do you think you could draw the house for me? I think Enza would love to see it on paper."

"I would be happy to. How long are you staying?"

"A week."

"It took you as long to get here as your visit will be."

"It's very hard to be away from Enza and Antonio."

"I understand," Giacomina said.

"I'm sure she explained about my health."

Giacomina and Marco nodded that she had.

"Antonio is a wonderful son. You would love him."

"We love him already," Vittorio said. "He's our nephew."

"He's an athlete. But he's intelligent too. I hope you will find a way to visit Enza and Antonio in Minnesota sometime."

Ciro did not want to make the pleasant visit somber in any way. He told funny stories about Enza, and described New York City, and living on Mulberry Street. He talked about the Great War and the decision to go to Minnesota. He told a few stories about Antonio, and what a wonderful young man he was. They shared photographs, and stories of Enza's youth. After dinner, the entire family took *la passeggiata* and went to the cemetery, where Ciro did as Enza had requested, kneeling to kiss the blue angel marking Stella's grave. He stood back and put his hands in his pockets. As the sun began to set, the sky turned the exact blue it had been the night he'd first kissed Enza, after digging the grave. It seemed so long ago, and yet, standing in this place, he felt as though it were happening all over again. It seemed to Ciro that so much of life was about not holding on, but letting go and in so doing, the beauty of the past and the happiness he felt then came full circle like a band of gold. The night sky, the cemetery, the memory of places past and the people who had been there to bear witness, provided all the constancy his heart required. This is what it means to be part of a family.

. . .

When Ciro went to hitch the horse that night, to return to Vilminore, Eliana went outside to help him. Ciro climbed up into the bench of the cart.

Eliana handed him a small leather-bound book, with endpapers of Florentine paisley. "This belongs to Enza. Will you take it to her?"

"Of course," he said.

The ride down the mountain to Vilminore filled Ciro with a deep longing for his wife. How he wished he could have made her come on this trip! But there had been no convincing her. As he put Rollatini in the barn and unhitched the cart, hung up the reins, and unbuckled the harness, he began to weep. He was ending where he began, and the irony was not lost on him.

Sister Teresa made up the bed in the guest room near the chapel. Ciro saw a nun kneeling inside, but he walked past the glass doors and into his room, closing the door gently behind him. He undressed, sat on the bed, and opened Enza's book.

As he turned the pages, he saw his wife's youth blossom all over again. She sketched dresses, wrote silly poems, and attempted to draw all the members of her family. As Ciro turned the pages, he smiled at her rudimentary attempts at portraiture.

He stopped when he saw "Stella" written at the top of the page. Enza had been fifteen when she wrote,

Stella

My sister died, and her funeral was today. I prayed so hard for God to save her. He did not listen. I promised God that if he spared her, I would not ask Him for children of my own later. I would give up being a mother to keep her here. But he did not listen. I am afraid that Papa will die from a broken heart. Mama is strong, he is not.

I met a boy named Ciro today. He dug Stella's grave. I wasn't afraid of him even though he was tall and twice my size. I felt sad for him. He doesn't have a father, and his mother left him. Someday I'll ask the sisters at San Nicola why his mother left him there.

Here's what I can tell you about him. He has blue-green eyes. His shoes were too small, and his pants were too big. But I never met a boy more handsome. I don't know why God would send him

up the mountain, but I hope there's a purpose in it. He doesn't believe in God very much. He doesn't seem to need anyone. But I think if he thought about it, he would realize he needs me.

My Stella is gone, and I will never forget her because I see how it goes when someone dies. First there are tears, then there is grief, and soon, the memory fogs and they disappear. Not Stella. Not for me. Not ever. E.

Ciro closed the book and placed it on the nightstand. He felt the hollow of his back, and it wasn't tender. Sometimes his pain was intense, and then, without explanation or warning, it would go, and there would be a reprieve. And in the moments without pain, Ciro believed he could heal.

Ciro lifted his hand to make the sign of the cross, something he had not done in years. He hadn't done it once during the war. He hadn't done it when his son was born. Enza would make a cross on the baby's forehead with her thumb, but not Ciro. He hadn't blessed himself when he left Enza for this trip. He felt it disingenuous to call upon God in desperation. But tonight, he wasn't making the sign of the cross so that God might grant him a wish, might have mercy and save him; he made the sign of the cross in gratitude.

Enza had loved him from the moment she met him, and he had not known it. He thought he charmed her on Carmine Street on the morning she was to marry another. He believed all his experience with beautiful girls had somehow formed a romantic confluence, so he might win the most beautiful girl of all, if only he chose her. Ciro thought it was he who had won his true love's heart. Now he knew that her heart was there for the taking all along.

No wonder she had been so hurt when he hadn't tried to find her, and no wonder she'd never come for him after she told him her feelings. She would never have wanted to make him uncomfortable. In fact, Enza's mission all along had been to give Ciro comfort, and in every way, she had succeeded, including making him go on this trip. He knew that if anything would heal him, it would be the mountain. As he turned over in the bed, he felt no pain in his body. As always, Enza knew best.

27

A BLUE CAMEO
Un Cammeo Blu

There was a loud and persistent knock on Ciro's door at the convent. He sat up, grabbed his pocket watch, and checked the time. He had slept uninterrupted through the night, a delicious nine hours. He had not slept this well since before his diagnosis at the Mayo Clinic.

"Yes?" he called out.

"It's Iggy."

Ciro leaped out of bed and threw the door open. Twenty-one years later, Ignazio Farino stood before him, wearing the same hat.

"Same hat, Iggy?"

Iggy shrugged. "It still fits."

Ciro embraced him.

"Be careful. My bones are like breadsticks," Iggy said. "I could snap in two right before your eyes."

"You look good, Iggy."

"You're thin."

"I know." Ciro pulled on his pants and shirt and slipped into his shoes. "I looked better before I was hit with mustard gas. But I still eat like a horse. Let's go raid the pantry for some breakfast."

Ciro followed Iggy down the hallway. Except for the bow in his knees, he moved well for a man in his eighties.

"Can you believe I'm not dead?" Iggy said. "I'm as old as the bell in San Nicola."

"You don't look it."

"I still visit my wife." Iggy's eyebrows shot up.

"Iggy, I just got up the mountain, and the first thing you tell me is that you still make love to your wife."

"I have not withered," Iggy promised him. "Besides, she says she doesn't mind."

"Well, if she doesn't mind, why not?"

"That's what I say—why not? It's one of the joys of marriage. I still get as hard as *torrone*. Not as often, but enough. How's Enza?"

"She's a great wife, Iggy."

"Good for you."

Iggy took a seat in the convent kitchen. He lit up a cigarette as the young nun came in from the main convent to make them breakfast. She poured them each a cup of coffee. Ciro poured cream into both cups, and Iggy ladled three teaspoons of sugar into his. The nun served them bread, butter, and jam, placed hard-boiled eggs in a clear glass bowl on the table, and sliced off a hunk of cheese for each of them. She picked up her moppeen and went into the main convent to help with the chores.

"Don Gregorio . . ." Iggy clucked.

"I know. Went to Sicily."

"I had words with him after you left."

"What did you say?"

"I told him, You'll have to answer to God someday for what you've done."

"Do you think he will?"

"Nah. He probably has every priest in Rome praying for him. That's how they do it, you know. They do a bad thing, they say they're sorry, and they get some *ninelle* to pray for them, wiping the slate clean. What a racket." Iggy handed the cigarette to Ciro, who took a puff. "If he's ahead of me in line to get into heaven, I'll raise holy hell. This guy we have now, he's all right."

"Don—"

"Yeah—Don Baci-ma-coolie. I see him kneel in the garden and say his rosary. I've been in his room, and there's nothing askew. He's neat as wire. I think he's all right. Finally after all these years, an actual pious priest. Didn't think *that* card trick was possible."

Ciro laughed. He took a sip of the coffee and turned to his old friend. "I don't pray, Iggy."

"You have to get it down to the bones, otherwise it doesn't work." Iggy waved his cigarette.

"What do you mean?"

"Be clear. Ask God for exactly what you want. Forget all the poor slobs of the world—their lot in life is not your problem. Who is starving has to find their own food. Who is broken-hearted has to find his own woman. Thirsty? Jump in a lake. Worry about yourself. You pray for what you need, and see if you don't get it."

"Did you miss me, Iggy?"

"I worried about you like a son. Eduardo too."

"Did you get my letters?"

"In twenty years, I got three. Not so good." Iggy smiled.

"Not so good. But you knew I was thinking of you."

"Yeah, yeah, I knew. I could feel it."

.   .   .

Ciro was walking the piazza as he waited for Eduardo to arrive with their mother. He paced under the colonnade, resisting the urge to run down the mountain to meet the carriage. He checked his watch repeatedly, hoping that time would pass more quickly if he did. He thought of this for a moment. Enza wanted to stop the clock, and here he was, bidding it to speed up toward the reunion he had dreamed about.

At the appointed hour, a black carriage pulled into the piazza, headed toward the convent. Ciro, at the far side of the colonnade, broke into a run to meet the carriage.

When it stopped, Ciro reached up and opened the shiny black door. Twenty-six years had come and gone since Ciro last saw his mother. She emerged from the carriage, dressed in blue, just as she had been when she left. Her hair was gray now, but still long, and braided, twisted into a chignon.

Her face was still beautiful. The arc of her nose, the fullness of her lips, all was as he remembered. Age had faded the intensity and colors of her beauty, but not the structure. Her long tapered fingers, graceful carriage, and slim figure were still hers. But her hands shook, and she was anxious, neither characteristics that had been apparent before.

"Mama," Ciro said. He cried, though he had promised himself he wouldn't.

"Help your mother, Ciro." She smiled as Ciro helped her to step out of the carriage and onto the cobblestones. He took his mother in his arms and rested his head against her neck. She still had the same scent of freesia. Ciro took it in and did not want to let go.

Eduardo emerged from the carriage, in the plain, mud-brown robe of the Franciscans. Ciro was so happy to see him that he shouted, "My brother!"

Eduardo threw his arms around Ciro.

"Please, let's go inside," Ciro said.

The sisters had prepared a room for Caterina, for Ciro would stay with Eduardo. Sister Teresa showed them to the library, where she had placed a tray with coffee and pastries. The Lazzaris thanked her, and she caught Ciro's eye before she left the room, closing both doors behind her.

Eduardo and Ciro knelt next to their mother as she sat in a chair. She began to weep, soft, quiet tears, like a gentle rainfall after years of torrents. She didn't want to be sad in front of her sons; she wanted to be a good mother before them, and act as though the suffering they had endured was over, and the wounds of their childhood had healed. She knew better, but she wanted to offer them as much solace as she could, knowing she herself would never find it.

She kissed each of her boys and then stood, walking to the windows to catch her breath. Ciro and Eduardo looked at one another. Eduardo had warned Ciro that sometimes their mother's behavior could be odd, but he was not to take it personally, as she had suffered from deep depression for so many years that she could not stand away from her own pain to ease theirs.

Caterina walked away from the windows to the bookshelves, where she perused the titles. "Some of these books were bound in our shop," she said. "I know the endpapers and the leather. The Montinis were meticulous."

"Would you like some coffee, Mama?" Eduardo asked.

"*Grazie*," she said.

Eduardo looked at Ciro, who watched his mother as though he were studying a work of art from a safe distance. "Mama, Ciro came all the way from America to see us."

Ciro could see that his mother had suffered mental trauma, but that she was still the same woman that he remembered in most ways. He decided to cling to those things that were wonderful about her, and to ignore the ravages of time and insecurity, instability, and anxiety. He had so much to say to her.

"I have something for you, Mama." Ciro reached into his pocket and removed the tracing of his father's grave, with the date of his death upon it. "My wife, Enza, made sure Papa had a proper gravestone. He died in the Burt-Sellers mining disaster of 1904. It was a terrible fire. But now he has a proper memorial," he said, handing her the paper.

She looked down at it. "It's beautiful. Thank you for this." She put her arm around Ciro.

"Mama, when he died, the company issued reparations. Stock. We cashed it and put it in the bank. This"—he gave her an envelope—"is the balance. I paid for my ticket with some of it."

She gave Ciro the envelope without opening it. "You keep this for my grandson. And kiss him for me."

"Mama, don't you need the money?"

Caterina put her hands on Ciro's face. "You're just like your father. He would give his last lira to someone if it might help them."

"Keep the money for your family, Ciro," said Eduardo. "Mama is provided for."

"I want to hear about you, Mama. Tell me how you've been."

"Tell Ciro where you were, Mama," said Eduardo.

"I worked at the convent in Montichiari-Fontanelle on Lake Garda."

He thought about how close his mother had been, and how as a boy, he could have hitched a ride to Lake Garda so easily and seen her. The loss of her was not only poignant; it was irreversible, and there was no healing his broken heart.

"I was too sick to find you boys again. By the time I was feeling better, you were in America, and Eduardo was in the priesthood. The sisters didn't tell me much, because they were afraid I would try to leave the hospital. They told me to imagine you on the mountain, healthy and happy and living with the good sisters. So that's how I got through. I prayed to be stronger and to get well so we could all be together again."

"Mama, you'll never be alone again. I am taking you to live near me, and I'll be able to see you," Eduardo promised her.

Caterina sat on the settee and pulled her sons close to sit next to her, holding their hands. "Eduardo and I will have many years together. And I'm so sorry, Ciro. We lost a lifetime. And it was all my fault. I see strong women everywhere, some with six or seven children, and I marvel at them. But I just wasn't well enough to do it. And I knew that if you were with the sisters, they would guide you to develop your talents, as I would have had I had the strength. But when your father died, I couldn't come up with a plan. It was only bleak and dark, and I was desperate. There was nothing."

Ciro hadn't known that his mother had tried her best. He had always assumed that he was too much trouble, and she couldn't handle him. Eduardo had taken the pain and turned it inward. It made him spiritually strong, as he believed that only sacrifice leads to redemption. He gave up the idea of his mother to earn a place closer to God, while Ciro was adrift.

That night, the Lazzari boys and their mother dined on *cassoeula*, a pork stew with onions, celery, and carrots in a thick broth, poured over fresh bread. Ciro showed his mother a picture of Antonio and Enza. He explained about her friend Laura, who had worked at the Metropolitan Opera, and how they were like sisters. He explained about baby Henry. And when his mother asked about Ciro's health, he didn't have the heart to tell his mother that he was dying; he would leave that to his brother, the priest. He wanted his mother to have as many happy moments as her sons could provide.

Ciro climbed into the cot in the convent guest room. Eduardo sat on the floor by his cot, as he had when they were boys. It didn't matter that they were older, nearing forty, grown men. They still longed for the comfort of their boyhood connection, which was as strong as ever. Whatever their mother had done or could not do, and no matter the fate of their young father, they had always had one another, and it had made all the difference.

"Eduardo, what do you think about our mother?"

"If she stops and realizes what she did, she will collapse."

"She seemed so prim."

"She is. It's her way of showing us that she's strong."

"She didn't cry when she saw the tracing of Papa's headstone."

"Mama is angry at him still."

"We should be angry with her."

"What good would that do now, Ciro?"

"I missed her."

"And so did I. By the time we were old enough to leave the convent to look for her, they had sent you away, and I was in the seminary. You have to understand that her heart is frozen. She needs love too, Ciro. We all do."

Ciro nodded. At long last, he understood his mother. The veneer had always been the thing that held her up. The surface had been strong, but beneath it, who knew?

Caterina brushed her hair in the chamber next door. Tears flowed freely and abundantly down her face, for all she had lost, all these many years. She'd believed that someone else could raise her sons better than she could. She'd thought the church knew best, and she, as a widow without savings, was worthless to her boys. She brushed her hair, one hundred strokes, and put the hairbrush in her duffel. That night, she did not sleep. She did not sit, and she did not read. She paced the chamber like a dutiful nun, hoping that the morning would bring some clarity, guide her to say something to the boys she'd left behind. She hoped that the words would come; that she would be able to explain why she had left them in the convent, changing the course of all of their lives.

On the other side of the wall, Ciro pulled the blanket over his legs and propped the pillow on the bed. He lay on his side, as he had during his youth when he needed to talk to his brother long into the night.

"Have you told her about me?"

"You should tell her."

"Can you believe my diagnosis, Eduardo?" Ciro asked. "Not one good thing came of that war."

"You can't say that. You had courage, you were brave."

"It was either that, or die then. And at the end, when I came in, when the Americans came in, there was nothing left to fight. We had food and guns, artillery, uniforms, tanks—the Germans had nothing. And we rolled over them like a leather presser. For what? I won't know the joy I fought for. I tell myself I did it for the future, for my son."

"None of us can know what God has in mind for us."

"There's the problem, brother. God doesn't have me in mind."

Eduardo began to speak, but Ciro stopped him.

"You are a good man, Eduardo. Whether you wear the black biretta of a priest, or the wool cap of a farmer, in my mind, you are a duke. What you believe doesn't matter as much to me as who you are. I have always been, in great measure, in awe of you. You're decent and strong, which makes for a good man, never mind a good priest. But don't try and convince me that God knows I'm here. I just don't think it's true."

Eduardo's look of concern softened to a smile. He held up his hands as the priest does during a blessing, giving up winning his brother over to the ways of the rosary. "Tell me about your son."

"He's glorious. He's his mother. Approaches life sensibly. Women will never be his downfall."

"And the sports?"

"Brilliant. Like a dance. But he is so even-tempered, even in the heat of competition. They call him a good sportsman. He has dignity even on the basketball court."

"And Enza? Tell me about my sister."

"Enza wanted me to come to Italy so I could keep the image of the juniper trees and the waterfall and the asters in the front of my mind through the dark days to come. But when I close my eyes, brother, all I ever see is her face. There is no place or time without her. Where I am doesn't matter when we're apart. All I want is her."

"You really love her."

"I don't know why she loves me, but she does."

"What are you afraid of, Ciro?"

"Now?"

"Now, in a few months—"

"When death comes," Ciro said practically.

"When the moment of your death comes."

"Well, I imagine I won't want to go. The doctors have told me this is a painful death. But Enza has learned how to boil the needles and fill the syringe, and I will have all the medicine I need to get through it. That, the doctors have promised me. But what do you say to God when you don't want to die? What if I want to raise my son and love my wife and live to be an old man?"

"I'm sorry, Ciro. I would do it for you if I could."

"I know you would." Ciro wiped away a tear. He had never doubted that his brother would die for him.

"You'll see the face of God before me."

"I'm sorry about that. I know how hard you worked to get there first."

Eduardo laughed. "There is no justice."

"True."

"Is there anything I can do?"

"Someday I hope you can show my son the mountain. I want him to know these roads, hike these trails, own these cliffs like we did. I want you to give him religious instruction—I want him to know God, even though his father doesn't."

"You know Him," Eduardo assured Ciro. "You know Him because you are part of Him. You always have been. Even when you tried your best to be bad, you were good. You're made of God's light. I didn't become a priest because I had this light; I became one because I saw it in you."

"Then why am I not the pope?" Ciro asked Eduardo. They laughed and laughed, the sound of one brother's laughter only making the other laugh harder, just as it had when they were boys, when they looked out for one another and believed no harm would ever come to them as long as they were together.

Through the convent wall, Caterina heard her sons' laughter. She listened at the wall for a few moments, taking in the sound, reminded of all she had lost. But a child's joy is doubled for the mother, and the sound of her sons' laughter began to heal her heart, a feat she had never believed possible.

.   .   .

Ciro woke early and looked over at his brother, who was fast asleep. He dressed and went to the convent kitchen. Sitting on a stool at the worktable was Caterina, dressed and ready for the day. She poured Ciro a cup of coffee.

"Good morning, Mama." Ciro kissed her on the cheek.

"How did you sleep?"

"Like the old convent cat," Ciro said. "It's so peaceful here."

"It's good to be together. You're a fine man, Ciro. I mean that. And I'm proud of what you have become."

The words that Ciro had hoped to hear all of his life had now been said. The strong boy who became a strong man had done so because goodness lived within him. He might not have ever left the mountain if his mother hadn't, and when he looked back over his life, the greatest joy he knew had come as a result of taking a risk. He couldn't change the past, but he could own it.

"Mama, do you know I call my shop the Caterina Shoe Company?"

Caterina's eyes filled with tears. "But I didn't do anything," she said sadly.

"It doesn't matter, Mama. Everything was for you. Everything."

Caterina poured Ciro a cup of coffee. She sat up straight. "Tell me about Enza." Caterina placed the bread and butter next to Ciro.

"She's beautiful and strong. Dark like the girls from Schilpario. Honest like them, too."

"Does she love beautiful things?"

"She creates beauty everywhere, Mama. She sews wool with the same care as she does satin. She's a good mother . . ." Ciro's voice trailed off.

"I want you to give Enza something from me. When your papa died, I sold everything. And I thought then that I only needed one thing to re-member my mother by. And I hoped that someday my sons would have a daughter, and it would go to her. But all I have heard about your wife leads me to believe that I've had a daughter all along." Caterina reached into her pocket and gave Ciro a velvet box. He opened it, and saw the blue cameo his mother had worn when he was a boy.

"She will like this very much, Mama."

"If I could give you the mountain for her, I would. But for now, this necklace will have to do." Caterina placed her hand on Ciro's; he let the soft warmth of her touch fill him up.

*   *   *

Enza waited at the harbor in lower Manhattan as the SS *Conte Grande* docked, and watched the passengers disembarking. When Ciro emerged from the gangplank, he looked handsome and robust. She waved to him.

Ciro made his way through the crowd and scooped Enza up in his arms. He kissed her a hundred times, and she him. As they walked to Colin's car, she told him about baby Henry, and how beautiful a boy he was, and how she had painted the nursery, sewed the layette, and taken care of Laura like a nurse.

Ciro told her about her parents, and the house in Schilpario—the house that Enza built. He told her it was yellow, and clean, and that it was high on the hill, set like a diamond in a crown. He told her about Eduardo and his mother, then reached into his coat and gave Enza a velvet box.

"From my mother," Ciro told her. "For the woman I love."

28

A SKYLIGHT

Un Lucernario

Ciro was able to work through the new year of 1932, but Luigi did most of the heavy lifting, and when long hours were required, he also picked up the slack. Ciro napped every afternoon, and could work at the table as long as he could sit, but standing was difficult.

Luigi tried to keep the chatter in the shop light, doing impressions of difficult customers and oddball salesmen to make Ciro laugh. Luigi also made sure the men came to play cards, as they had every Thursday since anyone could remember. Enza put out the grappa and the cigarettes as always, and late in the night would serve coffee and cake, but Ciro was getting worse, and everyone could see it. The poker games became shorter, but the players never acknowledged it.

Saint Patrick's Day was a big holiday in Chisholm because it held the promise of all things green, including the Minnesota spring. The bars on West Lake Street ran specials, and the stools were filled to overflowing, as the miners, from Eastern Orthodox to Lutheran, celebrated the Roman Catholic feastday.

That night, the din from the street was so loud, Enza closed the drapes in the front room and closed the bedroom door. She climbed on the stool and snapped the open skylight shut. "It's too cold, Ciro," she said as she placed another blanket over his body. He was growing thinner by the day.

"*Grazie*," he said. "What would I do without you?"

Enza lay in bed next to him. "You would have married the May Queen. What was her name?"

"I don't remember."

"Philomena? It sounded like that."

"I said, I don't remember," Ciro teased.

"Felicitá! That's it. The Sicilian bombshell. She would have made you buy her diamonds. No, no. That wouldn't have been good enough. She would have made you dig for them, and when you brought her the biggest stone, she'd look at it and say, 'I said a rock, Ciro. Not a pebble. A rock.' "

"You would have married Vito Blazek."

"I would have been his first wife. He's had three since."

"Really?"

"Laura keeps up with him. So see, you saved me from a life of glamour and sophistication. I was rescued by the shoemaker."

"I feel sorry for you," Ciro said.

"Don't you dare," Enza said, leaning over to kiss him. "I have my dream."

On his deathbed, Ciro realized he'd chosen Enza because she was strong alone; she did not *need* him, she *wanted* him. Enza had chosen Ciro, forsaking her own sense of security, which, he had come to know, was the need that drove her. Everything his wife did, and every decision she made, was about holding life together, and creating safety in a world where there was little.

Ciro was sad that he and Enza would never know what it might have been like to love each other their whole lives long, but the gift of what had been, the risks taken and endured, would have to be enough. They had received their portion. It was useless now to have hoped for more time.

But what about their son?

Ciro was bereft that his own son would live with the grief he had known all of his life. The loss of his own father had never left him.

A man needs his father more as life progresses, not less. It is not enough to learn how to use a lathe, milk a cow, repair a roof; there are greater holes to mend, deeper wells to fill, that only a father's wisdom can sustain. A father teaches his son how to think a problem through, how to lead a household, how to love his wife. A father sets an example for his son, building his character from the soul outward.

Ciro sought his father in the face of every man he met—Iggy at the convent, Remo in the shoe shop, and Juan Torres during the war. Each man gave what he could, but none of them, despite their best intentions, could be Carlo Lazzari.

In the last moments of his life Ciro realized that a truly good man is a rarity, a speck of gold in a mountain of slag. All around him during the war, Ciro saw men lie, engage in acts of cowardice, create feeble attachments to women, only to leave them—men acting in pursuit of their own comforts, men behaving without grace. And now Ciro was about to do to his son the terrible thing that had been done to him— die without raising him properly to adulthood. Ciro could not forgive himself for failing his son.

"Thank you for taking care of me, Enza."

She turned to him. "You've been a terrible patient."

Ciro laughed. "I know. Come and sit with me. I just want to look at you."

Enza sat next to Ciro on the bed. He reached out and took both of her hands. She closed her eyes and felt the warmth of them. Enza loved Ciro's beautiful hands; for all the hard labor he had done all of his life, he still had the long, lovely fingers of a musician or a painter.

His hands had created art. She had watched when he measured leather, suede, and silk, cut patterns, sewed shapes, and pressed the assembled boot he had sewn against the brushes. She could spend hours watching him make shoes. It was theater to her; every movement of his mastery had meaning and magic to it.

His hands had fed them. She had watched as he deftly carved *stelline* in delicate quick movements to make soup for their baby. Sometimes he made cheese, an elaborate operation that turned milk and rennet into ropes of mozzarella.

His hands had protected them. The hand that had first taken hers in the dark on the Passo Presolana was the same hand that eventually cradled her newborn son. The same hands that had encircled her body for the first time when she became his wife. "I'm going to miss your hands, Ciro. What will you miss?"

He looked up through the skylight, as if some bird would sail past with a ribbon in its beak, an aphorism written upon it in Latin, like the scrolls held by the cherubs over the tabernacle in San Nicola. Ciro knew what he would miss about this world, but he didn't want to share it with his wife. He didn't want to acknowledge that the life he loved so dearly and desperately was ending. But there was also part of him that wanted her to know. So he said, "I love the straight seam of a cut of good leather. I like to make shoes with my hands. I like the feeling when I've polished a pair of boots I've repaired and the lemon wax is fresh, and I look at the boots and think, I've made some fellow's long walk into that mine more comfortable. I'll miss making love to you, and knowing, after all these years, that there's always something new about your body that delights me all over again. I'll miss our son, because he reminds me of you."

"I want you to pray, Ciro."

"I can't."

"Please."

"When I was in France, I was talking with a man in my regiment that I respected so much. His name was Juan Torres, and he had a wife, and three daughters. He was Puerto Rican, and he talked a great deal about one of his girls, Margarita. He would tell stories about her, and we would laugh, and he would remember."

"You told me about him, honey. But you never told me how he died."

"One night, when we were talking, we could hear the grind of the tanks in the distance, and he stood up to see what was coming toward us. We were so involved in our conversation, he forgot he was in a trench, and that there was a war going on around us. He was just a father telling a story about the daughter he loved, as though we were at a bar, and passing time on any ordinary Friday night. I reached up to pull him back down, and he was shot.

"He died soon after, and I buried him. On my way to Rome after the war, I wrote to Margarita and told her that the last thing her father said was how much she delighted him. I can't pray to God to save myself, when others haven't the luxury."

"Papa." Antonio appeared in the doorway. He took in his mother and father, and a look of concern crossed his face. He didn't know whether to enter the room or run away, and a great part of him wanted to run. The moment Antonio had dreaded was approaching.

"There's room here." Ciro patted the side of the bed.

Antonio slipped off his shoes and lay next to his father. Enza reached across Ciro's frail body and held her son's hand. Ciro placed his hand on theirs.

This was the legacy of the only child: no matter how old he grew, there was always room in the bed for him. Antonio was the sole focus of the mother and father, as much a part of their relationship as they were for one another. Their small trinity had been sacrosanct, and it would always remain so. They had keenly observed their boy, and they had been better for it.

"Antonio, be good to your mother."

"I will."

"And take her home to the mountain. My brother will help you. Write to him."

"I will, Papa."

"Enza, you'll go home with our son?"

"Yes," she said softly.

"Good." Ciro smiled. "Antonio, I am proud of you."

"I know, Papa."

"And remember that I always will be. I can't believe that out of all the angels in heaven, God decided to send you to me. I'm the luckiest man you will ever meet."

Antonio nestled against his father, as he had when he was small. He buried his face in his father's neck, not thinking his father very lucky at all.

Enza got up and went to the kitchen. She lifted the sterile needles from the pot, filled the syringe with morphine, snapped the needle into place, and went back to her husband.

Antonio wept quietly into his father's shoulder now, as Ciro encircled his son with his arms to comfort him. Ciro was now so weak, he could barely hold his boy.

"I'm going to give Papa a shot, honey," Enza told her son. Antonio sat up and looked away, holding his father's hand. Antonio had not been able to abide the needles these last weeks, and was heartsick as his father needed them administered more and more.

Enza gently cleaned a patch of skin on what were once had been Ciro's muscular arm and administered the morphine. A look of serenity crossed her husband's face as the medicine took over.

Enza climbed back into bed with her husband and son, and gently ruffled Ciro's thick hair, now fringed with a few gray hairs at the temples.

"So many things I didn't do," Ciro whispered.

"You did everything right, my love," Enza told him.

"I never learned how to make women's shoes." He tried to smile.

"It doesn't matter. I never learned how to dance."

"It's not so great." He smiled.

Ciro did not speak again. He lived through that night. Enza administered the morphine through her tears. The chore she was loath to learn became the only thing she could hold on to as her husband slipped toward death. The routine of the boiling of the needles, pouring the liquid into the syringe, checking it, and walking it back to the bedroom had given her a purpose in the final days of Ciro's life. It made her feel useful, and it also made her feel that she was helping him as the morphine eased his pain.

That night, Antonio slept in the chair, facing his father in bed. Enza would check on her son as she watched Ciro sleep.

That night she cried about all the things she did not have. She had hoped for more children; as her husband lay dying, she realized that there should be more aspects of him in the world, not less. She had done the best she could, but in those hours, she did not believe it.

When the sun came up, she bathed her husband, cut his hair and nails, and gently shaved his face. She massaged his feet with lavender oil, and patted his face with a cool cloth. She lay beside him and listened as his heartbeat became more faint with each *tup, tup, tup.* She looked up through the skylight at dawn that morning, saw a pink sun in a blue sky, and took it as an omen.

Antonio woke up and sat bolt upright in the chair. "Mama?"

"Come," she said to her son.

Antonio climbed into the bed with his father and mother. He put his arm across his father's chest and, placing his cheek next to his father's, he began to cry.

Enza reached across, and with one hand on her son's face, she placed the other on Ciro's, leaned down, and put her lips to his ear. "Wait for me," were the last words Ciro Lazzari heard as he took his last breath.

March 18, 1932
Dear Don Eduardo,

This is the most difficult letter I have ever had to write. Your beloved brother Ciro died in my arms today at 5:02 a.m. Monsignor Schiffer came to anoint his body and administer last rites. Antonio was with us in the room when his father passed away.

Eduardo, my heart is full of so many feelings, and so many images and stories of things that Ciro told me about you. I hope you know that he looked up to you, and if ever an example of piety and honesty was needed in any situation, Ciro would always look to you.

I wish you could be here for the funeral. Already, the stairs up to our home are filled with flowers; I had to create a path to navigate them. The veterans hung a flag outside our house, and the drum and bugle corps played on the street when they heard he was gone.

Your brother made me the happiest woman that ever lived. I had loved him since I was fifteen years old, and the years did not diminish the depth of my feelings. I cannot imagine life without him, so I humbly beg you to please pray for me, as I will for you, and your mother. Please share this terrible news with her, and send her my deepest condolences.

Your sister-in-law,
Enza

29

A PAIR OF ICE SKATES
Un Paio di Pattini da Ghiaccio

Enza pulled on her gloves as she stood next to the Chisholm ice rink and watched as Antonio sailed on the outskirts of the silver ice with such dexterity, it looked as though he was building up speed to fly. The dark woods beyond the rink hemmed the oasis of ice lit by the bright white floodlights. It was as though the full moon had embedded itself in the ground of the north woods. The scent of roasted chestnuts and buttery baked sweet potatoes filled the air.

Every teenager in Chisholm seemed to be at the rink that night, skating to popular music piped over the ice. The kids spun to "The Music Goes Round and Round" by Tommy Dorsey; waltzed to "These Foolish Things" by Benny Goodman and created a daisy chain; and snaked around the rink to "Moon Over Miami" by Eddy Duchin.

Enza purchased a roasted sweet potato from a girl who was raising money for the high school band. She unwrapped the tin foil and took a bite without taking her eyes off her son.

Antonio was seventeen, at the top of his class at Chisholm High School, but every bit as athletic as he was brilliant at his studies. Skates felt as natural to his body as snow skis. Even the slow sport of curling—"chess on the ice," Antonio called it—was mastered. His basketball skills were famous throughout the Iron Range, and he was in line for scholarships to attend university.

At the age of forty-one, Enza could look back over her life confident that she had raised her son well, especially under the circumstances. She knew Ciro would be proud of their son. It had been five years since her husband died, and yet it seemed as though it was yesterday.

Enza wrestled with the promise she had made to Ciro to return to the mountain to raise Antonio among family and friends in the Alps. She gave it serious consideration, but the world had changed quickly in the months after Ciro's death. Italy was in the midst of political tumult, and it would not have been prudent to take her American son back to where she came from. Observing the social changes in her homeland, she knew she had made the right decision to stay in Minnesota. She chose America because it had been good to them.

Enza was loyal to the town Ciro had chosen for them, and business was steady. She did alterations for the department stores and built wedding gowns, coats, and dresses for the ladies of Chisholm. She sewed draperies, slipcovers, and layettes. Customers marveled at her skill and returned time and again.

Luigi ran the shoe shop alone. The constant flow of company provided by the Latinis, especially Pappina, but also their sons and Angela, who was now nearly ten years old, had been a tonic for Enza. Only when she climbed the stairs and closed her bedroom door at night did her loneliness at the loss of Ciro consume her. Eventually her tears stopped, giving way to a dull ache that Enza accepted as the natural pain of widowhood, one for which there was no cure.

Antonio skated by, grinning and waving at his mother. Enza leaned against the wall and watched as Betsy Madich, also seventeen, in a short red velvet skating skirt, white tights, and a matching sweater, took Antonio's hands and skated with him. Enza smiled, remembering when the pair had gone roller skating together down West Lake Street when they were children.

Antonio was madly in love with Betsy, a willowy Serbian beauty with her mother's chestnut hair and blue eyes. She planned to attend nursing school at the University of Minnesota, one of the schools where Antonio hoped to play basketball. Enza had many talks with her son about girls, but she always found them difficult. During those conversations, she felt Ciro's absence like a missing limb. Sometimes she even felt annoyed at her husband for leaving her behind to raise their son alone. It seemed that she needed Ciro more as time went by, not less.

Antonio and Betsy skated over to the wall where Enza stood.

"Mama," Antonio said, "I'd like to go Betsy's after skating."

"Mom is making *povitica*," Betsy added.

"Aren't you going to help Mr. Uncini flood the rink?"

"Yeah. After that, I'd like to go to Betsy's."

"Okay. You have your key?"

"Yes, Ma."

"Not too late, *va bene*?"

"*Va bene*, Mama." Antonio winked at his mother. Her native Italian had become a secret language between them. When they closed the door at 5 West Lake Street, mother and son spoke as though she had never left the mountain.

Later that night, Mr. Uncini, nicknamed "Oonch," played "Goodnight, Irene" and closed the rink for the night. The teenagers piled into their cars to go home, or to Choppy's Pizza, which had just opened on Main Street.

"Clear the ice for me, Antonio," Mr. Uncini said.

Antonio lifted a long-handled wire broom from the storage bin next to the rink and skated in a circular pattern, clearing the loose shavings and chunks of ice off the rink. While Antonio smoothed the surface as best he could, Mr. Uncini unspooled the fire hose.

Antonio came off the ice and removed his skates. He pulled on his work boots and helped Mr. Uncini crank the wheel to release water onto the rink. Flooding the rink took some time. Antonio would sit with his father's old friend and talk.

"How are you doing in school?" Mr. Uncini asked.

"Great except for calculus. I might get a B," Antonio said.

"You're getting serious with Betsy."

"Have you been talking to my mom?"

"I have eyes, Antonio."

"I'd like to marry her someday."

"That's pretty serious."

"Not yet. After college."

"That's a good plan. A lot of things will change in four years. It's a lifetime."

"That's what Mama says."

"You know, your father came to see me before he died. And now that you're going off to college, I think there are some things I should tell you. You know, he wanted me to look out for you."

"And you always have, Oonch."

"I hope I haven't been too obvious."

"You cried when I sang 'Panis Angelicus' at Saint Joseph's—that was pretty obvious."

"I just wanted you to know I was standing in for your father. It's not the same, I know, but I promised him I would be there for you."

"What was he like, Oonch? Mama cries when I ask her. I remember a lot about him, but I wonder what I would think of him now that I'm older."

"He was a decent man. But he loved to have fun. He was ambitious, but not to the extreme. I liked him because he was a true Italian."

"What's a true Italian?"

"He loved his family and he loved beauty. For a true Italian, those are the only two things that matter, because in the end that's what sustains you. Your family gathers around and shores you up while the beauty uplifts you. Your father was devoted to your mother. He made boots like I make scrambled eggs. You'd be talking to him, and he'd be measuring and pinning pattern paper on a sleeve of leather, and in no time, he was sewing and then polishing and buffing. It was as if it was nothing. But it was hard work."

Antonio looked out over the ice as Mr. Uncini turned the water pump off by cranking the wheel in reverse. The clear water had settled above the old layer of blue ice, filling in every pit and crack. The air was so cold, the surface had already begun to harden, making patterns that under the lights looked like lace. The woods were quiet, and once the water was turned off, there was no sound.

Antonio's nose burned, and tears came to his eyes as he thought about his father, and how he'd gone around Chisholm, hat in hand, asking his friends to fill in for the times to come when he could not be there. The realization of this made Antonio long for his father and miss him more. He wiped his tears on his sleeve as he closed the gate to the rink.

"You all right?" Mr. Uncini asked.

"Just cold," Antonio answered.

. . . .

"You are six-three, Antonio," Dr. Graham said, scribbling on the report. "You weigh two hundred and fifteen pounds, all muscle." The doctor chuckled. "Have you decided where you're going to go to school?"

"The University of Minnesota offered me a four-year scholarship."

"Of course they did."

"But I'm going to Notre Dame."

"Good for you."

"I want to play professionally once I graduate."

The phone rang in Dr. Graham's office. "I'm on my way." He hung up the phone. "Antonio, please, go get your mother. Tell her Pappina Latini is in the hospital."

Antonio ran a mile swiftly; in a matter of minutes, he'd pushed the shop door open, called for his mother, and told her to come with him to the hospital. By the time they made it up the hill, Luigi and his children were in the waiting room. They were holding one another, weeping. Angela let out a wail, and called out for her mother.

"What happened, Luigi?" Enza put her hands on his shoulder.

"She's gone, Enza. She's gone. There was trouble with the baby and they tried to save her, and they couldn't. Pappina never came out of it . . . and our baby son died."

Pappina was a year or two younger than Enza, and this baby had been a surprise. Pappina had been going through the change of life early, and hadn't thought creating another life was possible. But the Latinis had been as happy with the news as they had the first four times. Enza, who had prayed for years for a sibling for Antonio, was always profoundly touched by the way Pappina included her at the heart of every pregnancy. Pappina never made a fuss, but she somehow drew Enza into the circle of happiness with her, involving Enza in every aspect of the new baby's life, so Enza might be filled up with joy despite her longing.

After leaving the hospital and ensuring that Luigi was capable of handling the final arrangements, Enza took the Latini children back to 5 West Lake Street with her. John Latini was eighteen and an apprentice in the shop. The older boys were stoic, but Angela could not stop crying for her mother. As they walked along the sidewalk beneath the bare winter trees, Enza tried to comfort them.

"Children come to us in many ways," she remembered Pappina saying. The thought sent a chill through her.

At home, Enza cooked for the Latini family, Antonio and John led them in games to distract them, and later on, Enza bathed Angela and prepared her school clothes. It was, of course, the least she could do for all the Latinis had done for her and Antonio when Ciro died. The children had always called her Zenza, a combination of Zia and Enza, and most of them had spent as many nights under her roof, playing with Antonio, as they had under their own.

Pappina's funeral was held four days later in a standing-room-only mass at St. Joseph's. Pappina had been beloved in the community, a wonderful baker, a beautiful wife and mother. Luigi was bereft at the loss of his wife and new baby. His life would never be the same, nor would his heart.

Each of her children took a turn reading the scripture. Enza knew her friend would have been very proud of her children that day.

Enza slowly eased the younger family back into their routine. After a few weeks, she moved them back to the Latini house, showing the boys how to do their own laundry and prepare meals.

Angela watched Enza carefully, and tried to do chores as her mother had done. Cleaning was not difficult, but cooking and baking for the entire family were too much for a child only ten years old, and she grew frustrated at the challenge. Enza stepped in and made the meals. She arranged to have the children come only on the weekends for lunch, and made sure they went to church on Sundays.

One morning, Enza had opened the shop and was sewing in the back. Luigi came in, and called out to her. He began to repair shoes as he had every morning. But something was different about him that day. He put down his tools, went back to the sewing workroom, and sat in front of Enza.

"I'm going back to Italy," he said.

"Luigi, it's too soon to make any decisions."

"No, I'm going to do it."

"You can't run away from what happened to you."

"I can't bear it. I want to start over. And the only way I can do that is go back to the beginning."

"But your children!"

"I'm going to take the boys with me."

"But what about Angela?"

"I was hoping you would take her. I don't know what to do with a girl," he cried. "She needs a mother."

Enza sat back in her chair. She understood Luigi's concern. In the coming year or two, Angela would begin adolescence. Without a mother in the home, there would be no one to guide her in the matters of womanhood.

Antonio was leaving for Notre Dame in the spring, to begin training for the basketball team. Enza would be alone, and now, if Luigi left for Italy, she would have to rent the workroom out.

"Leave her with me," Enza said. "I'll take care of her."

"*Grazie*, Enza. *Grazie*."

"Pappina would have done the same for me." Enza was sure of it.

*   *   *

Enza prepared the spare room for Angela. She painted it pink, sewed a white chenille coverlet, and made lampshades with some leftover chintz. She made sure that Angela had photographs of her mother, father, and brothers on the dresser. Knowing what it was like to live in someone else's home, Enza vowed that she would make Angela comfortable and secure; it would be nothing like her own experience in Hoboken with the Buffa family.

Enza went to the school to make certain that the teachers were aware of Angela's needs. Angela stayed in her room a lot, but that was to be expected. The ten-year-old girl was making the transition from life with a big family to the serenity of the Lazzari home. Luckily she had been in and out of the shop all of her life, and had many happy memories of shared holidays upstairs in the Lazzari apartment. Enza checked on her, and would find Angela reading, or sitting quietly and looking off in the middle distance. It was heartbreaking for Enza; she understood every nuance of what the little girl was feeling. At least Enza knew her mother was alive, and she could write to her. Angela did not have that luxury.

One Sunday afternoon, Enza was making pasta in the kitchen when she heard singing. Enza smiled, happy that Angela felt comfortable enough to play the phonograph without asking.

As the recording continued, Enza realized that the orchestra was not joining in after the first a cappella stanza. A single voice continued to cut through the quiet. Enza stopped kneading the pasta dough, wiped her hands on the moppeen, and followed the sound down the hallway. Enza moved toward Angela's room, then stopped, frozen by what she saw. Angela was singing. Enza had not heard a voice like it since Geraldine Farrar back at the Met.

Angela did not slide into a note as she sang, she hit it and held it. The crystal quality of her tone was natural and God given. Enza closed her eyes and followed the sound, picturing the moment she first heard the same aria at the Met years earlier. Enza stepped away and listened until Angela finished singing the phrase, then tiptoed back to the kitchen.

.   .   .

Enza pulled on her coat and gloves and her best hat and walked up West Lake Street for her appointment with Miss Robin Homonoff, Chisholm's only piano and voice teacher. Her first name was not written out on the mailbox, rather it was a sketch of a tweeting bird.

Miss Homonoff answered the door. She had soft gray hair, and was in every way prim. She invited Enza to sit in the parlor by the baby grand Steinway piano, the only shiny object in her blue cottage.

"I want to talk to you about Angela Latini," Enza began.

"I think she has talent. If she begins to study now with me in earnest, and works very hard, I think she could be a professional singer someday."

"I think she sounds like Geraldine Farrar."

"You studied opera?"

"I worked at the Metropolitan Opera when I was a girl."

"You sang?"

"Sewed. But I love music, and I think this would be good for her. She's endured a lot in her young life, and I think this would give her confidence."

"We'll get started right away, then." Miss Homonoff extended her hand.

"How much are the lessons?"

"Not one penny. In a matter of months, she'll be teaching me, Mrs. Lazzari; that's how good she is."

Miss Homonoff closed the door and smiled. She lived for these moments, when raw talent was entrusted to her to refine and shape. She would make a world class soprano out of Angela Latini.

·   ·   ·

Angela knelt in the living room at 5 West Lake Street. She fiddled with the dial on the radio until WNDU out of South Bend, Indiana, came through clear and sharp without static. Enza shook the pan on the stove in the kitchen, and soon the popcorn was crackling inside. She held the lid down as the puffs exploded.

"Hurry, Zenza! Antonio is in the starting five!"

Enza threw the popcorn into a bowl, and just as they had every Saturday since the Notre Dame basketball season had begun, she and Angela listened to the game on the radio. Notre Dame was playing Army in South Bend.

Angela and Enza listened as Antonio scored. They laughed because the announcer mispronounced Lazzari. Angela corrected the announcer. "I know he can't hear me," Angela said, her eyes flashing. "But I wish he could."

·   ·   ·

When Antonio graduated with honors from Notre Dame in 1940, Veda Ponikvar, the editor of the *Chisholm Free Press*, wrote a profile about him, with his picture. The headline read:

HIS FATHER'S SON

As soon as Antonio arrived home to Chisholm with his diploma, a letter from the draft board was waiting for him. Antonio was summoned to appear with his mother in Hibbing. Angela was in school when Enza took the trolley with Antonio to Hibbing. She had a heavy heart, knowing that her son would be sent to fight in the second world war. She thought of the stories Ciro had told her about the Great War, and she couldn't help but feel that history was repeating itself. She tried not to show her apprehension to Antonio, but it couldn't be helped.

"I've called you here today because you're in a unique situation." Corporal Robert Vukad looked at Enza, then Antonio, in the small, spare storefront office on the main street of Hibbing.

"I understand that your father served in the Great War. You're the only son in the family, and your mother is a widow. We don't have to send you into action. In fact, you can be exempt from it entirely. It's the government's way of holding families under these circumstances together."

"I want to be in the war, sir. I want to serve my country. I don't want to be benched."

"Your mother may disagree with you. Mrs. Lazzari?"

Enza wanted to tell the officer that she wanted her son to take the exemption. As a mother, she couldn't imagine offering her only son to the war. She had already lived through the loss of her husband; the thought of losing her son as well was devastating. Enza looked at Antonio, who had the calm confidence that begat courage. So instead of taking the offer, she said quietly, "Sir, my son goes like every other young man. He should not be exempt from the war to take care of me. It means more to me as a mother that he wants to emulate his father. It means he understands the great debt we have to this country."

"I'll be all right, Mama."

Enza and Antonio walked back to the trolley from the recruitment office. They didn't say much on the ride back to Chisholm, and walked in silence from the trolley station. Enza's heart was heavy as she unlocked the door. Antonio pushed the door open. The scent of tomato and basil gravy simmering on the stove permeated the hallway.

"Angela?" Enza called out.

"I made dinner, come on up!" she hollered.

Enza and Antonio entered the kitchen. The table was set with a cloth, candles, and china. Antonio's girlfriend, Betsy—beautiful and collegiate in a Pendleton wool skirt, blouse, and loafers who was home from nursing school—was tossing the salad, wearing an apron.

Angela, now fourteen, had tied a moppeen around her head and wore faded blue jeans and one of Antonio's old jerseys. "Sorry," she apologized to Enza. "I didn't have time to change. And I didn't want to get tomato sauce on my good blouse."

Betsy put her arm around Angela. "I told her she was beautiful just as she is."

Antonio kissed Betsy. "And so are you."

That night, they feasted on spaghetti pomodoro, fresh salad, and chocolate cake. They told stories of the ice rink, high school basketball games, and the night Betsy fell in the dance competition during Serbian Days. Enza sat back and watched her son, taking in every detail of him, wishing the night would never end and praying he would be very, very lucky and return home safely to her someday.

.   .   .

Antonio shipped out from New Haven with the navy the following summer. He called his mother the night before. She buckled under the anxiety of his decision, and hers. She fretted so much, and so deeply, that within a year of Antonio's leaving, her raven hair had turned quickly and completely white.

Month after month, she waited for Antonio's letters, opening them as soon as they were placed in her hands. She'd remove a hair clasp from her head, then rip open the envelope with the sharp metal end. After poring over the words a dozen times, she would carry each letter in her apron pocket until the next letter arrived. The most recent letter he sent had given her cause for concern. He spoke of his father in it, which he had never done before.

February 15, 1943
My dearest Mama,
    I can't tell you exactly where I am, but every morning all I

*see is blue. It's hard to believe that something so beautiful could
hide the enemy with such depth and dexterity.*

*I have been thinking of Papa a lot. I miss you terribly, and
don't like that you are alone in Chisholm. Mama, when I come
home, let's go to your mountain. I want to see the fields of Schilpario and see the convent where Papa lived. He wanted us to
go, and we should. Please don't cry yourself to sleep. I am safe
and with a good regiment, very smart fellows. There are recruits
from the University of Minnesota, a few from Texas, others from
Mississippi, and one fellow from North Dakota who we call No
Dak. He tells long-winded stories about the history of the moose
in middle America. Sometimes we tell him we can't take it, and
other times, we just let him talk. It's almost like the radio.*

I love you Mama, you have my heart, and I will be home soon,

Antonio

P.S. Give Angela a hug for me.

*   *   *

Enza put aside her alterations, neatly folding a coat from Blomquist's.

She checked the mailbox each morning, hoping for word from her
son. When no letter came, she pulled on her coat and took the long walk
up the street to the post office building to check the rosters of the war
dead. She was not alone in this habit; every mother in Chisholm with a
son or daughter in the war did the same, though they would pretend to
be running an errand, or dropping off a package. But when one mother
looked into the eyes of another, she knew.

*   *   *

In the spring of 1944, Laura Heery Chapin returned to Chisholm, Minnesota. Her son Henry was in boarding school, and Laura was free to
accompany Colin around the country, as he was now in charge of production for the Metropolitan Opera's road companies.

As soon as Angela was accepted to the Institute of Musical Art,
Enza had called her old friend, who was going to be in Chicago for the

opening of *La Traviata*. Laura had agreed to visit and take Angela safely back with her to New York City, because that's what friends were for.

Laura was still tall, slim, and grand, though her red hair had faded to a shiny auburn. Her suit was Mainbocher, and even her suitcases had style, French made and Italian trimmed.

"I wish Colin's mother could see you now. She would say you were to the manor born."

"Probably not. She'd think that I should've chosen white gloves instead of blue."

"Hasn't Chisholm grown since your last visit?"

"I think it's not Hoboken."

Enza and Laura laughed. Through the years, whenever they liked something, they would say, "At least it's not Hoboken."

"But you know, this is where Colin came to claim me. It will always be a special place to me."

Enza smiled and remembered the exact place she had stood on Carmine Street when Ciro came for her on the sidewalk in front of Our Lady of Pompeii. It's funny how a woman remembers exactly where she stood when she was chosen.

"Miss Homonoff sent quite a letter to the Institute. She believes your goddaughter is a talented soprano."

"We brought her down to the Twin Cities, and the professors at the University of Minnesota agreed. Laura, she would never be able to go to New York if you weren't there."

"I'm lonely with Henry away at school. You're giving me a gift."

"Oh, Laura, she's so shy sometimes. She misses her mother, and there's nothing I can do to comfort her. It brings up all my feelings about home and how much I miss my family. Her father and brothers are in Italy, and she's afraid for them. They're unfounded fears, but they're real to her."

"Angela needs to focus on her work. You and I made it because we stayed busy and we had goals. Look, she can live with me and walk across the park to her classes at the Institute. Colin is close to the dean. We'll make her feel at home."

"Is it all too easy?" Enza said worriedly.

"You just said the kid has had a terrible childhood. I didn't say she could come to New York and nap. She'll have to work hard, but why can't we give her that little bit of security we know she needs? Didn't Miss DeCoursey give it to us at the Milbank? How many times did we fret about the rent, and she'd give us a few extra days to go and wash dishes? I won't pamper Angela, but I can encourage her—and she can learn. I'll be her Emma Fogarty. I'll make the connections for her like Emma did for us."

Enza took a deep breath. Every fear she had for her ward was now assuaged. The truth was, she trusted Laura with her life, and with anyone that she loved. "What would my life have been, had we never met?"

"I have a feeling you would have been just fine." Laura embraced her old friend for a long time. "I, on the other hand, would have been in a suite at Bellevue, eating crushed bananas, singing 'Tico Tico' on a loop."

. . .

Enza and Laura sat on the shore of Longyear Lake, sipping wine in paper cups while they ate figs and cheese Enza had wrapped in a starched moppeen.

"This is when I miss Ciro. You know, we're at the stage of life where things get quiet, and when you're a widow, that silence is painful."

"I think of you when I want to push Colin out the window."

"Enjoy him."

"Come and stay with us!"

"I do miss New York. I'm sorry so much time has passed without a visit. But now I'm waiting for Antonio to come home, and when he does, I can make some big decisions, and one of them will be to come and see you for a nice long visit."

"I have a bedroom for you. We could go to the opera every night of the week. Colin has a box."

"The diamond horseshoe."

"Can you imagine? Remember the first time we walked in there? And now I sit up there and I complain if I can't see the stage-left wings from my seat. And back then, we would have scrubbed floors to be anywhere in the building. And we did! But ultimately we didn't have to, because you were an artist and could sew better than any machine. And it didn't hurt that you were Italian. That went so far in the opera house—as it should."

"I still play Caruso's records."

"You cooked for Caruso. I washed his dishes! The man would not eat raw tomatoes." Laura clapped her hands together. "We've lived in the days of Caruso at the Met."

"I wonder what he'd say if he saw my white hair."

"He would have said, 'Vincenza, you may have white hair, but I will always be older than you.' "

"You know, whenever I pick up a pen, I think of you. You taught me how to read and write English. You never got impatient and snapped at me."

"You were so smart, I worried you'd teach me a thing or two about grammar."

"No, it was the most generous thing anyone's ever done for me. You have a way of finding out what people need and giving it to them."

"All you needed is what every girl needs, a good friend. Someone to talk to, to share with, to run things by . . . You were always that person for me."

"I hope I always will be."

"As long as there are telephones." Laura laughed.

*   *   *

Angela walked to her classes at the Institute of Musical Art carrying her sheet music in a newspaper boy's burlap tote which she wore across her body. The sun in late March was hot, but the air was cool. She hummed as she walked, imagining the musical notes of her audition piece in succession, visiualizing them in her mind's eye, and rehearsing as she went. Whenever she reached a crosswalk and the trolley would speed by, clanking on the tracks, drowning out all sound, Angela would practice her high register and test her vocal power by singing her scales as loudly as she could.

Heads turned as Angela walked; young men would whistle, but she didn't hear them. Her long black hair ruffled in the breeze as did her long pleated skirt which she wore with bobby socks and Capezio flats. She didn't need lipstick, as her lips were deep pink without it. Like her unstudied, effortless beauty, singing came naturally. Angela was a delicate soprano, known in her class for her perfect pitch and crystal tone.

Angela was a small-town girl. She lacked the sophistication, and therefore the cunning, of her fellow students. She didn't fight for the best parts, but was happy to be in the chorus. She sang because it was a gift, not because she wanted to gain something more from it. Singing made her feel close to her mother, who had sung to her. Music was a way of holding on to Pappina.

The Institute was housed in the Vanderbilt family guest house on East 52nd Street. Angela loved the marble entry; shades of deep cherry and pink offset by slashes of black reminded her of the inside of a candy box. The auditorium, where Angela took lessons in Vocal Technique, Dramatic Expression, and Italian for Singers, was stately, but small. It could have fit on the stage of the Metropolitan Opera House.

Angela handed her sheet music to Frances Shapiro, the rehearsal pianist, and her closest friend. Frances was a lean, stylish young woman of twenty-two with light brown hair and a wide grin who played for the voice classes at the Institute. She attended Brooklyn College at night to study secretarial science. Frances laid the sheet music across the piano. As she began to play the introduction to *Batti, batti bel Masetto* from *Don Giovanni*, Angela took the stage and stood before her, closed her eyes, opened her hands, stood up straight, and lifted her chin, singing out to the back of the theater. Frances smiled and nodded as Angela hit every note. Angela's high soprano was like a cool breeze through an open window.

"How was it?" Angela asked.

"Professor Kirshenbaum is going to be amazed."

"I hope so. I need his recommendation."

"Sing like that, and you'll get it," Frances assured her.

Angela Latini left the Institute and went for coffee as she often did at the end of the day. She used the time to study and write letters. Her father and brothers received a long letter every week. She sat in the window of the Automat and opened a notebook. Her long dark hair was tied back with a silk scarf. She tucked her full skirt around her, and buttoned her sweater.

"You were splendid in there today," Frances said, dropping her purse on the table as she stood eyeing the pie selection. "I mean, never better."

"Thanks. I have to be. I need a letter from Professor Kirshenbaum to get into La Scala."

"Have you told your aunt yet?"

"It would crush her if she thought I wasn't coming back to Minnesota."

"The sooner you tell her, the better."

"I want to be near my dad and my brothers. They're all I have left." Angela still could not think of Pappina without becoming emotional. She wondered if she would ever be able to move forward, and there were times when she doubted it. Angela's talent was inborn and natural, and therefore she valued it only as a gift, and not with a sense of purpose. She loved to sing, but she would have gladly traded this ability to have her mother back. Zenza had done her best, but she too had a hard time figuring out how to make this lonely little girl happy, and now that Angela was grown, she felt it was her own responsibility to seek happiness in any way that she could.

"When are you going to tell her?"

"Once her son comes home."

"She has a son? Is he single?" Frances sat up in her seat like a curious hen.

"He's had a girlfriend all of his life. He's so handsome. And older."

"I like older."

"Not for anything, Frances, but I think you like all ages."

"As long as he's Jewish."

"You're out of luck—this one's a Catholic."

"I will entertain the idea of bending the rules, even if my parents won't." Frances threw her head back and laughed. "Where is he?"

"He's fighting in the Pacific theater."

Frances's face clouded over. She knew many boys from her neighborhood in Brooklyn who had been drafted and were in the South Pacific. "Oh, Angela . . . " Frances said softly.

"Don't even say it. I know. He'll be lucky if he makes it home." Angela sighed.

"You can't live your life to make anyone happy, including your honorary aunt who took you in. You need to be with your family."

"I know." Angela sipped her coffee. "But first I have to decide what a family is."

"Or maybe you'll do what every Shapiro, Nachmanoff, and Pomerance has done since the beginning of time: you'll invent it."

Laura lit the candles in the Tiffany holders on the mantel in the soft green and beige living room of her Park Avenue penthouse. The city lights twinkled below, beyond the black pool of Central Park, like a collection of small stars in the distance. In the years that the Chapins had lived in the apartment, the lights around the park had multiplied. The neighborhood borders of Manhattan had swelled—more people, better business, and more seats sold at the Metropolitan Opera House.

Angela, wearing a chiffon chemise, her long hair grazing her waist, sat at her vanity table in the guest room where she had lived since she became a student at The Institute of Musical Art.

She brushed her long hair, leaned forward, and applied a pale pink lipstick to her mouth. Angela was a southern Italian beauty, brown-eyed with waves of dark hair and a trim figure with curves like carved marble.

Laura swept into Angela's room and gave her a bracelet to wear. Angela thanked her as she put it on her arm. "It works on you. Keep it."

It occurred to Laura as she looked at Angela's reflection that she possessed the natural elegance that Enza Ravanelli always had, even in the tenements of Hoboken. Angela was graceful, she spoke well, directly and softly; she was helpful when called upon, yet assertive when she needed to be. Her second mother had taught her well.

Angela had been a delight in every way for Laura. With Henry now in college, Angela had filled the quiet as she rehearsed at the piano, singing scales and mastering phrases for her singing classes at the Institute. In Enza's absence, Laura went to Angela's recitals and rehearsals. She consulted with Angela's professors and made sure she got extra attention when she needed it.

Colin had made sure Angela had a job in the ticket office and ushered during performances, so she might have exposure to the full menu of what it took to present an opera. Angela would never take the Chapins for granted, or their generosity.

Laura had exposed Angela to a world she would have never known had she stayed on the Iron Range. She took Angela shopping and to parties for the board of the Met. She introduced Angela to all the star points of a gracious life. Angela's natural talent and regal bearing had only made her more humble and grateful for the opportunities Laura presented. Angela had been a good student.

The doorbell rang.

"Angela, will you get that?" Laura called out.

"Yes, Aunt Laura," Angela called back. She took one last look in the mirror before she opened the door, smoothing her hair over her ear and adjusting the pearl on the drop necklace she wore with her gown.

Angela's heart beat fast when she opened the door to see Antonio Lazzari standing in the doorway in his dress uniform. He pushed his hat off his forehead and then removed it. His dark good looks were dazzling against the bright white of his uniform.

"I'm looking for Mrs. Chapin," he said, taking in the beautiful girl from the top of her head to the tips of her silk moiré shoes.

Angela put her hands on her hips. "Antonio," she chided him. "It's *me.*"

He heard her voice and remembered. He squinted. "Angela?"

"Who else?" She threw her arms around his neck.

"What happened to you?"

"I grew a foot and got into the Institute of Musical Art. And then I learned to sing high notes." She laughed. "And hold them."

"That's just the beginning of what's different about you."

Laura rushed to the door to greet Antonio.

"Aunt Laura!" Antonio embraced her.

"Welcome to New York."

"You didn't tell Mama, did you?" Antonio asked.

"Not one word. But you have to call her. Right now."

·   ·   ·

Enza went through the apartment, making sure all the skylights were snapped shut. A thunderstorm was raging outside. The lightning streaking through the sky cast an eerie green glow over Chisholm.

Enza wrapped her robe tightly around her. She'd had a bad feeling all day, convinced that Antonio had come into harm's way in the Pacific. The more she tried to distract herself, the worse her anxiety became.

She heated milk on the stove, poured it into a cup, added some brandy and a pat of butter. She said a quick prayer for her mother, who used to make her the drink, then took the mug and went back to her room.

Sitting up in bed, she watched the storm through the skylight, slowly sipping the warm milk and brandy. Soon she became tired, put out the lamp, and placed the cup on the nightstand.

Enza dreamed of her family. She was fifty-one years old in the dream, the age she turned on her last birthday, but her brothers and sisters were small. Stella was in the dream, as were her mother and father.

Giacomina came through the door of the house on Via Scalina with a bouquet of white daisies and pink asters from the cliffs on the mountain. It was an enormous bunch of flowers, beautiful, fresh, fragrant.

"I will see you again, my Enza," her mother said.

"Where are you going, Mama?"

"I have a place now, and I must go."

"But you can't leave me, Mama."

"Keep these flowers and think of me."

The phone rang on the nightstand. Enza sat up in bed, clutching her chest at the shock of the loud ring.

"Enza? It's Eliana. Mama died this morning."

Enza paced through the house alone, wishing that she were in Schilpario with her family, angry that she hadn't braved the ocean and brought Antonio to the mountain as she had promised Ciro, and brokenhearted at the loss of her mother.

Life was changing again, and there was nothing she could do to stop it. The loss of one's mother was devastating, and echoed in every chamber of her heart.

The phone rang. Enza leaped for it.

"Mama?"

"Antonio!" The only balm for Enza in this moment of loss was her son's voice, and it had been sent to her.

"What's wrong, Mama?"

"Your Nonna Ravanelli died, honey."

"I'm sorry."

"She loved you, Antonio."

Antonio swallowed. He had never met his grandmother and now he never would. He had been halfway around the world, and yet he had never been to the mountain.

"I'm in New York, Mama. I'm home. Stateside. Safe as can be."

Waves of relief rushed over Enza. Every nerve within her released, and she had to sit down. "When will I see you?"

"Mama, I've never been to New York. Aunt Laura and Angela want to show me the town."

"Good, good, make sure they take you to the opera."

"I will. Mama, what can I bring you?"

"Just you."

"That's easy, Mama."

"Let me know when you've made your plans. Should I call Betsy?"

"Oh, Mama, I didn't write to tell you. She fell in love with a doctor in Minneapolis and married him."

"I'm sorry, honey."

"No, no, it's all right, Mama. I'm fine with it. I just want to come home and see my favorite girl."

Enza wept for joy. This terrible day had just become wonderful, with one phone call from her soldier son.

Enza went into the kitchen, cleared the table, and began to make fresh pasta. She needed to *do* something, before getting on the phone and calling everyone from Ida and Emilio Uncini to Veda Ponikvar to Monsignor Schiffer. Everything felt wonderful in her hands, the silky flour, the eggs—the well was deep as she kneaded the dough. She delighted in the textures as she never had before.

She played the radio as she worked, leaving fingerprints of flour on the dial when she raised the volume. She was thrilled when a recording of "Mattinata" sung by Enrico Caruso poured out of the cloth speakers. It was a sign—everything good was a sign; the war was over, Antonio was coming home, he was alive, he had made it through, he'd done the right thing and it had paid off, for him, his character, and the country of his birth. Her mother had kept Antonio safe for her. She was sure of it now. There were no coincidences.

If only Ciro had been here to share this day with her. He knew exactly how to manage sadness, and he knew how to embrace joy. If only he were here.

⋅   ⋅   ⋅

Enza set about freshening up the house. She opened the skylights and let in the spring breezes as she changed the sheets, scrubbed the floors, put out plants and photographs, and made the entire place shine. She flipped the sign on the shop door every day at lunch and locked up. The sign read, "Back in one hour," and everyone in Chisholm knew exactly where she was; Enza went up and down West Lake Street buying all the ingredients to prepare Antonio's favorite foods and returning home to prepare them. She baked anisette cookies, rolled fresh skeins of linguini, baked bread, and made his favorite chicken pastina soup. She was sure he would be thin, and as anxious as she was for him to come home, she was happy that Laura and Angela were showing him New York, which gave her an extra week to prepare for his homecoming.

"Mama!" Antonio took his mother in his arms, after the four longest years of her life. She kissed her son's face over and over again, unable to believe her good fortune.

"Mama, I got married," Antonio said.

"What?" Enza put her hand over her mouth. She imagined a war bride, an Asian beauty, a girl rescued from an island, a place that Antonio found enchanting and therefore wanted to possess forever in a romantic way. "Where did you get married?"

"In New York."

"Well, where is she?" Enza's happiness turned to trepidation.

"She's downstairs."

"Well, I'd love to meet her." Enza's heart raced. She had not counted on this. What if she wasn't a wonderful girl? What if he'd married his version of Vito Blazek? What if, in the thrill of having made it through the war, he simply snap-judged the biggest decision of a person's life? She couldn't imagine it. And yet as she turned to go down the stairs to meet her new daughter-in-law, she remembered that Ciro had raced from the pier to the Milbank House to the church to claim her before she married another man. War, evidently, makes a man think and spins the hands of a clock speedily as if the inner springs are broken.

Antonio, who knew his mother so well, read her expression of worry.

"Mama, I know for certain you will love her."

"How?"

Antonio called down the stairs, "Honey?"

Angela Latini, in a crisp periwinkle wool suit and matching hat, walked up the stairs in her high-heeled pumps. She was beautifully turned out, a New York deb gracing the Iron Range.

"Zenza!" Angela put her arms around the woman who'd filled a void so deep that the job seemed impossible. Enza was her mother and her friend, and now, she was her mother-in-law.

"But, how did this—"

"We were at Aunt Laura's apartment and we looked at one another . . . ," Antonio explained.

"And we realized how similar we are," Angela said. "And we spent a long week on the town, talking."

"And we decided to surprise you."

"I'm surprised—and I'm so happy!"

"Zenza, I was afraid you wouldn't be happy."

"Why?"

"Because no one would be good enough for Antonio."

"Ah," Enza said. "You are." She put her arms around Angela.

Angela, who had never felt that the loss of her own mother had healed, began to cry in the arms of the woman who had stepped in to fill that void and love her. "I'll be a good wife. I learned everything from you."

"No, you came to me well trained in all things. Pappina was your mother, and she was the best mother any girl could ever have."

"The truth is, I've loved Antonio since I was a little girl. I prayed that someday he would come back to me, and I would be old enough, and he wouldn't have fallen in love with someone else. I prayed he would wait for me. I know it sounds crazy—"

"No, it doesn't. Not at all. Sometimes a childhood dream is the best dream of all."

Enza embraced her son and her new daughter-in-law. She thought about Ciro and how she'd loved him from the first moment she saw him, and how tradition, properly cared for, nurtured, honored, and respected, continues to feed the soul of a family. Antonio saw love so he could eventually choose it. So had Angela, and she, too, recognized it and waited for it to find her just as it had found Luigi and Pappina.

Enza wrote to Luigi Latini with the news. He had remarried in his village and was, by all accounts, happy. This letter would delight Luigi; he learned that Antonio and Angela would take their honeymoon in Italy and visit him and his sons and their families. Luigi would remember to tell Antonio all the stories about how Ciro became his partner, but in fact, Ciro had been the leader, and Luigi would have followed him wherever he wanted to go.

Enza smiled when she thought of her son joining the Latini family, with its growing numbers, and climbing the Passo Presolana to see Vilminore and Schilpario, where Enza and Ciro's story had begun. Enza would write to Eduardo and Caterina, who would know Antonio upon first sight, as Ciro always called his boy a Montini.

.   .   .

"You wanted to see me, Zenza?" Angela stood in the doorway of Enza's bedroom in her robe. Enza looked up at her and for a moment saw Pappina's face, as she was the first time she'd met her on Mulberry Street. Enza remembered Angela as a little girl, and could hardly believe she was a woman now, and her son's wife.

"Yes, yes, honey, come and sit with me."

Angela sat on the edge of the bed.

"I couldn't be happier for you."

"I know." Angela put her arms around Enza. "That means everything to me."

"I want to give you something." Enza gave Angela a small velvet box.

Angela opened the box and lifted out a delicate blue cameo, suspended on a string of pearls. "It's exquisite."

"It belonged to my husband's mother. She was once a privileged girl from a good family, and when she was widowed young, they lost everything. But through all her troubles, she managed to hang on to this necklace. This is the family you have married, Angela. They are strong, and resilient, and they hold on. Wear it and think of them." Enza fastened the necklace on to Angela's neck.

"And I'll wear it and think of you," Angela said.

"What are you girls talking about?" Antonio appeared in the doorway. Enza patted the bed next to her. Her son sat down beside her and watched his new bride look at her reflection in the mirror.

"Zenza, I mean, Mama . . . gave me this cameo. It belonged to your grandmother."

"I don't know if it's beautiful on its own or lovely because you're wearing it," Antonio said.

Angela kissed her mother-in-law on the cheek. "I'll take good care of it," she promised. She touched Antonio's face before leaving the room.

"You'll never know what it means to me to see you so happy," Enza said.

"I want you to be happy, Mama."

"I've had so much." Enza smiled.

"I promised Papa that I would take you home to the mountain someday. Angela and I are planning a trip to Italy. She wants to see her family and then we planned a trip north to meet my grandfather and aunts and uncles. Papa's mother. Papa's brother. I have so many cousins."

"You go for me."

"Mama, they have medication now. During the war so many men got seasick, and they took a pill. You'd be fine."

Enza imagined the thrill of seeing her father and brothers and sisters again, but it wasn't the Passo Presolana, or the lake at Endine or the stone bridge over the Stream Vò where the waterfall meets the rocks that she missed. It was the air on the mountain. The crisp, fresh Alpine air, that brought the scent of spring with fragrant freesia, or the scent of autumn with the pungent juniper nettles, or the scent of snow before the storm began in winter. That was what she missed, the air that filled her with possibility and yearning, the air that she breathed with Ciro the first night they kissed. That blue air. The night air as rich as a treasure chest of lapis, shimmering, inviting and made smooth over time.

To breathe the mountain air would make the final days of her own life sweet in memory. It would be a priceless gift to look back on the trip with her son and daughter-in-law someday, when she too would breathe her final moments on this earth.

"Please, Mama? Will you come with us?"

Enza put her arms around her son. "I'd do anything for you. Yes, I'll go with you."

Antonio kissed his mother good night and went to bed.

Enza sat in the chair in her room and tried to read, but her thoughts interrupted the words on the page, and she imagined the past, and tried to make some sense of all the moments of her life that had built the days that became the years she shared with Ciro. She remembered that she had always felt an underlying urgency when she was with him, she never thought there was enough time. She had felt it that night on the pass when she drove him back to the convent. The trip went too fast, and there was so much more to say. In the years that followed, when they were apart, she'd see something that reminded her of Ciro, and she'd make a note to tell him about it someday, even when he'd fallen in love with another girl and she thought she'd never see him again. And once she married Ciro, and Antonio was born, the years sped by even faster, like the overtime clock in any of Antonio's basketball games. When Ciro died, he was so young, but then again, so was she. And in the years since, she had not met a single man who could turn her head. The memory of Ciro had not faded. While she would like to think that she could return to the mountain, in her heart, she wondered if she could climb the pass without the man who had been and would remain her true love.

Later that night, long after Antonio and Angela were asleep, Enza made herself a cup of tea. She brought it back to her bedroom. She propped open the skylight to let in the cool night air, looking around the room, and taking in the familiar walls and corners of it. Enza remembered Ciro there, and thought about the night he came home late from a party after dancing with a pretty girl. Those hours without him seemed an eternity. It was funny to her that when she thought she might lose him, time seemed to stop, yet, when they were happy, it flew.

Enza did something she had not done in years. She opened Ciro's drawer in the dresser, the one she hadn't had the heart to empty when he died many years ago. Now, though, she felt lucky. Antonio was home safely, and he'd married a wonderful girl. Enza felt Ciro would be proud of her; she had done a good job raising their son alone and honored his memory by always doing her best for their family. She took in the lingering scent of cedar and lemon that still permeated the cover of her husband's missal and his leather belt. She opened the leather pouch of tobacco, and inhaled the sweet remainder of the leaves, remembering Ciro's face when he smiled and squinted at her through the puffs of smoke.

Enza sorted Ciro's socks, and held the leather belt, which had been wrapped neatly into a coil. She pulled out the small calfksin sleeve that contained his honorable discharge papers, which he had carried in his pocket every day of his life, as if to say, *See how much I loved this country?* As if anyone would have ever doubted it.

Enza placed his passport on the dresser top. She lifted out the prayer missal that Eduardo had given to Ciro when they were parted as young men. Enza had carried it on her wedding day, and remembered how heavy it felt in her hands. She found a photograph of the Latinis and the Lazzaris tucked inside, taken by Longyear Lake when the children were small. How young Pappina looked, and how happy Luigi was as he held baby Angela!

Enza also removed a photograph from her own wedding day, to give to Angela and Antonio as a gift. She looked at her stern young face in the photograph and wondered why she had been so serious. After all, it was the happiest moment of her life. If only she had been giddy with possibility instead of worried about all the things that might go wrong! She saw, as she looked back, that there would have been no stopping the terrible things that happened to them, any more than there was a way to contain all the joy they had known.

Enza looked at Ciro's face, and wondered how she had managed to marry a man so beautiful. His sandy hair, obvious even in sepia, was thick and wavy, as it was until the day he died. His straight nose and full lips fit beautifully with her own, as if it was fated that they would become one.

She missed her husband's kisses most of all.

Enza was about to close the drawer when she saw something shimmering at the bottom of the drawer, in a small cup where Ciro kept extra bolts and screws for the machines in the shop. An unused penny stamp peeked out of the cup. Enza pulled the small cup from the drawer.

She emptied the contents onto the bedspread. An ivory collar stay, a few screws, a bobbin, a couple of buttons, and, finally, a gold coin tumbled out. Enza picked it up, taking the coin to the bedside lamp to examine it.

It was the coin Enrico Caruso had given her on the closing night of *Lodoletta*. When Antonio was a boy, Enza had allowed him to hold it, and, when times were tough, she'd thought about selling it. But she needed one thing to remind her of where she came from and who she once knew, so she kept it, just as Caterina had held on to that blue cameo. Enza placed the coin on the nightstand next to the photograph, thinking Antonio would be thrilled to have it as part of his wedding gift. She twisted the gold ring Ciro had placed on her hand so many years ago on the day they were married. She had never taken it off. Enza remembered Ciro's words: *Beware the things of this world that can mean everything or nothing.*

Love.

Gold.

Somehow, Ciro had managed to give Enza both, but the love had been the everything.

ACKNOWLEDGMENTS

I had long been enchanted by my grandparents' love story. Lucia Spada and Carlo Bonicelli were from villages in the Italian Alps five miles apart, but they met for the first time in Hoboken, New Jersey. This novel is being published during the 100th anniversary year of Carlo Bonicelli's immigration. He arrived in New York City from Le Havre, France, on the S.S. *Chicago* on February 19, 1912. Imagine my elation when I first visited their villages on the mountain where they were born.

My great uncle, Monsignor Don Andrea Spada, was the first person to show me the Pizzo Camino. I took in the snow-capped peaks and the Italian sky, which was so blue that I still look for the exact shade of it everywhere, in fabric swatches, on walls, and in books. Don Andrea was my grandmother Lucia Bonicelli's baby brother. He was born in 1908 to a big, hardworking family. He left the mountain to be educated and was ordained a priest in 1931. He became a respected and renowned journalist in Italy, where his worldview was focused through a prism of compassion and a firsthand knowledge of what it meant to be poor. He returned to the mountain and Bergamo as soon as he could. He was editor of the *L'Eco di Bergamo* newspaper for fifty-one years. He was a *padrone* of language like no other. His newspaper articles were specific, clear, and truthful; his headlines plain and direct. He went on to write glorious books of power and scope. He died in Schilpario at the age of ninety-six in the house where he was born, in the shadow of the mountain he loved.

I am grateful to be published by HarperCollins, led by the great Brian Murray and my champion, Michael Morrison. Jonathan Burnham is a publisher with exquisite taste and clear vision. He encouraged me to write this novel, and gave me the best tools to do the job. He is also good-looking and British, two of my favorite food groups.

My beloved editor, Lee Boudreaux, has skill and heart, a rare combination. This is our thirteenth book together and I don't know what I would do without her. She is gentle and strong, and so gifted. Abigail Holstein is a treasure, and takes care of the details effortlessly. I am indebted also to the great marketing team led by the razor-sharp Kathy Schneider, including Leah Wasielewski, Mark Ferguson, Katie O'Callaghan, Danielle Plafsky, and Tom Hopke, Jr.

The Harper publicity team gets the word out beautifully: thank you, Tina Andreadis, (Greek girls rule), Kate Blum, (the best), Sydney Sherman, Alberto Rojas, Joseph Papa, and Jamie Brickhouse (yes, Jamie I will go . . . there). Thank you, Camille McDuffy and Grace McQuade. Virginia Stanley, queen of the libraries, never fails me. My gratitude also to Kayleigh George and Annie Mazes.

The sparkling design and production group, who created this glorious cover art and interior design, includes Amanda Kain, Robin Biardello, Cindy Achar, Lydia Weaver, Miranda Ottewell, Leah Carlson-Stanisic, and Eric Levy. The team who gets the books into your hands via sales includes the fabulous Josh Marwell, Andrea Rosen, Jeanette Zwart, Doug Jones, Carla Clifford, Kristin Bowers, Brian Grogan, Jeff Rogart, Mark Hillesheim, Caitlin Rollfes, Erin Gorham, and Diane Jackson. Thank you, Amy Baker, Erica Barmash, Regina Eckes, and Jennifer Hart (who goes the extra five miles).

At William Morris Endeavor, thank you and my love always to the gamine powerhouse: Suzanne Gluck. The gamine's team is the best: Caroline Donofrio, Eve Attermann, and Becca Kaplan. I adore Nancy Josephson, who has been in my life as long as my sisters, reads as soon as she gets a draft, and provides unconditional support when it's most needed. Alicia Gordon drives the movie bus splendidly.

Thank you and love to: Sarah Ceglarski, Shekar Sathyanarayana,

Erin Malone, Tracy Fisher, Pauline Post, Eugenie Furniss: (the elegant duchess), Claudia Webb, Cathryn Summerhayes, Becky Thomas, Jamie Quiroz, Raffaella de Angelis, Amanda Krentzman (Global), Graham Taylor, Casey Carroll, Michelle Bohan, Matt Smith, Juliet Barrack, Stephanie Ward, Ellen Sushko, Joe Austin, Carrie Brody, Sarah Ceglarksi, Jessica Lubben, Natalie Hayden, Philip Grenz, Arielle Datz, and Brandon Guzman.

In Movieland, thank you to the brilliant producer Larry Sanitsky, Claude Chung and the team at the Sanitsky Company. My love and thanks to Lou Pitt and Michael Pitt. I will be ever grateful to Ann Godoff for opening the door to my literary career. Thank you to the fabulous Jackie Levin who has been so kind to me over the years.

At Simon and Schuster UK, my love to my publisher, Ian Chapman, my divine editor, Suzanne Baboneau, and the irreplaceable, unforgettable Nigel Stoneman.

Thank you, Allison Van Groesbeck (you're a star); Kelly Meehan (so talented and now engaged!); Antonia Trigiani, queen of the gift shop; Gina Casella, our fearless leader and fabulous president of our tours; Nikki Padilla, who leads the walking tours with panache and style.

My love and gratitude to Jake and Jean Morrissey, Mary Murphy, Gail Berman, Debra McGuire, Cate Magennis Wyatt, Nancy Bolmeier Fisher, Carol and Dominic Vechiarelli, Jim and Mary Deese Hampton, Suzanne and Peter Walsh, Heather and Peter Rooney, Ian Moffitt, Anne Weintraub, Gene Stein, Aaron Hill and Susan Fales-Hill, Kate Benton Doughan and Jim Doughan, Ruth Pomerance and Rafael Prieto, Joanna Patton and Bill Persky, Angelina Fiordellisi and Matt Williams, Michael La Hart and F. Todd Johnson, Richard and Dana Kirshenbaum, Hugh and Jody Friedman O'Neill, Rosalie Ciardullo, Dolores and Dr. Emil Pascarelli, Sharon Hall, Mary Ellen Gallagher Gavin, Rosanne Cash, Liz Welch Tirell, Rachel Cohen DeSario, Charles Randolph Wright, Constance Marks, Mario Cantone and Jerry Dixon; Nancy Ringham Smith, Sharon Watroba Burns, Dee Emmerson, Elaine Martinelli, Kitty Martinelli (Vi and the girls), Sally Davies, Sister Karol Jackowski, Jane Cline Higgins, Beth Vechiarelli Cooper (my Youngstown boss), Max and Robyn Westler, John Searles, Robin Kall, Gina Vechiarelli, Barbara and Tom Sullivan, Brownie and Connie Polly, Catherine Brennan,

Joe O'Brien, Greg D'Alessandro, Jena and Charlie Corsello, Karen Fink, Beata and Steven (the Warrior) Baker, Todd Doughty and Randy Losapio, Craig Fisse, Anemone and Steve Kaplan, Christina Avis Krauss and her Sonny, Joanne Curley Kerner, Bina Valenzano, Christine Freglette, Veronica Kilcullen, Lisa Rykoski, and Iva Lou Johnson. Cousin Evangeline "Eva" Palermo, wife, mother, and teacher, turned ninety as I wrote this book, and if you want to be an active, amazing ninety-year-old, check out my cousin Eva.

Thank you Michael Patrick King, the chairman of my mental health board. Thank you for being true and being you. Cynthia Rutledge Olson, I'm putting in an 800 number so people can call you with their problems worldwide. You will have help: Mary Testa can run the switchboard, while Wendy Luck passes out pamphlets; thank you both. Thank you Elena Nachmanoff and Dianne Festa, my honorary sisters.

Many months of research went into the history woven through this book. I am indebted to the experts who guided the process and did the heavy lifting. Thank you

Anthony Tamburri and Joseph Sciorra of the Calandra Institute, experts in Italian American history including life in Little Italy and turn-of-the-century immigration. My dear friend Betsy Brazis was generous, specific, and selflessly on call for her knowledge of the Iron Range. My mother, Ida, as always, gave priceless insight into life with her parents in Chisholm.

My gratitude to Nadia Sammarco for her insight into the Metropolitan Opera in New York City; Richie Sammarco for his memories of the opera; the (divine) Sisters of the RSCJ (*Religieuses de Sacre Coeur de Jesus*), including Sister Angela Bayo, Sister Judy Garson, and Sister Maura Keleher, Susan Burke-O'Neal at the Convent of the Sacred Heart; archivist John Pennino at the Metropolitan Opera; Andrea Spolti, my cousin an expert of all things Schilpario; and the great writer/editor Veda Ponikvar of *The Chisholm Tribune-Press*, Chisholm, Minnesota.

Samantha Rowe did an amazing job with the history of the Milbank House, Otto Kahn, and James Burden mansions, Ellis Island, and life at the turn of the last century. Luca Delbello researched use of language and currency. The Italian translations in the text were provided by Professor Dorina Cereghino.

During the final phases of writing this book, I lost some dear friends and family that I hope to honor here. Michele O'Callaghan Togneri, Tommy's beloved wife, was a total original. She was a wonderful mother to Julia, T.J., and Mia. Tommy told me that my books were always on Michele's nightstand. She will always be in my heart. My cousin Cathy Peters was a fabulous wife to Joe and mother to Lauren and Joey; Rebecca Wright Long from Big Stone Gap was my honorary sister (along with her sister Theresa Bledsoe), and would drive hours to come to a reading; she was also a beautiful wife to Stephen and mother to Adam and Christina. The great Theo Barnes, actor, playwright, and director began his career at the Judson Poets Theater, and when I moved to New York he took me under his wing and shared his every talent to encourage mine. Abner "Abbey" Zalaznick was a wonderful husband and father who took such delight in the world it was infectious. Lily Badger, our daughter's classmate at Chelsea Day School was a beautiful girl, along with her sisters Grace and Sarah. Madonna and Matthew are their loving parents, and we will never forget their three beauties.

It is fitting that many of the names in this novel came from donations made to the good nuns at the Caroline House in Connecticut. They do all manner of good works for immigrants; most important, they teach them to read and write English. My grandparents would be thrilled that elements of their story were woven with the current generation of immigrants. In that spirit, I'd like to thank my family, all of us descendents of strong, hardworking immigrants with big dreams.

Finally, on the dedication page, Don Andrea Spada, signed the photograph of himself, taken in the seminary in 1930. He wrote to my grandmother Lucia: *For my dear sister in America with my immense affection always.* He was able to visit his sister in America many times over the years, which thrilled her. When we visited him on the mountain fifty years later, the walls of the family home were filled with photographs of us, his family in America. No ocean, country, or war kept the Spada family from remaining close and connected. The love was always there and it endures evermore, just like the mountain.

ABOUT THE AUTHOR

ADRIANA TRIGIANI is an award-winning playwright, television writer, and documentary filmmaker. The author of the bestselling Big Stone Gap series; *Very Valentine; Encore, Valentine; Lucia, Lucia; The Queen of the Big Time;* and *Rococo,* she has also written the bestselling memoir *The Wisdom of My Grandmothers* as well as the young adult novels *Viola in Reel Life* and *Viola in the Spotlight.* Her books have been published in thirty-six countries around the world. She lives in New York City with her husband and daughter.

Adriana Trigiani
Very Valentine

Meet Valentine, an unforgettable and passionate woman with a heart and a dream as big as New York City. Her dream? To design the perfect pair of shoes ...

The Angelini Shoe Company, makers of exquisite wedding shoes since 1903, is one of the last family-owned businesses in Greenwich Village. Now the company run so devotedly by Valentine and her grandmother Teodora faces financial ruin.

Juggling a relationship with dashing chef Roman Falconi, her duty to her family and a design competition for a prestigious department store, Valentine accompanies her grandmother to Italy to find inspiration. There she discovers her artistic voice and much more, turning her life around in ways she never expected.

'Charming, charismatic and addictive, this tale of love, life and shoes is an absolute treat' *Company*

'A funny, heart-warming tale of a woman looking for love, family harmony and the perfect shoe. Surely, just what every girl wants, right?' *Heat*

ISBN 978-1-84739-111-7
PRICE £7.99

Adriana Trigiani
Encore Valentine

Family secrets, tantalising love and new possibilities throw Valentine's life into chaos in this dazzling tale.

Snow falls like glitter over Tuscany at the wedding of Valentine Roncalli's grandmother, and Valentine is expecting more good news - but her dreams are dashed when her grandmother names her brother and nemesis Alfred her partner at Angelini Shoes. A long-distance romance with the sexy Gianluca in remote Tuscany also seems impossible, so heartbroken Valentine devotes herself to her work.

A once-in-a-lifetime business opportunity takes her to the sun-kissed cobblestones of Buenos Aires, where she finds a long-buried secret hidden deep within a family scandal. Once discovered, the truth shakes the Roncallis, while Valentine is torn between a past love that nurtured her and a new one that promises to last a lifetime...

'Trigiani is as charming as ever' *Elle*

'Hilarious and romantic'
Sarah Jessica Parker

ISBN 978-1-84983-079-9
PRICE £7.99

Adriana Trigiani
Milk Glass Moon

A daughter's first love, a mother's heartbreak, an enduring marriage facing its own on-going challenges, and a community faced with seismic changes, all are deep at the heart of Adriana Trigiani's new novel. As she faces the joys and demands of motherhood, Ave Maria continues her life story with her trademark humour and honesty.

Reaching into the past to find answers to the present, Ave Maria is led to places she never dreamed she would go, and to people who enter her life and rock its foundation.   *Milk Glass Moon* is about the power of love and its abiding truth, and captures Trigiani at her most lyrical, affectionate and heartfelt.

'The warmth seeps out of the pages ... Trigiani's talent is not so much writing page-turners as writing page-lingerers... you won't want this to finish' *Daily Mirror*

ISBN 978-0-74345-088-1
PRICE £6.99

Adriana Trigiani
Big Cherry Holler

It's been eight years since Ave Maria Mulligan married Jack
MacChesney. With her newfound belief in love and its
possibilities, she has made a life for herself and her growing
family. What she hasn't counted on is that the ghosts of the
past will return...

Here we have the story of a marriage, the deep secrets, the
power struggle, the betrayal and the unmet expectations that
exist between a husband and wife. And here too we have the
story of a wonderful community and an extended family, the
people of Big Stone Gap, Virginia, who are always there for one
another.

Full of humour, honesty, drama and local colour, *Big
Cherry Holler* has at its core two lovers who have lost
their way and struggle so compellingly to find each other
again.

'A charming, moving and beautifully observed tale'
Daily Mirror

ISBN 978-0-74343-034-0
PRICE £6.99

Adriana Trigiani
Rococo

Makeover specialist Bartolomeo Di Crespi is all his name suggests – stylish, sophisticated, a legend in his own time. From the Mediterranean to Manhattan his taste reigns supreme. When the renovation of his hometown church comes up for tender, Bartolemeo assumes only he can do justice to the task ahead. But the local pastor, Father Porporino, has other ideas . . .

Captivating, hilarious, bursting with effervescent life, as fanciful as flocked wallpaper, *Rococo* is a comic masterpiece with a heart of goldleaf from Richard & Judy favourite Adriana Trigiani.

'Yum yum – if novels were food, this one would be fudge. A joyous blend of Italian-American warmth and whiplash New York wit' *The Times*

ISBN 978-0-74349-588-2
PRICE £6.99

Adriana Trigiani
Big Stone Gap

Big Stone Gap, Virginia, is the sort of sleepy hamlet in the Blue Ridge Mountains where kids get married and start families at eighteen, and stay forever. So thirty-five-year-old Ave Maria Mulligan is something of an oddity. A self-proclaimed spinster, as the local pharmacist she's been keeping the townsfolk's secrets for years.

Now Ave Maria is about to discover a scandal in her own family's past that will blow the lid right off her quiet, uneventful life.

With an unforgettable cast of characters and a heroine with an extraordinary story to tell, *Big Stone Gap* is a wonderfully vibrant, unashamedly feel-good debut.

'As warm and sweet as Southern Comfort' ELLE

ISBN 978-0-74344-012-7
PRICE £6.99

Adriana Trigiani
Lucia, Lucia

'The perfect feel-good read' *Glamour*

Lucia Sartori is the most beautiful girl in Greenwich Village. Never short of suitors, she is sought after as a potential wife by the best Italian families in New York. But it is 1950, a time of great opportunity for ambitious girls with dreams of a career, and Lucia is no exception. She has a glamorous job in a chic Fifth Avenue department store, which she's not yet ready to swap for a role as wife.

Until a handsome stranger comes into her life and she falls desperately and passionately in love at first sight. But in order to be together, they must first win over her traditional family. Their love affair takes an unexpected turn as secrets are revealed, Lucia's family honour is tested, and her own reputation becomes the centre of a sizzling scandal.

ISBN 978-0-74346-226-6
PRICE £6.99

Home of the sassiest fiction in town!

If you enjoyed this book, you'll love...

978-1-84739-111-7	Adriana Trigiani	Very Valentine	£7.99
978-1-84983-079-9	Adriana Trigiani	Encore Valentine	£7.99
978-1-84983-106-2	Santa Montefiore	The House by the Sea	£7.99
978-1-84739-261-9	Sandra Howard	Ex Wives	£7.99
978-1-84983-294-6	Helen Warner	RSVP	£6.99
978-1-84739-853-6	Tara Hyland	Fallen Angels	£6.99
978-1-84739-852-9	Tara Hyland	Daughter of Fortune	£6.99
978-1-84739-962-5	Colette Caddle	Every Time We Say Goodbye	£6.99

For exclusive author interviews, features and competitions log onto
www.booksandthecity.co.uk